"*I can't believe he ever fooled* me." Squirrelflight shuddered. "I've known Bramblestar my whole life. I should have known that something was wrong." She lifted her head, her nose twitching as the scents of ThunderClan's camp washed over them.

Bristlefrost followed Squirrelflight through the tunnel; her leader's words were muffled as the thorns swallowed them.

"I'm going to make it right," Squirrelflight mewed. "I have to."

Dread pressed at the edges of Bristlefrost's thoughts. *A cornered fox is more dangerous than a whole warrior patrol.* This impostor seemed more like a fox than any cat Bristlefrost had ever known. She admired Squirrelflight's courage, and she wished she could be more like her, yet she couldn't help feeling that something was about to go terribly wrong.

WARRIORS

THE BROKEN CODE

THE BROKEN CODE

WARRIORS

DARKNESS
WITHIN

ERIN
HUNTER

HARPER

An Imprint of HarperCollinsPublishers

Darkness Within

Copyright © 2020 by Working Partners Ltd.

Series created by Working Partners Ltd.

Map art © 2020 by Dave Stevenson

Interior art © 2020 by Owen Richardson

Library of Congress Cataloging-in-Publication Data

Names: Hunter, Erin, author.

Title: Darkness within / Erin Hunter.

Description: First edition. | New York : HarperCollins, [2020] | Series: Warriors: the broken code ; book 4 | Summary: "Exiled after a battle that left all five Clans devastated, ThunderClan's deputy, Squirrelflight, reveals the identity of the fake Bramblestar and fights for the return of the real one"— Provided by publisher.

Identifiers: LCCN 2020008885 | ISBN 978-0-06-282374-8 (pbk.)

Subjects: CYAC: Cats—Fiction. | Fantasy.

Classification: LCC PZ7.H916625 Dav 2020 | DDC [Fic]—dc23

LC record available at https://lccn.loc.gov/2020008885

Typography by Jessie Gang

23 24 25   PC/BRR   12 11 10

❖

First paperback edition, 2021

Special thanks to Kate Cary

ALLEGIANCES

THUNDERCLAN

ACTING LEADER **SQUIRRELFLIGHT**—dark ginger she-cat with green eyes and one white paw

ACTING DEPUTY **LIONBLAZE**—golden tabby tom with amber eyes

MEDICINE CATS **JAYFEATHER**—gray tabby tom with blind blue eyes

ALDERHEART—dark ginger tom with amber eyes

WARRIORS (toms and she-cats without kits)

THORNCLAW—golden-brown tabby tom

WHITEWING—white she-cat with green eyes

BIRCHFALL—light brown tabby tom

MOUSEWHISKER—gray-and-white tom
APPRENTICE, BAYPAW (golden tabby tom)

POPPYFROST—pale tortoiseshell-and-white she-cat

BRISTLEFROST—pale gray she-cat

LILYHEART—small, dark tabby she-cat with white patches and blue eyes
APPRENTICE, FLAMEPAW (black tom)

BUMBLESTRIPE—very pale gray tom with black stripes

CHERRYFALL—ginger she-cat

MOLEWHISKER—brown-and-cream tom

CINDERHEART—gray tabby she-cat
APPRENTICE, FINCHPAW (tortoiseshell she-cat)

BLOSSOMFALL—tortoiseshell-and-white she-cat with petal-shaped white patches

IVYPOOL—silver-and-white tabby she-cat with dark blue eyes

EAGLEWING—ginger she-cat
APPRENTICE, MYRTLEPAW (pale brown she-cat)

DEWNOSE—gray-and-white tom

THRIFTEAR—dark gray she-cat

STORMCLOUD—gray tabby tom

HOLLYTUFT—black she-cat

FLIPCLAW—tabby tom

FERNSONG—yellow tabby tom

HONEYFUR—white she-cat with yellow splotches

SPARKPELT—orange tabby she-cat

SORRELSTRIPE—dark brown she-cat

TWIGBRANCH—gray she-cat with green eyes

FINLEAP—brown tom

SHELLFUR—tortoiseshell tom

PLUMSTONE—black-and-ginger she-cat

LEAFSHADE—tortoiseshell she-cat

SPOTFUR—spotted tabby she-cat

FLYWHISKER—striped gray tabby she-cat

SNAPTOOTH—golden tabby tom

QUEENS

(she-cats expecting or nursing kits)

DAISY—cream long-furred cat from the horseplace

ELDERS (former warriors and queens, now retired)

GRAYSTRIPE—long-haired gray tom

CLOUDTAIL—long-haired white tom with blue eyes

BRIGHTHEART—white she-cat with ginger patches

BRACKENFUR—golden-brown tabby tom

SHADOWCLAN

LEADER **TIGERSTAR**—dark brown tabby tom

DEPUTY **CLOVERFOOT**—gray tabby she-cat

MEDICINE CATS **PUDDLESHINE**—brown tom with white splotches

SHADOWSIGHT—gray tabby tom

MOTHWING—dappled golden she-cat

WARRIORS **TAWNYPELT**—tortoiseshell she-cat with green eyes

DOVEWING—pale gray she-cat with green eyes

HARELIGHT—white tom

ICEWING—white she-cat with blue eyes

STONEWING—white tom

SCORCHFUR—dark gray tom with slashed ears

FLAXFOOT—brown tabby tom

SPARROWTAIL—large brown tabby tom

SNOWBIRD—pure white she-cat with green eyes

YARROWLEAF—ginger she-cat with yellow eyes

BERRYHEART—black-and-white she-cat

GRASSHEART—pale brown tabby she-cat

WHORLPELT—gray-and-white tom

HOPWHISKER—calico she-cat

BLAZEFIRE—white-and-ginger tom

CINNAMONTAIL—brown tabby she-cat with white paws

FLOWERSTEM—silver she-cat

SNAKETOOTH—honey-colored tabby she-cat

SLATEFUR—sleek gray tom

POUNCESTEP—gray tabby she-cat

LIGHTLEAP—brown tabby she-cat

GULLSWOOP—white she-cat

SPIRECLAW—black-and-white tom

HOLLOWSPRING—black tom

SUNBEAM—brown-and-white tabby she-cat

ELDERS   **OAKFUR**—small brown tom

SKYCLAN

LEADER   **LEAFSTAR**—brown-and-cream tabby she-cat with amber eyes

DEPUTY   **HAWKWING**—dark gray tom with yellow eyes

MEDICINE CATS   **FRECKLEWISH**—mottled light brown tabby she-cat with spotted legs

FIDGETFLAKE—black-and-white tom

MEDIATOR   **TREE**—yellow tom with amber eyes

WARRIORS

SPARROWPELT—dark brown tabby tom

MACGYVER—black-and-white tom

DEWSPRING—sturdy gray tom

ROOTSPRING—yellow tom

NEEDLECLAW—black-and-white she-cat

PLUMWILLOW—dark gray she-cat

SAGENOSE—pale gray tom

KITESCRATCH—reddish-brown tom

HARRYBROOK—gray tom

CHERRYTAIL—fluffy tortoiseshell and white she-cat

CLOUDMIST—white she-cat with yellow eyes

BLOSSOMHEART—ginger-and-white she-cat

TURTLECRAWL—tortoiseshell she-cat

RABBITLEAP—brown tom
APPRENTICE, WRENPAW (golden tabby she-cat)

REEDCLAW—small pale tabby she-cat

MINTFUR—gray tabby she-cat with blue eyes

NETTLESPLASH—pale brown tom

TINYCLOUD—small white she-cat

PALESKY—black-and-white she-cat

VIOLETSHINE—black-and-white she-cat with yellow eyes

BELLALEAF—pale orange she-cat with green eyes

QUAILFEATHER—white tom with crow-black ears

PIGEONFOOT—gray-and-white she-cat

FRINGEWHISKER—white she-cat with brown splotches

GRAVELNOSE—tan tom

SUNNYPELT—ginger she-cat

QUEENS   **NECTARSONG**—brown she-cat

ELDERS   **FALLOWFERN**—pale brown she-cat who has lost her hearing

WINDCLAN

LEADER   **HARESTAR**—brown-and-white tom

DEPUTY   **CROWFEATHER**—dark gray tom

MEDICINE CAT   **KESTRELFLIGHT**—mottled gray tom with white splotches like kestrel feathers

WARRIORS   **NIGHTCLOUD**—black she-cat

BRINDLEWING—mottled brown she-cat
APPRENTICE, APPLEPAW (yellow tabby she-cat)

LEAFTAIL—dark tabby tom with amber eyes
APPRENTICE, WOODPAW (brown she-cat)

EMBERFOOT—gray tom with two dark paws

BREEZEPELT—black tom with amber eyes

HEATHERTAIL—light brown tabby she-cat with blue eyes

FEATHERPELT—gray tabby she-cat

CROUCHFOOT—ginger tom
APPRENTICE, SONGPAW (tortoiseshell she-cat)

LARKWING—pale brown tabby she-cat

SEDGEWHISKER—light brown tabby she-cat
APPRENTICE, FLUTTERPAW (brown-and-white tom)

SLIGHTFOOT—black tom with white flash on his chest

OATCLAW—pale brown tabby tom

HOOTWHISKER—dark gray tom
APPRENTICE, WHISTLEPAW (gray tabby she-cat)

FERNSTRIPE—gray tabby she-cat

ELDERS **WHISKERNOSE**—light brown tom

GORSETAIL—very pale gray-and-white she-cat with blue eyes

RIVERCLAN

LEADER **MISTYSTAR**—gray she-cat with blue eyes

DEPUTY **REEDWHISKER**—black tom

MEDICINE CATS **WILLOWSHINE**—gray tabby she-cat

WARRIORS **DUSKFUR**—brown tabby she-cat

MINNOWTAIL—dark gray-and-white she-cat
APPRENTICE, SPLASHPAW (brown tabby tom)

MALLOWNOSE—light brown tabby tom

HAVENPELT—black-and-white she-cat

PODLIGHT—gray-and-white tom

SHIMMERPELT—silver she-cat

LIZARDTAIL—light brown tom

    APPRENTICE, FOGPAW (gray-and-white she-cat)

SNEEZECLOUD—gray-and-white tom

BRACKENPELT—tortoiseshell she-cat

JAYCLAW—gray tom

OWLNOSE—brown tabby tom

GORSECLAW—white tom with gray ears

NIGHTSKY—dark gray she-cat with blue eyes

BREEZEHEART—brown-and-white she-cat

<u>QUEENS</u>   **CURLFEATHER**—pale brown she-cat (mother to Frostkit, a she-kit; Mistkit, a she-kit; and Graykit, a tom)

<u>ELDERS</u>   **MOSSPELT**—tortoiseshell-and-white she-cat

THE BROKEN CODE

WARRIORS

DARKNESS
WITHIN

TWOLEG NEST

GREENLEAF TWOLEGPLACE

TWOLEG PATH

TWOLEG PATH

CLEARING

SHADOWCLAN CAMP

SMALL THUNDERPATH

HALFBRIDGE

GREENLEAF TWOLEGPLACE

HALFBRIDGE

CAT VIEW

ISLAND

STREAM

RIVERCLAN CAMP

HORSEPLACE

MOONPOOL

ABANDONED
TWOLEG NEST

SKYCLAN
CAMP

OLD THUNDERPATH

THUNDERCLAN
CAMP

ANCIENT OAK

LAKE

WINDCLAN
CAMP

BROKEN
HALFBRIDGE

TWOLEGPLACE

THUNDERPATH

KEY
To The
CLANS

THUNDERCLAN

RIVERCLAN

SHADOWCLAN

WINDCLAN

SKYCLAN

STARCLAN

NORTH

SANCTUARY
COTTAGE

HAREVIEW
CAMPSITE

SADLER WOODS

LITTLEPINE ROAD

LITTLEPINE
SAILING
CENTER

TWOLEG VIE

LITTLEPINE
ISLAND

RIVER ALBA

WHITECHURCH ROAD

KNIGHT'S
COPSE

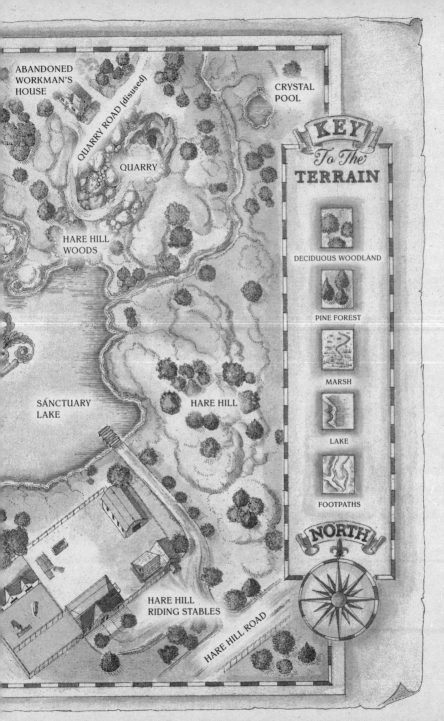

PROLOGUE

Leafpool shivered. A cool wind streamed around her, fragrant with the scent of the wide green fields of StarClan's hunting grounds. Clouds pressed at the distant hills. She fluffed out her fur, drawing her gaze back to where Firestar was sniffing the pool that marked the heart of StarClan territory. Bluestar crouched nearby, paws tucked under her chest, while Tallstar sat stiffly beside her, his amber eyes dark with worry.

Despite the moons that had passed since she had come to StarClan, Leafpool still found it strange to be around cats she'd only heard about in nursery tales growing up. And yet she felt at home in the tranquil forests and meadows of her ancestors, reunited with Firestar and Sandstorm, caring for the kits Squirrelflight had lost before they'd had a chance to know their mother. She felt a sense of acceptance that she'd rarely felt in her final moons in Thunderclan. Back there, she'd known that some cats would never truly forgive her for lying about being the real mother of Lionblaze, Jayfeather, and Hollyleaf. The secret she'd kept for so long, and the guilt she'd felt after it had been revealed, had stuck like thorns in her heart. Here, all was forgiven, and for the most part her heart was free of pain.

But even in the midst of her joy, worry managed to find her. She'd promised to watch over Squirrelflight until her sister could join her. But how could she keep that promise now, when a shadow had fallen over StarClan? As she stared at Firestar, fear pressed harder in her belly.

Her father sniffed again at the pool, where branches twined and snaked into the water. "There's still no way to see the Clans," he growled.

Leafpool remembered how she and Squirrelflight had watched their Clanmates in the waters of this pool when they'd first come to StarClan. Squirrelflight had dived in and swum back through the murky depths to return to the cats she loved so much. But now that route was blocked.

Branches crisscrossed the water, vines knotting them into an impenetrable web. No cat could see through such a tangle, and there would be no chance for any cat to reach the living Clans now.

Even Squirrelflight wouldn't be able to make it through. Leafpool's heart fluttered with alarm. She was losing track of how long the branches had covered the pool, but she knew it had been too long. Squirrelflight, Jayfeather, and Lionblaze were alone with no cat to watch over them. She saw Firestar's fur prickle along his spine. He must feel the same way, as anxious about Squirrelflight and the Clan he'd left behind as she was. Where had the branches come from? Why were they blocking StarClan's way? She knew her father was as mystified as every other cat in StarClan.

She padded closer. "I keep hoping they'll have disappeared each time I come here," she mewed.

Firestar's pelt twitched nervously. "What if we never make it past them?"

"We have to," she breathed. "We can't be separated from the living Clans forever. They need us."

Bluestar pushed herself to her paws. "Have faith," she mewed. "They are warriors, and they're resourceful. They might not need us as much as we think."

Panic sparked in Leafpool's belly. "What if *we* need *them*?" A thought flitted at the edge of her mind, too frightening to reach for. And yet she couldn't resist. "Will we disappear if we have no connection to the living Clans?"

"Of course not." Firestar blinked at her. She saw doubt in his emerald eyes. *He doesn't believe what he's saying.* Firestar's gaze flitted back to the water. "Why did we allow a cat like that to go down there?"

Bluestar snorted. "We were going to keep an eye on him, remember?" she mewed wryly.

Firestar poked a vine angrily. It shivered, sending ripples over the water. Leafpool caught her breath. Had he managed to dislodge something? She peered hopefully into the water, but there was still nothing to see except the gray mist that seemed to swirl beneath the surface.

"It was too important to put in the paws of such a cat," Firestar growled. "We should have sent some other cat."

"It doesn't matter who we sent—" Tallstar began.

"Really?" Firestar swung his gaze toward the WindClan leader. "Don't you think it's strange that we trusted a cat we should never have trusted in life and *this* happened? We've lost our connection to the Clans. Do you think it's a coincidence?"

Tallstar's ears twitched. "It's no coincidence that this has happened when the Clans have been breaking the code whenever it suits them. They're the ones who have caused this mess." He jerked his muzzle toward the knotted branches obscuring the pool.

"The code has been broken before," Firestar retorted. "In worse ways, and nothing like this has ever happened." He frowned. "There's only one cat responsible for this. We must find a way to fix it. If we don't, the living Clans might be lost forever."

Leafpool's mouth grew dry. Was he right? Could this be the end of the connection between the lake Clans and their ancestors? And, if it was, how long could the living and the dead survive?

CHAPTER 1

As *Squirrelflight's mew rang across the* island, Bristlefrost's heart seemed to skip a beat.

"I know who has taken over Bramblestar's body!"

Who? Bristlefrost jerked her muzzle toward the acting Thunderclan leader, who stared down from the Great Oak, her orange pelt milky in the moonlight.

"But I can hardly believe it," Squirrelflight mumbled, beneath other cats' exclamations of surprise.

The Clans stopped in their tracks. Mistystar had ended the Gathering abruptly, angry at demands that she allow Harelight and Icewing to rejoin RiverClan from their exile, and the Clans had been preparing to leave the island. But now every cat seemed to halt as though snared by the same thought, ears pricked, faces lifting toward Squirrelflight. Warriors who had been heading toward the tree-bridge turned back and pushed their way from the long grass, their eyes glittering anxiously as Squirrelflight went on. Graystripe, one of Thunderclan's elders, turned back, his ears angled forward with curiosity.

"And if I'm right"—in the moonlight, shadows darkened the Thunderclan leader's face—"it's even worse than we

thought. This warrior will not stop until every Clan cat has
paid for what he believes was stolen from him when he was
alive."

Bristlefrost's pelt sparked with dread. It sounded as though
the cat who'd stolen Bramblestar's body was well known to
Squirrelflight. She flattened her ears. Only part of her wanted
to know who it was. Clearly some dark spirit had possessed
the Thunderclan leader, dividing the Clans and turning
Clanmate against Clanmate, until a bloody battle had left
warriors dead and the impostor a prisoner of ShadowClan.
Bristlefrost didn't want to believe that a *warrior* could wreak
such horrors on the Clans. Once Squirrelflight named the cat
who'd driven out Bramblestar's spirit and left it to wander the
forest, neither living nor dead, the Clans would have to accept
that one of their ancestors had betrayed them.

Squirrelflight hesitated, her gaze flitting nervously over
the waiting cats. Was she scared to say the warrior's name out
loud?

"Well?" Tigerstar shouldered his way through the gathered
cats and stopped at the base of the Great Oak. "Who do you
think it is?"

Bristlefrost's belly tightened. She saw pelts spike around
her. Would naming the cat who had stolen Bramblestar's body
divide the Clans once more? Would they fight again? Here?
Now? She glanced back at Squirrelflight. There was fear in
the Thunderclan leader's gaze; it seemed to spark like lightning through the Clans, setting whiskers twitching and fur
on end.

"Tell us," Tigerstar demanded.

Squirrelflight glanced at the ShadowClan leader, then took a deep breath. "I know this is going to sound crazy," she began.

Tigerstar's tail twitched ominously.

"But I'm *sure* I'm right." Squirrelflight's mew grew more certain. "It has to be. It can't be anyone else." She lifted her chin. "I think Ashfur has returned."

Bristlefrost frowned, puzzled. *Ashfur?* He had been a Thunderclan warrior, she thought. He'd died, many moons ago, in an accident. She tried to remember the times she'd heard older warriors talk about him. There had been something strange about his death, hadn't there?

"Why would Ashfur come back?" Mistystar was threading her way between the cats. When she reached the Great Oak, she scrambled up beside Squirrelflight.

Tigerstar followed her. "He wanted to be your mate, didn't he? Before you chose Bramblestar." As Harestar and Leafstar hurried to take their places beside the others once more, the ShadowClan leader went on. "Is that why you think he's returned?"

Squirrelflight avoided Tigerstar's eye. "He might feel he has unfinished business here," she mewed.

"Maybe with *Thunderclan*." Harestar looked unconvinced. "But not enough to stir up trouble with the rest of us." He glanced at the other leaders.

Bristlefrost's paws prickled with unease, and her claws started to flex with anger at hearing a hint of accusation in the WindClan leader's voice. That the Clans' current problems were somehow all the fault of Thunderclan. Then she saw Squirrelflight's forlorn expression. Her muzzle clamped tightly shut, and she felt a wave of pity. Squirrelflight clearly believed she was right: But did she really think a cat would try to destroy all the Clans just because she'd chosen Bramblestar over him?

Squirrelflight shifted self-consciously. "I know it sounds far-fetched," she mewed. "But you didn't know him as well as I did."

Leafstar looked puzzled. "Who is Ashfur?"

"He was a Thunderclan warrior," Squirrelflight replied. Her mouth moved, but no more words came out. It was as if her disbelief was keeping her from finishing her own thought.

"He tried to kill Hollyleaf," Tawnypelt called from among the cats pressing closer beneath the Great Oak, eyes wide with interest.

"That's what we heard in RiverClan." Willowshine looked around at her Clanmates. Shock sparked in the gazes of the younger warriors, but many of the older warriors nodded, exchanging knowing glances.

Reedwhisker flicked his tail. "Mousefur told me at a Gathering that he attacked Hollyleaf when she was alone. That's how he died: He slipped and hit his head when she fought him off."

Bristlefrost remembered a night, many moons ago, when Graystripe had told some of the younger apprentices all about Ashfur, whom he'd called "a bad cat." But however much she trusted the Thunderclan elder, she'd found it hard to believe that a warrior could turn on his Clanmate like that. Was it actually true?

"We heard that in WindClan too." Crowfeather padded toward Lionblaze, blinking anxiously as he met the golden warrior's gaze. "He threatened to kill you and Jayfeather once, didn't he?"

Lionblaze nodded.

Emberfoot blinked. "I thought he was a loyal Thunderclan warrior."

Sedgewhisker glanced at his denmate. "Don't you remember the rumors?"

"Of course." Emberfoot looked surprised. "But I didn't believe them."

"They weren't lies," Squirrelflight mewed. "Ashfur even helped Hawkfrost lure Firestar into a trap."

Leafstar frowned. "And you think he's found his way back from the Dark Forest?"

"He's in StarClan," Squirrelflight told her. "I saw him there."

Leafstar swished her tail. "If StarClan accepted him, he must have changed. He can't still be bad."

Lionblaze narrowed his eyes. "He was my mentor, so I knew him better than most," he meowed. "I can't imagine him ever changing."

Leafstar frowned. "But surely this happened moons ago! What's it got to do with us now?"

Bristlefrost couldn't help agreeing. Even if Ashfur had been bad when he was alive, he was in StarClan now. Why would a long-dead warrior want to leave StarClan to steal the body of another cat and cause trouble for all the Clans? She glanced around at the younger Clan cats, who were looking at one another, clearly as puzzled as she was.

Squirrelflight's pelt prickled across her shoulders. "Just because a cat gets accepted into StarClan doesn't mean they don't bring their old resentments and hurts with them. Ashfur never forgave me for choosing Bramblestar over him," she mewed uncomfortably.

Mistystar's gaze hadn't wavered. "And you think he's come back for revenge?"

Squirrelflight nodded eagerly. "That's why he possessed Bramblestar, don't you see? That was the best way to get close to me and my kin."

Harestar looked unconvinced. "That still doesn't explain why he's been causing trouble for the rest of us."

Jayfeather called from below the oak. "When he was alive, Ashfur was willing to kill me and my littermates to make Squirrelflight suffer. He knows hurting the Clans would hurt her more than anything else."

"But he's just a warrior," Tigerstar pointed out. "How could he have found his way back from StarClan? He wasn't a medicine cat. He's not that powerful."

"I found my way back," Squirrelflight told him. "When I was injured in the fight with the Sisters . . . when Leafpool . . ." Her breath caught in her throat, and her head drooped sadly for a moment, before she went on: "I spent time in StarClan, and I found my way back as a spirit." She ignored the murmurs of astonishment rippling through the crowd. Instead her gaze flashed toward Tree. "You saw me," she urged. "You know I came back."

"Yes, you did," Tree agreed. "There are things about StarClan we don't fully understand," he mewed. "If it's possible for Squirrelflight to return, then why not Ashfur?"

Tigerstar flicked his tail decisively. "Squirrelflight didn't steal another cat's body."

"I didn't try to," Squirrelflight argued. "I never would. But Ashfur might. He's capable of anything."

Leafstar's eyes went round. "Do you think this cat is the reason why we can't communicate with StarClan?"

Squirrelflight nodded. "Maybe."

Kestrelflight pushed his way through the crowd and stopped beside Jayfeather. "No one cat could be powerful enough to break our connection with StarClan."

Jayfeather blinked at him. "Why not?"

"It's never been done before," Kestrelflight argued.

"Perhaps no cat has *tried* before," Jayfeather answered.

Around the clearing, cats exchanged glances. Bristlefrost noticed that the older cats, who must remember Ashfur, were looking worried. It was clear they were beginning to believe that this Thunderclan warrior might have returned. She felt a strange, curious flush of heat run through her pelt at seeing the cats of other Clans sharing glances—some concerned, some shocked, and some a little angry. Could this really *have* been Thunderclan's fault, that StarClan was now absent?

Anxiety sparked in her chest. She supposed it was possible

that one of their ancestors had turned against them and found a way to break their connection with StarClan. Her thoughts spiraled. *Can we survive without StarClan? And if we do, will we even be warriors anymore?*

Squirrelflight shifted on the branch. "Whether or not you agree with me about who's stolen Bramblestar's body, we can all agree that a spirit is pretending to be him." The gathered cats stared back at her uncertainly. "I know how it sounds, but it's the only explanation that fits the facts. A dead warrior has found a way back and is trying to hurt us," she pressed. "Right?"

At the back of the crowd, Shimmerpelt began to nod. Around her, the other RiverClan warriors dipped their heads. Their agreement spread as a murmur through the other Clans until Tigerstar whisked his tail.

"Okay," the ShadowClan leader meowed. "An ancestor has found a way to come back."

Mistystar nodded. "It seems like it could be Ashfur."

"I wouldn't put it past him," Lionblaze called from below.

Harestar narrowed his eyes. "Why didn't StarClan put a stop to it?"

Squirrelflight's tail swished angrily. "Let's accept that we don't know how this has happened, but it has. And I'm sure Ashfur's behind it. He wants revenge, and if I'm right, revenge against me won't be enough for him. As Lionblaze said, he'll want every cat to suffer. I can't let that happen because of me."

"Let Thunderclan deal with it." The WindClan tom Breezepelt was standing up straight, his tail in the air. "We shouldn't have to suffer just because Squirrelflight couldn't decide who she loved."

"I never—"

Squirrelflight's protest was drowned out by Cherryfall's hiss, as the ginger she-cat got to her paws and aimed her amber eyes at Breezepelt: "Do not speak to our leader like that!"

"She's *not* your leader!" Breezepelt broke from the Wind-Clan group and stalked ominously toward Cherryfall—who strode out to meet him. All around the Gathering, cats shifted their paws, murmuring uneasily. "Thunderclan doesn't *have* one right now."

"Yeah . . ." Stonewing, the white ShadowClan tom, stretched his neck as he called out: "And Thunderclan doesn't have their leader because Squirrelflight's former mate is causing trouble."

"He's not my mate!" Up on the branch, Squirrelflight was standing up straight, risking losing her footing. "He never was!"

"It is not Squirrelflight's fault that Ashfur developed an obsession." Jayfeather's blind eyes were roving the Gathering, as though he was prepared to fight every cat if he had to, to defend his adopted mother.

A heavy, uneasy silence fell. One or two cats looked embarrassed at having almost gotten into fights, while Bristlefrost couldn't help noticing that SkyClan looked mostly confused at hearing the other Clans discuss trials of a different time, before they had arrived at the lake.

After a moment, Thornclaw bowed his head solemnly. "If

it's Ashfur, he'll never feel satisfied."

Blossomfall and Cinderheart murmured in agreement. Birchfall glanced at Poppyfrost.

As Bristlefrost saw worry flash between them, she suppressed a shiver. The older Thunderclan warriors clearly remembered Ashfur and were wary of him.

"If it is Ashfur who's possessed Bramblestar, at least we know who we're fighting," Squirrelflight mewed. She stared over the heads of the cats on the ground, her eyes flitting left and right for a moment, before she turned to face Leafstar. "And I think I know a way to prove it's him."

Leafstar blinked. "How?"

The Thunderclan leader's eyes lit up. "I have a plan." Harestar tipped his head and Squirrelflight went on. "I think I can trick him into admitting who he is."

"Okay." Tigerstar pricked his ears. "Let's hear it."

Moonlight drenched the trees, pouring down through the canopy and silvering the forest floor as Bristlefrost followed her Clanmates home from the Gathering. They'd reached Thunderclan territory, but their muscles were still taut, their ears pricked. The air here was fragrant with familiar woodland scents; the undergrowth rustled with prey. But none of the patrol glanced toward the sounds. They padded in silence behind Squirrelflight.

Bristlefrost guessed they were all considering the plan their leader had outlined at the meeting. Could it really work? Her heart was racing. Even if it did work, would proving that

Ashfur had stolen Bramblestar's body help them fix this? She stopped and watched her Clanmates, her tail twitching anxiously. "What difference will it make if we know who it is?" she called after them.

Squirrelflight looked back. Shadows pooled around her, and, as she hesitated, the air seemed to quiver as though it were waiting for her answer, too. "The Clans need to know that the warrior who's done this is acting alone," she mewed at last. "It will restore their faith that the rest of StarClan is still on our side."

"But what if he's not acting alone?" Bristlefrost struggled to keep up with her racing thoughts. "What if StarClan's *not* on our side? The impostor might have divided StarClan just like he divided us. Maybe that's why we can't reach them."

The others had stopped beside Squirrelflight. Cinderheart and Finleap exchanged glances while Thornclaw and Poppyfrost looked nervously at their leader. Finchpaw's eyes glittered anxiously in the darkness.

Lionblaze lifted his muzzle stiffly. "No cat could divide StarClan."

Squirrelflight blinked gratefully at her deputy. "Especially not Ashfur." She signaled to Lionblaze with a flick of her tail. "Take the patrol back to camp," she told him. "Share our plan with the others. The sooner every cat knows who our enemy is, the better. I want to speak with Bristlefrost alone."

Bristlefrost stiffened. *Is she angry that I questioned StarClan?* Her paws felt rooted to the earth as the rest of the patrol padded silently into the shadows and disappeared. "I didn't mean to scare any cat," she told Squirrelflight, meeting her leader's gaze apologetically. "But I don't see how knowing who's stolen Bramblestar's body will help. If one ancestor can turn against us, couldn't any of them?" She fluffed out her fur, fear making her cold.

"Our ancestors won't turn against us," Squirrelflight told her.

"How do you know that?"

"They were warriors once. They are warriors still. They believe in loyalty."

"So you're sure he's acting alone?"

"Yes," Squirrelflight assured her. "Ashfur is the only cat in StarClan who would put his own needs above his Clan." She blinked reassuringly at Bristlefrost.

But Bristlefrost didn't feel reassured. She'd tried to help this impostor when she'd still believed he was Bramblestar, and even after she'd realized he wasn't, she'd been too scared to confront him. She remembered with a shiver how ruthless he had been, and the dark menace that had sometimes crept into his voice. "But what if he finds a new way to hurt us?" she mewed nervously. "He loved you, but he still wanted to hurt you. What will he do to cats he's never loved?"

"It wasn't love," Squirrelflight growled. "It was obsession. To love another cat is to put their needs first. But Ashfur only ever put himself first. He will do anything to make me sorry I chose Bramblestar over him. He's already found a way back to the lake, and I'm sure he's the one who destroyed the connection between the Clans and StarClan, all to get his own way." Determination lit her gaze. "But we won't let him. We'll fix what he's broken and rid ourselves of him once and for all, okay?"

"Okay." Bristlefrost dipped her head. Squirrelflight seemed suddenly much more powerful than any spiteful dead cat. *Of course* Ashfur couldn't win this battle. He was one cat against many. And yet, as Squirrelflight turned and headed after the others, doubt began to worm in Bristlefrost's belly. If Squirrelflight's plan worked, would it make Ashfur *more* determined to get his revenge?

"Come on." Squirrelflight picked up the pace as Bristlefrost hurried after her. "I know my plan sounds a little . . . well, *very* dangerous. But once the Clans know who the impostor is, they'll know he can be defeated. We can work out a way to get rid of him so that Bramblestar can return."

What will Ashfur do when he realizes you're choosing Bramblestar over him again? Bristlefrost swallowed back the words. Squirrelflight must realize the danger, surely.

"I can't believe he ever fooled me." Squirrelflight shuddered. "I've known Bramblestar my whole life. I should have known straight away that something was wrong." She lifted her head, her nose twitching as the scents of ThunderClan's camp washed over them.

Bristlefrost could see the entrance before her. She followed Squirrelflight through the tunnel; her leader's words were muffled as the thorns swallowed them.

"I'm going to make it right," Squirrelflight mewed. "I have to."

Dread pressed at the edges of Bristlefrost's thoughts. *A cornered fox is more dangerous than a whole warrior patrol.* She remembered her mentor's words, learned moons ago. This impostor seemed more like a fox than any cat Bristlefrost had ever known. She admired Squirrelflight's courage, and she wished she could be more like her, yet she couldn't help feeling that something was about to go terribly wrong.

CHAPTER 2

♣

The pungent scent of rosemary filled Shadowsight's nose as he pushed his way through the entrance tunnel, a few stems bunched between his jaws. He was looking forward to tucking them away in the herb store, where the smell would be lost among the other leaves. And yet he hesitated at the edge of the clearing and scanned the ShadowClan camp, noting Mothwing, the RiverClan exile, laying out yarrow leaves in a patch of sunshine near the medicine den. Cloverfoot and Berryheart murmured softly to each other at the head of the clearing, while Tawnypelt and Stonewing shared a starling nearby, and Grassheart and Pouncestep picked at the fresh-kill pile. Flowerstem was working with Whorlpelt to patch a hole in the elders' den, where Oakfur peered out. It seemed like an ordinary morning, and yet Shadowsight could see his Clanmates exchanging occasional worried glances. Whorlpelt stopped work and sat back on his haunches, peering at the sky as though judging how close to sunhigh it was.

They're waiting for it to begin. Shadowsight pushed back a tremor of foreboding and eyed the hollow tree. It stood, dark and gnarled, in the densest part of the camp wall, where brambles twined so thickly against it that even a mouse couldn't slip through. There was a hole in the trunk that looked like a wailing mouth. Kits used to explore the gloomy den inside, and when greenleaf was very hot, ShadowClan stored prey there to keep it cool. Now it was Bramblestar's prison. Trailing branches bounded a narrow stretch of earth in front where Bramblestar was allowed to stretch his legs from time to time. Even though he was separated from the rest of the camp, Shadowsight felt the impostor's presence like the memory of a bad dream that tainted a new day.

Scorchfur and Sparrowtail sat stiffly at the entrance to this bramble enclosure, guarding the defeated Thunderclan leader—or whoever had possessed his body. Scorchfur glanced at the hole in the trunk, where something moved in the darkness, then turned quickly back toward camp. He caught Sparrowtail's eye, and the two warriors held each other's gaze for a moment before looking away, shifting their paws uneasily.

They're nervous. Shadowsight's pelt prickled. Even the most experienced warriors were scared of the impostor. He pushed the thought away and carried the rosemary to the medicine den, where he dropped it beside Mothwing.

She sniffed it. "That's strong. Where did you find it?"

"Near the lakeshore," he told her. "Where we collect mallow."

"We'd better dry it a little before we put it in the store," Mothwing mewed.

"Really?" Shadowsight blinked at her. "Won't it lose its power if it dries out?"

"Some, but it'll keep longer and save us another trip to the lake." Mothwing began to spread out the stems, but Shadowsight was hardly listening. His thoughts had flitted to his father. "Where's Tigerstar?"

Mothwing nodded toward the leader's den. "With Dovewing."

"I'll go and check that they're ready." It couldn't be long now. Beside the clearing, Cloverfoot's tail was flicking restlessly. Blazefire's pelt twitched next to her. Shadowsight padded past them and paused outside Tigerstar's den. He could hear his father's mew within.

"Do you really think the impostor will admit he's Ashfur?"

Shadowsight leaned closer to the brambles screening the leader's den as his mother answered.

"Squirrelflight will find a way to make him," Dovewing promised.

"And what if she can't?" Tigerstar's voice was taut with worry.

Shadowsight felt fear flutter in his belly. If his father was uncertain, perhaps this plan wasn't such a good one after all.

Dovewing answered calmly. "She will. Don't forget, I used to be a Thunderclan cat. I've known her my whole life, and I trust her."

Tigerstar frowned, considering her words. He gave a slow shake of his head. "It just feels too risky," he murmured. "What if he escapes? I don't see what difference it will make, knowing whether he's Ashfur or not."

"Knowing who's causing this problem might be the key to

solving it," Dovewing soothed. "If it is Ashfur, at least we'll know who we're dealing with. And if we can get him talking, he might let slip why StarClan has gone quiet."

"Or we might just be sucked in by another pack of lies."

"We've agreed to go ahead with the plan," Dovewing mewed firmly. "There's nothing we can do now except wait for Squirrelflight."

Shadowsight shifted his paws nervously.

"Shadowsight?" His father's mew made him jump. The brambles rustled as a paw drew them aside. Tigerstar stared at him. "Have you got something to add?"

"Sorry." Shadowsight blinked at him. "I didn't mean to eavesdrop. I was just coming to see if you were ready."

"How long have you been listening?" Tigerstar's voice was low but steady.

Shadowsight dropped his gaze. "Not long. You sounded so worried. I just—"

"Don't be angry with him." Dovewing nosed Tigerstar out of the way and beckoned Shadowsight inside with a nod. "We're all worried." She ran her tail protectively along Shadowsight's spine. "But it will be okay," she told him gently. "I trust Squirrelflight."

"Her plan might go wrong." Shadowsight thought of the stories his mother had told about the dead Thunderclan warrior as they'd trekked home from the Gathering last night. "You said Ashfur was a fox-heart."

"That's just what the older cats used to say," she mewed.

"I knew him a little," Tigerstar grunted. "When I stayed

in Thunderclan as a 'paw. There was always something dark about him. Like he had something on his mind."

"What I don't understand"—Dovewing turned to Tigerstar—"is why he was allowed into StarClan in the first place."

"Perhaps StarClan thought he could change." Tigerstar shrugged, looking unconvinced by his own answer. "But if Squirrelflight is right, then apparently he spent his time there just waiting for a chance to get revenge on the Clans."

Dovewing moved closer to Shadowsight. "We don't know for sure that she *is* right."

"I don't know why we're bothering to find out," Tigerstar sniffed. "We should just drive him from the lake for good, like we would any rogue."

"But what about Bramblestar?" Shadowsight wondered again what had become of Bramblestar's ghost. According to the SkyClan warrior Rootspring, he hadn't been seen for more than a moon. "He needs his body back."

"Let's not worry about that now," Dovewing mewed. "Squirrelflight will be here soon, and, one way or another, we'll have an answer. That will help us figure out what to do next."

Shadowsight tipped his head to one side. A thought had been nagging him since Squirrelflight had first suggested the impostor was Ashfur. He hadn't mentioned it before, in case he was wrong. But he was alone with Dovewing and Tigerstar now. "What did Ashfur look like?"

Tigerstar met his gaze, puzzled. "He was a gray tom," he mewed.

"Did he have blue eyes?" Shadowsight pressed.

"Yes." Tigerstar's pelt prickled across his shoulders. He glanced at Dovewing. "Why?"

"I think I saw him." Shadowsight's mouth felt dry as he remembered the blue-eyed tom he'd seen in a dream.

"When?" Dovewing thrust her muzzle closer, her whiskers trembling.

"When I ate the deathberries." Shadowsight had swallowed deathberries in an attempt to put himself into a deep enough sleep that he could search for Bramblestar's ghost in the realm beyond the living. "While I was sleeping, I saw a ghost cat leave Bramblestar's body. It was a gray tom I'd never seen before. He had blue eyes."

Dovewing and Tigerstar exchanged glances again. A thought seemed to pass between them.

"Is it him?" Shadowsight asked nervously.

"We don't know." Dovewing touched her muzzle to his head. "It could be, but we'll have to wait for Squirrelflight before we can be sure."

Paw steps sounded outside the den. Cloverfoot's mew rang through the brambles. "I'm taking the border patrol out." Her voice was louder and brighter than usual, as though she were announcing the patrol not just to Tigerstar, but to the whole camp.

"Okay." Tigerstar raised his voice to match hers.

Shadowsight's chest tightened. It was starting. They were going through with Squirrelflight's plan. He dipped his head to Tigerstar. "Good luck," he breathed as he hurried out of the den.

"Good luck," Dovewing called softly after him, a tremor in her mew.

Outside, Cloverfoot was already leading Blazefire and Yarrowleaf out of camp. Around the clearing, his Clanmates watched the patrol leave, eyes glittering with trepidation. Shadowsight padded toward the medicine den, his breath shallow. Whoever the impostor was, he'd attacked Shadowsight as he'd traveled to the last half-moon meeting and had thrown him over the edge of a gorge, leaving him for dead. A cat who could do that was capable of anything. Especially if he was a spirit who could come back from the dead and steal a living cat's body. He must be more powerful than any cat the Clans had ever known. *And we've lost contact with StarClan.* Shadowsight pressed back a shiver and began to straighten up the rosemary stems Mothwing had laid out. *This impostor has the power of the stars in his paws, and we have to fight him alone.* Was it possible that, this time, the Clans faced an enemy they couldn't defeat?

As morning slid into afternoon, the sun burned hot where it penetrated the thick pine branches. Shadowsight shifted away from the heat when sunshine reached the patch where he was sitting. He'd stripped the needlelike leaves from the rosemary stems and spread them out on the earth behind him to catch the sunshine that had made him move. If Mothwing wanted them dried, he might as well do it thoroughly. He needed something to distract him while he waited.

The exiled RiverClan medicine cat had gone inside, disappearing into the medicine den only a few moments ago to consult with Puddleshine about which herbs still needed to be gathered. Shadowsight sat up and began to wash the rosemary scent from his paws with his tongue. He pricked his ears, listening for paw steps outside the camp. It couldn't be long now, surely. Flowerstem and Whorlpelt were still working on the elders' den. Stonewing was nibbling at the shrew he'd taken from the fresh-kill pile. Their gazes flitted toward the camp entrance from time to time, and Shadowsight wondered if they were nervous too.

His heart seemed to beat in his throat as he washed between his claws. Then he froze. There it was: the sound the whole camp had been waiting for. Paws were thrumming beyond the camp walls. Cloverfoot's yowl rang through the forest. "We're under attack!"

Shadowsight leaped up. Whorlpelt and Flowerstem dropped the vine they'd been threading through the wall of the elders' den. Stonewing was already on his paws as Tigerstar and Dovewing raced into the clearing.

Tigerstar's eyes were round as Cloverfoot hurtled into camp. Blazefire and Yarrowleaf skidded to a halt at her tail. "What is it?" he demanded, as though he didn't already know.

Shadowsight held his breath. The whole camp was aware that the attack had been planned. His Clanmates listened, fur bristling, ears pricked, anticipating what Cloverfoot would say next.

"Thunderclan warriors are on the border, with SkyClan and RiverClan." She feigned wide-eyed terror. "And Wind-Clan warriors are on their way!"

Movement caught Shadowsight's eye as a shadow slid from the hollow tree. The impostor was crossing the bramble enclosure outside his prison. His fur was still ragged from the battle, and the wounds he'd suffered had not yet healed. Sparrowtail and Scorchfur turned to face him, their tails twitching a warning as he padded to the opening and stared out across the camp. His eyes flashed with interest as Cloverfoot went on.

"They say that they're coming to kill the impostor." Cloverfoot's pelt spiked impressively.

Tigerstar looked outraged. "But we agreed he would be spared for now."

"They say they don't care what their leaders have agreed." Cloverfoot turned, alarmed, toward the hollow tree, and looked the impostor in the eye. "They say Bramblestar has to die."

Shadowsight searched the impostor's gaze for signs of fear. But the dark tabby stared impassively back. *Isn't he scared?* Perhaps death held no fear for a cat who'd died already. *Or perhaps he knows something we don't.* Shadowsight's paws felt heavy with dread.

Tigerstar lashed his tail. "We must defend our territory!"

He nodded to Mothwing, who had hurried from the medicine den with Puddleshine. "Stay with Oakfur," he told her. "Shadowsight, guard the herb store. Puddleshine, come with me. There might be injuries." He swung his head toward his warriors, who were already clustering into a patrol. "I want every ShadowClan warrior to fight. We must not let these invaders reach the camp."

The ShadowClan leader charged through the entrance tunnel, his warriors at his heels. Mothwing raced to the elders' den and nosed Oakfur inside, hauling loose brambles from the walls to block the entrance. Shadowsight froze as pelts whisked past him. A moment later, the clearing was empty. Bracken swished beyond the camp walls as ShadowClan crashed away through the forest.

Shadowsight's paws seemed to fuse with the earth. Heart pounding, he stared at Sparrowtail and Scorchfur, knowing what they would do next.

"Should we go with them?" Sparrowtail asked.

Scorchfur nodded. "They'll need our help."

"What about . . . ?" Sparrowtail flicked his tail toward the prisoner.

"Where would he go?" Scorchfur shrugged. "Every warrior in the forest wants him dead. This camp is probably the safest place for him."

Shadowsight watched, heart sinking, as the two warriors headed for the entrance and raced into the forest. This was the moment he'd been dreading most. The deserted camp stretched around him, seeming emptier than he'd ever known, and he forced his whiskers not to tremble as he turned his head toward the impostor. He was alone with the cat who'd tried to kill him.

The dark warrior met his gaze. His eyes gleamed mischievously. "Don't worry," he meowed. "You're safe with me." Shadowsight wanted to back away, but he forced himself to hold his ground as the impostor began to pad toward the fresh-kill pile. "I might as well make myself at home."

"Aren't you scared?" Shadowsight asked. "Warriors are coming to kill you." He knew his father wouldn't let that happen, but the impostor didn't.

The false Bramblestar shrugged. "It's your Clanmates who are fighting them, not me." Was he enjoying this?

Shadowsight watched him sniff the fresh-kill pile, pushing aside the mice at the top and tugging out a fat pigeon to examine it more closely. Then the impostor straightened, clearly uninterested in the prey after all, and looked toward the entrance. Was he planning to escape? Shadowsight's belly tightened. *Squirrelflight, where are you?* Surely she should be here by now! That was what she'd planned. *How can I stop him if he tries to run away? I'm a medicine cat!* He forced his breath to slow as the dark warrior looked back lazily at the fresh-kill pile.

"Do you want a mouse?" he meowed silkily.

Shadowsight swallowed back panic. "N-no, thank you."

"Aren't you hungry?"

"No." Shadowsight's mew was hardly more than a whisper. Why *wasn't* the impostor trying to escape? *Is he planning to finish what he started? Does he want to kill me properly this time?*

As his thoughts whirled, movement caught his eye. Orange fur rippled in the shadowy entrance. *Squirrelflight!* She'd come. Relief washed Shadowsight's pelt. *At last!* Did that mean the other leaders were here, ready to hear the impostor's confession? Were they already in place outside the bramble walls?

The prisoner stiffened, his gaze sharpening. "What are you looking at?" He followed Shadowsight's gaze, his hackles lifting as he spotted Squirrelflight.

The Thunderclan she-cat hurried across the clearing, keeping low, her ears flattened against her head. Shadowsight held his breath as the impostor's attention focused on her, and he prayed that he wouldn't pick up the other leaders' scents.

Squirrelflight flashed him a look, and Shadowsight remembered what he was supposed to do. He leaped in front of the impostor, blocking her way. "Keep back!" he warned her. "He mustn't be hurt!"

"I can defend myself!" Claws hooked his scruff. The impostor had grabbed him and was dragging him off his paws. Shadowsight scrabbled at the air as the dark tabby lifted him like a kit and flung him to one side. He landed with a thump, scrambling up as the false Bramblestar faced Squirrelflight. Would he attack her before she had a chance to speak?

Squirrelflight drew up short. "I'm here to help you!"

The impostor stared at her. Disbelief lit his amber eyes. "Why?"

"I know who you are now!" Squirrelflight's face showed excitement. "Why didn't you tell me before?"

The impostor looked wary. "Tell you?"

Shadowsight watched, holding his breath, willing the prisoner to believe Squirrelflight's lie. He could see Mothwing peeping through a gap in the wall of the elders' den. *Please let the plan work!* He wondered if StarClan could hear him.

Squirrelflight's eyes rounded eagerly. "We need to leave. Now. Together. That's why you came back, isn't it? That's why you stole Bramblestar's body? To be with me?"

Hope and suspicion seemed to tussle in the impostor's gaze. For the first time, Shadowsight saw him look uncertain. *Is the plan working?*

Squirrelflight pressed on, slowly moving closer, allowing a purr to hum in her throat. "I'm sure now," she mewed gently. "I'm sure it's you. I knew there was something different about Bramblestar from the moment he got his new life. But it wasn't *his* life, was it? It was yours." She stopped suddenly, her gaze swinging toward Shadowsight.

He stiffened. *Don't look at me! Look at him!*

"I have you to thank for that," she meowed. "It was your treatment that killed Bramblestar and let this happen." She turned back to the impostor. "Without Shadowsight's help, you would never have come back," she went on as the dark warrior stared at her in wonder. "You're the tom I always loved, much more than Bramblestar. And now we can be together, forever." Her eyes shone with such love that Shadowsight felt panic spark beneath his pelt. She was pretending, right? She didn't really love this fox-heart!

"You love me?" The impostor spoke weakly, as though he was scared he was dreaming.

"It is you, right?" Squirrelflight's gaze bored into his. "Tell me it's you. Say your name, so I know I'm not making a fool of myself. Tell me it's you."

Shadowsight stared at the impostor, blood roaring in his ears. He no longer saw Squirrelflight. He forgot about Mothwing. He held his breath as Bramblestar's body seemed to change. Not its color or its shape, but its posture shifted, its hindquarters hunching down and leaning to one side, the shoulders sharpening so that they seemed to strain at the skin and fur that covered them, the head lowering, the muzzle questing forward like a snake's. Before Shadowsight's eyes, Bramblestar seemed, despite the tabby pelt and amber gaze, to become another cat.

"It *is* me. It's Ashfur." This stranger spoke with a voice harsher than Bramblestar's. It had an edge that seemed to carry a sneer. And yet he spoke softly, uncertainty gone as hope seemed to triumph. "I knew you'd realize eventually. I knew you'd see the truth."

"Ashfur!" Delight shone in Squirrelflight's eyes.

Shadowsight felt sick to see it. *She's pretending,* he told himself sharply. *This is the plan.*

"If only you'd told me sooner," she mewed breathlessly. "We could have saved a lot of time."

Ashfur padded closer, his eyes wide with joy. "I had to make sure you'd be on my side." He hesitated, frowning suddenly. "You acted like you didn't want any cat to replace Bramblestar."

"I didn't know it was you," Squirrelflight mewed breathlessly. "I could have helped you, if you'd told me."

"I didn't need help," Ashfur sneered. "It's been so easy, turning the Clans against one another as they scramble to obey me and rid themselves of *codebreakers*." He purred loudly, clearly pleased with himself, then looked at Shadowsight. "All I had to do was visit that little mouse-brain and give him *visions*." Shadowsight burned with shame as Ashfur went on. "Telling him how to treat Bramblestar's sickness. He was so eager to believe that he was StarClan's chosen one. He really believed he could cure Bramblestar by letting him freeze to death on the moor."

I killed him. Shadowsight wanted to crawl away and hide. He *had* wanted to be the medicine cat StarClan most trusted. *Ashfur's right! I am a mouse-brain. And a traitor!*

Squirrelflight was still gazing fondly at Ashfur. "You're so clever. Of course you didn't need my help. You found your way back from StarClan. That couldn't have been easy."

"I did it for you," he mewed urgently. "I only ever wanted you, and I wasn't going to let anything get in my way."

"Didn't StarClan try to stop you?" Squirrelflight asked.

"StarClan!" Ashfur grunted in disgust. "That bunch of do-gooders didn't stand a chance. And they won't be getting in my way ever again. I've seen to that."

No! Rage flashed like lightning through Shadowsight's pelt, driving out fear. "What have you done?" He crossed the clearing, pushing Squirrelflight aside, and glared at Ashfur. "Have you hurt them?"

"Stay out of this!" Ashfur unsheathed his claws and swung

a paw at Shadowsight. As Shadowsight ducked, Squirrel-flight tugged him backward by the scruff and bundled him behind her.

"Don't waste time on him," she told Ashfur. "We need to get out of here."

Ashfur grunted. "I should have killed him last time."

"Last time?" Squirrelflight's eyes widened.

"On his way to the Moonpool." Ashfur glared threaten-ingly at Shadowsight as he crouched behind Squirrelflight. "Berrynose lured his Clanmate away, and I attacked him. I should have checked he was dead before I threw him down the gorge. He's tougher than he looks."

Squirrelflight was staring at him. "Berrynose lured Puddle-shine away?"

"Of course." He looked surprised. "He was my deputy. He was following orders."

Squirrelflight didn't move, but Shadowsight could see that she was struggling to keep the fur along her spine smooth. "I didn't think Berrynose would have the courage to do any-thing as brave as trying to kill another leader's kit."

"He didn't know we were trying to kill him," Ashfur growled. "I told him we were just going to scare him. Berry-nose pretended to be wounded so I could get that little goody-four-paws alone and deal with him. Afterward I told Berrynose I'd scared him so much he'd run away."

The brambles at the camp entrance swished. Shadowsight's heart lurched as paws pounded over the clearing. He turned as Tigerstar leaped past him and hurled himself, spitting, at

Ashfur. "You tried to kill my son!" Rage turned the Shadow-Clan leader's yowl into a hiss as he sent Ashfur tumbling across the clearing. He plunged after the impostor, hooking his claws deep into his flesh.

Ashfur's eyes lost their glitter of shock and narrowed to slits. He twisted in Tigerstar's grip, pushing up with powerful hind paws, and shook the ShadowClan leader from his back. Eyes blazing with hate, he aimed a vicious blow at Tigerstar. The ShadowClan leader met his attack with a snarl, raising his forepaws to slash at Ashfur's muzzle. Ashfur ducked clear, darting beneath Tigerstar and knocking his legs from under him.

Leave him alone! Desperate with terror, Shadowsight prepared to leap at the impostor. Before he could, Harestar's yowl echoed across the clearing.

"Stop them!"

Shadowsight froze as warriors streamed around him. The leaders and their deputies were surging into the ShadowClan camp.

Reedwhisker and Hawkwing raced ahead to drive Ashfur back, while Cloverfoot dragged Tigerstar away. The Shadow-Clan leader spat with fury, struggling in Cloverfoot's grip until Crowfeather grabbed his scruff and pressed him to the ground.

"Calm down," hissed the WindClan deputy.

Ashfur ducked and slipped past Reedwhisker, hissing when Hawkwing tried to drag him onto his side. Blood showed on Ashfur's flank where a wound from the Clan battle had reopened. But the impostor seemed impervious to pain. He fought wildly as Lionblaze darted in and grasped his churning hind legs while Hawkwing pinned his tail so fiercely to the ground that he couldn't move.

Ashfur snarled in their grip. His gaze flashed around the leaders before stopping on Squirrelflight. "You lied." Hurt showed in his face for a moment before it twisted into hate. "You betrayed me!" Thrashing in vain, he tried to get free. "You think you've won, but you don't know how powerful I am! You're all going to suffer!" His yowl was wild with fury. "And not just you. Your descendants will pay for what you've done to me. And your ancestors! The Clans are going to get a taste of *real* justice, the kind they've avoided for far too long!"

"Take him back to the hollow tree." Tigerstar hauled himself to his paws as Crowfeather and Cloverfoot released their grip.

"You can't hold me forever!" Ashfur screeched as Crowfeather and Hawkwing dragged him, writhing, toward the bramble enclosure. Blood trailed behind him as Cloverfoot and Reedwhisker hurried to help.

Shadowsight swallowed. What had Ashfur meant? How could he harm their descendants? Or their ancestors? Then he remembered Ashfur's boast to Squirrelflight about StarClan. *They won't be getting in my way ever again. I've seen to that.* Had he already hurt StarClan?

Perhaps he's just trying to scare us. And yet Ashfur could move between the living and the dead. Shadowsight had seen it with his own eyes. Could he really be powerful enough to sink his claws into StarClan's hunting grounds?

Tigerstar shook out his pelt. "He'll never see reason."

Shadowsight blinked in surprise. His father was staring hollow-eyed at Ashfur as the deputies shoved him into the brambled enclosure. Ashfur had clearly shaken him.

"What do we do?" Harestar meowed. "We can't hold him prisoner forever."

Squirrelflight flicked her tail. "Of course we can't. Bramblestar needs his body back."

Mistystar and Leafstar exchanged glances, as though unsure what to say.

"We need to act quickly," Tigerstar meowed.

"But we still don't know what we're dealing with," Mistystar mewed. "How has he done this?"

Leafstar nodded. "He clearly has powers we don't understand. We need to think about what to do."

"It's clear what we have to do," Tigerstar growled darkly.

Shadowsight's fur lifted along his spine. He knew what his father was about to suggest. Tigerstar wanted to kill Ashfur.

"Let's not do anything rash," Mistystar mewed quickly. Had she also guessed what Tigerstar was thinking? "We need to make sure Ashfur can't escape. He mustn't be allowed to hurt any more cats, living or dead." She looked around at the other leaders. "It's too much to expect ShadowClan to shoulder this burden alone." Leafstar dipped her head in agreement as she went on. "Each Clan should send two of its strongest warriors to guard Ashfur until we figure out what to do."

"Really?" Tigerstar looked surprised. "You think we can

guard him forever?"

"Just until we've decided what to do," Harestar mewed.

"But you heard what he said!" Indignation sparked in Tigerstar's eyes. "He's confessed to everything. Why do you want to keep him around? He's dangerous."

Squirrelflight blinked at him. "What else can we do?"

"We can kill him," Tigerstar meowed bluntly. "Keeping Ashfur alive is like keeping deathberries in a nursery. Some cat is going to get hurt eventually."

Mistystar looked away. Harestar shifted his paws. Only Leafstar met Tigerstar's gaze. Was she going to agree?

Squirrelflight's hackles lifted. "You can't kill him!" she gasped. "We need him alive until we can work out a way to get Bramblestar back into his body!"

Shadowsight stared at her. How in StarClan could they possibly do that?

Leafstar dipped her head. "Okay," she meowed. "For now. Ashfur should remain under guard, and as long as we know where he is, there's no need for us to do anything hasty."

Mistystar whisked her tail. "We'll try to hold out until Bramblestar's ghost returns, or StarClan can give us guidance."

Harestar grunted. "StarClan's been gone so long, I wonder if they're ever coming back."

Shadowsight thrust his muzzle toward the WindClan leader. "Of course they're coming back!" he blurted. "They must. They have to!" The thought that the Clans would have to survive without StarClan forever sent a ripple of panic through his fur.

Tigerstar's gaze darkened. "Perhaps they can't return as long as Ashfur is here in the forest, alive in Bramblestar's body."

Shadowsight stared at his father, pressing his paws into the ground to stop them from trembling. A darker thought struck him. What if it made no difference whether Ashfur was alive in Bramblestar's body or not? He'd seen Ashfur's spirit. He knew that it didn't need a body to exist. His breath caught in his throat. What if the Clans' last resort—killing Bramblestar's body—wasn't enough to prevent Ashfur from destroying the Clans? Would they be sacrificing the only chance the Thunderclan leader had of returning, only to discover that Ashfur was still powerful enough to break the connection between them and StarClan forever?

CHAPTER 3

Rootspring's heart felt heavy as he nosed his way through the long grass that edged the island. He could smell the scents of the other Clans in the clearing ahead. Each Clan had already buried its own lost warriors on its territory, but it felt right that they should come together to hold a vigil for all the warriors who had died at the paws of their Clanmates in the battle to drive the impostor from the lake. Rootspring hoped that this vigil would bring peace and reconciliation to those left behind.

His Clanmates moved like shadows in the grass around him. Violetshine and Tree padded at his side, while Frecklewish and Macgyver trailed a few tail-lengths behind with Palesky and Sagenose. Leafstar and Hawkwing were already filing into the clearing. He could hear Squirrelflight and Harestar greet them, their mews ringing in the soft night air.

Violetshine leaned closer to Tree. "She's hardly slept since Sandynose died," she whispered, nodding toward Plumwillow. The dark gray she-cat's tail grazed the earth as she followed Hawkwing, Dewspring, and Reedclaw, their heads low.

Tree watched them pad into the clearing. "I'll miss him."

Rootspring was surprised to hear his father sound so fond

of any SkyClan cat. Less than a moon ago, he'd been talking about leaving the Clans and taking Rootspring, Needleclaw, and Violetshine with him.

"The Clan seems strange without him," Violetshine mewed. "I still can't believe he died."

"I can't believe any cat died," Tree murmured. "How could *warriors* fight on the side of that impostor?"

"They believed he spoke for StarClan," Violetshine reminded him.

Rootspring's pelt bristled. "Why would *StarClan* order warriors to fight against their Clanmates?"

Palesky mewed from behind. "Enough. This vigil is about forgiveness," she reminded Rootspring.

Sagenose grunted. "It'll take more than a vigil to forget that Sandynose was killed by warriors for the sake of a traitor."

Violetshine glanced back at the pale gray tom. "No cat will forget," she told him. "But that doesn't mean we can't forgive."

Rootspring blinked at his mother. How could she be so kind? And yet she was right. It wouldn't help to blame the Clans. The *impostor* was responsible, and now they knew who he was and that he hadn't been trying to defend StarClan or the warrior code when he'd turned the Clans against one another. He'd only wanted revenge for something that had happened moons ago. Anger sparked afresh in Rootspring's belly. Did Ashfur really want to destroy the Clans just because Squirrelflight had rejected him? Could any cat be so selfish? If every cat tried to kill their Clanmates after they had been dumped, there would be no Clans left.

Rootspring followed Violetshine and Tree into the clearing. Warriors milled about in the moonlight. The Thunderclan patrol stood silently together, and Rootspring wondered if the impostor who'd pretended to be their leader had left rifts in the Clan.

Bristlefrost caught his eye from where she stood beside Blossomfall and Spotfur. She blinked at him warmly and Rootspring felt his grief ease, but only a little. The secret rebellion against the impostor was over now; peace between the Clans meant he wouldn't see her as often. He blinked a greeting in return, then looked away self-consciously, wondering who she shared a den with now. Was her nest beside a warrior she'd fought only a quarter moon ago?

He guessed there weren't such divisions in ShadowClan. They'd all fought side by side in the battle. WindClan had been united too, admittedly in defense of the impostor. Only Breezepelt and Crowfeather had rebelled. And WindClan was now mingling comfortably with ShadowClan. Dovewing was talking to Heathertail, while Cloverfoot and Crowfeather shared news, their heads bent close. Hope surged in Rootspring's chest. Perhaps this vigil would allow the Clans to forgive one another and themselves, just as Violetshine had hoped.

And yet the clearing wasn't crowded. Moonlight rippled in the empty spaces between groups of cats. Rootspring noticed that hardly any RiverClan cats had come. Mothwing was here, with Harelight and Icewing, but they weren't River-Clan cats anymore. Mistystar had refused to take Harelight and Icewing back after they'd joined the rebels. Mothwing had been a rebel too, but Mistystar had invited the medicine cat back into the Clan. Mothwing had declared she wouldn't go until their leader extended the same invitation to Harelight and Icewing.

They stood now with the ShadowClan cats, their gazes mournful as they watched the pawful of RiverClan cats that had come to the vigil: only Reedwhisker, Willowshine, Lizardtail, and Gorseclaw. Rootspring realized with a jolt that the RiverClan leader wasn't in the clearing. He hurried toward Harelight, Icewing, and Mothwing.

Harelight saw him and flicked his long white tail in greeting, just as he'd done when they'd met as rebels outside the Clans. "How are you?"

"Good, thanks." Rootspring scanned the gathered cats distractedly. "Is Mistystar here?"

"I haven't seen her," Harelight answered.

Icewing sniffed. "I guess she doesn't want to be part of a vigil that honors rebels."

"But Reedwhisker came." Rootspring glanced across the clearing at the RiverClan deputy.

"Mistystar had to send some cat so she wouldn't offend the other Clans," Harelight pointed out. "And to honor Softpelt." Rootspring's chest tightened. Would Mistystar's absence cause more friction they couldn't afford?

"Besides," Icewing growled, "what do we care who she sends? We're ShadowClan cats now." Her mew was bitter.

Mothwing arched her tail to touch her Clanmate's spine.

"We'll always be RiverClan cats at heart." As she spoke, her gaze reached toward Willowshine. Her former apprentice returned it eagerly; Reedwhisker dipped his head, while Gorseclaw and Lizardtail blinked warmly at the dappled medicine cat. Mothwing lifted her tail. "It looks like they still want to talk to us." She padded quickly toward her former Clanmates. "Are you coming?" she asked Icewing, not looking back.

Icewing sniffed again. "It's okay for her. Mistystar asked her to come back to the Clan."

Harelight glanced sympathetically at the white she-cat. "She might forgive us eventually and ask us back too."

Rootspring's heart ached at the hurt and hope mingled in the warrior's words. He didn't want to think what it must be like to be banished from his Clan. "Mistystar let Softpelt's kin come to the vigil," he offered encouragingly. "That's close to forgiveness, isn't it?"

"Softpelt fought for the impostor, not against him," Icewing reminded him. "Do you suppose she would have let them come if Dappletuft had been the only warrior to die?"

"I would have been here for them both, whatever happened," Harelight mewed mournfully.

Rootspring blinked at him, sharing Harelight's sorrow. Dappletuft and Softpelt had been the white tom's littermates. "Mistystar must realize by now that we were all trying to defend the Clans in our own way."

As he spoke, Squirrelflight lifted her tail and gazed around the gathered cats. "Let's begin," she mewed.

Rootspring hesitated as Harelight and Icewing followed ShadowClan toward the middle of the clearing. He frowned, puzzled. How could the Gathering begin? The leaders hadn't climbed into the Great Oak yet. They stood in the clearing, gazing expectantly at their Clanmates. *It's a vigil, not a Gathering,* Rootspring reminded himself. He hurried to join his Clanmates, wondering what would happen next.

Solemnly, the cats formed a circle around the center of the clearing, where the Great Oak cast a shadow across the empty earth.

As Rootspring slid in beside Tree and Violetshine, Squirrelflight padded forward. "We have come here tonight," she mewed grimly, "to remember our Clanmates who died fighting for what they thought was right."

A murmur of approval rippled around the encircling cats.

Harestar joined Squirrelflight, his pelt sleek, his head high. "Every warrior who fought that day believed they were fighting for StarClan."

Nodding, Tigerstar joined them. "Every cat who died, died for their Clan."

"We can ask no more of our warriors than that." Leafstar padded to the ShadowClan leader's side. "We come to honor those who gave their lives to defend the way of life they believed in."

Rootspring saw eyes glitter with sadness around the clearing. He felt the Clans' grief like a weight, and knew it must be reaching as cold and heavy as rain through every cat's pelt. Snowbird leaned, trembling, against Scorchfur. Their kits

Conefoot and Frondwhisker had died in the battle.

Squirrelflight spoke again. "This is a time for remembrance and forgiveness. . . ."

Rootspring let his attention drift around the clearing, searching for ghosts. He used to be so panicked when he spotted one; now he wanted to see them. It had become instinct to look out for them. He wondered if this was how Tree had lived his whole life. The shadows between the trees were no longer places he scanned only for prey. Ghosts might move there. And yet he hadn't seen one since the battle. Bramblestar's spirit had disappeared, and none of the cats who'd died had appeared in the forest. He wanted to believe they were safe in StarClan now, but he doubted it. When Harestar had lost a life in the battle, he'd traveled to StarClan to be given another. *I was in StarClan's hunting grounds,* he'd told the Clans afterward. *I heard only distorted voices, and saw only the haziest figures, no more than a blur. Our warrior ancestors were still there, but it was like they were fading into nothing.*

The memory sent a fresh shiver through Rootspring's pelt. If StarClan was fading, where could the dead warriors go? And if there was no StarClan to go to and they weren't ghosts in the forest, where were they? The leaders could stand here and talk of honor and forgiveness, but the impostor might have already done more damage than could be fixed. He might have severed the Clans' connection to StarClan forever and taken from the dead their last place to wander. What were warriors without StarClan? They were no more than rogues.

Rootspring gazed harder into the shadows around the

clearing, willing himself to glimpse a ghostly pelt moving beneath the trees, but he saw only darkness. He felt suddenly hollow, as though claws had ripped out his heart. He flinched as Snowbird let out a wail. Squirrelflight had finished talking, and Spotfur and Blossomfall lifted their voices to join Snowbird in her grief. Rootspring stared at them, his mouth dry. Without StarClan, they might never see their loved ones again. Without StarClan, this grief might just be the beginning.

Rootspring was thankful for the warmth of Violetshine's pelt as he huddled beside her. They had kept vigil all night, and dawn was beginning to show itself in the surface of the lake.

In the middle of the clearing, Squirrelflight stood and stretched. Tigerstar straightened beside her. Harestar lifted his gaze to meet the ShadowClan leader's and nodded as though agreeing. Together they headed for the Great Oak, picking their way through the circle of cats who still crouched in the pale dawn light. Squirrelflight and Leafstar followed, and the four leaders stopped beneath the ancient tree and began to talk softly among themselves. Rootspring watched them, interest pricking through his fur. Were they discussing what to do with the impostor?

Around Rootspring, the Clan cats were moving, stretching away the stiffness of the long night's vigil.

Tree was lapping at Violetshine's pelt. "You'll feel warmer once we head home," he told her.

"I hope the sun comes up soon." Violetshine fluffed out her

fur, as though soon wasn't quick enough.

A pale gray pelt caught Rootspring's eye as Bristlefrost stretched, arching her back until her tail trembled. Spotfur was hunched beside her. Bristlefrost nosed the warrior gently to her paws.

Rootspring hurried to speak to them. This could be the only chance he had to talk to Bristlefrost until the next Gathering, and he'd grown used to spending time with her. Standing shoulder to shoulder with her against the impostor, he'd felt they were almost Clanmates. "I'm sorry for your loss," he told Spotfur as he reached them. "Stemleaf was a brave warrior."

"Thank you." Spotfur returned his gaze, grief glittering afresh in her eyes. "He was." She turned away and headed toward Blossomfall, who'd found a spot at the edge of the clearing where sunlight was beginning to filter between the trees.

Bristlefrost gazed sadly after her. "She's so upset," she mewed.

Rootspring wished he could think of something to say to cheer Bristlefrost up. "She loved him a lot," he mumbled awkwardly.

Bristlefrost looked at him suddenly. "I feel kind of guilty."

Rootspring blinked, surprised. None of this was her fault. She'd done everything she could to protect her Clanmates. "Why?"

"I feel like I should have mourned him more."

"Who? Stemleaf?" Rootspring was puzzled.

"I feel bad that I got over him," she explained. "I had such a crush. I thought I'd love him forever, like Spotfur does. But seeing the way Spotfur is still grieving for him makes me think that what I felt wasn't love at all." She looked again at her Clanmate, who was staring blankly across the lake now.

"I guess you've just grown up," Rootspring suggested. "We all change as we get older." He went on without thinking. "I remember what it was like to have an apprentice crush."

She turned back to him. "Did you get over yours?" They both knew he'd had a crush on her since she'd rescued him from drowning as a 'paw. Was she worried he didn't like her anymore? She must know that wasn't true.

"Of course not," he mewed, surprised that he no longer felt embarrassed by his feelings for her. He'd been teased about them for moons, but he knew now that she shared them. There was no point telling her again. They'd decided ages ago that they could never be mates because they were from different Clans. There was enough trouble for the Clans to deal with without the two of them causing more.

She returned his gaze fondly for a moment, then glanced at Snaptooth and Flywhisker as they padded past. "It's weird in Thunderclan right now," she confided as her Clanmates moved out of earshot. "Everyone is trying to get along, but it's hard to forget that some of us left the Clan and some of us stayed. No cat says anything, but you can feel it."

Rootspring's pelt twitched guiltily. SkyClan had never felt more united. They'd stood against the impostor together. "I'm sure Squirrelflight will fix it."

"I hope she can." Bristlefrost didn't look convinced. "But

how can she lead Thunderclan when StarClan hasn't given her nine lives yet? What if the Clan loses faith in her?"

"They won't," Rootspring told her. "She's strong. We've all seen that. And she has warriors like you to support her."

"I guess," Bristlefrost conceded. "But there are tough times ahead. Knowing who the impostor is doesn't mean that we can defeat him."

"We can." Rootspring hoped it was true. He tried to push away the fears that had haunted him last night. "We'll defeat him and StarClan will come back and everything will go back to normal."

"What about Bramblestar?" Bristlefrost asked nervously. "Will *he* ever come back?"

"Of course," Rootspring told her breezily. "Once we've gotten rid of Ashfur." He held Bristlefrost's gaze, trying to look positive, but he could see she felt as doubtful as he did.

She lifted her chin suddenly. "Yes," she stated firmly. "It'll all be okay."

"There's no harm in hoping for the best," Rootspring said.

She purred, only her eyes betraying worry. "Even if it's not possible."

The leaders had finished their discussion. Squirrelflight's Clanmates were following her toward the tree-bridge. Tigerstar had called his warriors close while Harestar headed for the long grass.

Bristlefrost turned away. "I'd better go," she mewed. "See you soon."

"Take care of yourself," Rootspring called after her as she padded behind her Clanmates.

"You too," she called back, swishing her tail. "Thanks for trying to cheer me up."

Leafstar lingered in the clearing as the other Clans headed home. SkyClan paced around her, clearly trying to warm themselves up. Violetshine stayed close to Plumwillow, her anxious gaze on her grieving denmate. Tree sat a little apart, watching the sun lift above the distant hills. Rootspring padded to his side and, as Leafstar finally began to lead the way from the island, stuck close to him. They hadn't talked properly since they'd met at the battle, and the vigil had given Rootspring time to think. Cats who had been among them a quarter moon ago were gone now, and their Clanmates might never see them again. He'd realized that there was so much he wanted to say to his father while he still had the chance.

As they padded through the long grass and crossed the tree-bridge, he didn't speak, but just let his pelt brush against Tree's. But once they reached the shore, he slowed his pace to let their Clanmates pull ahead, and he was relieved when Tree slowed too. Violetshine stayed close to Plumwillow, and before long, Rootspring and Tree were trailing behind the rest of the patrol.

"It was a long night," Rootspring began casually, his gaze on the tiny waves rippling over the beach.

"Yes." Stones crunched beneath Tree's paws.

"I was hoping I'd see some spirits." Rootspring glanced at

Tree. Had his father seen any ghosts?

"I guess they didn't want to be at their own vigil," Tree mewed grimly.

"I guess not." Hope pricked in his heart. Perhaps they'd come later. Or perhaps they'd found StarClan after all. They walked on in silence for a while longer as Rootspring searched for words. At last he found them. "I wanted to thank you for sticking up for me," he mewed softly.

Tree glanced at him. "Sticking up for you?" He looked puzzled.

"When you pretended to be the one who was speaking to the ghost so I didn't have to admit that I could see it too."

Tree shrugged. "I just wanted to make it easy for you," he mewed.

"But you didn't have to." Rootspring stopped. "And I wanted you to know I appreciated it."

Tree paused and looked back. Affection shone in his gaze. "It's what any father would do," he mewed huskily. "You'll find out when you have kits of your own."

Ahead, the patrol had left the shore and disappeared into the forest where the path led toward SkyClan's camp in the hills beyond Thunderclan's land. Tree flicked his muzzle toward the ferns, which were still shivering where their Clanmates had passed. "Come on," he mewed. "We'd better catch up."

As Rootspring nodded and began to head toward the trees, a shape shimmered at the edge of his vision. Jerking his muzzle toward it, he froze, his pelt spiking along his spine.

"What's wrong?" Tree stared at him, then followed his gaze.

Rootspring held his breath. Could his father see it?

Tree's hackles lifted and Rootspring knew it must be real. A ghost cat was watching them from farther up the shore, its outline so hazy it was hard to see.

Bramblestar? Had the Thunderclan leader's ghost returned at last? He squinted harder, peering past the haze. *No.* It wasn't Bramblestar. It was a she-cat.

The ghost cat noticed them watching it and padded closer. As she neared, she seemed to grow more solid, as though she had decided to let herself be seen. Her ears pricked with interest. Rootspring guessed she was a kittypet. Her pelt looked as soft as a kit's, and a warrior—even a ghostly one—would never approach so carelessly.

Tree let his hackles fall. As he lifted his tail in a friendly greeting, Rootspring did the same.

"Hi," Tree mewed. "I haven't seen you before."

The kittypet looked surprised. "I'm surprised you can see me now." She looked from Tree to Rootspring, her eyes growing even wider as she seemed to realize that Rootspring was staring at her too. "Can you *both* see me?"

"Yes." Tree dipped his head politely.

"But how?" The kittypet frowned, clearly puzzled. "Living cats usually can't."

We're different. Rootspring stopped himself before he could say it out loud. He was used to seeing ghosts now, but he wasn't ready to admit to this strange kittypet that he wasn't an ordinary warrior. Instead he shrugged. "I don't know. We just can."

"You're warriors, right?" the kittypet mewed.

Rootspring nodded. "Have you seen warriors before?"

"Of course." She blinked. "They're all around the lake."

"What's your name?" Tree asked.

"Cheddar."

Rootspring's ears pricked. *What a weird name.*

Tree didn't seem surprised. "I'm Tree, and this is Rootspring."

"Hi." She lapped her shoulder fiercely as though responding to a sudden itch.

Rootspring wondered if ghost cats had ghost fleas. His thoughts began to quicken. If she was a ghost, and he was seeing her, then he could be sure he still had the power to see the dead. So where were the warriors who'd been killed in the battle? If they weren't in StarClan, perhaps they were just keeping their distance from their living Clanmates. "Have you seen any other spirit cats around here?" he asked Cheddar.

Her gaze flitted along the shore, as though she was searching. "No," she mewed at last, bringing her gaze back to Rootspring. "It's just me most of the time."

Tree leaned forward. "Most of the time?" he echoed.

"I've seen some other cats around recently, but they fade in and out." Cheddar frowned. "It's like they can't decide whether to be ghosts or not."

They fade in and out. Dread pressed at the edge of Rootspring's thoughts. Did that mean they were close to disappearing altogether? "What did they look like?" he pressed.

"Some were gray; some were tabby," Cheddar told him. "There was a brown tom with ginger legs."

Sandynose? Rootspring's heart lurched.

Tree must have recognized the description as well. He glanced at Rootspring.

"Do you know them?" Cheddar's eyes widened.

"We lost some Clanmates recently," Tree explained.

"I've never seen ghosts fade like that before." Cheddar's ears twitched nervously. "Do you know what's happening to them?"

"They might be trying to join their Clanmates in StarClan," Tree suggested.

"Is that where dead warriors go?" Cheddar asked.

Rootspring nodded, wondering if Tree might be right. Were the dead warriors trying to get to StarClan?

"StarClan must be a creepy place, because they looked scared." Cheddar's pelt was spiking across her shoulders now.

Scared? Rootspring's heart quickened.

"Perhaps they were just fading into nothing." The kittypet's eyes rounded with fear. "Will that happen to me too? Dying was bad enough—I don't want to disappear forever!"

"You won't disappear," Tree promised.

Rootspring wondered how his father could be sure. Did cats without StarClan stick around forever because they had nowhere else to go?

Cheddar blinked at Tree anxiously. "How do you know?"

"You're not a warrior," Tree told her.

Do warriors disappear if they can't find their way to StarClan? Fear dropped like a stone in Rootspring's belly. With StarClan out of reach, was it possible the dead warriors might simply fade into nothing?

As his thoughts spiraled, Cheddar turned away. Rootspring watched her climb the shore. "If you see them again, tell them we're trying to help them!" he called after her.

Cheddar looked over her shoulder. "Okay."

But how? What could he do to make sure the dead Clan cats found their way safely to StarClan? Frustration sparked through his fur. What was the point of having a weird power like seeing ghost cats if he couldn't help them when they were in danger?

CHAPTER 4

❦

The mouse moved beneath the scattered leaves, making them quiver. Bristlefrost tensed. *I'll catch it this time.* She slammed her paws down, her heart leaping, then felt the mouse slither from her grasp. *Again? How?* She'd hooked it for sure! *Fox dung!* Her pelt burned with frustration. Why couldn't she catch it? She'd caught countless mice before. What was wrong with this one?

Hunger was gnawing at her belly as she hunted for food. She felt like she hadn't eaten, or slept, for days. If she could just catch this mouse, she'd break her run of bad luck—and then she'd catch another and another. No cat need ever go hungry again. She just had to catch this one mouse.

The scattered leaves rippled again. The mouse was moving beneath them once more. Bristlefrost watched it, following her training, keeping her tail still even though it wanted to whip back and forth as excitement gathered beneath her fur. *This time.* Determination hardened every muscle. Her claws itched in their sheaths. When the mouse moved, she leaped for it, throwing out her forepaws, grabbing for the shape she could see beneath the leaves. She'd keep hold of it this time! Blood pounded in her ears, bursting into fury as she felt empty earth beneath her claws again. The mouse had vanished.

Her heart sank. How could she catch prey that became invisible in a moment? As she fell back onto her haunches, her ears twitched. Sounds were pawing at her ears—voices, whose words were clear but who sounded oddly . . . distant.

"StarClan will never come back if we don't do things right!"

Thornclaw's angry yowl tugged her wide awake, blinking as the camp swam into view, her memories of hunting mice fading fast. Lionblaze's sharp reply set her fur prickling.

"Who even knows what's *right* anymore?"

"A true warrior knows!" Thornclaw's growl sounded like an accusation.

Bristlefrost sat up in her nest. Guilt twisted her belly. She'd slipped away for a nap before her border patrol at dusk. She should have stayed awake. She knew how fragile the Clan was at the moment. Now a fight was breaking out. Quickly, she hopped from her nest and poked her head out the entrance of the warriors' den.

Lionblaze was facing Thornclaw in the middle of the clearing. Afternoon sunshine had turned the Thunderclan deputy's pelt to gold, but Bristlefrost could see he was fighting to keep his hackles down. Thornclaw stared back at him, ears half flat, anger shining in the tabby's blue eyes. Their Clanmates watched from the edge.

Ivypool was staring at the two warriors in dismay. Sorrelstripe's and Dewnose's eyes rounded with worry. Twigbranch leaned forward, her ears pricked, as though ready to join in; Finleap tried to calm her with a touch of his tail as

Bumblestripe paced anxiously beside Flywhisker, Snaptooth, and Flipclaw. The three young warriors' gazes were sharp with interest.

No sign of Squirrelflight. Bristlefrost glanced up at the Highledge, toward Bramblestar's den, where Squirrelflight slept alone now. But she didn't see the acting Thunderclan leader. She must be heading a patrol. Bristlefrost slid out of the den, keeping her distance from Lionblaze and Thornclaw. She wouldn't intervene yet. An argument might clear the air, as long as it didn't get out of control.

Lionblaze glared at Thornclaw. "Are you accusing me of not being a true warrior?"

Bristlefrost held her breath. She'd been wrong. This was more than a petty squabble. All around the camp, cats had stopped what they were doing to listen. Even Graystripe had appeared at the entrance to the elders' den, watching everything with wide eyes.

"Of course not." Thornclaw looked away, and Bristlefrost breathed out a little as he backed down. But the warrior hadn't finished. "I just mean, we're floundering like fish on a riverbank when we should know what to do," he grunted.

"How *can* we know?" Lionblaze challenged. "No Clan has had a leader stranded between life and death before."

"Exactly," Thornclaw snapped. "And no Clan should. Our leader should be *here*, leading us."

"How?" Lionblaze looked confused.

Thornclaw ignored the question. "A Clan isn't a Clan without a proper leader."

"We have Squirrelflight!"

"She's our deputy."

"*I'm* your deputy for now!" Lionblaze thrust his muzzle toward the golden-brown tabby.

"Which is why you're so happy with the way things are." Thornclaw's eyes flashed accusingly. "You were a warrior a moon ago, like the rest of us."

Bristlefrost's pelt pricked with tension as Twigbranch marched forward. "Is that what this is about?" She stared boldly at Thornclaw. "Is that the real reason you're so angry? You think you should be acting deputy?"

Thornclaw shrank back, ears flattening as though he were offended. "That's not what I said!" he snapped.

Bristlefrost saw Bumblestripe and Ivypool exchange glances. Sorrelstripe snorted. They clearly weren't convinced by Thornclaw's denial. *Neither am I.* Thornclaw had been ordering cats around since she was a kit. He'd grown worse after the battle, and Bristlefrost suspected Twigbranch might be right. He was an experienced warrior and still strong despite his age. Why shouldn't he set his sights on being Thunderclan's deputy?

Bumblestripe wove between Lionblaze and Thornclaw. "The Clan doesn't need cats competing to be deputy," he mewed soothingly. "We've got bigger problems."

"I know!" Thornclaw glared at the striped warrior. "That's exactly why we need to think about who should be making our decisions. I'm thinking of my Clan, not myself."

More cats were gathering at the edge of the clearing.

Myrtlepaw and Flamepaw had slid from the apprentices' den, and Lilyheart had padded over from the shady patch where she'd been resting beneath the Highledge. Alderheart nosed his way through the brambles at the entrance to the medicine den and watched as Lionblaze thrust out his chest.

"Do you think you'd make better decisions than me?" the golden warrior demanded.

"No, but I *do* think the only reason you're the one making decisions is because you're Squirrelflight's kin."

Pelts ruffled uneasily around the clearing as Thornclaw stared at Lionblaze. The tabby warrior was accusing Squirrelflight of choosing favorites instead of putting her Clan's needs first. Bristlefrost curled her claws nervously into the earth as Lionblaze lashed his tail angrily.

"Take that back!" the golden warrior hissed.

"How can I take back the truth?" Thornclaw retorted. "Since Firestar's time, there's been no question about who Thunderclan's next leader might be."

"Thunderclan's leadership has always passed from leader to deputy, as the warrior code says it should!" Lionblaze reminded him sharply.

Thornclaw held his gaze. "So it's just a coincidence that Firestar made his daughter's mate deputy."

"Bramblestar was the strongest warrior in Thunderclan!" Lionblaze objected.

"And Bramblestar named his own mate deputy," Thornclaw went on. "And now—"

"She deserved to be deputy!"

Thornclaw was clearly determined to finish his point. "And *now* Firestar's kin—a cat Squirrelflight and Bramblestar raised as their own kit—is Thunderclan deputy. Are we supposed to believe that only one family in this Clan can raise kits to be leaders? Are the rest of us just here for them to order around? Who will *you* name deputy? Sparkpelt? Flamepaw?" He glared at Sparkpelt's kit. Flamepaw seemed to shrink beneath his fur, moving closer to his denmate.

"Don't be mouse-brained!" Lionblaze growled.

But Thornclaw didn't seem to hear him. He was looking at his Clanmates. Bristlefrost guessed he was gauging their reactions.

Flywhisker's tail had been twitching throughout Thornclaw's outburst; Snaptooth's eyes were wide. Both looked conflicted, their muzzles twisting with concern. Elsewhere, Flipclaw was nodding.

Flipclaw? Bristlefrost tried to catch her brother's eye. Surely he couldn't agree with the old warrior—Thornclaw was threatening the stability of the whole Clan with his accusations! But Flipclaw's gaze was fixed eagerly on the tabby tom. The whole Clan was staring at him, but no cat spoke out.

Should I say something? Bristlefrost's mouth felt dry. *But what?* Every word Thornclaw had spoken had been true. And yet Thunderclan's leaders and deputies had always been the strongest warriors in the Clan. This was what she'd been taught and she was certain of it. Of course it wasn't a coincidence that they were related; one generation had passed on its skills to the next. Before she could point this out, Lionblaze spoke.

"Why are you trying to stir up trouble in the Clan?" he demanded, glowering at Thornclaw. "Don't we have enough to worry about?"

Thornclaw turned on him. "Should we blindly trust you without asking questions?" he demanded. "The way we trusted Bramblestar?"

"I'm not asking you to blindly trust any cat—"

Thornclaw cut Lionblaze off. "It's trusting our leaders that got us into this trouble in the first place. Our faith in Bramblestar allowed the impostor to get away with his crimes for moons! It almost destroyed Thunderclan."

Lionblaze's pelt spiked with rage. "The only cats who might destroy Thunderclan now are featherbrained warriors starting trouble for no reason!" He padded menacingly closer to Thornclaw. "Like you!"

Bristlefrost's heart seemed to skip a beat as she saw both warriors unsheathe their claws. Were they really going to fight about this? Frustration jabbed her belly. Clearly Ashfur could still hurt Thunderclan, even though he was a prisoner in ShadowClan's camp.

Out of the corner of her eye she saw Jayfeather emerge from the medicine den and pause beside Alderheart. Could the blind medicine cat stop what was happening? He was never one to hold his tongue when something needed saying. She looked at him hopefully, but Jayfeather didn't speak.

Before she had time to talk herself out of it, Bristlefrost

padded forward and yowled. "Stop this! Can't you see this is just what Ashfur wanted? To have us fighting one another?"

"Stay out of this, Bristlefrost," Thornclaw hissed, a growl rumbling in his throat as he eyed Lionblaze. The golden warrior glared back at him, his spine beginning to arch. Bristlefrost swallowed. If she could push her way between them, she might be able to stop them fighting. As she hurried forward, the camp entrance rustled. She paused, turning her head to see Squirrelflight duck into camp.

The Clan leader was carrying a pigeon between her jaws. Her eyes widened as she saw Thornclaw and Lionblaze glaring at each other. Behind her, Poppyfrost, Birchfall, and Spotfur hurried in, prey between their jaws. They froze as they saw what was happening.

Squirrelflight put down her catch and crossed the clearing quickly. "What's going on?" Her gaze flicked from Thornclaw to Lionblaze.

Lionblaze's gave a low growl. "Thornclaw is questioning Thunderclan's leadership."

Squirrelflight's muzzle jerked toward Thornclaw. "What does Lionblaze mean?"

"I'm not ashamed to say it." The tabby tom was unrepentant. "If we'd questioned our leader earlier, we might have avoided a lot of trouble."

Squirrelflight's gaze hardened. "It's pointless worrying about what we should have done," she mewed firmly. "It's what we do next that's important. And right now, Thunderclan must stick together. Until we can find a way of getting Bramblestar back, we need to trust one another."

Thornclaw snorted. "You didn't seem to think that when you abandoned your Clan."

"I never *abandoned* my Clan," Squirrelflight snapped. "I had no choice but to leave. And it's because I spent time in exile that I understand why it's so important we pull together now."

Thornclaw's gaze flitted back to Lionblaze. "I suppose you mean we should support all your choices without question," he mewed sourly. "However unfair they seem."

Squirrelflight's ears twitched angrily. "I am being as fair as I know how," she growled. "And like it or not, I am the Clan's best option until Bramblestar returns."

Thornclaw narrowed his eyes. "And what if he doesn't return?"

"He will!" Squirrelflight's eyes suddenly glistened with emotion. "Of course he will. He has to."

Bristlefrost noted the way the other cats looked around quietly, clearly feeling that Squirrelflight was being delusional. Bristlefrost had her doubts too, but she trusted Squirrelflight. Wasn't any cat going to support her?

Bristlefrost swished her tail. If no other cat would speak up for Squirrelflight, she would. "We know he's around somewhere," she mewed. "We just have to find a way to get him back where he belongs."

Twigbranch nodded eagerly, her gaze switching to Jayfeather. "If we could just get in touch with StarClan," she mewed hopefully. "Then maybe we would know whether our paws are on the right path. We could all relax a bit."

Jayfeather grunted. "Do you think we haven't been trying? What do you expect me to do? Fly up to the stars and drag them down by their tails?"

"There's nothing more we can do until they're ready to share with us," Alderheart mewed, more gently.

Bristlefrost felt her heart sink. *Unless it wasn't their choice to stay away,* she mused. It was clear that the false Bramblestar wanted to cause chaos in the Clans. Had he done something to send StarClan away permanently?

Snaptooth swished his tail crossly. "What's the point of ancestors who only turn up when it suits them? They could have saved us a lot of trouble if they'd warned us that Ashfur had come back. Surely they noticed he was missing?"

Jayfeather looked exasperated. "If they did, they clearly couldn't or didn't want to share with us."

Flipclaw glowered at the medicine cat. "Perhaps they don't care about us anymore. Or maybe they never did. Perhaps we imagined all their prophecies."

Jayfeather's blind blue eyes flashed with indignation. "Are you saying we've been inventing visions all these moons?"

"That's not what he means." Squirrelflight looked sharply at Jayfeather. "He's just worried about StarClan's silence, like we all are."

Flipclaw's hackles lifted. "I can speak for myself," he told Squirrelflight angrily. "Whatever StarClan thought in the past, it's pretty clear they're not here for us now. Perhaps they won't ever be here for us again. We might have to live without them."

Twigbranch looked horrified. "How?"

Flipclaw shrugged. "We all know the Clans were born before there was even a StarClan. We existed without them once; we can do it again."

Bristlefrost felt suddenly cold despite the warm afternoon sunshine. How could her own littermate say such a thing? Her Clanmates exchanged anxious glances as Flipclaw stared defiantly around the gathered cats. Did they think he might be right?

Lilyheart was the first to break the silence. "Can we even *be* Clans without StarClan?"

Poppyfrost shifted her paws nervously. "Surely, without StarClan to guide us, we'd be rogues?"

"Of course we wouldn't," Squirrelflight argued. "We'll always have the warrior code."

"What's the point of following it with StarClan gone?" Flipclaw countered.

Lionblaze lifted his chin. "Because that's what makes us warriors. Without it we'd be no better than Darktail and his Kin."

"So we carry on, following a code no cat cares about but us?" Flipclaw demanded. "What's the point?"

Lilyheart whisked her tail. "The point is that we take care of one another. We're loyal. We protect one another. We defend our own, and we make sure they are safe and well fed whether they are weak or strong. Do you really believe that if

StarClan stops caring about us, we should stop caring about one another?" She stared at Flipclaw angrily.

"I'm just saying that things need to change," Flipclaw answered. "If our ancestors have abandoned us, why bother following traditions they invented? We don't even live in the forests they were born in. We can make up our own codes to suit our new life beside the lake."

Lilyheart stared at him in disbelief. "Do you really think the warrior code should change?"

"I don't know what I think," Flipclaw answered. "But isn't StarClan's absence a perfect opportunity to work out what we believe?"

Bristlefrost was lost for words. What was wrong with her brother? Had he rejected everything he'd been taught?

Lilyheart's pelt was rippling uneasily, but she didn't speak. Instead she glanced nervously at Squirrelflight, as though hoping Thunderclan's leader would say something to settle this.

But Squirrelflight shifted her paws, and as she looked at Flipclaw, confusion clouded her gaze. "Our beliefs have always served us well enough," she mewed, a little uncertainly.

Lionblaze pushed past her and glared at Flipclaw. "We need to stick to our beliefs more than ever, now that StarClan is silent."

Dewnose nodded eagerly. "They're all we have."

"It's the only way StarClan will return," Bumblestripe added.

Lilyheart seemed to find words at last. "If StarClan sees we have abandoned the code, they might never come back."

Flipclaw lifted his muzzle. "I'm not talking about abandoning the code. I love being a warrior. I would die to protect my Clanmates. But after everything that's happened with the false Bramblestar, I need a chance to think about what being a warrior really means." He met Squirrelflight's gaze. "I think we all do."

She narrowed her eyes, determination quickly sweeping away doubt. "I already know what being a warrior means," she growled.

"Then perhaps I should go for a wander," Flipclaw answered. "Alone. To think things through, and decide whether to come back to Thunderclan. Maybe I can find better, less dangerous territory where we can live. Or maybe it's time we all stopped living like this, in Clans."

Bristlefrost could barely concentrate on what her Clanmates were saying, her littermate's words shocked her so thoroughly. *He would leave?* she wondered. *Leave not just his family, but the Clans entirely? To find a "better" way to live?*

She felt as though a thorn had pierced her heart. "Flipclaw, you don't mean that!" she yowled.

"Maybe he does," Snaptooth retorted. "And maybe I agree with him."

"Then maybe you should both go." Squirrelflight's tail flicked angrily.

Thornclaw padded to Flipclaw's side. "I want to go for a

wander too." His mew was soft, his anger gone now.

"Me too." Flywhisker joined them, speaking over Clanmates' protests.

Snaptooth crossed the clearing and stood beside his littermate. "And me."

Bristlefrost stared at them. Thunderclan was falling apart. She glanced around at her other Clanmates, her breath shallow, praying that no other cats would join Flipclaw's group.

No cat moved. Lionblaze had stepped forward and was saying something to Squirrelflight and his kits. But she could tell by their reactions that they weren't dissuaded.

Ivypool hurried forward. "You can't abandon your Clan," she mewed to Flipclaw.

"I'm just going to do some thinking," he told her.

"But you'll come back?" Her plea was desperate.

"I don't know." Flipclaw's answer felt like a heavy rock on Bristlefrost's chest. She hurried to her mother's side and pressed against her. Ivypool was trembling.

Squirrelflight padded closer, her gaze flitting between Snaptooth, Flywhisker, and Thornclaw. "Are you planning to come back?"

They exchanged glances.

"I don't know," Flywhisker murmured.

Thornclaw dipped his head to Blossomfall. "If I decide to leave," he told her, "I'll return to say good-bye."

As Bristlefrost steadied her breathing, paws brushed the earth behind them. Lionblaze's gaze flashed across the clearing; Flipclaw and Lilyheart turned to look.

Bristlefrost's belly tightened. Was another cat going to join Thornclaw and desert the Clan? She jerked her muzzle around to see who it was. Relief washed her pelt. Graystripe was padding from the shadow of the elders' den. He'd been a Thunderclan warrior since Firestar was leader. He knew the importance of loyalty. He'd reason with Thornclaw and the others. He'd persuade them to stay.

Poppyfrost shifted to let him pass. Finleap dipped his head as the elder brushed past him.

As Graystripe stopped beside Thornclaw, silence gripped the Clan. *They're waiting for him to stop this.* Bristlefrost leaned forward, willing him to speak.

Graystripe looked around the Clan solemnly. "I'm going to leave too."

Bristlefrost could hardly believe her ears. "No!" she cried, her yowl rising above the shocked murmurs that rippled around the Clan.

Squirrelflight stared at the elder for a moment, her eyes suddenly hollow with grief. "You told me you'd support me," she mewed huskily. "You said I could count on you."

Graystripe's ears twitched awkwardly as he bowed his head. "I'm sorry. I can't keep that promise."

"But why?" Squirrelflight didn't move, but her pelt was rippling along her spine. "You made a promise to my father too, that you'd never leave Thunderclan—or have you forgotten that?"

"Too much has changed," Graystripe told her. "I've been through so much with Thunderclan: the destruction of the old forest, being lost and living as a kittypet, then finding you again. But the Thunderclan I see today isn't the same one I served under Firestar. I don't know that I still belong here. I need time to think."

Bristlefrost couldn't imagine life in Thunderclan without Graystripe. How would he take care of himself in the forest alone? He was an elder. The Clan had been hunting for him for moons. What if he got sick? There'd be no medicine cat to help him. She wanted to point this out, to persuade him to stay, but the old gray warrior looked determined. She guessed she wouldn't be able to change his mind.

Squirrelflight's pelt smoothed. She stepped back and lifted her muzzle. "If this is your decision," she told the leaving cats, "then go with my good wishes. You know your own minds and I won't try to change them." Her tail flicked ominously. "But remember, a warrior takes care of their Clan. If you go, you are letting down your Clanmates. I will tolerate this for now, but if you do not return within a moon, do not come back at all."

Alarm shrilled beneath Bristlefrost's pelt. Would this be the last she'd ever see of Flipclaw? And the others? Would they never return? The air around her felt heavy as she watched Graystripe head for the camp entrance. Flipclaw, Thornclaw, Snaptooth, and Flywhisker followed at his tail. She wanted to yowl good-bye, but Squirrelflight was watching them darkly, and her Clanmates stood in silence as though their paws were frozen to the earth. Despair swept over her as though an icy flood had engulfed the camp.

Ashfur might be in the ShadowClan camp now, but he had still succeeded in tearing Thunderclan apart.

Squirrelflight turned wordlessly and headed for the rock tumble.

Bristlefrost hurried after her. This wasn't as bad as it seemed, surely? Squirrelflight must know that this was just temporary. "They'll be back, won't they?" she mewed breathlessly, following Squirrelflight up the stony slope.

"That's up to them." Squirrelflight didn't look at her.

"But this happens sometimes, right?" Bristlefrost stopped as Squirrelflight reached the ledge.

Squirrelflight turned on her, her ears twitching with irritation. "I don't have time to reassure you," she mewed sharply. "You're a warrior, not a kit." She must have seen the shock in Bristlefrost's eyes at her harsh tone, because she added more gently, "I'm sure everything will be okay."

"Will it?" Bristlefrost's heart ached for comfort. Could Thunderclan survive this? What if the Clan fell apart? What would become of them all?

Squirrelflight didn't answer. "You should focus on being a loyal warrior right now," she said.

Bristlefrost searched her gaze for a sign that Squirrelflight was truly hopeful. But the Thunderclan leader's eyes were dark with worry.

Bristlefrost backed away. Squirrelflight didn't know. She scrambled clumsily back down the rock tumble, sending stones clattering into the clearing.

Spotfur jumped out of the way as a pebble bounced onto the earth in front of her.

"Sorry." Bristlefrost pulled up in front of the gray-and-white she-cat.

"It's okay." Spotfur shook out her spotted pelt coolly, but her eyes glittered with such unease, Bristlefrost felt her paws flex and her resolve harden. Spotfur was taking this worse than she was.

"Are you all right?" Bristlefrost asked.

"Sure." There was brittleness in her mew, as though something was worrying her.

Bristlefrost sympathized. "It's unnerving seeing Clanmates leave." She glanced at the camp entrance. The shadowy tunnel seemed suddenly different, no longer a place where warriors returned home with prey and stories of triumph. Now it was the way warriors left their Clan.

Spotfur shrugged, seeming distracted. "It's weird. But if that's what they want, there's no point in making them stay."

Surprise sparked in Bristlefrost's belly. Didn't Spotfur care? She looked at her denmate again. Spotfur's pelt was fluffed out like a kit's. Her paws were drawn in. Her tail trembled at the tip. The she-cat seemed suddenly very small. *Don't be mouse-brained. She's a warrior like me.* And yet there seemed something vulnerable about Spotfur as she stood in the fading afternoon light. Compassion surged in Bristlefrost's heart. She felt suddenly protective of Spotfur—of *all* her Clanmates. How could any cat leave them to fend for themselves? If Thunderclan was falling apart, Bristlefrost was sure that she could never turn her back on the cats who'd fed her and raised her and trained her to become the warrior she'd always longed to be. She was going to stay, whatever it took, and make sure her Clan became whole again.

CHAPTER 5

Shadowsight's heart sank as he watched Mothwing reach into the herb store. She was frowning, a frown that grew deeper as she pulled out a bundle of comfrey.

What is it this time? Shadowsight wondered wearily as River-Clan's former medicine cat looked disdainfully at the withered leaves.

"Did you gather these?" she asked, turning to look at him.

Shadowsight tried to remember. He and Puddleshine had gathered so many herbs since the start of newleaf, he'd lost track of who'd gathered what. "I'm not sure."

"Well, whoever it was, they didn't dry them properly before they stored them." Mothwing sniffed the bundle, her nose wrinkling as she gave a sigh. "I'll put them in the sun now and see what I can salvage." She picked up the bundle and headed for the entrance.

"Puddleshine prefers them with a little sap still left in," Shadowsight told her. "He says they keep their goodness longer."

She dropped the bundle. "They'll rot if you keep them like this."

"It's greenleaf. We can collect more." Shadowsight swallowed back his frustration. He knew it must be hard for Mothwing, trying to fit into a new Clan, and he admired her for standing by Icewing and Harelight, but he wished she didn't have to find fault with everything. Why couldn't she just accept that ShadowClan did things differently from RiverClan?

She wasn't the only RiverClan cat finding it hard to adjust. Puddleshine was taking watermint to Icewing right now, to settle her belly. The white she-cat wasn't used to eating more forest prey than fish. Shadowsight eyed Mothwing sullenly. At least Icewing didn't try to tell the ShadowClan warriors how to hunt.

Mothwing's ears twitched. "Rot spreads," she mewed. "If these leaves get mildew, the whole herb store could be ruined."

"That might be true in the marshland," Shadowsight replied. "But it's drier here. We don't get mildew."

Mothwing wasn't convinced. She picked up the bundle and began to head outside.

She stopped short at the entrance, backing away as Scorchfur limped into the den. Shadowsight could smell forest scents in his fur. He also smelled blood.

He hurried to see why the dark gray tom was limping. Mothwing must have smelled it too. She dropped the comfrey and followed Scorchfur to the middle of the den, where the warrior held his paw out for Shadowsight to examine.

"I jumped down from a tree stump and landed on a sharp

stone," he mewed, wincing.

As Shadowsight leaned down to sniff the gash in the war-rior's pad, his cheek grazed Scorchfur's pelt; it was warm. He touched his nose to the warrior's pad to be sure that his fur had been warmed by sun and not fever, relieved to find the paw cool. The fur around it was drenched with blood from a wide cut that was still dripping. "Sit down," he told Scorchfur. "I'll fetch marigold."

"Marigold?" Mothwing stared at him. "You'll want oak leaves for a wound like that."

"Marigold will prevent infection," Shadowsight told her.

"Oak leaf would be better," Mothwing argued.

"I agree." Shadowsight was careful not to contradict her. "But only once infection has set in. This cut is fresh and looks clean. Marigold will be fine." *And will sting less.* He kept the last thought to himself so as not to alarm Scorchfur.

"Let me look." Mothwing lifted Scorchfur's paw with her own and inspected the wound. She seemed not to notice Scorchfur's wince. "It's a long cut. I'd use oak leaf to be safe."

Shadowsight flexed his claws but didn't argue. "Okay," he conceded. "I'll fetch oak leaf." *Puddleshine would have used mari-gold.* He wished his mentor were here to back him up but, since he wasn't, he padded to the gap in the brambles and reached his paw into the herb store. He hooked a bundle of leaves from the back, surprised to find, as he tugged them out, that they were mallow. What was mallow doing in the space they kept for oak? His pelt prickled irritably as he guessed that

Mothwing had been rearranging the store again. He reached farther in and felt around for the scalloped edges of the oak leaves, grunting with relief when he finally found them tucked between the nettles and rosemary.

He pulled out the bundle and eased one from the stack, which had been held together with a long grass stalk. As he turned back to Scorchfur, he saw with a ripple of irritation that Mothwing was hunched over the dark gray tom's paw, stuffing cobweb around the wound.

"What about the oak leaf?" He dropped it beside her indignantly. She'd stolen his patient. He leaned close to Scorchfur, trying gently to ease Mothwing aside, but she pushed him back and began trailing cobweb across the gash.

"It's important we staunch the bleeding first," she told him without looking up. "I'm surprised you wandered off and left Scorchfur to bleed."

"I was fetching oak leaf, like you said," Shadowsight snapped. "I was going to put a poultice on. That's what you wanted, wasn't it?"

Mothwing rolled her eyes at Scorchfur. "It's pointless putting any sort of poultice on while it's bleeding so heavily," she told him.

"It was barely a claw deep." Shadowsight felt rattled. He'd worked hard to show his Clanmates he was a skillful medicine cat, and here was a cat from another Clan undermining him. "The bleeding won't last long. But if there's any dirt in there, it needs to be cleaned out."

Mothwing snorted. "Well, of course I cleaned it out. Perhaps that's what you should have done before you went to the herb store. Then you wouldn't have needed oak leaf *or* marigold."

"Puddleshine taught me that infection is a cat's greatest enemy," Shadowsight snapped. Mothwing was rolling cobweb thickly around Scorchfur's paw. He wouldn't even be able to check the wound now. "Why couldn't you have waited?"

"You were taking forever."

"Only because you've moved the herbs again!"

Scorchfur pulled his paw sharply away and stared accusingly at Shadowsight and Mothwing. "I came here for help, not to watch a fight. I thought you were meant to treat your Clanmates, not squabble over them."

Shadowsight bristled. "There wouldn't *be* a fight if Mothwing didn't keep interfering."

"*Interfering?*" She turned on him, raising her voice. "I've been treating cats for more moons than you've been alive. You should be grateful I'm here!"

"How would you like it if I came into your medicine den and started messing with your herb store and giving you orders?"

A shadow blocked the sunshine streaming through the entrance.

Cloverfoot stood there, frowning. "What's going on?" The ShadowClan deputy marched into the den. "I could hear your yowls halfway across the clearing."

Shadowsight glared at Mothwing. "She's messing up the

medicine den and stealing my patients."

"He doesn't know his oak leaf from his marigold," Mothwing retorted.

"I do so!"

"And his herb store is a shambles."

"Because *you* messed it up!"

Cloverfoot's ears flattened. "Be quiet!" Her yowl rang around the den, shocking Shadowsight into silence. "You're meant to be looking after Scorchfur, not arguing like a pair of kits!"

Shadowsight glanced at her sheepishly.

Mothwing puffed out her chest. "I wasn't arguing. I was fixing Scorchfur's paw."

"Then I suggest you finish fixing it," Cloverfoot told her, "and then report to Tigerstar's den."

Shadowsight felt a rush of triumph. His father would remind this RiverClan cat she was a guest here.

Cloverfoot looked at him sternly. "And you can go too. Tigerstar will want to speak to both of you."

Shadowsight stared at her in disbelief. Had Cloverfoot forgotten they were Clanmates? *Why would Tigerstar need to speak to me? I've done nothing wrong.* She was supposed to be on his side, wasn't she?

Mothwing sat back on her haunches. "I'm finished here." She sounded satisfied. "How does it feel?" she asked Scorchfur.

The gray warrior touched his tightly wrapped paw to the ground.

"Don't put weight on it for a while," Mothwing warned

him. "And come back in the morning so I can re-dress it and see if it needs a poultice."

"If you'd put a poultice on it now, he wouldn't have to come back in the morning," Shadowsight grumbled.

Mothwing blinked at him, unfazed. "It's always best to check a wound the next day." She got to her paws. "I'm ready to see Tigerstar now," she mewed. "Are you?"

Shadowsight glowered at her as she headed for the entrance, then padded after her, avoiding Cloverfoot's gaze.

Sunshine filled the clearing, and the pines creaked around the bramble wall as a soft breeze stirred their tips. Tawnypelt and Snowbird were sharing a mouse in the long grass at the edge of camp. Snaketooth and Whorlpelt practiced battle moves beside the rocks. Outside the bramble enclosure, where Ashfur must be keeping cool in the hollow tree, two SkyClan warriors, Mintfur and Sagenose, stood guard. Leafstar had sent them to take their Clan's turn guarding the impostor.

Outside the warriors' den, Puddleshine was running his paws over Icewing's belly. The medicine cat glanced at Shadowsight as he followed Mothwing across the camp. Shadowsight shot him a pleading look. He wanted his mentor to defend him. It wasn't fair he was being sent to Tigerstar too. But Puddleshine hardly seemed to notice, and, peeling a few watermint leaves from the pile he'd taken with him, he gave them to Icewing.

Disappointed, Shadowsight stopped beside Mothwing as she reached his father's den.

"Tigerstar?" she called through the brambles.

"Come in, Mothwing." Tigerstar sounded brisk, as though he was expecting her. As Shadowsight followed her inside, his father dipped his head. "Good," he mewed. "You've both come."

Shadowsight blinked at him, puzzled. Had his father *wanted* to see them?

"You must know why I'm here," Mothwing mewed smoothly.

Does he? Unease began to flutter in Shadowsight's belly.

Tigerstar's gaze flicked to Shadowsight for a moment, then back to the RiverClan medicine cat. His ears were twitching uneasily.

"I know you don't want to hear this," Mothwing went on, "but it's best to have it out now before some cat gets hurt."

Anxiety rushed up from Shadowsight's paws and set his heart racing. What did she mean?

"I don't think Shadowsight should be treating cats unsupervised."

Shadowsight's pelt spiked with shock. "Why not?" He looked at his father. Surely he would object!

Tigerstar's expression was unreadable. "I know you've felt this way for a while."

Shadowsight could hardly believe his ears. Why hadn't Tigerstar said anything? How many of his Clanmates knew about this?

His father went on. "But I think Shadowsight should have a chance to defend himself—"

"Defend myself?" Shadowsight cut him off. Outrage surged in his chest. "I haven't done anything wrong!"

"No cat is saying you have," Tigerstar soothed. "But Mothwing is an experienced medicine cat, and if she has concerns, I think we should discuss them."

Shadowsight couldn't believe his ears. "She's not even *ShadowClan!*"

Tigerstar didn't respond to that. Instead, he went on, "We should hear what Puddleshine has to say." As Shadowsight struggled to keep his breath steady, Tigerstar padded to the entrance and called across the clearing. "Puddleshine! Can you spare a moment?"

Shadowsight glared at Mothwing. "What have I done wrong?" he demanded. "I've been treating cats unsupervised for moons!"

"I think you received your medicine-cat name too early." Mothwing's mew was gentle now. "I can see your inexperience in the way you use herbs before they're properly dry, and you're too slow about tending to wounds. I only say this because I'm concerned for your Clanmates. You're still very young."

"No younger than Puddleshine was when he became a medicine cat!" Shadowsight objected.

"Two wrongs don't make a right," Mothwing persisted. "You must know, ShadowClan had no choice but to make Puddleshine a medicine cat early. He was the only trained healer they had at that time. Luckily, his skills and judgment were exceptional, so every cat trusted him. The truth is, we can't say the same about you right now. It's become clear that some of the cats in the Clan have been waiting until you're away to come to the medicine den to have me or Puddleshine treat them."

Shadowsight fluffed out his fur. "Are you saying that my Clan doesn't need me because you're here now?"

"No," Mothwing mewed. "But you remember why you were given your medicine-cat name, don't you?"

Shadowsight frowned, puzzled. What did she mean?

"Puddleshine made you a full medicine cat because you saved Bramblestar's life," she went on.

Dread pulsed in Shadowsight's belly. He knew what she was about to say.

"But you didn't save it, did you?" Her gaze was clear. There was no hostility there. "We know that now. You told Jayfeather and Alderheart to leave him on the moor to freeze the fever out of him."

Shadowsight's mouth was dry. "I thought it was the right thing to do. StarClan told me to do it."

"*Ashfur* told you to do it," Mothwing corrected. "And you were too inexperienced to know any better."

Shadowsight felt sick. It was true. He'd been wrong and his mistake had cost Bramblestar a life—*all* his lives if he never got his body back. *I killed him!* He'd allowed Ashfur to steal the Thunderclan leader's body, and now even more cats had *died*. Shadowsight stared wordlessly at Mothwing, despair circling his thoughts like a fox.

"No cat is blaming you." Tigerstar was at his side now, running his tail along Shadowsight's spine. "You didn't realize what you were doing."

Puddleshine pushed his way through the brambles as Mothwing added, "You were just an apprentice. There was no reason why you should have known it was Ashfur and not StarClan who spoke to you."

Puddleshine frowned. "They were unusual visions. I don't know if any medicine cat would have realized they were from Ashfur. And don't underestimate Shadowsight's experience. Even if he was an apprentice, he'd been having visions since he was a kit."

Shadowsight felt a flash of relief. His mentor was defending him.

"We don't know whether the visions he had as a kit were from StarClan, either," Mothwing argued. "Ashfur might have been grooming him from the beginning. He may have been trying to earn our trust. Why else would a kit have visions?"

The ground seemed to sway beneath Shadowsight's paws. Could it be that StarClan had *never* spoken to him? Had everything he believed about himself been a lie?

Tigerstar pressed against him. "I still believe Shadowsight is a special cat."

"He's a gifted healer," Puddleshine added.

"I'm sure he is," Mothwing pressed. "But after what happened to Bramblestar, is he really ready to take sole responsibility for other cats' lives?"

Puddleshine stared at her.

"I know you've had your doubts too, Puddleshine," Mothwing mewed. "We've discussed them."

Shadowsight stared at Puddleshine, feeling sick with betrayal. His mentor had been talking about him with Mothwing? For how long? Puddleshine, Mothwing, and Tigerstar glanced at one another. *You all agree!* Did the whole Clan think him unfit to be a medicine cat? He wanted to run and hide in the deepest part of the forest.

Puddleshine broke the silence. "Perhaps you should take a break, Shadowsight," he mewed softly. "We would still have two medicine cats in ShadowClan. More than enough to treat every cat. Perhaps it's best for you to go back to your apprentice duties for a while. Just until you've had a little more experience. A little extra training won't do you any harm."

"All of us can do with reminding ourselves of our skills from time to time," Mothwing put in. "Even experienced healers like me." She spoke gently, softly, and Shadowsight felt a flash of fury. *It's a bit late for her to try to be nice.*

He could hardly look any of them in the eye. "Will I lose my medicine-cat name?" he mewed weakly. The humiliation of being called Shadowpaw again would kill him.

Tigerstar touched his nose to Shadowsight's ear. "You will always be called Shadowsight," he promised. "But if Puddleshine thinks a little more training will help, perhaps you should go along with it. You want to be the best medicine cat you can be, don't you?"

"Yes." Shadowsight's mew cracked. "Of course I do." *But I want you to trust me again.*

Mothwing shook out her fur. "It's for the best," she mewed, suddenly brisk. "You'll see."

If only he hadn't listened to Ashfur. If only he'd known. None of this would have happened. "How long do I have to train for?" Shadowsight stared hopelessly at his father.

Tigerstar looked uncertain. "Let's see how it goes," he mewed. "When we've figured all this out and decided what to do about Ashfur, we'll make a decision." He looked at Puddle-shine. "Right?"

"Let's wait until StarClan returns," Puddleshine mewed. "They'll know better than us if you're ready to become a full medicine cat."

What if they say I'll never be ready? Shadowsight swallowed. *What if they think I can never be trusted after the mistake I made with Ashfur?* His chest tightened in panic. *Or what if StarClan never comes back?* Then this temporary "break" would become per-manent. He looked helplessly at his father.

Tigerstar blinked at him fondly. "No cat is blaming you," he repeated. Shadowsight had to clench his jaws to stop him-self from yowling that the more his father said this, the less he believed it.

"We just have to be cautious," Puddleshine chimed. "Until we know who we can trust."

Shadowsight stared at his paws. This morning he'd been a medicine cat of ShadowClan. Now he was nothing. He'd really thought that when Ashfur had been exposed, every-thing could go back to normal. Now he realized that as long as Ashfur was controlling Bramblestar's body and StarClan remained silent, nothing could be normal. Darkness suddenly seemed to cloud the future like a coming storm. He stared miserably at Tigerstar. "So what do I do now?" Was he going to have to follow Puddleshine and Mothwing around and fetch herbs for them like a 'paw?

Tigerstar met his gaze, brightening a little. "We've been thinking about that, and Puddleshine has an idea."

Shadowsight walked stiffly past Sagenose and Mintfur. The SkyClan warriors nodded as he passed but didn't question why he'd come. They probably guessed from the herbs bunched between his jaws. Did they know he was an apprentice again? Would they spread word to SkyClan? Shame burned his pelt as he dipped his head and carried the herbs into the bramble enclosure, eyeing the hole in the hollow tree warily. Ashfur must be resting inside. *At least I'm still allowed to treat one cat unsupervised,* Shadowsight consoled himself. *Even though it's only Ashfur.* He grunted bitterly to himself. *Perhaps Tigerstar and Puddleshine are hoping I'm so useless, I'll accidentally kill him.*

He dropped the herbs on the ground and began to sort them into piles. Marigold for wounds, poppy seeds in case Ashfur was still in pain from his battle injuries, and some nettle leaves, soaked to remove their sting, to reduce any swelling around the impostor's cuts and bruises. Shadowsight's fur pricked resentfully. Why did he have to treat the cat who'd ruined his life?

The sun was dipping behind the trees, and it was chilly in their shadow. As Shadowsight fluffed out his pelt, fur brushed over bark behind him. He spun around.

Ashfur was sliding from the hollow tree, interest shining in his eyes. His pelt was still ruffled and bloody from the battle and his more recent tussle with Reedwhisker and Hawkwing. He'd made no effort at all to groom himself, and Shadowsight wondered if the prisoner simply didn't care about the body he had stolen.

Ashfur's gaze flitted to the herbs. "You're still a medicine cat, then?"

"Why wouldn't I be?" Shadowsight tried to ignore the sting of his words.

"I thought your Clanmates might think twice about trusting you after you'd passed on my messages so helpfully."

"I didn't know they were *your* messages!" Anger flared in Shadowsight's chest. The impostor had known exactly what would happen to the cat he chose to speak for him.

Ashfur looked amused. Shadowsight's anger hardened into hate. He grabbed marigold and nettle leaves between his teeth and began to chew them into an ointment. He wished he'd brought oak leaves instead of marigold. Ashfur deserved to feel their sting. He pushed the thought away. *I'm still a medicine cat, no matter what Mothwing or Puddleshine—or my father—says. I'm going to behave like one.*

He spat the ointment onto a paw and nodded at the largest wound on Ashfur's flank. "Has it been giving you any pain?" he asked.

"No more than you'd expect." Ashfur was watching him intently.

Shadowsight tried to ignore his gaze as he approached and applied the ointment to the gash, checking for swelling as he smeared it over the broken flesh. The wound was drying. It would be healed quite soon.

"Why didn't Puddleshine come to treat me?" Ashfur asked.

"He's busy." Shadowsight glanced toward Sagenose and Mintfur. Would they wonder what the impostor was saying to him? "I'm only here to take care of your wounds."

Ashfur must have noticed him look at the guards. "Are you scared they'll think we're friends?"

"No!" Shadowsight sat up. "No cat would ever think I'd be your friend."

"But you've helped me so much." Ashfur's eyes sparkled knowingly. "Aren't your Clanmates worried you'll help me again?"

"They know I'd never help you now that I know who you are and what you want," Shadowsight snapped.

"And what do I want?"

"You want to hurt us!"

Ashfur watched him thoughtfully for a moment, then spoke again. "We're quite alike, you and me," he mewed softly.

"No, we're not!" *This warrior has bees in his brain.* "We're not alike at all!"

"Are you sure?" Ashfur tipped his head to one side. "Neither of us really belongs."

"I belong!" Shadowsight glared at him.

Ashfur looked unconvinced. "Do all the other cats in ShadowClan hear messages from dead cats?"

"Puddleshine does."

"But not from dead cats like me." Ashfur looked amused. "What did your Clanmates say when they found out you'd been passing on messages from me, and not from StarClan?"

"I thought you *were* StarClan!"

"I'm sure your Clanmates find that very reassuring," Ashfur murmured. "Is that why they only trust you to take care of traitors now?"

Shadowsight growled as frustration pulsed through him. Was Ashfur always going to be like this? He glared at the impostor. He didn't even *look* like Bramblestar now, even though he was still using the Thunderclan leader's body. He had the slinking, furtive look of a rogue. "Why?" he hissed.

Ashfur looked puzzled. "Why what?"

Shadowsight fought the rage that was pressing in his throat. "Why did you choose me?"

Ashfur frowned, as though considering the question.

Shadowsight watched him, curling his claws deep into the earth to keep his paws from trembling.

At last, Ashfur answered. "You were young and impressionable," he told him simply. "And you could already share with StarClan. It helped that you were Tigerstar's son. Anyone who questioned you would have had to answer to him. And Tigerstar is so stubborn and loyal, he'd defend you no matter how crazy your visions sounded." Ashfur sniffed the ointment Shadowsight had smeared along his flank.

Shadowsight felt a tingle in his belly; relief at Ashfur confirming that he could share with StarClan. But then sadness swarmed that feeling, and seemed to set his chest on fire. All the moons he'd spent thinking he was special . . . But he wasn't special. He was just young and stupid. Tigerstar and Dovewing had been wrong. Or they'd just been humoring him. He had *never* been special. He was a mouse-brain who *thought* he was special. How had he not realized he was being used? "Didn't you care what would happen to me?" he mewed miserably.

Ashfur narrowed his eyes. "Not at the time."

"And now?" Shadowsight looked at him. "Don't you feel guilty that you've ruined my life?"

"I never feel guilty," Ashfur told him. "And I don't think I've ruined your life."

"*I* feel like you have."

"Maybe you should stop feeling sorry for yourself," Ashfur mewed coolly. "You're still a medicine cat, aren't you?"

A medicine-cat apprentice, Shadowsight thought bitterly.

Ashfur pressed on. "And you're a natural."

"I am?" Shadowsight pricked his ears.

"You've had visions from StarClan since you were a kit," Ashfur reminded him. "And you were perceptive enough to hear *my* messages." He paused, as though thinking. "I may have been smarter than I thought in choosing you."

Shadowsight leaned closer, eager to hear more. Some cat

still had faith in him. He knew Ashfur was a liar, but perhaps his time in StarClan had taught the dead warrior something living cats didn't know yet.

"I'm beginning to see that there may be something about you after all." Ashfur lowered his voice. "Something very special indeed."

CHAPTER 6

❧

Leafstar's den was stuffy. A thick layer of clouds had rolled in overnight, and it seemed to have gathered the heat of the past few days, pressing it so close that Rootspring's pelt itched. He wished he could have this conversation with Leafstar outside, but the air there was barely fresher, and besides, Tree had insisted they talk in private. He didn't want to alarm their Clanmates.

Leafstar blinked at Rootspring expectantly, her amber eyes shining in the gloom of the den. Rootspring glanced at Tree, hoping he'd speak, but Tree only returned his gaze, as expectant as Leafstar.

Rootspring lifted his chin and reminded himself that he was a warrior now and could speak for himself. "We haven't seen any ghosts," he began.

"So?" Leafstar looked puzzled.

"After the battle . . ." Rootspring wished he'd planned what he was going to say. "With so many dead, we thought there would be ghosts at the vigil." He searched Leafstar's gaze. She was watching him, eyes dark with concern. *Does she think I'm weird for wanting to see ghosts?*

"Surely they've gone to StarClan?" Leafstar didn't seem to understand.

"But I saw ghosts after the first attack on Bramblestar," Rootspring explained. "When Conefoot and Stemleaf died. And I saw Bramblestar—"

"Recently?" Leafstar leaned forward.

"No." Rootspring dropped his gaze. *I'm explaining this badly.* "I haven't seen Bramblestar in a moon."

Leafstar's shoulders drooped. Rootspring took a breath and tried again.

"After Ashfur stole Bramblestar's body, I saw ghosts," he mewed. "Like Bramblestar and Stemleaf. They were still in the forest. But this time, none of the warriors who died seem to be around."

"But that's a good thing, isn't it?" Leafstar still seemed puzzled. "It means they've found their way to StarClan."

Rootspring stared at her. She was still missing the point.

Tree dipped his head politely. "I don't think that's possible now."

"But dead warriors always go to StarClan. It's the way things are." Leafstar blinked at him.

"But we haven't been able to reach StarClan for so long," Tree pressed. "There might be nowhere for them to go." He hesitated as Leafstar closed her eyes.

She seemed to understand at last. "You think they can't reach StarClan, either."

"I don't know," Tree mewed. "But it seems likely, doesn't it?" He didn't wait for an answer. "And, if it's true, the dead should still be here in the forest, where we can see them." He glanced at Rootspring.

"That's why we thought we would see them at the vigil," Rootspring mewed. "But none of them showed up."

"Perhaps they simply didn't want to watch their own vigil." Leafstar seemed determined to be hopeful.

Rootspring felt a pang of pity for his leader. He didn't want to upset her, but she had to know the truth. "We saw a kitty-pet ghost on our way back from the island," he told her. "She said she'd seen a few warrior ghosts, but they kept fading." He met her gaze solemnly. "She said they looked *scared*."

Tree leaned closer. "We think they're disappearing."

"Into nothing." Rootspring's mew grew husky as he finished his father's thought.

Leafstar stared at them for a moment, then sighed. "You need to tell the other Clans," she mewed. "They must know what's happening to their dead Clanmates."

Rootspring's heart dropped. It had been hard enough telling her.

"I'll send word to the Clan leaders to meet me today," Leafstar went on. "We'll travel to the island this evening. You and Tree can tell them what you told me."

Rootspring dipped his head to Leafstar. "Okay," he mewed. He glanced at Tree, relieved that his father would be with him.

". . . so we think they might be fading into nothing." Rootspring looked around apprehensively at the leaders. They'd brought their medicine cats, and as the light faded over the lake, they listened with pricked ears. Water lapped the shore a few tail-lengths away. The cats had gathered at the far edge of the island, a short distance from the clearing, unwilling, perhaps, to break the silence of yesterday's vigil.

A cool breeze had swept away the oppressive heat, bringing an oncoming rainstorm that already showed as a shadow over the distant moor. Rootspring fluffed out his fur as he waited for someone to speak.

Tigerstar shifted his paws. The ShadowClan leader looked strangely satisfied, as though the news settled something that had been weighing on his mind. "If it's true, and the dead are disappearing, we must accept that Bramblestar's ghost is already gone."

Squirrelflight stared at him in disbelief. "How could you say such a thing?"

Harestar's hackles lifted. "If our dead Clanmates are disappearing," the WindClan leader growled, "we have to help them."

"How?" Leafstar directed her question to the medicine cats.

Willowshine blinked back at her. She didn't seem to hear; she was clearly still struggling with the news. "Surely StarClan would not abandon the dead even if they've abandoned us!"

Kestrelflight's eyes were wide. "How can we help them without StarClan?"

"We must try harder to contact them," Frecklewish mewed.

Jayfeather stared blindly ahead. "We've tried everything we know."

Tigerstar swished his tail. "Ashfur is the one who's caused this. If we deal with him, it might solve everything."

Rootspring's heart quickened. There was grim determination in the ShadowClan leader's mew. The other leaders exchanged wary glances.

"You wanted to kill my mate before we knew about this," Squirrelflight growled. "Don't try to convince any cat that this is about the Clans."

Tigerstar met her stare. "We're keeping Bramblestar's murderer alive for no reason."

"He has Bramblestar's body!" Squirrelflight argued.

"It sounds as though Bramblestar doesn't need it anymore," Tigerstar growled darkly.

"We don't know that." Leafstar padded between the two warriors, her pelt lifting along her spine.

Rootspring's breath caught as Tigerstar's gaze swung toward him.

"You said it's been a moon since the last time you saw Bramblestar, right?" the ShadowClan leader demanded.

Rootspring hesitated, seeing anguish in Squirrelflight's eyes. "Yes," he mewed quietly.

Tigerstar's tail flicked. "See?" He stared at the other leaders. "If cats who died a quarter moon ago are already fading, Bramblestar must be gone. Why are we keeping Ashfur alive, when he could be blocking our link to StarClan? We should kill him and be done with it, then everything can go back to normal."

Harestar frowned. "Are you sure it's so simple?"

"Of course I'm not sure," Tigerstar snapped. "But you heard Ashfur's threat. He's promised to cause trouble, for the living and the dead. We have to stop him!"

Mistystar tipped her head thoughtfully to one side. "Tigerstar has a point. If we're too late to save Bramblestar, we still might be able to stop our dead Clanmates from disappearing."

"But Rootspring wasn't the last cat to see Bramblestar." Squirrelflight looked stricken, her forepaws grinding into the earth. "Shadowsight saw him in the Dark Forest. His ghost must still be around somewhere." She stared desperately at Jayfeather, and when he didn't speak, her gaze flitted around to the other medicine cats. She stiffened. "Where *is* Shadowsight?" Had she only just noticed that ShadowClan was missing a medicine cat?

Tigerstar shifted his paws. "Shadowsight has decided to focus on training and improving his skills for the time being."

Mothwing dipped her head. "He felt he was getting a little ahead of himself and needed to get back to basics for a while."

Squirrelflight flattened her ears. "Is he being punished for passing on messages from Ashfur?"

"Of course not," Tigerstar mewed. Rootspring narrowed his eyes. The ShadowClan leader had answered a little too quickly.

Squirrelflight seemed unconvinced too. "If any cat should hold a grudge against Shadowsight, it's me," she mewed. "But I don't. He thought he was doing the right thing. He's young. How could he have known better?"

"Exactly," Mothwing mewed. "He's a little too young to be a full medicine cat. Some extra training won't do him any harm."

Rootspring's heart ached for Shadowsight. They'd become close over the past few moons. How humiliating to be made an apprentice again. All this trouble wasn't Shadowsight's fault; Ashfur had caused it. The dark warrior had deceived everyone.

Squirrelflight's tail was flicking ominously. "Whatever you've decided about Shadowsight's training, the fact remains: He saw Bramblestar in the Dark Forest, which means his ghost is still out there. We can't harm Ashfur until we've given Bramblestar a chance to reclaim his body."

Tigerstar grunted. "So how long do you want us to wait? One moon? Two? How long is enough?"

"How *long*?" Squirrelflight stared at the ShadowClan leader.

Beside Rootspring, Tree shifted uneasily. Harestar stared at the ground as an awkward silence gripped the gathered cats. It was unfair to ask Squirrelflight when she'd be ready to let go of a cat she loved. And yet the other leaders did have a point. Ashfur had threatened the living *and* the dead. And now it seemed as though their Clanmates were fading into nothing. Surely they had to do something before the fallen warriors vanished forever.

Squirrelflight turned to Leafstar. "Do *you* think we should kill Ashfur while there's a chance Bramblestar will return?"

Leafstar avoided the Thunderclan warrior's gaze. "There

might not be time to wait if we want to stop our Clanmates from disappearing."

Tigerstar gazed imploringly at Squirrelflight. "What else *can* we do except kill the one cat we are sure has caused all this trouble?"

Alderheart stepped forward and looked around at the gathered cats. His tail twitched nervously. "We don't even know if killing Bramblestar's body will stop Ashfur."

"What do you mean?" Mistystar pricked her ears.

"Can we be sure Ashfur really needs Bramblestar's body?" Alderheart asked. "Shadowsight said he saw Ashfur's spirit leave it. What if, by killing Bramblestar, we simply drive Ashfur out of one body and into another?"

Rootspring stared at the Thunderclan medicine cat. Did that mean Ashfur could never be killed? Dread pricked through his fur as Alderheart went on.

"If Ashfur can't die, then we'd be murdering Bramblestar for no good reason."

Tigerstar was suddenly very still.

Harestar blinked. "Perhaps killing Bramblestar's body will let Bramblestar back in," he mewed hopefully.

Mistystar leaned forward. "*You* found your way back to your body after you died in the battle. Why can't Bramblestar do the same?"

Harestar nodded eagerly. "He might be waiting for his body to die so he can return to it."

"And if he isn't?" Squirrelflight snapped. "If he *can't* return to his body? What then?"

Tigerstar's gaze darkened. "Then we'll know he's truly gone."

Squirrelflight flinched as though the ShadowClan leader had lashed out with unsheathed claws.

Rootspring's thoughts whirled. Would Tigerstar risk killing a Clan leader? What if he destroyed Bramblestar's body only to find that Ashfur's spirit went on causing trouble for the Clans? Surely the ShadowClan leader wouldn't be so reckless. . . .

Leafstar lifted her chin. "Before we do anything, we have to figure out if Bramblestar is really gone."

Squirrelflight seemed hardly to be listening. Her pelt twitched as though she was trying to stop herself from shivering. Jayfeather moved closer and pressed against her as Leafstar looked questioningly around at the other leaders.

"Are we sure we have waited long enough for him to return?" the SkyClan leader asked.

"He's had plenty of time to show himself," Tigerstar growled. "We have more medicine cats than ever before." His gaze flicked toward Tree and Rootspring. "And *those* two." Rootspring felt only a mild tingle of embarrassment at the ShadowClan leader's tone. At least no other cats had shown Tigerstar's disdain for the powers he and his father shared. "Surely one of them would have seen Bramblestar if he were still around."

Mistystar looked uneasy. "Maybe he really is gone."

Squirrelflight was trembling now without hiding it. Her eyes were hollow with dread. "You all think we should kill Bramblestar?"

"We have to do something," Tigerstar mewed softly.

"And what if you're wrong?" She glared at him accusingly. "You don't know! You admitted you weren't sure. And yet you'd kill a warrior on the chance that it might fix things you don't even fully understand!"

Rootspring's heart seemed to press in his throat. "She's right." He was the reason this meeting had been called. He couldn't risk letting the Clan leaders make a decision that could cost Bramblestar everything. He had to make sure they truly understood what was at stake. He went on, hoping his mew didn't tremble. "I was the first one to see Bramblestar's ghost. I didn't want to see him at first, but he kept following me. He wouldn't give up until I admitted I could see him. He won't have given up now. And I can't give up on him, not after he fought so hard to make me see him. I wish I understood more. I wish I knew what was happening. But I'm not an expert. . . ." As his words ran out, Rootspring stared imploringly at the leaders. "Please, give him more time."

Tree padded forward. "Rootspring is right. We need to be sure we know what we're doing." Rootspring blinked gratefully at his father. "There are cats who know more about wandering spirits than we do," Tree went on. "You know who I mean.."

Rootspring's heart leaped as he understood. "The Sisters?" The group of strange she-cats—his kin and Tree's—were born with the ability to see ghosts. They accepted it as part of their everyday lives.

Tigerstar rolled his eyes. "That bunch of troublemakers."

Tree ignored him. "I don't know for sure that they can help, but they might at least understand what's happening." His gaze flitted around at the medicine cats. "You know StarClan. But the Sisters know about the dead who stay with us to walk the forests. If any cat can find out if Bramblestar is truly gone, it'll be them." He met the ShadowClan leader's contemptuous gaze. "We need advice," he mewed. "And they are the best to give it."

Leafstar frowned. "But we tried one of their ceremonies before the battle," she reminded them. "It didn't work. Why will it work this time?"

"We're no longer trying to bring him back," Tree told him. "We're trying to find out if he's still beside the lake at all."

Rootspring nodded, trying not to look in the direction of Squirrelflight, whose jaw clenched as though she had been scratched by claws. "Besides, copying a Sisters ceremony isn't the same as asking them to perform one themselves," he mewed. "They know how it works."

Tree nodded. "And they are more powerful."

Kestrelflight snorted. "*Rogues* aren't more powerful than StarClan."

"The Sisters aren't rogues!" Squirrelflight meowed hotly.

Tree's calm gaze remained fixed on Kestrelflight. "StarClan isn't with us right now," he reminded him. "We need all the help we can get."

Squirrelflight's tail was twitching. "Tree's idea is a good one," she mewed. "I spent time with the Sisters. I trust them. And I will respect whatever *they* have to say about

Bramblestar"—she glanced scornfully at Tigerstar—"even if they say he's gone."

Harestar looked dubious. "Why should we bring in outsiders to solve our problems?"

"What if their meddling makes things worse?" Mistystar agreed.

Leafstar glanced at her. "Can it get worse than a dead warrior taking over a leader's body to harm the Clans?"

When no cat answered, Rootspring fluffed out his pelt. The wind was getting colder. Rain had reached the far shore and was speckling the surface of the lake. The leaders didn't seem to notice. They stood impassively, pelts smooth.

"Okay." Leafstar gave a decisive nod. "Let's ask the Sisters. We are dealing with things we don't understand. And we would never forgive ourselves if we made the wrong decision. We must take a little more time and get advice from cats accustomed to dealing with ghosts."

Tigerstar huffed softly to himself but didn't object. Harestar and Mistystar exchanged glances. When they didn't speak, Leafstar went on.

"Tree." She blinked at the yellow tom. "Do you know where we could find the Sisters now?"

"It's hard to know for sure," he told her. "But with greenleaf nearly here, they will be in search of land away from Twolegs, which means they'll probably head across the hills." He looked past the forest, where trees met the moors and the Moonpool lay beyond.

Squirrelflight leaned closer. "How far will they have gone?" she mewed.

"I can't be sure," Tree told her. "But the Sisters are hard to miss. Some cat will have seen them pass."

Mistystar's pelt ruffled. "The sooner we find them, the better," she mewed briskly.

Tigerstar growled. "More delays."

"It's better to delay than make a mistake we can't take back," Harestar told him. "Let's find these Sisters, see what they have to say, and then deal with Ashfur once and for all."

Rootspring hoped it was that simple. He wondered if his father would be able to find the Sisters as easily as he hoped.

Mothwing looked troubled. "And if the Sisters can't find Bramblestar either?"

"Then we'll have no choice," Tigerstar mewed. Behind him, the lake was disappearing behind a fine gray mist. "We'll have to kill Ashfur. It may be our only hope."

Squirrelflight curled her claws into the earth, as though steadying herself.

Harestar dipped his head in agreement. "With any luck, it'll mean Bramblestar can begin a new life as himself, just as I did during the battle."

"Okay." Leafstar nodded. "We'll find the Sisters and get their help."

"They're not coming onto ShadowClan land," Tigerstar growled.

Harestar puffed out his chest. "Nor WindClan."

Leafstar looked weary. "Very well. They may only set paw on SkyClan land."

"And talk to SkyClan cats," Mistystar added.

Leafstar waited as the other leaders murmured in agreement; then she nodded to Tree. "When can you leave?"

The yellow tom met her gaze. "*I'm* not going," he told her. "I owe the Sisters nothing and they owe me nothing, and that's the way I like it."

Rootspring stared at his father as rain began to pound the earth around the gathered cats. "But you have to go! You're their kin. You can persuade them to help us better than anyone else."

Tree blinked at him. "You're their kin too. And your relationship with them is far less complicated than mine."

"You want *me* to go?" Rootspring shook raindrops from his eyes. "I haven't seen them since I was a kit! I've never left Clan territory before. Do you think I can do it?"

"Of course you can." Tree gazed at him warmly. "There's no one I'd trust more with this mission."

He really believes in me. Rootspring was sharply aware of the earth pressing up against his paws. It felt deep and strong. *I think I can do this too.* "Okay." He turned to Leafstar. "I'll find the Sisters."

Her eyes lit up. "Thank you, Rootspring." Pride swelled in his chest as she went on. "Take Needleclaw with you." She shook raindrops from her whiskers. "She is the Sisters' kin too. Hopefully they will welcome you both." The SkyClan leader turned her muzzle toward the other leaders. "Does any other Clan want to send cats on this mission?"

Tigerstar and Harestar avoided her gaze. Mistystar didn't speak, but Squirrelflight straightened.

"Bristlefrost will go with them," the Thunderclan leader mewed. "And Spotfur."

Rootspring blinked at the Thunderclan leader. She sounded very certain. "Isn't Spotfur still mourning Stemleaf?"

"A mission will remind her that that she is a warrior and her Clan needs her," Squirrelflight told him. "Bristlefrost will take care of her."

Butterflies seemed to flutter like leaves in Rootspring's belly. He would get to spend time with Bristlefrost again. He tried to push away his excitement, hoping the others couldn't sense it. Would it be hard being so close to her? *No.* They were both warriors now, and they were being entrusted with an important mission. Neither of them would let their feelings get in the way of that. Besides, it wasn't like they'd be alone; Spotfur and Needleclaw would be there too.

We're friends. He and Bristlefrost had already decided that was all they could ever be. He stood in the rain as the others began to head for the cover of the trees. *I just hope I'm strong enough to stick by that decision.*

CHAPTER 7

❧

Bristlefrost hurried to the top of the rise, excited by fresh scents carried on a wind untainted by the lake, pine, or heather. Her heart swelled with joy. This was the first time she'd set paw outside Clan territory. The rain, which had drenched the forests and moor for the past two days, had cleared in time for the journey, and now, at last, the patrol had left the forest behind. Ahead, sunlit valleys and grassy hills rolled toward a blue horizon.

Her fur had been fizzing with excitement ever since Squirrelflight had told her she would be going on the patrol to find the Sisters with Rootspring. She'd thought, after the battle, that they would only see each other at Gatherings, and she'd resigned herself to living in Thunderclan while he stayed in SkyClan, even though they'd admitted they had feelings for each other. But suddenly it didn't matter so much that they could never be mates. They would be together for the next few days. That was enough. She would just have to keep her feelings in check. She could do that, surely? She wasn't a fluff-brained apprentice anymore. She was a warrior, and her Clan was relying on her to bring the Sisters back.

She would focus on that. She felt almost sure the mission would be a success, because she and Rootspring worked so well together—almost as though they were Clanmates. *Clanmates!* The thought sent happiness flowing like warm honey through her veins.

She looked over her shoulder to where Rootspring, Spotfur, and Needleclaw trailed behind. "It's beautiful!" she called.

The wind must have whipped away her mew, because the others didn't seem to hear her. Rootspring was keeping close to Spotfur, whose gaze barely lifted from the ground, while Needleclaw glanced around warily, as though a fox might be stalking them. Her heart sank. Weren't they excited too?

Guilt jabbed Bristlefrost's belly. Was she the only one who felt pleased to be away from her Clan? In the days since Flipclaw and the others had left, Thunderclan had seemed lost. Every paw-length of the camp reminded Bristlefrost of the long moons when Ashfur had posed as Bramblestar and brought chaos to the Clan turning Clanmates against one another. She knew that every warrior in Thunderclan felt ashamed of some of the things they'd done; they'd been taken in by a fox-heart and had fought with one another because of him. But she couldn't help feeling relieved to be away from the forest for a while—and to be on a quest that might put everything right.

Shaking out her fur, she hurried back to the patrol. "It looks like open country ahead," she reported. "I can't see any Twolegplaces; just a few dens dotted here and there."

Rootspring lifted his muzzle, brightening as she spoke.

"The Sisters must have headed this way," he mewed. "We may find them by sunset."

Needleclaw grunted. "That's not what you said last night," she mewed. "Before we left, you said we could be looking for them until leaf-fall."

Bristlefrost's pelt twitched crossly. "He was probably trying not to get your hopes up." She swished her tail. "You know how cautious Rootspring can be."

Rootspring stared ahead. "Let's focus on finding them. Tree told us to look for a kittypet called Pancakes. He knows the Sisters and he can tell us if . . ." His mew trailed off as they reached the top of the rise and he gazed at the valleys and grassy hills. Had the view taken his breath away?

Bristlefrost watched him expectantly.

"It's big," he mewed quietly.

Spotfur stared across the hills. "I didn't know there was so much land beyond Clan territory," she breathed.

Needleclaw blinked. "Do you really think we're going to find the Sisters in all *that*?"

"We have to," Bristlefrost told her, determined to be hopeful. She remembered the huge she-cats who'd come to the Clans when she was an apprentice. "They're our only chance of finding Bramblestar's ghost again."

Needleclaw swished her tail. "Where should we start?"

"Let's head down that way." Bristlefrost nodded toward a valley crowded with ferns. "There's a Twoleg nest at the bottom. Pancakes might be there."

Needleclaw stared at her sourly. "Rootspring's in charge," she mewed. "He decides where we go. I know you're used to bossing your Clanmates around, but on this patrol, Rootspring is the leader."

Bristlefrost blinked at her. "We each have a voice," she snapped. "There's no harm in any cat making a suggestion." She tried to catch Rootspring's eye, hoping he'd back her up, but he was gazing down the hill.

"Tree said Pancakes lives in a Twoleg nest in a valley beyond the Moonpool," he mewed thoughtfully. "Bristlefrost might be right. That could be Pancakes's Twoleg nest."

Triumph sparked in Bristlefrost's pelt as Needleclaw fluffed out her fur and stalked away. "Thanks for backing me up," she murmured as Spotfur headed after the SkyClan warrior.

Rootspring's pelt prickled self-consciously. "It might take a while to find the Sisters." He avoided her gaze. "We should all try to get along."

Okay. Bristlefrost followed him as he padded after the others. *But only because she's your littermate.* Needleclaw could act like she'd swallowed a wasp if she liked. Bristlefrost was determined to enjoy this mission. She lifted her gaze to the horizon. They were going to find the Sisters, no matter where they'd wandered. For the first time since the battle, confidence pulsed in her paws. This was what she was meant to do. She was going to save Thunderclan and bring StarClan back.

* * *

Her paws ached by the time the sun dipped behind the horizon. Dusk had spread deep blue shadows across the hillside as she followed Rootspring and Needleclaw along a ridge and headed down into yet another valley. She'd lost count of the hills they'd climbed and the tiny Twoleg nests they'd stopped at, looking for Pancakes. They'd found three plump, pampered kittypets: One had been a queen, close to kitting, another a bad-tempered she-cat. The third was a tom, but he'd smelled different from the toms she knew, and he'd had the narrow forehead of a young 'paw. None of them had seen any strange, large she-cats traveling in a group past their nests, and none had heard of a kittypet named Pancakes.

Perhaps we've come the wrong way. Doubt tugged in Bristlefrost's belly. She should have let Rootspring decide which route to take from the start. *Why did I let him listen to me?* He was walking beside Needleclaw now, as he'd done for most of the day. She was disappointed that they hadn't had time to talk alone, but she thought it might be for the best. They'd agreed they could never be mates, hadn't they? Perhaps it was easier not to get too close now.

"Mouse dung!" Spotfur's mew was pained.

Bristlefrost's heart quickened. Was she hurt? She turned back to help as the other she-cat stumbled to a halt and lifted her forepaw. "What happened?"

"It's okay." Spotfur lapped between her claws, then placed them gingerly onto the grass. "I didn't see the dip." She nodded toward a tiny hole where some creature must have burrowed.

Bristlefrost saw weariness in Spotfur's eyes. "Rootspring!" she called out.

He turned, his eyes widening. "Are you two okay?"

"Spotfur hurt her paw," Bristlefrost told him.

"It's not bad," Spotfur mewed quickly.

"Can we make camp soon? She's getting tired," Bristlefrost mewed, ignoring Spotfur's denial. "And my pads hurt." She hated to mention her own aching paws, but Spotfur needed rest. Who knew how many days' walking they had ahead of them? There was no use wearing themselves out at the start.

Rootspring gazed around the valley. The grass ran down to a small Twoleg den, nestled among trees. A willow draped the hillside a few tree-lengths from where they stood. Rootspring nodded toward it. "We could make camp there."

Needleclaw was already padding toward the willow. She nosed her way through the hanging leaves. "There's space between the roots to make nests," she called from inside.

Rootspring followed her, and Bristlefrost slid after him, Spotfur at her heels. Inside, branches shielded a small stretch of grass, hidden like a cave behind a waterfall. A sandy hollow opened among the roots of the tree, sheltered enough to defend. It would be easy to build nests here.

"This looks like a good place to sleep," Rootspring mewed.

"I can hunt," Bristlefrost offered.

Rootspring shook his head. "I'll hunt with Needleclaw." He looked down at his paws shyly. "We've been hunting together since we were kits. We kind of make a good team."

Needleclaw whisked her tail. "We'll be able to catch enough for every cat," she mewed. "You and Spotfur can build the nests."

Bristlefrost forced her fur not to ruffle. *We're not your apprentices.*

"Or you could check out that Twoleg den," Rootspring suggested. "Pancakes might be there."

"Okay." Bristlefrost dipped her head. She'd begun to lose hope of ever finding Pancakes. "But if we see prey, we'll catch it," she added. "Just in case you can't find any."

Needleclaw purred. "We'll find some," she mewed confidently, and pushed her way through the willow leaves.

"Good luck," Rootspring called, following his littermate.

Bristlefrost ignored the pang of jealousy that tugged in her belly. She ducked under the branches and headed downhill, toward the Twoleg nest.

Spotfur caught up to her. "Wait for me."

Bristlefrost was relieved to see that her Clanmate wasn't limping. "Is your paw okay now?"

"I told you, it was nothing."

"We should all be careful where we tread," Bristlefrost told her. "We can't risk getting hurt. We don't have a medicine cat with us."

"I guess." Spotfur gazed ahead.

"It's a shame we couldn't hunt," Bristlefrost mewed. "I bet there's some great prey around here." When Spotfur didn't respond, she went on. "At least SkyClan cats like the same sort of prey we do. Imagine if Rootspring and Needleclaw were

RiverClan cats. They'd bring back fish instead of mice. Or ShadowClan cats!" She pulled a face. "I've heard ShadowClan warriors eat frogs."

Bristlefrost glanced at her Clanmate, hoping for a response. But Spotfur didn't twitch a whisker. Squirrelflight's words echoed in her mind. *Spotfur needs a distraction from her grief.* Perhaps she'd feel better if she remembered why they'd come. "If we find the Sisters, we might be able to get Bramblestar back soon." When Spotfur didn't answer, Bristlefrost pressed on. "Wouldn't it be great if we found Pancakes here? He could tell us where the Sisters have gone and then—"

Spotfur cut her off. "Why don't we stop talking and focus on finding him."

Bristlefrost's heart sank. Wasn't there anything she could do to cheer her friend up? She padded on in silence. Maybe grief was something you couldn't rush.

A stone wall peeked through a stretch of ferns. *A Twoleg boundary.* She signaled to Spotfur with a flick of her tail and ducked low, moving like a snake through the long grass to the foot of the wall. Spotfur hurried behind her, belly brushing the ground. They stopped and Bristlefrost tasted the air. Catscent was nearly hidden beneath the sweet scent of flowers, stronger than any she'd smelled beside the lake. She nodded at Spotfur and leaped silently onto the wall. Fur brushed stone as Spotfur jumped up beside her, and together they scanned the stretch of smooth grass that ran around the Twoleg nest. Something rustled from the shadows at one side. *Pancakes?*

Hope flickering in her chest, Bristlefrost jumped down,

landed on the soft lawn, and straightened. "Try to look friendly," she whispered to Spotfur as she landed beside her.

"I know." Spotfur shot her a look. "This is the fourth time we've done this."

Bristlefrost's pelt prickled self-consciously. "I'm just trying to be careful." She led the way across the grass, keeping her pelt smooth and her ears pricked, as though she were greeting an old friend. "Hey," she mewed as they neared the nest. The moon had risen behind the hills, and she narrowed her eyes against its glare as she peered into the shadows. Something moved there. She nodded for Spotfur to stop and spoke again. "We're just passing through," she meowed breezily. "We're looking for some friends."

She waited, her heart quickening as paws brushed the earth. She hoped it was a friendly kittypet. She was too tired for a fight. Bright, round eyes glittered from the darkness. Then a new scent touched her nose. Through the sharp fragrance of flowers, she smelled dog.

Her pelt spiked as a low growl sounded in the darkness. It must have disguised its scent by rolling in petals. She could see its outline now: a stocky dog, trembling with excitement.

The air seemed to split as it let out a howl. Bristlefrost pressed against Spotfur. "Run!" As she felt Spotfur turn, fear-scent pulsing from her pelt, she followed, racing across the grass so fast it blurred beneath her paws.

Barking exploded behind them. Heavy paws thumped the earth. Hot breath bathed her tail, and foul stench of crow-food almost made her gag. Spotfur streaked up the wall ahead of her, pausing only long enough to glance back at Bristlefrost before leaping down the other side. Bristlefrost jumped after her, praying that the dog couldn't follow.

She followed Spotfur up the slope, relieved that Spotfur was heading away from the willow. If the dog found their trail, it might track them back to their temporary camp. She let out a shaky breath when she realized that the dog's bark had not followed them over the wall. A Twoleg yelp made her turn, and she saw a figure in the moonlight, moving toward the dog and hooking it with a paw before hauling it inside the nest.

As Bristlefrost stood panting, her fur slowly flattening, Spotfur stalked back to her side. The gray-and-white she-cat was breathing heavily, her eyes sparking with fear. They stared at the Twoleg nest. Bristlefrost heard the grass swish farther up the slope and her heart lurched. Were there more dogs here? As she turned, she saw two kits racing toward her, their fluffy pelts pale in the moonlight.

The kits bundled to a halt in front of them and blinked with wide, excited eyes.

"Did you see Spike?" the larger kit asked.

"Did he scare you?" asked the other.

Both kits burst into purrs, as though the idea were hilarious.

Bristlefrost blinked at them. Why did these kits think dogs were funny? "He chased us!"

"He probably wanted to say hello," the larger kit mewed.

"Spike loves cats," the other kit told them. "We live with him."

Bristlefrost flattened her ears, horrified. "Cats don't live with dogs."

"Why not?" Both kits stared at her.

Bristlefrost stared back without answering. These kits were weird.

Spotfur shook out her pelt. "Why does Spike smell like flowers?" she asked.

"Our Twolegs wash him," the larger kit explained.

Bristlefrost shivered. Twolegs were even crueler to dogs than they were to cats. "Does a cat called Pancakes live around here?"

The kits looked at each other. "He used to," the larger one mewed. "But he's gone now."

"We're his kits," the other told her. "I'm Bacon."

"I'm Eggs."

Bristlefrost tried to catch Spotfur's eye. *Those are the dumbest kittypet names yet.* But Spotfur didn't seem to find it amusing— she looked like she'd rather be curled in her nest.

"Do you want to play tag?" Bacon asked eagerly.

"No thanks," Spotfur told him. "We're looking for some friends."

"We can be your friends," Eggs told her.

"We're looking for *old* friends," Spotfur mewed wearily. "Not new ones."

Eggs looked crestfallen.

Bristlefrost shot Spotfur a warning glance. These kits might know something useful. "I'm sure you'd make great friends," she added. "But we can't stay, I'm afraid. We're on a mission—"

Spotfur's tail flicked impatiently. "Have you ever seen any big, furry she-cats?"

The kits looked at each other thoughtfully.

"No," Eggs mewed. "I don't think so."

Spotfur leaned closer. "What about toms?"

Bristlefrost watched as the kits frowned, clearly trying to remember. She tried prompting them. "They might have had funny names like Stone or Branch or—"

Bacon's ears pricked. "Leaf!"

Bristlefrost's heart leaped. Leaf sounded like the sort of name the Sisters would give to a kit.

Eggs' fluffy tail shot up excitedly. "We know a tom called Leaf," he mewed. "He stopped here and played tag with us once."

"Are you sure you don't want to play tag?" Bacon asked. "It's really fun."

"No thanks," Bristlefrost told him.

Spotfur's pelt was rippling along her spine. "Did this Leaf say where he came from or where he was going?"

"He said he'd left a group of cats that was heading toward the river to make their camp for the warm season," Eggs replied.

"Which river?" Spotfur asked.

"He said it was that way." Eggs nodded toward the fern-pelted hillside.

Bristlefrost could hardly keep her paws still. She couldn't wait to get back to the willow and tell Rootspring. They'd been heading the right way after all. All they had to do now was find the river and follow it.

She just hoped they could persuade the Sisters to return to the lake. For the first time, a chilling thought flashed through her mind. What if the Sisters refused to come?

"Of course they'll come," Needleclaw mewed when Bristlefrost shared her fear. The black-and-white she-cat leaned back contentedly, pushing away the remnants of the mouse she'd been eating.

"Why should they?" Bristlefrost had hardly touched any of the prey Rootspring and Needleclaw had brought back. The idea that the Sisters might refuse to help made her belly tight with worry.

"We'll persuade them." Needleclaw half closed her eyes.

Rootspring tore a strip of flesh from a thrush and laid it on the ground in front of Bristlefrost. "Needleclaw always gets her way in the end," he murmured, wryly. "If any cat can persuade the Sisters to come back, she can." He nudged the strip closer. "You persuaded warriors from all different Clans to fight Ashfur," he reminded her. "Between the two of you, you'll make them see that it's the right thing to do."

Bristlefrost blinked at him. The moon had risen high above the willow, its light filtering like water between the leaves. Spotfur, who'd said she was too tired to eat, was already sleeping in the fern nest Bristlefrost had made for her. A mouse lay beside it, for when she woke up. "But they've got no reason to help Bramblestar," she mewed. "Or us. After all, he wasn't so kind to them when they last sought to settle near the lake, even though that was only temporary. If they're still upset—"

"Eat." Rootspring nudged the strip of flesh again. "You'll need your strength tomorrow. We don't know how far away this river is."

"Or how long ago the Sisters passed through," Needleclaw added.

"But we'll find them." Rootspring regarded them both with a determined gleam in his eyes. "And we'll persuade them to come back with us."

Bristlefrost wanted to believe him. She was touched that he was trying so hard to convince her that it would be okay. She searched his gaze. Did he believe it? His eyes shone. He seemed really excited. She took a bite of the flesh, her belly growling as it suddenly seemed to remember how hungry it was. She took another bite, swallowing it eagerly.

Rootspring purred and hooked the rest of the thrush closer. He'd been right about hunting well with Needleclaw. They'd brought back enough prey to feed a whole warriors' den. There would be plenty left for the morning.

Needleclaw stretched. "I'm sleepy."

"Some cat needs to guard the camp," Rootspring mewed.

Bristlefrost swallowed her mouthful. "I can take the first shift."

"Good." Needleclaw yawned.

Bristlefrost glanced at Spotfur, wondering if she should

take Spotfur's shift too. The gray-and-white she-cat had seemed exhausted.

"I'll sit with you," Rootspring offered. "I'm not really tired."

"Shouldn't you sleep while you can?" Needleclaw got to her paws and padded to her nest, plucking at the ferns to soften them.

Rootspring didn't answer. Instead he told her, "I'll wake you when it's your turn."

She glanced at him but didn't argue, just wound herself into the nest and closed her eyes.

As Bristlefrost finished the thrush, she heard the black-and-white she-cat's breathing deepen into sleep. She swallowed the last mouthful and licked her lips. "There's no need for you to stay up," she told Rootspring.

"I want to." He got to his paws and padded out through the trailing willow branches.

Bristlefrost followed, her heart fluttering like a bird in her chest. She felt suddenly awkward. What would they talk about? Perhaps they shouldn't talk at all. They'd agreed to be friends and nothing more. But it was hard to be just friends alone in the moonlight. Especially when being near Rootspring made her fur tingle like this. Perhaps she should wake Spotfur and ask her to change shifts.

Rootspring sat on the grass outside the willow den and gazed along the valley. Around him, ferns stirred in the breeze, swishing like the lake stirring pebbles against the shore. Bristlefrost sat down stiffly beside him. She'd wanted to be alone with him and now she was. But this wasn't how she'd imagined it. She'd thought it would be wonderful. And yet he seemed suddenly like a stranger. How his pelt gleamed. How broad his head had grown. And his shoulders. She pressed back a shiver and tried to remember him as the gangly apprentice she'd rescued from the lake. Or the awkward young 'paw who'd once crossed the Thunderclan border to bring her prey.

As he fluffed out his pelt against the chill, his fur brushed hers. She tried not to flinch as her own pelt seemed to spark where they touched, and stared ahead, not daring to catch his eye.

"It's a relief to be away from the Clans for a while, isn't it?" Rootspring mewed.

She felt him looking at her and wrapped her tail tighter around her paws, unable to stop herself from thinking about how the Clan she'd left was now missing several warriors. "I guess . . ."

"What's wrong?"

She could feel his gaze like the heat of the sun on her fur. Slowly, she turned to meet it.

"Some of our Clanmates have left." His eyes widened, but he said nothing. "With everything that's been going on, not every warrior in Thunderclan thinks it's the right place for them anymore. They've . . . 'gone for a wander,' whatever that means. . . ."

She felt his tail rest gently on her back, felt the chill of the night be chased away like a trespasser on a Clan's border. "Oh no . . ." He shifted so that his flank pressed right up against hers. "Do you think they're going to come back?"

"I don't know," she admitted. "I hope so, but . . . I don't know. Even Graystripe left. Squirrelflight took that hardest of all."

Rootspring sat with her in silence for a moment, until he finally murmured, "That must be very worrying."

She nodded. "It is, but . . . I'm glad to be here with you."

His eyes shone with warmth, unchanged from the first time they'd met. "The moon seems bigger out here," he mewed softly.

"Yes." Bristlefrost's shoulders loosened. "Yes, it does." Sitting beside Rootspring, fur touching, suddenly seemed as natural as sleeping. *I was right,* she thought happily. *This is wonderful.*

CHAPTER 8

Shadowsight stretched and climbed out of his nest. Morning sunshine streamed through the medicine-den entrance as he headed for the herb store. Mothwing and Puddleshine had already left. Were they gathering herbs? Or perhaps one of their Clanmates had needed their help. Frustration stabbed Shadowsight's belly. They used to share things like that with him, but now that he'd lost his full medicine-cat status, they murmured to each other as though they were scared he'd overhear. He never knew now where his denmates had gone or which Clanmate was sick.

At least they still let him treat one cat. Shadowsight headed for the herb store, wondering which herbs the prisoner would need today. *Not poppy seed or marigold.* Ashfur's battle wounds had closed up well and weren't inflamed anymore. He could take some goldenrod and dock, to speed up the healing. He crouched beside the store and reached his paw in.

"What are you doing?" Mothwing's sharp mew made him jerk around. She stood in the den entrance, frowning at him.

"I was getting herbs for Ashfur." Shadowsight's pelt grew hot with embarrassment, as though he'd just been caught stealing from the fresh-kill pile.

"I left you a bundle." Mothwing nodded toward a leaf wrap at the edge of the den.

"Is there any goldenrod in it?" Shadowsight asked. "Or dock?"

"There's everything you need." Mothwing grabbed the bundle between her jaws and carried it across the den. She dropped it at his paws. "You'd better stay out of the herb store for now."

He blinked at her as though she'd raked his muzzle. Puddleshine had encouraged him to study the herb store so that he knew where everything was kept. "But I'm still a *medicine-cat* apprentice," he reminded her.

"You're under supervision," she mewed sourly. "Stay away from the herb store unless Puddleshine or I tell you otherwise." She slid past him and peered into the store, as though checking for any damage he might have done.

Angrily, Shadowsight grabbed the herb bundle and stalked out of the den.

He passed Scorchfur and Snowbird sharing a mouse beside the long grass at the edge of the clearing. Blazefire and Berryheart were play-fighting nearby, while Gullswoop and Hollowspring dragged old nests from the warriors' den. Shadowsight's pelt twitched self-consciously. Were they staring at him? He kept his gaze on the hollow tree. The whole Clan must know by now that he'd lost his medicine-cat status. It made him feel as though he were walking around camp without his fur.

Breezepelt and Sedgewhisker were guarding the bramble enclosure this morning. The two WindClan warriors looked small and sleek beside the ShadowClan cats.

Breezepelt stretched deeply, as though sitting had made him stiff. "I'm looking forward to getting back to the moor and feeling the wind in my pelt again."

"And sunshine," Sedgewhisker mewed wistfully. "This forest makes me feel like I'm living underground." She glanced at the strips of blue showing between the tips of the pines. "I'm surprised ShadowClan cats don't have moss growing between their claws."

Breezepelt purred with amusement, then stopped as he noticed Shadowsight padding toward him. He sat up stiffly. Sedgewhisker straightened and stared ahead.

Shadowsight's paws pricked. Had they stopped talking because a ShadowClan cat was approaching? *Or is it because* I'm *coming?* He felt a chill run through his pelt as he neared. He'd been so focused on the possibility that every cat in his Clan knew about his change in status, he hadn't considered how far the news might already have spread into the other Clans. *Does every cat know?* He nodded a greeting as he passed. "Hey."

"Hi." Breezepelt's reply was barely a mumble.

Sedgewhisker grunted, avoiding Shadowsight's eye.

Shadowsight padded past them, shrinking beneath his pelt. He felt sure now. *All the Clans know I'm a failed medicine cat, and they blame me for Ashfur coming to Thunderclan.* As misery crowded his thoughts, Ashfur squeezed out of his den in the hollow tree.

The dark warrior blinked at Shadowsight as though he, at

least, was pleased to see him. "Hi, Shadowsight." He waited for Shadowsight to drop his bundle, then sat down in a patch of sunshine near the enclosure wall. "What have you got for me today?"

I don't know yet. Shadowsight unrolled the leaf, irritated once more as he saw a few damp nettle leaves inside. These drooping leaves wouldn't be much help. He would go through the motions anyway and make an ointment for Ashfur's worst scratches. Bitterly, he began to chew the leaves.

Ashfur settled onto his belly and waited, accustomed now to the daily routine. "I need some exercise," he meowed absently.

Shadowsight spat nettle pulp onto the unrolled leaf and dabbed some onto his paw. "It's best for you to rest until your wounds are completely healed."

"I need to stay fit," Ashfur complained.

"Why?" Shadowsight parted the fur on Ashfur's flank with a paw and began to spread the pulp onto the long scab that ran along it.

"The Clans can't keep me trapped here forever," Ashfur mewed.

Just until they work out a way to help Bramblestar get his body back, Shadowsight thought. He still found it strange to treat a warrior who looked like one cat but talked like another.

Ashfur spoke again. "Have you heard any news from Thunderclan?"

Shadowsight stiffened. *Why does he want to know?* "No," he answered. The leaders and medicine cats had met on the island three days ago, but he hadn't been allowed to attend. He swallowed back anger.

"What about Squirrelflight?" Ashfur's eyes narrowed with interest.

"No cat's mentioned her." Shadowsight felt wary. What was the dark warrior planning?

"Do you think she'll visit me again?"

Did he want a chance to get revenge on the Thunderclan leader for tricking him? Shadowsight dabbed his paw into the pulp once more and began to smear a bitemark at the back of Ashfur's neck. "I'm surprised you want to see her again," he mewed casually.

"She couldn't help what happened last time." Ashfur shook his head. "The other leaders must have forced her into betraying me like that." He shifted so that Shadowsight could reach a scar on his hind leg. "They were listening to every word she said. If she hadn't betrayed me, they'd have made her a prisoner too." His eyes sparked, as though he enjoyed the thought of having Squirrelflight as his denmate in the hollow tree.

Shadowsight sat back on his haunches. Did Ashfur really believe she hadn't wanted to betray him? "I don't think Squirrelflight will visit you again."

"If she could, we could talk things out." Ashfur's gaze drifted thoughtfully. "We might be able to come to an agreement."

Shadowsight's eyes widened. Was Ashfur crazy? "Like what?"

"If she agreed to leave with me, I wouldn't bother the Clans anymore." His gaze suddenly fixed on Shadowsight. Alarm sparked in Shadowsight's belly as he saw determination in it. "Then no cat would have to suffer." There was menace in the dark warrior's tone.

Shadowsight turned away and dabbed more pulp onto his paw. He padded around Ashfur and spread it along the scar on his tail. "What if Squirrelflight doesn't want to leave with you?" he asked tentatively.

"She must." A growl rumbled in Ashfur's throat. "She's a warrior. She'll do anything for her Clan."

Shadowsight felt sick. Ashfur would clearly be willing to take Squirrelflight with him against her will. Did he hope that threatening the Clans would make her agree to go? *Would she sacrifice herself like that?* Shadowsight's heart lurched. *She might.* He rubbed the last of the pulp over Ashfur's shredded ear tips. Squirrelflight must never find out. The Clans mustn't let her destroy her life to save them. There had to be another way. He rerolled the empty leaf. "I'm done," he told Ashfur.

Ashfur got to his paws and glanced at the wounds Shadowsight had treated. "You're still a good medicine cat," he mewed. "But what's the point of being good at healing if you're not allowed to heal anymore?"

"I'm healing you." Shadowsight met his gaze, refusing to be provoked.

"And when I'm gone?" Ashfur pursued. "What will you do then? Are you going to spend the rest of your life cleaning other cats' bedding?"

"Of course not." Doubt wormed in Shadowsight's belly. Tigerstar and Puddleshine would let him go back to real medicine-cat work eventually, wouldn't they? "As soon as StarClan returns—"

Ashfur's whiskers twitched with amusement. "StarClan isn't coming back."

"They will." *They have to.*

"Do you really think your Clanmates will believe any message you pass on from StarClan ever again?" Ashfur's gaze burned into Shadowsight's.

Shadowsight swallowed back panic. *Will they?*

Ashfur leaned closer. "And it's not like you can become a warrior," he murmured. "You're not trained. You have no skills."

"I could learn!" Shadowsight puffed out his chest.

"I suppose you could be a mediator." Ashfur sneered. "Or whatever it is Tree calls himself so that he can stay in the Clans without becoming a *real* warrior."

Shadowsight stared at the impostor. "Why do you enjoy making other cats miserable?"

"We're more alike than you think," Ashfur murmured.

"No, we're not!" Shadowsight lashed his tail.

Ashfur tipped his head, clearly unimpressed by Shadowsight's anger. "I'm a warrior who's not a warrior, and you're a medicine cat who's not a medicine cat."

"You mean you *were* a warrior. You've been dead a long time!" Shadowsight grabbed the empty leaf and marched out of the enclosure.

"I don't *feel* dead, thanks to this body!" Ashfur called after him.

Shadowsight ignored him and padded past Breezepelt and Sedgewhisker, who were still standing guard outside. Breezepelt blinked at him in surprise. The WindClan warrior was staring at him as though he had two tails.

Shadowsight spat out the leaf. *"What?"* he demanded angrily.

Breezepelt looked curious. "Are you really allowed to treat him alone?" He nodded toward Ashfur, who had padded to the back of the enclosure and lain down in the shade.

"Of course I am!"

Breezepelt glanced at his Clanmate uncertainly.

Shadowsight spun around and glared at Sedgewhisker. "Do you have a problem with that?"

"We just thought you weren't a medicine cat anymore," Sedgewhisker mewed.

So the rest of the Clans *did* know that Tigerstar had stripped him of his status. Fury pulsed in Shadowsight's paws. "I'm still a medicine-cat *apprentice!*" Was he going to have to tell every cat he met now?

Sedgewhisker frowned. "But you killed Bramblestar."

Breezepelt nodded. "What cat is going to let you treat them after you've killed a leader?"

Shadowsight's mouth went dry. He felt light-headed as his anger turned to shame. Dropping his gaze, he hurried away, leaving the empty leaf lying between the two WindClan warriors. *Is that what every cat thinks? That I killed Bramblestar?* Shadowsight pulled up short before he reached the medicine den. Why bother? He didn't belong there anymore. He didn't belong anywhere.

If the real Bramblestar comes back, then they'll know I didn't kill him. And yet Shadowsight knew Bramblestar's ghost was missing. Even though he'd released him from the vines that had held him fast in the Dark Forest, Bramblestar hadn't returned to the living forest. What if he was gone forever? *Then I'll know I did kill him.*

Lost in his thoughts, Shadowsight blindly watched Lightleap, his littermate, drag an old nest from the warriors' den. She dropped it beside the pile Hollowspring and Gullswoop had made and began to rip them apart. *How could any cat forgive me? I have no future here. I'd be better off as a loner.*

Despair swirled like fog around him, choking him until he could hardly breathe.

"Shadowsight?" Lightleap's mew sounded somewhere outside his haze of misery. "Are you okay?"

He watched her pad toward him, feeling as though he were very far away, even as she reached him and lapped between his ears. "You look lost," she mewed, leaning closer.

He blinked at her, the fog receding as he clung to her gaze.

"Do you need something to do?" she asked gently.

He nodded numbly.

She stepped back and shook bracken dust from her fur. "Blazefire and I were planning to hunt with Hollowspring and Gullswoop. Do you want to come with us?"

Shadowsight gazed at the pile of half-dismantled nests. "Don't you have to finish cleaning out the den?"

Lightleap sniffed. "We're not apprentices," she mewed. When Shadowsight winced, she hurriedly added, "I just mean we can finish that later." She glanced over her shoulder to where Gullswoop was dragging fresh ferns into camp. "Can Shadowsight hunt with us?" she called.

Gullswoop dropped the ferns, her eyes bright. "He's welcome to try."

"Try what?" Hollowspring padded into camp behind her, carrying more ferns.

"Shadowsight's coming hunting with us," Gullswoop told him.

Was that irritation glittering in the black warrior's eyes?

Blazefire popped his head out of the den. His whiskers were flecked with scraps of bracken. "Are we hunting *now*?"

"Yes!" Lightleap purred eagerly. "We've done enough cleaning for today."

Shadowsight felt a glimmer of happiness, and his misery began to melt. Gratitude surged in his chest. "Thanks, Lightleap."

"We might be able to teach you a thing or two," she mewed, leading the way out of camp.

Shadowsight followed. "You can teach me a lot. I don't know anything about hunting."

Gullswoop fell in beside him. "The first thing you have to learn is how to sit still."

As they headed into the forest, Blazefire and Hollowspring fanned out. Shadowsight could see them tasting the air. Were they searching for prey already? He copied them, opening his mouth to let the air bathe his tongue. He could smell the mint that grew close to camp and a patch of comfrey that sprouted between the bracken in this part of the forest. Another scent touched his tongue. Was that sage? He hadn't realized it grew this close to camp.

"Rabbit!" Hollowspring's yowl made him jump. Shadowsight's heart seemed to skip a beat as the black warrior hared away, crashing through a wall of ferns. Blazefire hurtled after him, veering away to one side.

"Won't they have scared it with all that noise?" Shadowsight whispered to Lightleap.

"It had already spotted us." His littermate's gaze was following a gray blur far ahead between the trees. A rabbit was pelting toward a thick swath of brambles. Her pelt bristled with excitement, and she didn't take her eyes from it as she explained, "It was running away. Watch what Blazefire does." She nodded toward the white-and-ginger tom. It was hard to believe Blazefire had been born in a Twolegplace. He was streaking over the forest floor like a swooping hawk. Taking the cleanest line between the trees, he rounded a ridge while Hollowspring leaped over it, the rabbit a few tail-lengths ahead of him.

"Why doesn't Hollowspring grab it?" Shadowsight asked. Surely, if the black warrior leaped now, he could catch the rabbit.

"Wait." Lightleap was as still as stone as she watched her denmates.

Blazefire had changed tack now and, picking up speed,

swung around to block the rabbit's path. If it reached the brambles, Shadowsight guessed, they'd lose it in the tangle of branches and thorns. As soon as Blazefire reached his Clan-mate's line of sight, Hollowspring leaped. The rabbit swerved, changing direction, but Blazefire had closed in. Deftly, he blocked the rabbit's path and lunged at it before it could reach the safety of the thorns.

Hollowspring skidded to a halt, his tail whisking with delight as Blazefire made the killing bite and lifted the rabbit by its scruff.

Lightleap purred. "Hollowspring couldn't be sure of catching it," she explained to Shadowsight now the hunt was over. "But he knew Blazefire would cut it off. A sure kill is better than a quick kill."

Shadowsight blinked at his sister. He hadn't realized she knew so much about hunting.

"Come on," she mewed, heading away happily. "Let's go help bury it. We can pick it up on the way home."

Shadowsight hung back as Lightleap scooped out soft earth between the roots of a pine. Blazefire laid the rabbit in the hole and covered it with loose dirt and leaves. Gullswoop padded around the tree, her white tail flicking with obvious satisfaction. The whole patrol seemed happy. Shadowsight hadn't known how much fun it was, being a warrior. He was used to working alone, gathering herbs or tending to sick Clanmates. His life as a medicine cat seemed suddenly solitary compared to this, especially now that he was allowed to treat only one patient.

"Will you teach me how to scent prey?" he whispered to Lightleap as she began to lead the patrol through the forest once more. "All I can pick out is herbs."

She purred. "I hadn't thought about that." She paused and tasted the air. "Can you smell what I smell?"

Shadowsight stopped beside her and opened his mouth.

Gullswoop, Blazefire, and Hollowspring pulled up behind them.

"What are we looking for?" Gullswoop whispered.

"We're smelling for prey," Lightleap told him.

Hollowspring sniffed. "I can smell a—"

"Hush!" Lightleap cut him off. "Shadowsight needs to practice."

Shadowsight breathed deeper, trying not to notice the dock scent that hung heavy in the air here. He tasted a musky scent beneath it—a familiar musky scent. He concentrated, trying to remember which piece of prey from the fresh-kill pile it smelled like. Excitement fizzed in his paws as he remembered. "Mouse?"

Lightleap flicked her tail happily. "Well done." She nodded toward a beech tree that had made a space for itself among the pines. "You often find mice around beech trees," she told him. "They eat the nuts, so it's a good place to hunt in leaf-bare, when berries are scarce."

"Look." Hollowspring hissed. The black warrior had dropped his tail. He was staring at a blueberry patch a few tree-lengths away. Four sparrows were hopping among the leaves, pecking at the fruit that was beginning to ripen there.

Lightleap nodded, and the patrol picked its way quietly between the trees. Gullswoop and Blazefire moved out in a wide arc around the sparrows, clearly planning to approach them from the far side of the blueberry patch. Shadowsight stuck close to Lightleap, hardly daring to breathe. He didn't want to scare the birds away.

As they neared, Lightleap nodded. "Stay back," she told him, her order barely a whisper.

Shadowsight waited as the others closed in on the unsuspecting birds. His heart was pounding. How would they catch the sparrows before they fluttered away? The patrol crept nearer until they were only a few tail-lengths from their prey. Another few paw steps and they'd be within leaping distance. Shadowsight watched, enthralled, willing them to make the catch.

Suddenly, a buzz sounded in his ear. His heart seemed to burst as a bee brushed his ear fur, its hum so loud that he hardly heard his own yelp of shock. He leaped backward, his fur spiking with panic. Crying with alarm, the sparrows fluttered into the trees, their feathers ruffled with surprise.

Hollowspring turned on him and glared through the trees. "You mouse-brain!"

"I'm sorry." Shadowsight blinked at the black tom, flustered with embarrassment. He glanced over his shoulder, hoping the bee was gone. There was no sign of it.

"It's okay." Lightleap headed back to Shadowsight, her mew calm. "We'll find some more."

Hollowspring grunted, following her with Gullswoop and Blazefire. "What scared you?"

Shadowsight looked at the ground. "A bee buzzed in my ear."

Blazefire's whiskers twitched. "A bee?" Shadowsight could tell he was trying to swallow back a purr.

"It was a *big* bee," Shadowsight mewed defensively.

Gullswoop's eyes shimmered with amusement. "Bees are a warrior's greatest enemy."

"More dangerous than foxes," Blazefire teased.

Shadowsight glanced at them ruefully. At least they thought it was funny, unlike Hollowspring, who was still glaring at him.

"I guess it's okay for *some* cats to ruin a hunt," the tom muttered resentfully. "I guess *some* cats can do whatever they like."

Lightleap stiffened. "What do you mean by that?"

"Nothing." Hollowspring looked away sullenly.

Lightleap glared at him. "Spit it out."

Hollowspring hesitated, then swung his gaze back at the brown tabby she-cat. "I'm not sure it's smart to criticize one of Tigerstar's kin."

Lightleap stared at him as though she didn't know what to say. Gullswoop and Blazefire shifted awkwardly.

Hollowspring turned away. "Come on," he growled. "Let's catch something. The Clan will be hungry if we don't."

Shadowsight's paws felt frozen to the earth. *Does every cat in ShadowClan resent me?* Dismay crept beneath his pelt like cold water. He'd assumed his Clanmates hadn't challenged him about Bramblestar's death because they liked and respected him enough to forgive him. But perhaps they *hadn't* forgiven him. They could be keeping quiet for fear of making Tiger-star angry. Shadowsight suddenly felt weak with dread. Had his Clanmates all turned against him without him realizing?

CHAPTER 9

❧

Rootspring hardly noticed the drizzle that fell on the patrol as he led it from the cover of the trees. He was thinking about Bristlefrost. She was trailing behind, staying close to Spotfur. The gray-and-white she-cat had complained she felt nauseous and had quickly grown tired as they'd climbed hill after hill, each one higher than the last, following the direction Pancakes's kits had given them.

Needleclaw fell in beside him and stared gloomily at the slope rising ahead. "Surely we should have found the river by now," she fretted. "Do you think those kits even knew where Leaf was headed?"

Rootspring followed her gaze without seeing. Sitting guard last night with Bristlefrost had made his fur tingle. It tingled now, despite the rain that slicked his pelt against his body. He reminded himself that they were just friends, but that didn't stop his heart leaping and racing like a playful kit. Far from the Clans, alone with the moon, the moment with Bristlefrost had seemed perfect.

Needleclaw jabbed his shoulder with her muzzle. "You're thinking about her, aren't you?"

Rootspring blinked at his sister, unable to stop himself from glancing guiltily back at Bristlefrost.

"I knew it!" Needleclaw looked dismayed. "You have to get over her. You two can never happen."

"We're just friends," Rootspring insisted.

"Friends don't keep staring at each other like moonstruck rabbits." Needleclaw mewed sharply. "I should never have let you stand guard together last night." She jerked her muzzle closer. "Did anything happen?"

"No." Rootspring bristled defensively. "I told you, we're just friends."

Needleclaw shot him a warning look. "When we get home, find a *friend* in your own Clan." She sounded more worried than angry. "If you keep trying to hang out with Bristlefrost, you'll both end up in trouble."

"But there's no cat like her," Rootspring protested. "She's so strong, and she's been through so much. Besides, the warrior code might change. The Clans are working together more and more now. You never know, one day—"

Needleclaw silenced him with a look. "You're fooling yourself *and* her if you think the Clans are ever going to allow you and Bristlefrost to be together."

"You don't know that." Crossly, Rootspring quickened his pace, breaking into a run to reach the top of the slope. His heart dropped like a stone as he saw what lay beyond.

Needleclaw caught up. "Do you see the river?"

Rootspring gazed down at the Twoleg nests crowding the valley. There was no river in sight. Too many huge gray dens cluttered the view. He'd never seen a Twolegplace this large. "The Sisters would never have come this way," he mewed, dismayed.

Needleclaw pawed the earth nervously. "The kits must have been wrong."

"Perhaps we misunderstood them." As Rootspring stared at the forest of rain-soaked Twoleg nests, Bristlefrost and Spotfur stopped beside them.

Spotfur's pelt spiked. "We're not going down there, are we?"

Rootspring looked at her. What was he supposed to say? They couldn't give up now. "I guess we have to."

Bristlefrost stared into the valley, her eyes rounding. "But there's no sign of the river."

Needleclaw swished her tail. "We should never have listened to those kits."

"Perhaps we should try a different route." Spotfur looked back the way they'd come.

Rootspring squared his shoulders. "This is the only lead we have," he insisted. "We should keep going. The river's probably down there somewhere. We just need to find our way through the Twoleg nests." He looked at the others.

Bristlefrost met his gaze. "We've come this far," she agreed. "Let's keep going." She headed for the wooden fence that bordered the first of the Twoleg nests and Rootspring followed, grateful for her support.

The edge of the Twolegplace was easy to navigate. Fences provided walkways between the gray stone nests, and the patrol followed them, running deftly along the ridges and leaping from one to another. Rootspring was relieved they could avoid crossing the grassy strips where the dog-scent was almost as strong as Twoleg stench. But at last the forest of fences ran out, and Rootspring stopped, his heart quickening as he saw a Thunderpath cutting its way like a river between the nests. There was no way around. They'd have to cross it.

Sleeping monsters lined the edge. He jumped onto the grass and crept closer. Needleclaw followed, narrowing her eyes as a growl sounded in the distance.

Rootspring followed her gaze, his heart lurching as a monster swung around a corner and rumbled toward them. Its glaring eyes sliced through the rain. "Look out!" Nosing Needleclaw away, he shielded her from the spray it threw across the grass.

She shuddered. "I hate Twolegplaces."

As they shook the filthy water from their fur, Bristlefrost and Spotfur landed beside them.

Spotfur eyed the Thunderpath nervously. "Perhaps we should turn back."

"We can't give up," Bristlefrost told her.

Rootspring glanced at the sky, wishing he could see where the sun was. It would tell them which direction they were heading. Frowning, he searched the clouds, hoping to see a lighter patch where the sun was trying to break through, but there was nothing but gray, each cloud darker than the next. He lifted his chin and tried to sound confident. "Let's keep going."

He looked along the Thunderpath, relieved to see it clear, and darted across, the stone scraping his paws. Needleclaw followed, Bristlefrost and Spotfur at her tail. On the other side, he led the patrol along a stone Twoleg path. The nests here were bigger; they kept growing higher as the patrol moved deeper into the Twolegplace, until Rootspring felt like he was in a forest of stone.

His chest tightened as the path opened onto a wider Thunderpath. There were no sleeping monsters here. Every monster was wide awake and grumbling, and they patrolled, nose to tail, along the gray strip of stone.

Rain fell between the towering Twoleg nests and dripped heavily from ledges where it gathered. Twolegs trudged along the paths, their eyes fixed on their paws. They seemed blind to one another, the monsters, and the warrior patrol.

Bristlefrost caught Rootspring's eye. "How can we cross it?"

Rootspring blinked back at her. "We'll figure it out," he promised. As he spoke, the entrance of a nest clattered a tree-length away, and Twolegs flooded onto the stone path, heading toward them.

"Look out!" Needleclaw dodged clear and crouched against the wall of the nest as the Twolegs streamed around them.

Rootspring pressed himself against the ground, praying that a Twoleg wouldn't crush him. His breath caught in his throat as he heard a yelp, and he jerked his muzzle around. Bristlefrost and Spotfur were teetering on the edge of the Twoleg path, their eyes wide with panic as monsters and

Twolegs hemmed them in on either side. A wide stream of filthy water swept past them, spilling over the stone and splashing their paws.

"Stay there!" he ordered.

As he darted toward them, zigzagging between the Twolegs, Spotfur's paws slipped over the edge. With a yelp, she tumbled into the water. Rootspring leaped for her, but Bristlefrost had already grabbed her Clanmate's scruff. She held her fast as water flooded over her muzzle. A Twoleg lunged down, reaching its pink paw toward her. Rootspring batted it away with outstretched claws. As it barked and shrank away, Rootspring hooked his claws into Spotfur's pelt.

A wall of spray blasted him as a monster roared past. Spitting out the foul water, he caught Bristlefrost's eye. She was straining to hold on to Spotfur's scruff. Fear glittered in her gaze as another monster veered toward them. Heart bursting with the effort, Rootspring heaved Spotfur up.

The Thunderclan she-cat's paws scrabbled to find a grip on the stone as he let go. "Thank you," she gasped, then staggered, her paws buckling beneath her.

Bristlefrost shoved her shoulder against her Clanmate's flank. Rootspring ducked around and pressed against her on the other side. Between them, they guided Spotfur around the Twolegs, who hopped and squawked like surprised pigeons as they passed.

"This is too dangerous!" Needleclaw yowled as they reached her, straining to be heard over the rumbling of the monsters.

Rootspring shook water from his pelt. "If we stay close to

the wall, we'll be okay," he promised, hoping it was true.

Bristlefrost sniffed her Clanmate's pelt. "Are you okay?"

Spotfur stared at her, stiff with shock, then shivered. "I'm fine," she rasped. "But let's get out of here." She looked expectantly at Rootspring.

"Come on." He hurried along the stone walkway, pressing himself against the wall until the Twolegs began to thin. Then he stopped and faced the others. "We need to cross the Thunderpath."

"How?" Needleclaw stared at the monsters filing past.

Rootspring's thoughts whirled. It would be too dangerous to dodge between them, but there was no other way to go on.

"Look!" Bristlefrost was staring toward a branchless tree. Three eyes stared from the top. As the red eye shone a warning, the monsters stopped, as though obeying it. A gap opened on the Thunderpath.

"Quick!" Bristlefrost darted forward. "We can cross!" She was already ducking in front of the unmoving monsters as they watched the colored eyes.

Rootspring stared after her, blood pulsing in his throat. Spotfur and Needleclaw raced at her tail and, pressing back panic, he pelted after them, his lungs burning from the acrid stench. As they reached the other side, the light blinked green and the monsters began roaring and lurched forward once more.

Rootspring blinked at Bristlefrost. "You could have been killed."

She lifted her muzzle. "It was the only way to cross."

He struggled to catch his breath. How could she be so reckless? And yet she'd been braver than any of them. He stared at her. "What if you'd died?" The thought horrified him. "What would I have done?"

Her eyes glistened for a moment as she met his gaze. "I'm sorry," she whispered. "I was only thinking about getting to the other side."

Needleclaw was scanning the Twoleg nests ahead. "Which way now?" she asked.

Rootspring tore his gaze from Bristlefrost, his heart aching. He couldn't let her take any more risks. "Follow me." He led them along another walkway, hoping he'd chosen the right route.

They kept moving, keeping low, learning quickly that red eyes meant the monsters would stop, and, before long they were crossing Thunderpaths as easily as they crossed streams. Rootspring soon felt as used to the Twolegs as he was to trees in the forest, and his heart no longer quickened each time they had to dodge one.

Bristlefrost caught his eye. "Are we still heading the right way?" Rain dripped from her long whiskers, and although she kept her mew bright, he could see uncertainty in her eyes.

"I think so." Rootspring wished he could be surer. He had tried to keep track of each turn and crossing. But they must be nearing the end. The nests were smaller now, as though the Twolegs had grown tired of building, and the Thunderpaths were narrower. Monsters had grown rarer, and the nests spread farther apart, until each was bordered by its own strip of grass with fences between.

As the rain eased, Rootspring's shoulders loosened. Above them, the clouds were tearing apart, and patches of blue sky showed through. The sun was still in the right part of the sky. With each paw step he grew more certain that they'd be out of the Twolegplace soon. Were those trees he could see beyond the nests?

"Let's try this way." He headed along a path between two nests and jumped onto the fence at the end, waiting for the rest of the patrol to catch up. Rootspring's heart leaped with joy. The grass, which encircled the Twoleg nest, stretched toward a hedge, taller than a camp wall. Trees sprouted beyond. "It looks like forest!"

Bristlefrost scrambled up beside him. "The river might be beyond those trees."

Spotfur climbed up the fence after Needleclaw and stared with tired, hollow eyes. Rootspring glanced at the Thunderclan warrior. Was she sick? He was responsible for her. He was responsible for the whole patrol, and there were no medicine cats here. He suddenly felt a long way from home.

"Come on." Bristlefrost leaped down onto the grass and began to head toward the hedge.

"Be careful!" Rootspring tensed. They hadn't checked for Twolegs.

Bristlefrost looked over her shoulder at him. "We're nearly there." She headed across the clearing, and Rootspring had no choice but to follow. Spotfur and Needleclaw thumped softly onto the grass behind him as he caught up to Bristlefrost.

She was already at the hedge, sniffing along the bottom for a gap that would open into the forest. She looked up as he reached her, dismayed. "There's no way through."

Rootspring's heart quickened. He scanned the bottom of the hedge. Surely there must be a space between the branches? Disappointment jabbed his belly as he saw shiny gray mesh lining the bushes. He ran his paw over it, realizing at once that it was Twoleg mesh, too tough to break. As Needleclaw and Spotfur reached him, he grunted. "We need to go back and try a different route." Frustrated at being pushed back when they were so close, he began to retrace his steps.

As he neared the middle of the clearing, a familiar scent touched his nose. He froze. Bristlefrost must have smelled it too. He felt her pelt brush his and jerked his muzzle around to see her eyes wide as she looked nervously around the clearing.

Needleclaw's fur lifted long her spine. "I smell dog."

An ominous growl made the air around them shiver. Rootspring's heart leaped into his throat. "Run!" He pelted for the fence, but it was too late. A large white dog had shot from the nest and was haring toward them, cutting off their escape. "Follow me!" Rootspring wheeled around, running blindly for the hedge. Perhaps they could scrabble into its branches and push their way over the top. As his thoughts whirled, vicious barking exploded from the other side of the clearing. A second dog charged, teeth bared and eyes blazing with excitement. Rootspring spun around, nearly crashing into Bristlefrost and Needleclaw, who were racing at his heels. Spotfur had frozen, pelt bushed, in the middle of the grass, her eyes darting from one dog to the other as they closed in on the terrified patrol from either side.

Rootspring couldn't breathe. If he couldn't get Spotfur moving, they might have to stand here and fight, and it wasn't a fight he was sure they could win. They needed somewhere to hide. He glanced around, looking for a way to escape the clearing. A small wooden den leaned against the Twoleg nest. Clutter had been piled beside it. If they could make it that far, they could climb clear of the dogs' reach.

He jerked his muzzle toward it, the dogs closing in fast. "Head for the den!" He held his ground as the others fled, then hared after them. He didn't dare look back, but he could feel the ground tremble beneath the pounding of heavy paws.

Needleclaw reached the pile of Twoleg clutter first, scrambling up it and leaping onto the wooden den. Bristlefrost nudged Spotfur up with her muzzle, and followed, turning to check on Rootspring as he neared.

He saw terror flash in her eyes as hot breath bathed his tail. Kicking out with his hind legs, he leaped for the pile and scrambled up. It rocked beneath his paws, and his heart seemed to explode. Then claws hooked his scruff and his paws churned empty air as Bristlefrost grabbed him and dragged him onto the roof.

Spotfur crouched miserably beside her as Needleclaw stared back at the hedge.

"Thanks for grabbing me." Rootspring blinked at Bristlefrost.

"Don't thank me yet." She was watching the dogs. The

smaller, white dog was jumping against the clutter. With a yelp of triumph, it managed to scrabble onto a ledge and lunged for the next. With each jump, it reached closer to a paw hold that it would use to haul itself onto the roof.

Rootspring stared in dismay. Could they fight the dog if it reached them up here? He glanced at Bristlefrost. Even if they could, one of them might get hurt, and they were too far from a medicine cat to get help. A single bite could become infected. He stared desperately toward the trees beyond the hedge. They'd been so close!

He stiffened. A shadow was slinking across the grass. Was he imagining it? A large gray tom was heading toward them, his eyes fixed on the dogs. As Rootspring watched, the tom glanced toward him and caught his eye with a tiny nod.

Rootspring frowned, puzzled. *What's he doing?*

Bristlefrost followed his gaze, her ears twitching in surprise as she spotted the tom. "Is he crazy?"

The tom crept closer as the dogs kept trying to fight their way up the pile of clutter. *They haven't scented him.* Rootspring held his breath.

Suddenly the tom fluffed out his fur. He flicked his tail in a signal and shot an urgent glance toward one corner of the hedge. "There's a hole over there!" he yowled to Rootspring. "The dogs can't get through it."

The dogs heard him and turned, menace in their eyes. The tom pelted forward, streaking past them with a snarl. Hackles lifting, they pounded after him as he fled toward the fence at the side of the Twoleg nest. He leaped onto it and hissed while the dogs hurled themselves against the wood, howling with fury.

Rootspring scanned the hedge and found a patch of shadow at one corner. Was that the hole? They'd have to risk it. The tom couldn't distract the dogs forever. "Follow me!" He leaped from the roof of the wooden den, landed heavily, and raced toward it, glancing over his shoulder to make sure the others were following. Spotfur and Needleclaw were at his tail, Bristlefrost behind them.

The grass blurred beneath Rootspring's paws as he charged across the clearing and slithered to a halt beside the hedge. The tom had been right. There was a hole! It was a small one, where the silver mesh had worn thin, but Rootspring squeezed through it easily, bursting through into the forest. Spotfur hauled herself out after him, Needleclaw and Bristlefrost behind her. Their eyes were bright with fear.

Relief flooded Rootspring's pelt for a moment, until paws thumped the grass beyond the hedge. His throat tightened. The dogs were trying to follow them. Rootspring backed away, staring in panic at the hole. Had the tom been right? Was the gap too small for them? Gray fur showed against the leaves as the tom shot through, his eyes sparkling with triumph. Behind him, heavy bodies thumped against the hedge, making the silver mesh rattle. A snout poked through, its lips drawn back in rage.

The tom spun around and slashed the dog's muzzle. With a yelp of pain, it disappeared, and the tom faced the patrol, purring.

Rootspring blinked at him. Was this a kittypet? *It can't be. He's too brave.* And he was huge, with broad, powerful shoulders and a lustrous pelt so thick that it reminded Rootspring of Tree.

The tom's gaze flitted around at the cats. "Are you okay?"

Rootspring glanced anxiously at his patrol, relieved as, one by one, they nodded.

"You saved our lives!" Bristlefrost was staring admiringly at the tom.

Rootspring ignored a prick of jealousy and struggled to find his breath. "Thank you," he panted.

The tom's whiskers twitched with amusement. "Those dogs will be angry about this for a moon."

Spotfur blinked at him. "They could have ripped you apart."

Bristlefrost whisked her tail. "You were so brave!"

The tom shrugged. "I've dealt with them before," he told her. "They're loud but they're slow." His gaze flitted around the patrol. "You don't look like everkits."

"Everkits?" Bristlefrost blinked at him, puzzled.

"He means kittypets," Rootspring explained, remembering the Sisters' name for cats who lived with Twolegs. *He has to be the cat that we're looking for.*

The tom was still staring at them. "What are you doing here?"

Needleclaw shifted her paws. "We're searching for someone."

"A cat called Leaf," Bristlefrost told him.

The tom's ears pricked in surprise. "I'm Leaf," he mewed.

Rootspring's heart seemed to leap like a fish in his chest. *We found him!*

Leaf looked puzzled. "Why are you looking for me?"

"We're trying to find the Sisters," Bristlefrost told him. "We thought you might know where they are."

The tom narrowed his eyes. "Why would *I* know that?"

"Because you look like . . ." Bristlefrost's mew trailed away as her gaze lingered on the handsome tom.

Rootspring flicked his tail. "You look like them," he finished curtly.

The tom purred. "You look like them too," he answered.

"They're my kin." Rootspring nodded toward Needleclaw. "And hers. We're littermates."

Leaf's eyes widened. "It's good to see the Sisters have spread their claws so wide." His gaze flitted suddenly to Spotfur. "Are you kin too?"

Spotfur's pelt ruffled. "Of course not."

He looked disappointed. "What a shame. New kits always bring a blessing to our ancestors."

"New kits?" Spotfur stiffened.

"You're expecting some, aren't you?" Leaf narrowed his eyes, as though looking at her more carefully.

Rootspring blinked at the Thunderclan she-cat in surprise. He suddenly noticed that her flanks did seem swollen. Was that why she'd been so tired?

Spotfur shook her head in panic. "I can't be!"

Bristlefrost's eyes clouded for a moment. "You're having

Stemleaf's kits?" She must be sad that her friend hadn't lived to see them, Rootspring thought. Then she swished her tail. "He'll live on through you now." Her eyes brightened. "You'll see him each day in your kits."

Spotfur looked horrified. "How will I raise them alone?"

"You won't be alone," Bristlefrost reminded her. "No cat is alone in a Clan. And I'll help you."

"A Clan?" Leaf pricked his ears. "Are you *warriors*?"

As Rootspring nodded, Leaf looked suddenly wary. "Why are Clan cats looking for the Sisters? Didn't you drive them from their camp?"

Rootspring met his gaze. "That was moons ago," he mewed. "We need their help now."

"We've lost a Clanmate," Needleclaw explained. "We hoped the Sisters could help us find him."

Leaf looked doubtful. "Why would they know?"

Because they can see spirits. Rootspring wasn't ready to explain about Bramblestar and Ashfur. "They roam so far," he mewed quickly. "They might know more than us. Do you know where they are now?"

Leaf tipped his head to one side. "They're traveling along the river."

Needleclaw leaned closer. "We've been looking for a river all day and haven't found one."

"Can't you hear it?" Leaf pricked his ears.

Rootspring listened but could hear nothing beyond the sighing of the wind in the trees.

"It's beyond this forest." Leaf nodded toward the trees.

"The Sisters were heading toward sunrise-place." He hesitated. "I can locate them for you, but it will take me a while."

Locate them? Rootspring felt puzzled. "What do you mean?"

"If I concentrate, I can feel where they are," Leaf explained.

Bristlefrost blinked. "How?"

Leaf shrugged. "I ask the earth, and the earth tells me."

Rootspring's eyes widened. What was this tom talking about? "The earth can't talk."

"It talks to me," Leaf mewed. "It talks to all toms born to the Sisters."

Rootspring stared at him.

"I'll show you." Leaf padded between the trees and stopped beneath an oak. Curious, Rootspring followed, watching as Leaf pushed his paws carefully, one at a time, into the earth, like he was taking a battle stance. He closed his eyes, his legs growing stiff while the muscles along his back softened and his pelt smoothed.

Bristlefrost padded to Rootspring's side. "Is that what talking to the earth looks like?"

"I guess so," he whispered. *Can Tree do this?* he wondered. *Could I, if I had been raised by the Sisters?* Rootspring curled his claws into the soft soil. If Tree could hear the earth, why hadn't his father simply asked it where the Sisters were and saved them all this searching? Frustration rippled through Rootspring's pelt.

Spotfur padded away and sat beside a beech. Her gaze drifted, as though she was lost in thought. Needleclaw began to sniff a patch of ferns sprouting nearby. They seemed uninterested in Leaf's ritual, but Rootspring couldn't take his eyes off the tom.

Leaf didn't move. Above, birds chattered and the clouds cleared overhead. After a while, Bristlefrost glanced at Spotfur and joined her Clanmate, leaning close as though asking if she was okay. Spotfur waved her away with her tail and Bristlefrost dipped her head and left her, joining Needleclaw in her search for prey. As the sun began to sink behind the treetops, and dusk gathered between the branches, Rootspring wondered if he should help them and give Leaf space to talk to the earth alone.

Leaf's eyes suddenly blinked open. "I know where they are."

Rootspring's heart quickened. He called the others, pricking his ears as Bristlefrost hurried to his side. Spotfur looked up but didn't move. Needleclaw, who'd wandered deeper into the forest, came bounding out of the trees.

Leaf blinked at him calmly.

"Where are they?" Rootspring pressed.

"You'll have to cross the water," Leaf told him. "It might be dangerous, but there's no rush. Sunshine is heavy with kits. The Sisters won't move for at least a moon."

Rootspring's paws pricked eagerly. "Then we'll be able to catch up to them."

Leaf looked at Rootspring. "I can take you to them if you like."

"That would be great—"

Needleclaw cut him off. "Can I have a word with you?" Needleclaw caught Rootspring's eye, then glanced warily at

Leaf. "In *private*." She didn't wait for an answer but steered Rootspring away from the tom with a nudge. "Are you really going to listen to this stranger?" she hissed when they were out of earshot. "We only just met him."

"He saved our lives," Rootspring reminded her.

"Yes, but he's weird," Needleclaw mewed.

Bristlefrost hurried to join them, whispering as she neared, "It was nice of him to help us escape from the dogs. But I'm not sure we should trust him. Cats can't talk to the earth."

"He's got bees in his brain," Needleclaw agreed.

"It's the only thing we've got to go on," Rootspring reasoned. Didn't they realize by now that some cats saw more than others? *Like ghosts, for example.* "Why don't we follow him and see where he takes us?"

"You sound like a sparrow chick," Needleclaw mewed sharply. "Why would you follow a tom you'd just met?"

Rootspring stared at her. She was clearly never going to understand what it felt like to be connected to something more than her own tail and claws. "Do you have a better idea?" he asked. When she huffed and fell silent, he continued, "Okay, then, let's see where this goes before you drive our only lead away." His pelt prickled self-consciously as he saw Leaf padding toward them and hoped Bristlefrost and Needleclaw weren't going to insult the tom.

Leaf dipped his head. "Forgive me for interrupting," he mewed, "but I can see you don't trust me. I understand. We might be kin"—he glanced at Rootspring—"but we have chosen different paths."

Rootspring dipped his head in return, grateful that Leaf understood.

Leaf went on. "I have no reason to mislead you. You might have trouble convincing the Sisters to help you, though," he warned, "after the Clans drove them from their camp. But as you say, that was moons ago. And your kin took in my kin after the battle, healed their wounds, and nursed their young. If they hadn't, my littermates and I would have died along with our mother, Moonlight."

Rootspring stared at him in surprise. He'd heard Tree say that Moonlight wouldn't have died at all if the Clans hadn't declared war on the Sisters. "How can you be so forgiving?"

"I don't judge one cat by another cat's actions," Leaf told him. "If your Clan is in trouble, I can't let you suffer. I will give you directions to the Sisters. You can travel there alone."

Rootspring dipped his head, grateful for this cat's generosity.

Bristlefrost was gazing warmly at the tom. "Will you camp with us tonight? We can hunt and share our catch."

Leaf blinked at her happily. "Thank you," he mewed. "I would enjoy that."

Chapter 10

Bristlefrost narrowed her eyes against the glare of the morning light as she watched Leaf cross the meadow. Sunlight lit his silhouette so that he seemed to glow like a spirit cat as he turned and dipped his head in farewell. The tom's gaze locked with Rootspring's for a moment, and she saw Rootspring's fur ripple as the SkyClan warrior lifted his tail in a respectful salute.

Bristlefrost's heart swelled with affection. Rootspring was loyal to his Clan and yet openhearted with a tom who was hardly more than a loner. A purr rose in her throat, and she swallowed it back, pulling her gaze away from Rootspring before Needleclaw or Spotfur could catch her.

She didn't need to worry about Spotfur, who stared unenthusiastically across the fields. Bristlefrost wondered if she'd even noticed Leaf leaving. Her Clanmate had been distracted since the tom had told her she was expecting kits. It was as though, the moment she'd realized, her thoughts had wandered far away. Surely she must feel *some* happiness? Kits were a new beginning, weren't they? It meant part of Stemleaf would live on.

Bristlefrost moved closer to Spotfur and ran her tail along

her Clanmate's spine sympathetically. Without looking at her, Spotfur moved away. Clearly, she was not ready to share what she felt.

"Let's hunt before we leave." Needleclaw's gaze flitted across the fields. "This looks like great territory, and there's no one to claim it but us."

Bristlefrost was suddenly glad to be here. A warm breeze was stirring her fur. There were no Clan boundaries to worry about and no grouchy old warriors to tell them what to do. This mission was fun. She shook out her pelt. "I'll hunt with Spotfur," she mewed.

"Good idea." Needleclaw was already heading away. "Clan-mates always hunt better together." Her gaze flitted pointedly toward Rootspring. "Are you coming with me?"

"I'll hunt with Spotfur and Bristlefrost today," he told her. "I want to learn some Thunderclan hunting skills."

Needleclaw sniffed. "Suit yourself." Pelt ruffled, she padded downslope toward a meadow specked with wild flowers.

Spotfur glanced after her. "I want to hunt alone today too."

Bristlefrost blinked at her. "Are you sure?"

"I need time to think," Spotfur told her firmly.

Bristlefrost's paws pricked as Spotfur headed away. Should she let Spotfur hunt alone? This was strange territory, after all.

Rootspring's mew cut through her thoughts. "You can hunt with me, if you like," he offered.

"Thanks." Perhaps Spotfur *did* need time to think. Hunt-ing might restore her spirits and help her come to terms with the idea of expecting kits. She blinked at Rootspring. "Which way do you want to go?"

Rootspring nodded to a beech copse a little way away. "There will be mice there."

"Or rabbits." Bristlefrost narrowed her gaze. Were those burrow entrances showing in the grass? She fell in beside Rootspring as he headed across the field. He gazed into the distance. Was he looking for signs of Leaf? "You liked him, didn't you?"

"He's my kin." Rootspring's eyes shone. "And he kind of reminded me of Tree."

Bristlefrost thought about the way Leaf and Rootspring had hunted together last night: the way they'd pushed through long grass, muzzles lifted and shoulders squared, and the way they'd crouched when they'd spotted prey. "He reminded me of you," Bristlefrost told him.

"Really?" Rootspring blinked at her happily. Fondness pricked Bristlefrost's heart. He seemed proud to have kin like Leaf. Rootspring whisked his tail. "It's weird to think that I might be wandering too if I'd been raised by the Sisters."

Bristlefrost glanced at him. "Wouldn't you hate being alone all the time?"

Rootspring frowned. "I don't know. Leaf seems to enjoy it."

Bristlefrost suppressed a shiver. "I can't imagine living without a Clan. It feels like part of me. More than kin, even. And would you know *how* to live without the warrior code to guide you?"

"The Sisters must have their own code," Rootspring

pointed out. "One that they teach their toms before they send them away. Otherwise they'd be no more than loners."

"Isn't that exactly what they are?" Bristlefrost argued.

"Of course not!" Rootspring swung his muzzle toward her. "Leaf was clearly more than a loner. The earth speaks to him. Perhaps it tells him how to live."

Bristlefrost wasn't convinced. The earth had never spoken to her, or to any cat in the Clans. But she didn't point this out. Instead she shrugged. "I guess I'm just happier in a Clan."

"Even now that everything's changed?" Rootspring asked.

Bristlefrost's fur prickled defensively. She didn't want to think about the rifts in Thunderclan. Flipclaw had left. So had Graystripe, Thornclaw, and too many others. But perhaps there was nothing wrong with cats taking time out to think. Wasn't that what Spotfur was doing now? "Things are getting back to normal now that Squirrelflight's in charge," she told him.

Rootspring frowned. "But she hasn't been accepted by StarClan yet."

"Maybe not, but she's doing her best," Bristlefrost mewed sharply. "And she'll keep doing her best until we can get Bramblestar back."

"What if we can't?" Rootspring asked softly. "What if things don't get better? Would you think about leaving Thunderclan?"

"Of course not." Why did he have to talk about the future? No cat knew what was going to happen, but it would have to get better. The Clans had been through so much. "I'll always be loyal to Thunderclan," she told him firmly. "Nothing would make me leave." As she spoke, doubt tugged at her belly. Was that true? As much as she tried to deny it, Thunderclan *had* changed. It no longer felt like the Clan she'd been raised in.

Rootspring gazed ahead once more, his pelt smoothing along his spine. "If we can persuade the Sisters to come back with us, and if they help us find Bramblestar, things might go back to normal."

"We have to find them first." Bristlefrost felt suddenly anxious.

"Leaf told us where they are," Rootspring reminded her. "I have faith in him."

Bristlefrost halted. "What if they won't come home with us?" Her heart began to pound. "What if they do, but they can't find Bramblestar?"

Rootspring met her gaze. "We have to find them first. Then we'll see what happens." He stiffened suddenly, his nose twitching. "Can you smell that?"

Bristlefrost's breath caught in her throat. "What?" she whispered. Was something tracking them?

Rootspring's eyes flashed with excitement. "Rabbit."

Bristlefrost followed his gaze as it flicked past her. Gray fur flashed in the grass a few tree-lengths away. She dropped into a crouch, her attention fixed on their prey. Her worries melted as moons of training guided her paws. Stealthily, she began to creep through the grass. She twitched her tail, signaling to

Rootspring to head the other way so they could outflank the rabbit, but he was already on his way, as though they'd shared the same thought. Triumph flashed beneath Bristlefrost's fur. She could hunt together with Rootspring as intuitively as Needleclaw could.

As they moved around the rabbit silently, carefully, they seemed to match each other, like a single cat reflected in a pool. The rabbit was nibbling in a patch thick with dandelions, its long ears twitching as it listened for signs of danger. *It hasn't heard us.* Excitement built in Bristlefrost's muscles. Her mouth began to water. In a few more paw steps they could attack. She kept her tail still, only a whisker above the ground, as she padded nearer. *Three more paw steps.* She caught Rootspring's eye and knew he was ready. Holding his gaze, she lifted a paw, preparing to attack.

A screech cut across the meadow, splitting the air. Bristlefrost's pelt spiked as she recognized the agonized shriek of her Clanmate. *Spotfur's in trouble!*

She spun around, scanning the meadow. Spotfur must be beyond the hedge. Bristlefrost's blood seemed to turn to ice beneath her pelt as the shriek sounded again. Surging forward, she raced across the field, hearing paw steps at her heels. Rootspring hurtled past her and she quickened her pace, keeping up with him as he streaked through a gap in the hedge. She burst into the clearing, her pelt spiking with alarm. Spotfur was struggling to free herself from the long, sharp talons of a hawk. The bird had grabbed her flanks, its massive wings beating the air as it tried to haul her from the ground. Panic glittering in her eyes, Spotfur clutched at the earth with out-stretched claws.

Needleclaw was pounding toward them as Rootspring leaped for the hawk and grabbed its wing. Unbalanced, the bird shrieked but clung harder to Spotfur. Blood streaked the Thunderclan warrior's pelt, and Bristlefrost saw pain flash in her eyes.

She leaped for the other wing, digging her claws into the feathers until she felt flesh, then bone. The hawk's fierce gaze jerked toward her, and, faster than a snake, it struck with its beak. Pain seared her neck as it hooked her flesh and tore out a lump of fur. She clung on, pressing back a yowl, but the hawk was strong. It heaved her away with a flap of its wing, and she tumbled across the grass.

Rootspring was crouching against the earth, blood dripping from his ear as Needleclaw reached them and reared to sink her teeth into the hawk's leg. Spotfur dropped to the ground as the bird released her; talon marks showed in her flanks.

"Spotfur!" Bristlefrost raced toward her as Needleclaw backed away. But Spotfur's eyes had lit with rage. She wheeled around and leaped at the hawk as it struggled into the air.

What are you doing? Bristlefrost couldn't believe her eyes.

Rootspring stared at her in shock. "Let it go!"

Spotfur didn't seem to hear. Darting beneath the hawk's beating wings, she reached for its belly and tried to drag it back to the ground. It lunged, ripping her pelt with a talon, and hooked its beak into her shoulder, but she twisted from its grip and raked at its neck with her claws.

Bristlefrost's paws seemed frozen to the earth. "Stop!"

"I've nearly beaten it!" Spotfur hissed back, her eyes wild.

Was Spotfur crazy? The hawk had already proved it was too strong to be caught.

Spotfur's claws were hooked into the hawk's belly. It flapped its wings, confusion showing in its eyes as it began to lift from the ground.

Bristlefrost's mouth was dry with horror as Spotfur's hind paws left the earth. "Let go!" Her yowl seemed to split the air as, with another flap of its wings, the hawk regained its balance and kicked Spotfur away, wheeling clear as she thumped onto the grass.

Bristlefrost darted to her friend's side, relieved as Spotfur staggered to her paws. "What were you thinking?"

Blood welled on Spotfur's flanks and stained the fur around her neck. She glared at Bristlefrost as though she felt no pain. "I nearly had it!" she snarled.

"Do you have bees in your brain?" Needleclaw's eyes were as wide as an owl's.

Rootspring hurried toward them. "It was too big for us to catch!"

"I could have—" Spotfur's mew became a gasp. Her paw buckled beneath her.

Bristlefrost's heart leaped into her throat. "What's wrong?" She thrust her muzzle close to Spotfur's.

"It's okay," Spotfur growled through clenched teeth. "I think I've wrenched my shoulder."

Needleclaw snorted. "Just be grateful that's the worst thing that happened," she scolded. "You could have been killed." She padded to Spotfur's side and glared at her as Spotfur pushed herself into a sitting position and caught her breath. "And what about your kits? Did you think of them? It's not just your life you're putting at risk now. Is this what Thunder-clan warriors do? Charge after prey too dangerous to catch? How will we find the Sisters if you can barely walk?"

Spotfur met the SkyClan she-cat's gaze fiercely. "I'm fine, okay?" she snapped.

Rootspring wove between them. "Yowling at each other isn't going to help." He steered Needleclaw away. "Let's leave Bristlefrost to take care of Spotfur and finish the hunt." He nosed her toward the hedge. "There are rabbits in the next field."

Growling crossly under her breath, Needleclaw let him guide her through the hedge, leaving Spotfur and Bristlefrost alone.

Bristlefrost began to lap at the wounds on Spotfur's flank, aware that there were unborn kits beneath. Would they be okay? What had made her Clanmate behave so recklessly? She washed Spotfur's wounds silently until Spotfur flinched, wincing at the pain.

Bristlefrost sat back on her haunches. "It's not like you to take unnecessary risks," she mewed softly.

"I was hunting," Spotfur muttered.

Warriors don't hunt hawks. "I know you're brave, but you're not foolish," she mewed. "And now that you're carrying kits, shouldn't you be more careful, not less?"

Spotfur narrowed her eyes. "And what if I don't *want* the kits?"

"Don't *want* them?" Bristlefrost flattened her ears. How could that be? Spotfur had loved their father more than any cat. "But they're Stemleaf's," she mewed.

"He's not here, is he?" Spotfur snapped. "We were supposed to raise kits together, safe in Thunderclan. But we can't do that now!" Her gaze hardened. "Stemleaf is dead and Thunderclan doesn't feel safe anymore."

Bristlefrost's heart ached with pity. She could understand why Spotfur felt so frightened. Their Clan *did* feel different. But that didn't mean they could give up. "Things will get better, I promise," she told her gently. But she didn't know if that was a promise she could keep.

Spotfur's eyes brimmed suddenly with sadness. "What if the kits only remind me of the life I should have had with Stemleaf?"

Bristlefrost leaned closer, resting her cheek snugly against Spotfur's. "Try to focus on the life you will have, not the one you should have had," she said. "The kits are lucky to have had a father as brave as Stemleaf, who was willing to die to save his Clan." She pulled away and stared into Spotfur's glistening eyes as she went on. "Everything will be okay. The kits will mean that you'll always have a connection to Stemleaf. He can watch over them from StarClan."

"StarClan is gone!" Spotfur blinked at her.

"We're going to get them back." Bristlefrost held Spotfur's gaze. "In the meantime, your Clan will help you raise your kits, and I promise I will do anything to protect them. They won't go hungry or face any danger until they're old enough to take care of themselves. We'll keep them safe." As she spoke, fear trickled through her fur. Could she make any of this happen?

The scent of rabbit touched her nose, and she turned as Needleclaw and Rootspring ducked through the hedge.

Rootspring held a fat rabbit between his jaws. He dropped it beside Bristlefrost. "How is she?" He glanced at Spotfur, who had lowered onto her belly and was gazing at the ground.

"She'll be all right," Bristlefrost murmured. As she spoke, paw steps sounded beyond the hedge. An unfamiliar scent bathed her muzzle, and as her pelt bristled in alarm, a large yellow she-cat pushed her way through the hedge, her fur spiking as she slid between the branches.

Anger flashed in her eyes. "What are you doing so close to our camp?" she demanded.

Bristlefrost pressed closer to Spotfur, unsheathing her claws. No loner was going to hurt her Clanmate.

But Rootspring had lifted his tail, his eyes widening with delight. "You're one of the Sisters!" Bristlefrost blinked in surprise as he hurried to meet the yellow she-cat. "We've been looking for you! Leaf told us you'd be nearby!"

The she-cat backed away hesitantly, then nodded. "I'm Sunrise," she said simply. "You saw Leaf?" She was huge, her fur so thick Bristlefrost wondered how she managed to groom it all. As Bristlefrost stared at her, Needleclaw nodded.

"Yes, and he's alive and well," she replied. Then she turned to Bristlefrost and Spotfur, her eyes lighting up as she gave a happy *mrrow*. "We've done it. . . . We've found the Sisters!"

CHAPTER 11

Miserably, Shadowsight followed the hunting patrol into camp. He knew he should lift his tail and try to look as pleased as his Clanmates, but the two mice dangling between his jaws weren't his catch. Lightleap had caught them and asked him to carry them home because she was carrying a plump squirrel she'd chased down near the ditches.

Every cat in the patrol had caught something except him, and shame shimmered through his fur with each paw step. The others had been sympathetic. Slatefur had pointed out that it was only his second hunting trip, and Blazefire had told him that *he'd* found it hard at first too, adjusting to warrior techniques when he'd moved to the forest from the Twoleg city. But Shadowsight couldn't push away the feeling that he was no use to his Clanmates now that he couldn't heal them.

He crossed the clearing, following Lightleap and Blazefire to the fresh-kill pile. Slatefur and Scorchfur were already laying their catch beside the other prey. His heart ached as he passed the medicine den. How long before Tigerstar allowed him to be a medicine cat again? What if he was stuck like this forever, neither a healer nor a warrior?

He tried to be hopeful. SkyClan and Thunderclan were looking for the Sisters for help locating Bramblestar's ghost. But what if the Sisters couldn't help? The dread lurking in Shadowsight's belly moved again, his thoughts spiraling. *Taking him to the moor was a dumb idea. I killed him and the Clans will never forgive me. I'll never be a medicine cat again.* Feeling light-headed, he dropped the mice on the fresh-kill pile and turned away.

"You did better today." Lightleap blocked his path, blinking at him encouragingly.

"That's not true." Shadowsight looked at his paws.

"You're the one who scented the rabbit," Lightleap told him. "That was definitely better than last time."

Shadowsight met her gaze, grateful for her kindness. But it sounded more like pity, which made him feel worse. "Thanks, Lightleap." He dipped his head and walked across the camp. At least there was one cat he could still be of use to.

He padded to the bramble enclosure and nodded at Whitewing and Cherryfall, who were guarding it. The two Thunderclan cats exchanged glances.

Cherryfall flicked her tail toward the hollow tree. "He's sleeping."

"He's been sleeping all day," Whitewing added.

Were they angry that the dark warrior could sleep so peacefully in his den? Their eyes gave nothing away, but their pelts prickled uneasily. Perhaps they still found it strange to see their leader held prisoner, knowing another cat lived inside him.

"He didn't even wake when Whorlpelt brought him food."

Cherryfall nodded toward the mouse still lying outside the hollow tree.

Shadowsight tensed. Was Ashfur okay? Feeling responsible, he hurried across the bramble enclosure and peered into the shadowy den. Ashfur was curled inside, his flanks moving as he breathed. But his breath was shallow, and the dark warrior's body was as still as stone. Shadowsight reached a paw in and touched Ashfur's shoulder, relieved to find no heat pulsing from his pelt. He wasn't sick. *He usually wakes when I arrive.* Shadowsight's ears twitched nervously. *Is he dreaming?* He remembered the deep sleep he'd brought on himself by eating deathberries. It had allowed his spirit to travel to the Dark Forest. *Can Ashfur do that?*

He shook the thought away. *Stop worrying,* he told himself. *He's just resting.*

Ashfur must have heard him. The dark warrior's ear twitched, and for a moment he looked like Tigerstar. Shadowsight's heart lurched. What if Ashfur had stolen Tigerstar's life instead? He swallowed. *I'm glad he didn't.* Ashfur might have tricked him into killing his own father.

Ashfur lifted his head and blinked. "Hi." His eyes brightened, as though he was pleased that Shadowsight was here.

Unnerved, Shadowsight backed away. He'd rather Ashfur see him as an enemy than a friend. He forced his pelt to stay flat as Ashfur slid from the hollow tree.

"You're late," Ashfur mewed. "I've missed you."

"I went hunting," Shadowsight told him.

Ashfur's gaze flitted around him, as though looking for

something. "You haven't brought any herbs. Aren't you going to treat me anymore?"

"You don't need herbs," Shadowsight told him. "Your wounds are nearly healed."

"Is that why you went hunting?" Ashfur narrowed his eyes. "Because there's no one left for you to help?"

"I went hunting to help my Clan," Shadowsight told him hotly.

"I'm sure they were very grateful." Ashfur's whiskers twitched with amusement. "But what do you know about being a warrior? Do you know to watch your paws to avoid making a sound? Can you taste which way the wind's blowing?"

"I'm learning!"

"A warrior needs to be aware of things you've probably never even thought about before."

Shadowsight lifted his chin. "Puddleshine taught me to be alert when I'm out gathering herbs."

Ashfur looked unimpressed. "I hope he didn't teach you to be too jumpy," he mewed. "There's so much that can startle a cat in the forest. Foxes, owls. Even butterflies and bees." His gaze sharpened. "The last thing a hunting patrol needs is a warrior who yowls every time he hears a noise."

Shadowsight stiffened. Did the dark warrior *know* a bee had scared him? *Was your spirit spying on me?* He pressed back a shudder, feeling like beetles were crawling through his fur. He met Ashfur's stare boldly. Whatever the impostor knew, Shadowsight wasn't going to confirm it. "I need to check your scars."

He circled Ashfur, touching his muzzle to the warrior's

scabs, smelling to make sure they were clear of infection and feeling for heat. As he sat back on his haunches, Ashfur met his gaze.

"You could have been a talented healer," the dark warrior mewed. "My wounds improved so *quickly*. It's a shame the Clans will never trust you again."

Rage surged in Shadowsight's chest. "Whose fault is that?"

"I just wanted to live." As Ashfur looked away, Rootspring thought he saw a flash of guilt in the dark warrior's eyes. "I didn't think about what it would mean for you." His voice was husky. "I'm sorry you can't be a medicine cat now." Was this remorse? Ashfur met his gaze, his mew hardening once more. "But you'll always have a place in ShadowClan as long as you have Tigerstar to protect you."

Shadowsight stared at him. So that's what he thought. That his Clanmates only tolerated him because his father was a leader. Shadowsight got to his paws. "I'll tell Puddleshine that you're healing well." He turned his tail on the dark warrior and headed out of the enclosure.

"Come back soon," Ashfur called. "You're the only cat I can talk to."

Shadowsight didn't look back. He avoided the gazes of Whitewing and Cherryfall as he padded past them, hoping they hadn't overheard Ashfur's words. Unease wormed beneath his pelt. Was it true? Was he only welcome in ShadowClan now because Tigerstar was protecting him? He paused and glanced around the clearing. What would happen if that was no longer enough?

* * *

Shadowsight pulled himself over the lip of the Moonpool hollow, relieved to be here at last. This was the first time he'd traveled to the Moonpool since Ashfur had attacked him, and his paws had twitched with every step. The dark warrior had nearly killed him. The memory of it had made Shadowsight catch his breath each time a shadow shifted on the moor or prey made the bushes rustle. But he was glad Puddleshine and Mothwing had allowed him to come. Now that he'd lost his full medicine-cat status, he'd been afraid they'd leave him behind. Tigerstar had said he was still an apprentice medicine cat, but Shadowsight wasn't sure. Puddleshine wouldn't let him treat any cat but Ashfur, and he hadn't been trying to teach him anything. But Tigerstar's gaze had been firm when he'd asked Puddleshine to take care of him on the journey, and it had been clear to every cat that he wanted Shadowsight to go.

Puddleshine and Mothwing had told Shadowsight to stay close as they'd traveled through the forest, but they hadn't included him in their conversation, keeping their voices low as they'd led the way. Hurt and ashamed, he'd guessed they'd been discussing cats they'd treated or cures they wanted to try.

He followed them now around the spiral of dimpled rock, worn smooth by countless moons of paw steps, and stopped beside the Moonpool. The other medicine cats were already here. Around them, the encircling cliffs sparkled in a wash of starlight. Would they treat him as a full medicine cat, or would he have to hang back and hold his tongue like an apprentice? *I'll say what I like,* he thought rebelliously, wishing he had the courage.

Jayfeather gave an irritable shake of his head. "You're late," he told Puddleshine.

"The moon is still high." Puddleshine dipped his head politely as Mothwing glanced at Willowshine. Shadowsight narrowed his eyes. It must be strange for the former River-Clan cat to attend this meeting as part of ShadowClan.

Willowshine held Mothwing's gaze sadly for a moment, then nodded curtly and padded to the edge of the water. "Let's begin." She touched her nose to the pool, and the other medicine cats followed.

Shadowsight was relieved they weren't going to talk first; there was too much he didn't want to talk about, and he guessed every medicine cat was eager to see if they could reach StarClan this time. He settled beside Puddleshine and stretched his muzzle forward, accustomed now to the prickle of disappointment when, as the chill of the water stung his nose, no vision flashed in his mind and no voice rang in his head. StarClan was gone.

They waited a long time, but nothing changed. Shadowsight lifted his head, watching the others as they sat up one by one. Had they really thought that StarClan would have returned, even though nothing in the forest had changed? Ashfur still possessed the Thunderclan leader's body. Bramblestar's ghost was still lost.

Jayfeather shook the water from his nose. "We need to get used to the idea that StarClan is gone for good."

Willowshine's pelt bristled. "That can't be true! They wouldn't abandon us."

"Perhaps we've abandoned *them*," Kestrelflight growled.

"What do you mean?" Willowshine blinked at him. "We've been trying to contact them for moons."

Kestrelflight met her gaze. "We might have strayed so far from the warrior code that we've broken the connection."

Mothwing grunted. "What's the difference whether they're with us or not?" she asked. "Does it really change how we live?"

"Of course it does!" Fidgetflake stared at her. "What's the point of being warriors if we're not guided by our ancestors?"

Mothwing blinked at him calmly. "We're still cats living together and taking care of one another," she answered. "Isn't that enough?"

The other cats exchanged glances.

Is it enough? Shadowsight frowned. After all, taking care of his Clanmates was all he wanted to do, if only Puddleshine and Mothwing would let him. Did he need StarClan to be able to clear the infection from a Clanmate's wound?

Alderheart looked at the star-specked sky. "StarClan has always guided the Clans. Without them, we would find our own path, but where could it lead if not closer to our ancestors?"

Frecklewish swished her tail over the cold stone. "It's pointless trying to guess what will happen next," she mewed. "We need to find a way forward." As Kestrelflight and Alderheart murmured in agreement, she went on. "I've been thinking about Ashfur. If he's the one who's severed our connection with StarClan—"

"It must be him," Willowshine cut in. "It's too much of a coincidence that they disappeared when he appeared."

Frecklewish nodded. "He might be the only one who can show us how to restore it."

Jayfeather snorted. "Do you actually think he would?"

No cat spoke, but Shadowsight guessed the answer. Why would Ashfur want to help the Clans?

Puddleshine's eyes had narrowed thoughtfully. "Do you think StarClan has moved too far away for us to reach, or is something blocking our connection?" He turned to look at Shadowsight. "Didn't you say that you'd seen something?"

Shadowsight's mouth went dry. Puddleshine was talking about his Dark Forest vision.

"You saw a barrier between StarClan and the living Clans . . . ?" Puddleshine pressed.

Shadowsight felt the gazes of the other medicine cats burning into him. He stared ahead, trying to keep his voice steady. "I saw something," he mewed, wondering if they'd believe him. He'd shared so many visions that turned out to be false. "When I slept after eating those deathberries, I followed Bramblestar's voice and dived into the Moonpool." He hesitated as Jayfeather's blind blue gaze narrowed. *I'm only telling you what I saw. You don't have to believe it.* He forced himself to go on. "It took me to the Dark Forest. There was a wall there, like a camp wall, dividing it from StarClan."

Jayfeather snorted. "Of course there's a barrier between the Dark Forest and StarClan!"

"But it was blocking the Moonpool, too, and the path between StarClan and us," Shadowsight insisted.

Willowshine padded closer, curiosity in her eyes. "How did *you* find your way through it?"

"I didn't." Shadowsight blinked at her apologetically. "I only managed to untangle Bramblestar from the thorns."

Mothwing lifted her chin. "It sounds like nonsense to me," she mewed.

"Everything sounds like nonsense to you," Jayfeather snapped.

Mothwing's fur ruffled crossly, but she didn't reply.

"He probably imagined the whole thing," Kestrelflight suggested. He looked at Shadowsight. "How can you be sure it was a vision? You've been wrong before."

"You'll have to decide that for yourself." Shadowsight lifted his muzzle. He wasn't going to try to convince these cats if they didn't want to believe him. All he could do was tell them what he knew. "I saw Ashfur, too, in another vision. I saw his spirit leave Bramblestar's body."

Kestrelflight looked unimpressed. "We already know Ashfur stole Bramblestar's body."

"But you didn't know that he can leave it if he wants," Shadowsight told him.

"We still don't," Jayfeather grunted.

"I *saw* him do it!" Frustration flared in Shadowsight's belly.

Jayfeather's ears flattened. "You've seen a lot of things."

Alderheart shifted beside his Clanmate. "Perhaps we shouldn't be asking Shadowsight about these matters," he murmured softly.

Shadowsight's heart sank. *They're sorry they ever listened to me.* He suddenly wished the rock would open up and swallow him. He'd rather be in the Dark Forest than here.

Jayfeather shook out his pelt. "Without StarClan to guide us, we're just guessing. Let's focus on the things we can control, like the health of our Clanmates." He turned to face the other cats. "Thunderclan has been well this past moon. Lilyheart had whitecough, but she recovered quickly, and it didn't spread to her denmates."

"Emberfoot's had whitecough too," Kestrelflight chimed.

"And Stonewing," Puddleshine added. "But it was mild."

Stonewing? Shadowsight fluffed out his pelt against the night breeze. He hadn't known a Clanmate had been sick. He glanced at Puddleshine. They'd always been so close. There had been a time when he couldn't imagine his mentor would keep something like that from him. Ashfur's words echoed in his mind. Would ShadowClan ever trust him to treat his Clanmates again?

Puddleshine went on. "Shadowsight has been taking care of Ashfur's wounds," he mewed.

"What a waste of herbs," Willowshine muttered under her breath.

"It's still Bramblestar's body," Jayfeather reminded her.

Alderheart's eyes seemed to spark with rage. "Ashfur should never have been allowed to steal it!"

Is he blaming me? Shadowsight looked away guiltily.

Frecklewish whisked her tail. "We can't change the past."

Fidgetflake nodded. "Let's focus on the present." He looked around at the others. "SkyClan is thriving," he reported. "Nectarsong's given birth to two lovely kits, Beekit and Beetle-kit. Mother and kits are in good health. It was her first litter, but an easy kitting."

"It's nice to hear some good news," Willowshine mewed. "RiverClan has been healthy too, although we've had a few upset bellies. I've been busy collecting watermint all moon." Her gaze flitted toward Mothwing. "An extra set of paws would have been helpful." When Mothwing didn't comment, Willowshine leaned forward. "Every cat misses you, Mothwing, and wants you back in the Clan."

Hope flickered in Shadowsight's chest. If Mothwing left ShadowClan, Puddleshine might relent and allow him to be a medicine cat again.

Mothwing stared stiffly at her former Clanmate. "I will not return while Icewing and Harelight aren't welcome."

"What if Mistystar never changes her mind?" Willowshine's eyes glistened sadly. "Will you stay in ShadowClan forever?"

Shadowsight watched Mothwing closely. Could a cat switch Clans so easily?

But Mothwing didn't flinch. "ShadowClan has been kinder to me than RiverClan," she mewed coldly. "I am loyal to Tigerstar."

Shadowsight's heart sank. Mothwing was clearly going to dig her claws in over this. She might never leave ShadowClan.

Kestrelflight shifted his paws. "WindClan has been well, but I agree with Willowshine: It's hard to run a medicine den with only one set of paws."

Jayfeather sniffed. "ShadowClan has plenty of medicine cats," he muttered. "I'm sure they'd be happy to lend you Shadowsight."

"No, thanks." Kestrelflight's tail twitched uneasily.

Shadowsight shrank beneath his pelt. *I'm the medicine cat no Clan wants.*

"I've been thinking about taking on an apprentice," Kestrelflight went on.

Shadowsight blinked at the WindClan medicine cat in surprise. How could he take on an apprentice without StarClan's approval?

"Whistlepaw seems interested in herbs," Kestrelflight mewed. "He's been helping me take care of Emberfoot. He appears to have the right kind of instincts."

"But how can you?" Shadowsight blurted. "Shouldn't StarClan guide you in your choice?"

"I can at least begin his training," Kestrelflight told him. "There's a lot to learn." He met Shadowsight's gaze. "You must know that better than any cat."

Shadowsight looked at his paws, his pelt ruffling uncomfortably. He shouldn't have spoken.

Jayfeather tipped his head. "Shadowsight has a point," he mewed. "Is this the right time to be choosing an apprentice?"

Willowshine nodded. "It might be better to wait until StarClan can share with us again."

"Nonsense." Mothwing flicked her tail irritably. "A cat can learn to make a poultice whether StarClan is watching or not."

Puddleshine shifted his paws. "Rowanstar didn't wait for StarClan's approval before he made me ShadowClan's medicine cat."

"That was different," Willowshine argued. "He had no choice. ShadowClan didn't have any medicine cat at all."

"Surely the lives of our Clanmates are too important to wait for StarClan?" Mothwing argued.

"But herbs in the wrong paws can be more dangerous than no herbs at all." Alderheart frowned. "I think Flipclaw proved that."

"I'm not going to let Whistlepaw teach himself," Kestrelflight snapped. "I'll be mentoring him. Besides"—he looked stiffly around at the other cats—"it's my choice, not yours."

"But you're the one who's worried we've driven StarClan away," Willowshine insisted. "If they find you've taken an apprentice they don't approve of . . ."

As the medicine cats bickered on, Shadowsight's attention drifted toward the Moonpool, where the light of the half-moon sparkled on the surface. Without StarClan, were the

Clans going to spend all their time arguing over what was allowed and what wasn't? His heart fluttered nervously in his chest. How would they ever really know what was right and what was wrong?

CHAPTER 12

❧

These are my kin. In the clearing beside the river, Rootspring
gazed at the Sisters. He could see clearly now why he and Tree
seemed different from their Clanmates, larger than other
warriors, broad where their denmates were lithe. The Sisters
were huge, and not just because of their thick pelts. There was
power in their wide shoulders and paws.

The white she-cat, to whom the others deferred, called
herself Snow. Sunrise had introduced the others: a ginger she-
cat called Furze; a tabby called Tempest; the ginger-and-white
littermates, Flurry and Sparrow; Sunshine, the plump cream
she-cat; the large ginger she-cat, Hawk; and two younger gray
cats, Moon and Squirrel. He had learned that Sunrise was
Tree's littermate, and he tried to remember the other Sisters
who'd recovered in the SkyClan camp after the battle. Memories of them seemed to echo in his mind, but hazily. And there
were others with them now. He'd felt outnumbered as he'd
led the patrol into the clearing where the Sisters had made
their camp.

The alders encircling it swished as Snow blinked at him.
She was clearly pondering the news he'd shared. Would she

believe that a dead warrior had stolen a leader's body and that the leader was a spirit now, wandering lost with other dead warriors somewhere Rootspring could no longer reach them?

He glanced nervously at Bristlefrost. She blinked back, encouraging, and he was grateful again that she was here. She had stayed close to Spotfur since Sunrise had led them into the Sisters' camp, protective of her Clanmate. Spotfur's wounds still glistened in the sunshine, and Rootspring noticed Flurry and Hawk glancing at the gray-and-white warrior, concern shadowing their gazes. But no cat offered help.

Needleclaw had hung back, letting Rootspring speak for the patrol. She padded forward now, stopping beside him. "We've come a long way to find you, but the Clans are in trouble—"

Snow silenced her with a flick of her tail. "The Clans' troubles are their own affair."

Rootspring met her gaze. "You're right," he mewed. "But we thought the Sisters would understand more than any cat how important the dead are to the living."

Snow narrowed her eyes. "Surely these lost spirits have simply moved on to the next place."

Bristlefrost stretched her muzzle forward. "We can't find out," she mewed. "We've lost contact with StarClan."

"That's where your ancestors go, right?" Snow tipped her head to one side.

"Yes," Bristlefrost mewed.

Spotfur shifted beside her. "Where do *your* ancestors go?" she asked Snow.

"Some of them stay around for a while," Snow told her. "Watching over the cats they've cared for in life. But others disappear. Perhaps they know where they want to be. Perhaps they've always known." The white she-cat shrugged. "But, if they have, they've never shared it."

Spotfur's eyes glistened for a moment before she looked away. Rootspring guessed that she was thinking about Stemleaf, wondering where he had gone if StarClan was beyond reach.

Snow's gaze flitted over the gray-and-white she-cat's wounds. "Let us treat your injuries," she mewed softly.

Spotfur lifted her muzzle. "They're not deep," she told the white she-cat. "They'll heal by themselves."

Snow didn't press but stared at Spotfur with interest, and Rootspring wondered for a moment if the white Sister had guessed, as Leaf had, that the Thunderclan warrior was carrying kits. Snow dipped her head, as though bowing to Spotfur's pride, and changed the subject. "What do you want from us?" she asked, looking back at Rootspring.

"We were hoping you'd come with us and help find Bramblestar's spirit." Rootspring searched her gaze. Would she help?

"We can't go anywhere right now." Snow nodded toward a plump cream she-cat. "Sunshine is expecting kits."

Rootspring could see that the queen's flanks were swollen and wondered how close she was to kitting. "Some of you could come with us, and the rest could stay behind," he suggested.

Sunshine blinked brightly. "The kits won't be born for another half-moon," she assured Snow. "I can still travel."

Tempest twitched her tail stiffly. "Why should we help the Clans? They drove us from our camp before Moonlight's kits had even opened their eyes."

"They didn't know Moonlight was kitting." Furze blinked at her campmate. "And they took us in when they realized what they'd done."

Moon, the youngest she-cat, nodded. "One of their queens fed me and my littermates," she mewed. "If they hadn't, we'd have died."

She must have shared a nest with Needleclaw and me. Rootspring couldn't remember her, but he tasted the air, wondering if he'd recognize her scent. When he didn't, he shook out his pelt, disappointed.

Furze's pelt bristled along her spine. "If their Clans hadn't killed Moonlight, you wouldn't have needed their milk," she mewed sharply.

Snow met the ginger she-cat's gaze. "Moonlight was killed by a rockfall."

"It killed one of their campmates too," Hawk added. "Leafpool died alongside her."

Sunrise's eyes were dark with distrust. "Perhaps it's good that Bramblestar is gone," she muttered.

Bristlefrost stiffened. "Why?" She sounded as though she couldn't believe her ears.

"When I was injured, he refused to let his medicine cats treat me," Sunrise told her. "I would have died if Leafpool hadn't gone against his orders." She stared at Bristlefrost. "Thunderclan may be better off with a new leader."

Rootspring saw Bristlefrost flex her claws and shot her a warning look. They couldn't afford to offend the Sisters.

Moon narrowed her eyes. "Perhaps we could help in exchange for something."

Rootspring shifted his paws self-consciously. The Clans had been clear that the Sisters would be tolerated but not welcomed. There was no way they would give the Sisters anything in exchange.

Moon went on. "Do they have catmint?" she mewed. "Perhaps they could share some with us."

Snow sniffed. "If we help, we will do it out of honor," she mewed. "Not for herbs."

"I'd like to see SkyClan again," Furze ventured.

Hawk nodded. "Squirrelflight was as brave as a Sister," she mewed. "I'd like to pay my respects to her."

Hope prickled beneath Rootspring's pelt as the Sisters exchanged glances, interest replacing the distrust in their eyes. Were they going to come? He lifted his chin. First he had to tell them of the conditions the Clans had put on their visit. His mouth felt dry. Asking for help had been hard enough. Telling the Sisters that they must follow the Clans' rules if they came felt like an insult. But he'd promised Leafstar that he'd do it. He cleared his throat. "I'm afraid you'll only be allowed on SkyClan land," he mewed apologetically. He wouldn't tell them that ShadowClan, WindClan, and RiverClan had forbidden them from even talking to their warriors.

Furze's pelt spiked with anger. Tempest flattened her ears.

Sunrise snorted. "How dare they tell us where we can go!"

"Do the Clans think we must serve them while they dictate rules?" Snow asked, glaring at Rootspring.

His heart sank. There was no way the Sisters would come back with them to the lake. As he gazed imploringly at Snow, wishing he could find the words to make her understand that the Clans could be kinder than they seemed now, a shape shimmered like a heat haze at the edge of the clearing and flickered into view. He stared in surprise. A large gray she-cat was crossing the grass. She stopped in the middle. Her pelt was translucent—an apparition so fragile that a shadow might dissolve it. *A spirit.* Rootspring's heart quickened, then quickened again as he saw the Sisters watching it. He wasn't the only one who could see her.

"Moonlight." As Snow dipped her head to the spirit, Bristlefrost gasped. Needleclaw and Spotfur followed the white she-cat's gaze, their eyes clouded with confusion.

"One of their ancestors is here," Rootspring whispered to Needleclaw.

Needleclaw's tail twitched nervously. "Here? Now?"

"She's a spirit." Rootspring stared at Moonlight. The gray she-cat was looking around the clearing, her gaze warm as it flitted from cat to cat. It met his and he felt a jolt of excitement. "You are Tree's kit, aren't you?" she mewed.

Rootspring nodded nervously.

Moonlight purred. "I am his mother."

He gasped, feeling a thrill of wonder flow through him. "I didn't think I'd ever meet you."

"Really?" Moonlight's whiskers twitched with amusement. "Even though you clearly have his gift?"

Rootspring bowed his head. "I only learned I had it recently," he admitted. He could feel Needleclaw, Bristlefrost, and Spotfur staring at him. They must be wondering what in StarClan he was talking about.

Moonlight turned back to Snow. "You should help them," she mewed.

The Sisters exchanged glances around her.

Snow's ears twitched. "But they sound like they haven't changed since they drove us from our camp."

"Squirrelflight and Leafpool were friends to us," Moonlight mewed. "If Squirrelflight has lost her mate, then we must help her find him again. We owe her that much. She stood up for us when no other cat would."

"But they say we can only set paw on SkyClan land," Furze mewed crossly.

Moonlight blinked at them. "The Clans love making rules," she mewed. "Let them if they must. You will not be with them long."

"They don't respect us," Sunrise argued.

Moonlight's eyes sparkled playfully. "Do we need their respect?" She gazed around her campmates once again. "Aren't you curious about what's going on?" she asked them. "If something is stopping spirits from wandering the forests, shouldn't we find out what it is?"

"Yes." Hawk nodded. "If it affects the Clans' ancestors, it might affect ours soon."

The Sisters shifted uneasily.

Snow dipped her head. "Moonlight is right," she mewed. "The Clans are arrogant and foolish. But their lost spirits might be important to us as well as them. We should go with these cats and find out what's happening."

Rootspring's heart lifted. "So you'll come?" He looked eagerly around at the Sisters. They might be able to save Bramblestar where the Clans had failed.

Flurry and Sunshine nodded. Hawk paused for a moment then said, "Yes."

Furze met Snow's gaze.

The white she-cat returned it silently.

"We will go," Furze told her.

Moonlight swished her tail. "I'm glad." She turned, purring, and blinked at Spotfur. "But first we must celebrate new life."

The Sisters glanced at one another, then turned toward Spotfur.

The Thunderclan she-cat's pelt twitched warily. "What do they want?"

Rootspring padded to the Thunderclan she-cat's side. "Don't worry," he whispered. "They know you're carrying kits. I think they're just congratulating you." His eyes widened as more spirits began to appear, filling the gaps between the living sisters like gleaming mist. Along with the Sisters, they moved closer, encircling Spotfur, who watched the living cats among them, fear showing in her eyes.

Rootspring pressed against her. "They don't want to harm you," he told her.

Snow stopped in front of the gray-and-white she-cat. "We call on our ancestors to bring your kits a good and long life," Snow told her. "Your kits are very special." Around her, the Sisters and their ghostly ancestors lifted their muzzles to the sky and purred. Their throats rumbled with warmth and love until the clearing seemed to reverberate with the sound.

Spotfur stiffened against Rootspring, clearly unnerved by the display, but as the Sisters went on, circling now, living and dead moving together, letting their pelts brush past the Thunderclan warrior, Spotfur slowly relaxed. Her eyes began to glow with gratitude as their purrs lifted into soft yowls and they raised their voices to the sky.

Rootspring's fur stood on end. Their chanting seemed to resonate deep in his belly. Bristlefrost's gaze was glistening. She padded close to her Clanmate and, with Needleclaw, raised her muzzle and joined the Sisters' song.

CHAPTER 13

❧

As the sun began to slip behind the alders and melt between their branches, Bristlefrost settled deeper into the grass. The Sisters' ceremony had left her feeling calm, and while Rootspring and Needleclaw had hunted with the she-cats, she had stayed in their camp with Spotfur.

Spotfur was calmer too, as though she had been reassured by the Sisters' song for her kits. For the first time since Stemleaf's death, the grief that had shadowed her gaze had softened. Maybe she was ready to accept their kits. Had she finally glimpsed the happiness they could bring? Bristlefrost hadn't asked. Spotfur had made it clear that she wanted to sit quietly and watch the river slide past the camp.

When the hunting patrol returned, Bristlefrost was impressed by the amount of prey they carried. The Sisters must hunt like warriors even though they didn't look like warriors. She'd thought the heavy she-cats would be too slow to catch more than the oldest prey. But the hole was filled with juicy mice and plump birds. Rootspring and Needleclaw had returned looking happy, their pelts fluffed, their eyes bright. Now, as Needleclaw eyed the prey, Rootspring padded toward Bristlefrost.

"How is she?" He glanced at Spotfur as the Thunderclan queen passed him, heading for the prey-hole.

"She seems better." Bristlefrost followed his gaze.

Snow dropped a rabbit at Spotfur's paws. "Eat well," she mewed.

Spotfur dipped her head in thanks. As she carried the rabbit to the edge of the clearing, Needleclaw took a blackbird from the pile and settled beside the queen.

Snow carried two mice to Rootspring and laid them on the grass. "It was good to hunt with you," she mewed. "Tree taught you well."

"Tree wasn't my mentor," Rootspring told her.

The white she-cat blinked in surprise. "Don't toms teach their kits how to hunt in the Clans?"

"I guess Tree taught me some things," Rootspring conceded.

"But our mentors train us mostly," Bristlefrost explained. "When we reach six moons old, we become apprentices, and we're each assigned a warrior to train us in hunting and battle skills."

Snow's eyes widened, but she didn't comment, turning back to find her own piece of prey while the rest of the Sisters shared their catch and settled around the clearing.

Rootspring nudged one of the mice toward Bristlefrost and sat down beside her to eat his.

"Thanks." She hooked it closer, happy to be near him, and let her tail rest across his as she took a bite of the mouse.

Sunrise glanced toward them. Affection warmed her

gaze as it fell on their tails.

Bristlefrost stiffened and flicked her tail away from Root-spring's, suddenly self-conscious.

Sunrise blinked at her. "There's no need to be shy." She exchanged glances with Hawk, whose whiskers twitched with amusement. "I'm glad the kin of my kin has found someone who's clearly so fond of him."

Shame washed through Bristlefrost. She could feel Needle-claw's sharp eye burning into her pelt. "We're just friends," she mewed quickly.

Sunrise eyed her indulgently, clearly unconvinced.

Bristlefrost's ears twitched. She liked Rootspring; she liked him a lot, but she hadn't meant to be so obvious. Had every cat noticed? She glanced at the others. Moon's eyes sparkled knowingly. Hawk and Tempest were focusing on the squirrel they were sharing, but she wondered if they silently agreed with Sunrise. Did every cat think they were *mates*? "We're just friends," she repeated.

Rootspring tucked his tail tightly beside his body. "Good friends," he mewed. "But that's all."

"They can't be anything else." Needleclaw's black-and-white pelt was prickling along her spine.

Sunrise looked puzzled. "Why not?"

"Rootspring would never be so disloyal to his Clan," Needleclaw told her.

Snow narrowed her eyes. "What does his Clan have to do with it?"

Bristlefrost shifted uneasily. "Warriors can't take mates

from a different Clan." She didn't look at Rootspring, but she was so aware of him beside her she had to fight to keep her pelt from ruffling. "We can be friends," she went on. "But not mates."

Hawk looked up from her squirrel. "But what if you fall in love with a cat from another Clan?"

"We're not supposed to," Bristlefrost told her.

Hawk stared at her. "But what if you *do*?"

Needleclaw's tail flicked crossly. "A true warrior is loyal to their Clan above all things," she mewed. "Even love."

"But why?" Snow's gaze flitted from Needleclaw to Bristlefrost.

Bristlefrost avoided it. "How can we protect our Clanmates if our heart lies in another Clan?"

"Each Clan has its own borders," Needleclaw added. "We couldn't defend them properly if cats we loved were on the other side."

"So you are only allowed to love what's inside your borders?" Hawk frowned.

"Who made such a rule?" Snow asked.

"It's part of the warrior code," Needleclaw told her. "It's part of what binds a Clan together and keeps it safe."

Tempest ripped a strip of flesh from the squirrel. "It sounds like it must make life harder, not easier," she mewed, chewing.

"The warrior code isn't there to make life easier!" Needleclaw glared at her. "It's to help us be the best warriors we can be."

Bristlefrost frowned. Would she really be less of a warrior if she loved Rootspring? How could that be? She'd fight to the death for him as well as her Clan. Didn't that make her stronger, not weaker?

Needleclaw hadn't finished. "I don't know why you're being so superior." She looked challengingly at Snow. "The Sisters have rules too. You don't allow toms to live with you at all!"

Rootspring shot his littermate a look. Bristlefrost guessed he was warning her not to pick a fight with these cats. They had agreed to help them find Bramblestar.

"It's true." Snow inclined her head. "Toms don't live with us, but we would never tell a Sister who she can love. If one of us wants to leave and travel with a tom, we don't stop her." She eyed Needleclaw. "Sunrise had another littermate besides Tree, called Ice. But she left us to travel with her mate. We miss her, of course, but we're not angry she chose him over us, and if she ever wants to return, we will welcome her without question. You make it sound like loving a tom is *betraying* your Clan."

"That's because it is!" Needleclaw snapped.

Bristlefrost felt she ought to defend the Clans. "Ice still had to *leave* the group to be with her mate. You wouldn't allow her to stay once she'd made her choice."

"Exactly!" Needleclaw swished her tail triumphantly. "There's no real difference between our rule and yours."

Snow returned her gaze coolly. "Except that we don't shame one another for what's in our hearts."

Spotfur suddenly looked up from her rabbit, meeting Snow's gaze. "Warriors haven't always followed the rules." Bristlefrost blinked at her. She didn't realize the queen had been listening so closely. The others jerked their muzzles toward Spotfur, as though they were surprised to hear her speak too.

Spotfur looked around the group of cats thoughtfully. "Cats from different Clans have fallen in love before," she mewed. "And they've followed their hearts. Finleap left SkyClan to be with Twigbranch in Thunderclan."

"That was different." Needleclaw glared at her. "They were living in the same Clan when they fell in love."

Spotfur blinked at her calmly. "What about Dovewing and Tigerstar? Dovewing left Thunderclan to become his mate."

Needleclaw sniffed. "It just proves that you can't love someone outside your Clan. Finleap and Dovewing abandoned their birth Clans to be with the cats they love. I doubt any cat will really think of them as true warriors again."

They won't? Bristlefrost's chest tightened. Dovewing and Finleap were certainly *different*, but only because they'd done something most warriors didn't dare to. "I think they were braver because they broke the rules for something they believed in more," she mewed quietly.

Needleclaw's eyes flashed with indignation. "Rules are rules!" she snapped. "They are there for a reason. If we *all* broke them, there'd be no Clans left and no warriors."

Rootspring poked his mouse. "Careful, Needleclaw. You'll be yowling about codebreakers next, like Ashfur."

Needleclaw stiffened. "I'm not suggesting any cat be *exiled*. I'm just saying Finleap and Dovewing caused a lot of trouble that could have been avoided."

Spotfur's gaze drifted away from the other warriors. She stared once more at the river. "If Stemleaf had lived in a different Clan, I'd have loved him anyway." Her mew was soft. "No matter what Thunderclan thought about it."

Bristlefrost watched the queen. Her eyes were glistening wistfully. Did Spotfur love Stemleaf more than her own Clan? The thought unnerved her. How could she? Bristlefrost's gaze drifted toward Rootspring. Suddenly, her heart yearned for him more than she could bear. *Would I leave Thunderclan for him?* She pushed the thought away. *Of course not. Thunderclan needs me.* Why should her feelings for Rootspring mean leaving her Clan anyway? She'd heard that Crowfeather was Lionblaze and Jayfeather's father, even though Squirrelflight and Bramblestar had raised them. And Crowfeather was Windclan's deputy now. So his Clanmates couldn't have been too troubled that he'd had a relationship outside his Clan. Surely it was possible for her to love Rootspring and stay in Thunderclan?

Her tail twitched. *I shouldn't be looking for an excuse.* Ashamed, she licked her chest, hoping no cat would guess her thoughts. She shot Rootspring a look, but he was staring stiffly ahead, his paws tucked awkwardly beneath him. Was he embarrassed too?

The sun had disappeared and the camp was swathed in evening shadow. Stars were twinkling overhead.

Snow stood up and stretched.

Sunrise swallowed her last piece of the shrew and got up too. She nodded toward Spotfur, whose eyes had closed. Her head was beginning to droop. "There are warm nests for all of you." She glanced toward a den woven into a dogwood bush. "Spotfur should get as much rest as she can. We've a long journey ahead of us tomorrow."

"We should all get some rest," Snow agreed.

Around the clearing, the Sisters stood up and began to head toward the bushes encircling the camp. Snow nodded her head to the warriors and followed them as Tempest padded over to Spotfur and gently nosed her to her paws. Sleepily, Spotfur followed her to the dogwood and disappeared inside.

Needleclaw sat up. She eyed Rootspring as the Sisters slid into their dens. "Are you coming?"

"In a moment," Rootspring told her.

Needleclaw's gaze flicked sharply toward Bristlefrost. The SkyClan warrior clearly didn't want to leave them together in the empty clearing.

Bristlefrost settled deeper into the grass. They would be traveling home tomorrow. This would be one of her last nights away from the Clans. She didn't want to sleep through it. The stars here were brighter than they were beneath the canopy of Thunderclan's forest. And she'd never slept beside a river before. She blinked at Needleclaw. "I haven't finished my mouse." The last few mouthfuls still lay in front of her.

Needleclaw held her ground. "You should get some rest before the journey tomorrow," she mewed.

Rootspring stared at her. "Don't you trust us?" he challenged.

Her pelt rippled as she stared back. Then she swished her tail, avoiding the question. "Don't be long," she told him, turning away from them.

"We won't be." As his sister headed for the dogwood den, he blinked at Bristlefrost. "She doesn't dare accuse me of being disloyal."

Bristlefrost looked away quickly. She couldn't help feeling guilty that they were staying out here alone. And yet the grass smelled so sweet and the river was chattering softly. Happiness bubbled in her chest.

"You'd better finish it." He nodded at the remains of the mouse. "She might come back to check." His eyes twinkled.

"I'm not hungry," Bristlefrost whispered. She tried to stop her pelt from twitching with excitement as Rootspring moved closer and pressed his flank against hers. It was warm and soft, and she nestled against him, a purr rumbling in her throat. "We shouldn't stay out long," she mewed huskily.

Rootspring moved his muzzle close to hers. "But we'll be home in a day or two, and then we might not see each other again for a moon."

She couldn't argue. She didn't want to.

He folded his tail around hers. "It's strange to think about cats like Finleap and Dovewing," he murmured. "How they changed Clans for their mates."

She stiffened. Was he suggesting they do the same?

Rootspring gazed at the river thoughtfully. "I don't know

if I could leave my kin behind in SkyClan, even for a mate."

Her heart dropped and she realized how much she'd been hoping he would feel differently. Guilt tugged at her belly. She shouldn't wish that he would. It was asking too much. And would she love him as much if he were the sort of warrior who could? "I couldn't leave Thunderclan, either," she breathed. "It's where I was born and raised. And being a good Thunderclan warrior has always been the most important thing to me." She searched his face, trying to read his reaction. Had she hurt him? "Whatever I feel, my Clan must come first."

"I know." He blinked at her, his eyes sparkling with moonlight. They were wide and green, and her heart felt as though it would split as she returned his gaze. *Being a good Thunderclan warrior has always been the most important thing to me.* Here, beside the river, far from the Clans, with Rootspring's warmth seeping through her pelt, she wondered if that was true anymore.

Bristlefrost paced beside the entrance to the Sisters' camp. Spotfur was eating a thrush, while the Sisters stuffed the entrances to their dens with ferns to keep foxes from settling while they were away. The morning had brought more sunshine. It would be a good day to travel, and yet, as Bristlefrost watched the Sisters preparing for the journey, foreboding loomed in her mind and made her tense.

She stopped beside Rootspring. "There are so many of them." She nodded toward the Sisters. Young cats, not yet six moons old, had joined them now, along with Sisters who'd made their dens farther down the river. "Are you sure Leafstar won't object to having them on SkyClan territory?"

"I hope not." Rootspring looked anxious. "But she can't really object. They are doing us a favor."

"But they're so big," Bristlefrost pressed. "Your Clan might feel invaded. Especially since your camp used to be their camp." She heard a nervous shake in her own voice. "And will there be enough prey on your territory to support so many extra mouths?"

Rootspring frowned. "Perhaps we can persuade some of them to stay behind."

Snow's ears perked up. She must have heard him. "We travel together," she told him firmly.

Rootspring's tail twitched, but he didn't argue. "I guess that's it, then," he whispered to Bristlefrost as Snow began beckoning her campmates to the entrance with her tail. He ducked out of the camp and Bristlefrost followed.

Needleclaw and Spotfur fell in behind them, and bushes swished as the Sisters padded in their wake. Bristlefrost glanced over her shoulder. So many cats! Was this how Clan leaders felt when they led their warriors to a Gathering?

She looked at the meadows stretching ahead. "How will we get so many cats across the Twolegplace?"

"Sunrise says she knows another route," Rootspring told her.

She felt his fur brush hers and moved away, conscious that Needleclaw was watching. Her paws felt suddenly heavy.

These days away from the Clans had been special. The moments she'd shared with Rootspring would live forever in her heart. As she led the Sisters across the fields, she felt the tug of the countryside behind them. Was she ready to return home?

CHAPTER 14

Shadowsight itched with frustration as he watched Mothwing slowly pulling herbs from the herb store. Was she going to check every leaf for mildew before she finally pulled out the rolled strip of dock into which he'd smeared honey only a moon ago?

Yarrowleaf had whitecough, and Puddleshine had suggested she sleep in the medicine den so she didn't disturb the other warriors. The sound of Yarrowleaf's coughing had kept Shadowsight awake half the night. Twice, Shadowsight had barely convinced himself not to go to the herb store to fetch honey for the sick warrior. Mothwing and Puddleshine seemed able to sleep through her hacking, but he had been scared Mothwing would wake to find him rooting about in her herbs. She'd only complain he had no business there.

Now morning sunshine was streaming into the medicine den, and Yarrowleaf was still waiting for Mothwing to find honey to soothe her sore throat.

As last the RiverClan medicine cat pulled out the honey-smeared dock leaf. "Perhaps I should give her tansy instead," she wondered out loud, glancing at Puddleshine.

Puddleshine looked up from the bracken he was shaping

into a fresh nest. "Give her both," he suggested. "It can't do any harm."

Shadowsight flicked his tail impatiently. He would have given Yarrowleaf honey ages ago, but since Puddleshine and Mothwing didn't want his help, he might as well check on Ashfur. With any luck, Ashfur would be too sleepy to talk. He stalked out of the den, noticing with a twinge of sadness that no cat asked where he was going. *They don't even care anymore.*

He narrowed his eyes against the morning glare as he crossed the clearing. Thriftear was sitting by herself at the entrance to the bramble enclosure. Shadowsight frowned. Had Squirrelflight sent only one guard today? The Thunder-clan warrior's pelt twitched uneasily. As she cast a guilty glance toward Shadowsight, foreboding spiked in his belly. He quickened his pace, ears pricking as he heard snarls coming from the enclosure. "What's happening?" He broke into a run, pushing past Thriftear as she stepped forward to block his way.

Beyond the bramble wall, Lionblaze loomed over Ashfur, his ears flat, his back arched. The golden warrior was hissing viciously as Ashfur cowered against the roots of the hollow tree.

"You're a coward!" Lionblaze snarled. "You tried to kill me and my littermates when we were too young to defend our-selves, and now you're murdering Bramblestar. You can't even fight fairly."

Ashfur's eyes were slits, dark with hate. "You'll never get Bramblestar back," he taunted. "He's gone for good."

Lionblaze's pelt bushed. "Give him back his body, you murderer!"

Ashfur caught Shadowsight's eye. Malice sparked in his gaze. "I didn't murder him *alone*."

With a yowl of rage, Lionblaze hurled himself at the prisoner, hooking his claws into the warrior's shoulders. He dragged Ashfur onto his spine and raked his claws across his belly. Ashfur swung out a paw defensively, but Lionblaze knocked it away with a hiss and swung a blow at Ashfur's cheek. Ashfur squirmed away and pressed himself harder against the hollow tree. But Lionblaze kept lashing out, blow after blow until Shadowsight could smell blood. "Get out of Bramblestar's body!"

"Stop!" Shadowsight raced toward Lionblaze, ducking to avoid the golden warrior's paw as he aimed another blow at Ashfur's muzzle.

Lionblaze hesitated, and Ashfur kicked out with his hind legs, catching Lionblaze in the belly. Eyes narrowing, Lionblaze reared. "I'll kill you!"

"No!" Shadowsight dodged in front of the Thunderclan warrior before he could attack again.

Lionblaze froze, staring at him. "Why are you defending him?"

"You can't kill Bramblestar's body!" Panic sparked through Shadowsight's fur. "We won't ever get him back." *And I'll be a murderer forever!* He gazed pleadingly into Lionblaze's eyes.

"Killing him might give Bramblestar the chance he needs," Lionblaze hissed.

"But Ashfur is the only one who knows how we can reach StarClan again," Shadowsight pressed.

"We don't know that!"

"It's the only hope we have right now." Shadowsight's breath was coming fast, his heart pounding in his ears as he faced the furious Thunderclan warrior. He held his ground, suddenly aware that his Clanmates were crowding at the entrance to the bramble enclosure, staring wide-eyed. *Why don't you do something?* Shadowsight pleaded with them silently, knowing it was pointless. No cat was going to lift a paw to save Ashfur.

He dragged his gaze back to Lionblaze. The warrior's flanks were heaving. Anger still contorted his face. "If you kill Ashfur now, we might lose Bramblestar for good."

Lionblaze let his hackles fall, his gaze suddenly bleak. Was he wondering if it was already too late? Shadowsight swallowed. *It might be,* he thought with a shiver of dread.

"You can't defend him forever." Lionblaze backed away.

Shadowsight slumped with relief as Ashfur slid from behind him and shook out his pelt, streaked now with blood.

The dark warrior glanced at the ShadowClan cats pressing close to the entrance. Then his gaze flicked back to Shadowsight. "Thank you for saving me."

I don't want your thanks! Shadowsight felt his blood turn to ice as his Clanmates eyed one another. Scorchfur narrowed his eyes suspiciously. Sparrowtail curled his lip. "I saved *Bramblestar!*" Shadowsight snapped. "Not you!" He crossed the enclosure, ignoring the stares of his Clanmates even though they seemed to pierce his fur like claws. He glanced back at

Ashfur. "I'm not going to look after you anymore," he growled. "You can fix your own wounds!"

"What in StarClan were you thinking?" Tigerstar glared at Lionblaze.

Thriftear stared at her paws.

As soon as Tigerstar had heard about the fight in the enclosure, he'd sent ShadowClan warriors to replace the Thunderclan guards and summoned Lionblaze, Thriftear, and Shadowsight to his den. Shadowsight eyed his father nervously. The gloom here couldn't hide Tigerstar's fury.

His father's pelt bristled. "Ashfur is in ShadowClan's care," he hissed at Lionblaze. "If you kill him, the other Clans will blame *us.*"

Lionblaze returned his gaze without speaking. The golden warrior was still trembling with rage after his encounter with Ashfur.

Tigerstar's gaze flashed toward Thriftear. "Why didn't you try to stop him?"

"It wasn't her fault," Lionblaze insisted.

Tigerstar ignored him, still staring at the dark gray she-cat. "You could have called for help."

Shadowsight felt a rush of sympathy for Thriftear as she lifted her gaze miserably. "I'm sorry," she murmured. How could she have stood up to her deputy?

"Ashfur deserves to die," Lionblaze hissed through gritted teeth.

"Maybe he does," Tigerstar growled. "But it doesn't matter

what you think or I think. The Clans still believe he is our best chance of getting Bramblestar back and finding StarClan. They want him alive for now, as you well know." He thrust his muzzle forward. "Do you want to cause another battle between the Clans?"

Lionblaze held the ShadowClan leader's gaze for a moment. "No." He nodded. "I'm sorry. I lost control."

"You're a deputy now," Tigerstar declared. "Your Clan looks up to you. If you can't control yourself, why should they?"

The golden warrior lowered his head in shame. Tigerstar's words had clearly stung.

Tigerstar flicked his tail angrily. "Go home," he snarled. "And tell Squirrelflight to be more careful who she sends to guard Ashfur next time."

Lionblaze dipped his head. "It won't happen again," he mewed quietly, and nosed his way out of the den.

Thriftear blinked apologetically at Tigerstar. "I'm really sorry." She hurried away, her ears twitching.

Shadowsight turned to follow. His father clearly needed time to calm down.

"Wait." Tigerstar beckoned him back with a nod.

Shadowsight shivered with dread. He knew what Tigerstar was going to say.

"You were brave to step in." His father's eyes glowed with pride.

Shadowsight dropped his gaze. "We need Ashfur alive for now."

"You were the only cat to defend him," Tigerstar went on.

Shame washed Shadowsight's pelt. He could still picture Sparrowtail's look of contempt as he'd stalked away from the bramble enclosure. His Clanmates had moved to let Shadowsight pass as though he'd stunk of fox dung. "I can't take care of him anymore," he mewed. "Please let me go back to being a medicine cat. I just want to help my Clan."

"You can help your Clan by helping Ashfur." Tigerstar straightened. "It's clear we can't trust other cats around him, so you're going to need to take more care of him, not less. From now on, I want you to be the one to take him food and clean out his bedding as well as take care of his injuries."

Dismay dropped like a stone into Shadowsight's heart. He'd have to spend more time with Ashfur, and he'd be carrying out more apprentice duties. "Why me?"

"I can trust you," Tigerstar told him. "You will be the only cat to enter the enclosure from now on."

Shadowsight couldn't meet his father's gaze. Was this how he rewarded trustworthiness? It felt like a punishment.

"Go and see to him," Tigerstar ordered. "He must be hurt after the fight."

Shadowsight dipped his head and padded into the clearing, his tail dragging along the ground as he headed for the medicine den.

"I need herbs for Ashfur," he grunted as he slid inside.

Mothwing was alone. She looked up from the leaf wrap she was rolling. "I heard about the fight. Is Ashfur badly hurt?"

"I don't know yet," Shadowsight muttered.

"He'll have quite a few claw marks if he was fighting with

Lionblaze." She padded to the herb store and reached inside.

"It wasn't really a fight," Shadowsight told her. "Lionblaze attacked him."

Mothwing glanced at him. "You sound sorry for him."

"I'm not!" How could she think that? Was she as mouse-brained as the rest of his Clanmates? Didn't they realize he only cared that they *needed* Ashfur? He swallowed back frustration. What was the point in explaining if they refused to understand? He waited sullenly while she gathered herbs from the store, then took the bundle she gave him and headed toward the bramble enclosure.

Ashfur blinked at him in surprise as he entered. "I thought you weren't coming back."

Shadowsight dropped the herbs and glared at him coldly.

"Did your father send you here?" Ashfur asked.

Shadowsight curled his claws into the earth. Was Ashfur going to rub it in? "He told me to take care of you." He began to chew marigold into a pulp. Blood had dried already on Ashfur's ear, but the gashes on his cheek and flanks were still wet. Padding closer, Shadowsight inspected the wounds. An old injury had reopened on the dark warrior's tail, and the wound on his shoulder was quite deep, but Lionblaze must have been trying to hold back, because the other scratch marks were light. They would heal in a few days. He spat the pulp onto his paw and rubbed it gently into a shoulder wound.

Ashfur winced. "Thanks." He caught Shadowsight's eye. "You saved my life." Was that gratitude in his eyes?

Shadowsight ignored it.

"You can see what will happen," Ashfur mewed quietly. "They're going to kill me."

There was certainty in the dark warrior's mew. Shadowsight's paws began to tremble. He knew he'd only seen the edge of Lionblaze's fury—and none of the Clanmates who had watched his attack had seemed all that eager to intervene. He turned away and grabbed another mouthful of marigold. *I couldn't stop them if they really tried to kill him.* Fear tugged in his chest as Ashfur went on.

"If I die, you'll never get Bramblestar back," he murmured. "And you'll never share with your precious StarClan again."

And I'll always be remembered as a murderer.

Shadowsight's blood turned cold as Ashfur stared at him, his gaze as hypnotic as a snake's.

"You have to get me out of here," the dark warrior breathed.

CHAPTER 15

"I'm going to win this time!" Rootspring glanced over his shoulder as he raced up the slope.

Bristlefrost was right behind him, her ears flat as wind streamed through her fur. "No, you're not!" She caught up. "Besides, you cheated!" she called as she passed him.

As she neared the top of the slope. Rootspring dug his paws harder into the earth, his lungs bursting as he fought to beat her there. She was right. He *had* cheated. This time he'd begun the race without warning, but she had still managed to outrun him. She pulled up at the top of the hill ahead of him, looking back, her eyes bright with triumph.

He skidded to a halt beside her. "I'm going to win one time before we get home." He gazed over the hills ahead, his heart sinking as he saw the top of WindClan's moor in the distance.

They'd raced to the top of every hill over the past day, leaving Needleclaw and Spotfur trailing with the Sisters, and had waited at the top for the others to catch up. Neither of them had said it, but Rootspring knew that they both wanted to make the most of their time away from the Clans. Each race seemed like the last chance they'd have to be alone together.

Or would it? Rootspring couldn't help imagining a future where they'd be together forever. Somehow they'd find a way. They had to. He couldn't bear the thought of living apart from her, not after everything they'd shared. Not after this mission. And yet now, as he glimpsed Clan lands once more, he knew the future he'd pictured could never come true. The Clans were real, and the way he felt about Bristlefrost was just a feeling. How could he sacrifice his loyalty as a warrior for a dream?

Bristlefrost was staring toward the moor too as they caught their breath. "We'll be home by tonight," she mewed.

"Yes." He searched her gaze and wondered if her heart ached at the thought of returning to her old life, just as his did. "Squirrelflight will be pleased we found the Sisters."

She blinked at him, pricking her ears. "Why don't we head straight for Thunderclan territory?"

Rootspring frowned. That wasn't the plan. "But the Sisters are only allowed on SkyClan land," he reminded her.

Paw steps sounded behind them. Needleclaw was racing up the hill.

"It makes sense," Bristlefrost gazed eagerly at Rootspring. "Squirrelflight's the one who wanted us to find them. It's her mate who's lost. And she's the one the Sisters want to see. She should be the first warrior they meet when we get home."

Needleclaw pulled up beside them, her eyes widening. "What are you talking about?" She stared at Bristlefrost. "We'd be breaking every rule the Clans have made about the Sisters."

Bristlefrost looked at her. "But don't you see? The Sisters will feel more at ease if Squirrelflight is the first leader they meet. And Thunderclan has been through such a difficult time. Seeing the Sisters might give them hope."

Needleclaw's pelt bristled. "That's exactly why we *shouldn't* take them to Thunderclan first. Your Clan is already in a mess. I don't see how bringing a big group of cats like the Sisters onto their land will help them."

"But it would!" Bristlefrost insisted. "When Squirrelflight sees for herself that they're here and they're willing to help, she'll know everything might be okay. The whole Clan will know." She swung her muzzle toward Rootspring, and he felt frozen by her hopeful gaze. She wanted him to agree with her.

Needleclaw scowled at him. "Tell her she's talking nonsense."

Rootspring shrank beneath his pelt. He wanted Bristlefrost to be right. He wanted her to be happy. He wanted the Sisters' arrival to fix everything for Thunderclan—for *all* the Clans. But he knew that it wouldn't. She was hoping for too much. "We can't go against the decision of the Clans." He avoided Needleclaw's gaze. If she was pleased that he'd sided with her, he didn't want to see it. "The Sisters have to stay with SkyClan." Guilt jabbed his belly as Bristlefrost's eyes clouded with disappointment. "You can fetch Squirrelflight as soon as we arrive," he added quickly.

"Sure." Bristlefrost turned away. "I'd better make sure the others are okay." She headed back down the slope to where

Spotfur was leading the Sisters through a patch of long grass and tangled weeds.

Needleclaw narrowed her eyes, watching her go. "Do you see why you need to make a new *friend* when you get back to the Clans?" she asked Rootspring.

He glared at her. "You don't understand."

"I understand more than you," she snapped. "Can't you see that she's only loyal to her Clan? She wants us to take the Sisters there even if it means breaking rules the other Clans have made."

"Isn't being loyal to your Clan a good thing?"

"Not when I can see how much you like her," Needleclaw mewed. "You're going to get hurt if you carry on thinking about her. She'll always choose her Clan over you."

"I'm glad she's so loyal." The words felt like nettles on his tongue. Had he been secretly hoping she'd give up Thunder-clan for him? He'd dreamed of a future together, but he hadn't pictured where that future would be. *Could I ever leave SkyClan?* He looked away, scared Needleclaw would guess what he was thinking. Perhaps that was the only way he'd be able to be with Bristlefrost.

As his fur began to crawl with worry, a low yowl sounded from the slope below. He stiffened. It sounded like a cat was in pain.

Needleclaw must have heard it too. Her pelt was prick-ing along her spine as she scanned the slope. The Sisters had bunched together in the thick grass, and Bristlefrost was nos-ing her way between them.

Rootspring bounded downhill, hurrying toward the gathered cats. Heart racing, he slid past Tempest and Hawk and tasted the air. He couldn't smell anything but the pungent weeds, which snaked through the grass here.

Bristlefrost looked up as he reached her. Moon was lying on her side, struggling to get to her paws while Snow crouched beside her.

"What's happened?" he mewed leaning down to sniff Moon's pelt. "Is she hurt?"

Snow was pawing at something tangled in the weeds near Moon's legs. "She's caught."

Moon let out a low wail of fear. "Something grabbed my paw, and when I tried to pull free, my other paw got caught in it."

As Snow pulled away the weeds, Rootspring saw a thin silver vine coiled around two of Moon's paws. It was pressed into the fur, and pressing tighter as Moon struggled to free herself.

"Don't move," he ordered. He could see that her tugging was pulling the vine tighter, fastening her hind paw to her forepaw so that she could barely move. More vine coiled away into the long grass. "Careful," he warned Snow. "Don't get tangled up too."

Snow glanced at the vine, her eyes round with alarm. "It must be Twoleg vine," she mewed. "It's too tough to break."

Bristlefrost crouched beside Snow. "Perhaps we can pull it clear," she suggested, running a paw along the vine trapping Moon's paws.

"It's too tight," Snow told her. "There's no way to loosen it."

Rootspring leaned closer. Now that Snow had cleared away the weeds, he could see that the piece of vine wormed into the ground. "Can we dig out the end and unwind it?" he mewed.

Snow clawed gingerly at the ground, scraping away the grass and soil until she'd unearthed a short stretch of the silver vine. "It's buried deep." She gripped it with her teeth and tried tugging it. With a grunt, she let go. "And it's stuck fast." Her eyes rounded with alarm.

Moon let out a low yowl. "I can't get free!" She was panicking.

"We'll get you out," Rootspring promised. He turned to the other Sisters, who crowded closer, murmuring anxiously. "Move them away," he told Tempest. "There's more vine here. It's not safe."

Tempest's eyes glittered with alarm. "What about Moon?"

"She's not hurt; she's just trapped," he told her. "She's going to be fine."

Tempest nodded and began to guide the other Sisters away, nosing them out of the long grass.

Rootspring inspected the small stretch of vine Snow had unearthed. He scraped at the soil where it disappeared into the ground, wondering how deep it was buried.

Sunrise padded toward them. She slid past Rootspring and inspected the vine, frowning. "It seems to be caught on something underground."

Sunrise's gaze slid to Rootspring. "*You* could find out what it's caught on," she mewed.

Rootspring looked back at her. "You want *me* to dig?" He was happy to try, but he didn't understand why she was acting like he should do it alone.

"Not dig." She stepped forward and placed her large paw over his.

What was she doing? He stiffened, ready to pull away, but she pressed his paw gently into the damp grass. "Listen to the earth," she told him. "Let it show you what's wrong."

He blinked at her, then remembered how Leaf had placed his paws carefully on the ground and let the earth talk to him. *Does she think* I *can do that too?* "I'm a warrior," he protested. "I can't talk to the earth." He was aware of Bristlefrost's gaze on him. She looked curious. He pulled his paw out from beneath Sunrise's.

Sunrise gazed at him so intently that he looked away. "Try it," she mewed.

Moon whimpered beside them. "Please."

Bristlefrost blinked slowly. "There's no harm in trying."

Rootspring hesitated. *Could* he talk to the earth the way Leaf had? Until a few moons ago, he hadn't known he could see ghosts. Bristlefrost was right. There was no harm in trying. Pelt rippling nervously, he pressed his paws into the grass, trying to imagine the rich, dark soil beneath and ignore the voice that told him that this was silly. That he was not like Leaf. *Just try it.*

Pressing harder, he closed his eyes, letting the scent of the earth reach through the stench of the weeds until it was all he could smell.

He waited and waited, wondering. What was he supposed to be seeing? How was he going to figure out what he should *do*? He pressed down on the earth more firmly, and then felt his head being tugged to the left, as though gentle paws were pulling him by the ears. When he opened his eyes again, he was staring right at a small mound in the earth. Something was buried there, not far beneath the ground.

Slowly he slithered forward and, using his claws to move the earth a little, revealed a block of wood. The vine was wrapped around it, and roots from the weeds held it fast in their tangled grip. His heart leaped. That was it! That was what was stopping them from being able to pull up the vine. He looked at Sunrise, who had bounded forward to join him. "The vine's attached to a piece of wood that's snared by roots," he told her.

"Let's try digging it up," Sunrise mewed.

Rootspring shook out his pelt and began clawing up the grass above where he'd seen the block of wood. Bristlefrost hurried to join him, and before long they were unearthing the roots that held the wood fast. "Let's chew through these," he told her. Ducking into the dip they'd made, he gnawed through one root, then another, earth pressing around his muzzle. Bristlefrost tore at the ground with her claws. Rootspring began to dig again, the soil crumbling easily now, freed from the roots. He dug faster, hope sparking in his fur as his claws struck a rotting lump of wood. He hooked his claws into it and eased it up a little. "Try pulling now," he told Snow.

The white she-cat gripped the vine between her teeth and

tugged. Earth shifted beneath Rootspring as the vine uncoiled and slid away from the wood. It loosened around Moon's paws, and with a yowl of relief, the young she-cat wriggled loose and scrambled away. She shook out her pelt.

"Are you hurt?" Snow sniffed her anxiously.

"Just a little bruised," Moon told her, testing her paws against the earth one at a time.

Bristlefrost blinked at Rootspring. "Did you really see what was holding the vine?"

He shrugged. "I didn't *see* it. But it was like I could *feel* where to look." *Kind of like Leaf.*

Sunrise purred. "All our toms have a connection to the earth," she told him. "There's no reason why Tree's kit should be any different."

Excitement fizzed in Rootspring's fur as he wondered what else he might be able to do.

They reached the high moor as the sun dipped behind the forest. Rootspring slowed as they neared the top, Bristlefrost at his side. Needleclaw and Spotfur followed at their heels, while the Sisters trailed behind. He could see the lake glittering below and stared at it, weary. The excitement he'd felt had faded.

Bristlefrost gave a nod. "I'd better head straight to Thunderclan." Rootspring's heart sank as she looked at him, her eyes glistening. "Squirrelflight will want to know the Sisters are here."

"Sure." He dipped his head. Would she miss these days

they'd spent together as much as he would? Had they meant as much to her?

She turned toward the Sisters. "Thanks for coming," she called. "See you soon." Without waiting for their good-bye, she hurried downslope toward Thunderclan's forest.

Rootspring watched her go. Was she really so eager to be home? He felt sick. His dreams of a future together had been only dreams. They were back among the Clans now, and it was over. He felt fur brush his pelt. Needleclaw stopped beside him and ran her tail along his spine. "Don't worry," she mewed, watching Bristlefrost's shape become no more than shadow against the hillside. "You'll get over her."

Rootspring blinked at his sister, his chest tight with longing. *Will I?*

CHAPTER 16

Bristlefrost was out of breath by the time she reached the Thunderclan border. She realized with a jolt that she'd left Spotfur
alone with Rootspring and Needleclaw. She'd been too eager
to reach Squirrelflight. *Spotfur will be okay.* There wasn't time to
go back now.

She crossed the scent line, happy to be following familiar
tracks once more as she wove between the trees. What would
Squirrelflight say when she heard that the Sisters were on
Clan territory? *She'll be glad.* This time tomorrow, they might
have found Bramblestar's ghost. They might even have found
a way to contact StarClan. Excitement surged beneath her
pelt.

Stars shone overhead, glittering between the leaves, and
she wondered why she'd thought they'd seemed brighter in
the Sisters' camp. They were so bright here that Bristlefrost
felt sure StarClan must be trying to reach the Clans. *They want
to return!* She raced faster along the forest floor, then bounded
down the slope toward the camp entrance. Would the Clan
still be awake? She ducked inside, relieved to see Mousewhisker and Alderheart in the clearing with Squirrelflight and

Lionblaze. Bumblestripe and Birchfall were up too, watching from the edge of the camp with Twigbranch and Finleap.

Bristlefrost scrambled to a halt, suddenly wondering why they weren't in their nests. She tensed as she realized their gazes were fixed on Squirrelflight and Lionblaze.

The Thunderclan leader loomed over her deputy in the middle of the clearing, her pelt ruffled in anger. Lionblaze's head was bowed.

What's going on?

Squirrelflight's eyes flashed in the moonlight. "You expect me to listen to you now? After you've spent so long trying to convince us we should kill Bramblestar's body? After you *attacked* him right in the middle of ShadowClan's camp?"

Lionblaze mewed, "I'm sorry. I didn't mean to—" But his weak words were knocked aside by his leader's.

"*Sorry* would not have brought back my mate if you'd killed him," she snarled.

"I know, but . . ." Lionblaze's head was still hanging low. "Ashfur was trying to provoke me. He's made it clear he won't listen to any cat—unless it's you. You're the only cat he cares about. You might be able to reason with him."

"Reason with *Ashfur*?" Squirrelflight's eyes widened.

Now Lionblaze looked up. "How else will we persuade him?"

"Do you realize what you're asking me to do?" Squirrelflight growled. "Ashfur's obsessed with me. Sure, I could persuade him, but what would he expect in return?"

Bristlefrost cleared her throat. She wanted to share her

news. But none of her Clanmates seemed to have noticed her arrival.

"You might find a way without giving him everything he wants," Lionblaze insisted.

Squirrelflight's tail bushed. "You *know* Ashfur!" she hissed. "He stopped being reasonable the first time I turned him down!"

Alderheart shifted nervously from paw to paw. "Perhaps you could trick him, like last time."

Squirrelflight glared at the medicine cat. "Do you really think he'd fall for that again?"

They'll stop arguing as soon as they know the Sisters are here. Bristlefrost edged forward, trying to catch Squirrelflight's eye, but the Thunderclan leader was still glaring at Alderheart.

Bumblestripe padded forward. "There's no way to reason with a cat like Ashfur."

"We won't know until we try," Lionblaze muttered.

Birchfall lashed his tail. "There's only one thing that foxheart wants," he growled. "And that's for Squirrelflight to be his mate. Do you really expect her to agree to that?"

"Of course not," Lionblaze snapped. "I'm just saying we have to try *something*."

Bristlefrost stuck out her chest. There was no need for this. The Sisters would help them find Bramblestar; then the Clans could find a way to get him back. Everything could return to normal. "The Sisters are here!" Her mew rang around the hollow.

Squirrelflight's gaze flashed toward her. "You're back!"

Relief glowed in her emerald gaze. "Is every cat safe?"

"Yes!" Bristlefrost hurried forward. "We found the Sisters and persuaded them to come with—"

Squirrelflight interrupted her. "Where's Spotfur?"

"I left her with Rootspring and Needleclaw." Bristlefrost realized that her Clanmates didn't know Spotfur was expecting kits. "She needed . . . rest."

Squirrelflight frowned. "But she's okay?"

Bristlefrost purred. "She's fine."

Jayfeather had padded from the medicine den and was staring at her, his blind blue gaze milky in the moonlight. "Where are the Sisters?"

"Rootspring's taking them to the SkyClan camp." Bristlefrost hoped the medicine cat would be pleased that they were a paw step closer to finding StarClan. She blinked eagerly at Squirrelflight. "I came to fetch you."

Hope sparked in Squirrelflight's eyes. "Did they say they could help us?"

"They're not sure," Bristlefrost told her. "But they're willing to try."

Lionblaze rolled his eyes. "It's a poor hunter who tries to trap a mouse with its weakest paw."

Squirrelflight jerked her muzzle toward him. "What do you mean by that?" she demanded.

The golden tabby tom seemed to hesitate for a moment, then nodded to himself and met his leader's gaze. "Why are we asking a bunch of rogues to find Bramblestar when it's obvious he's gone?"

"You don't know that!" Squirrelflight's gaze burned with fury.

"He hasn't been seen in a moon!" Lionblaze snapped. "If you won't talk to Ashfur, perhaps the only sensible thing to do is kill the body Bramblestar left behind." His eyes sparked with grief. "It might be the only way to drive Ashfur out."

"'The only sensible thing'?" Squirrelflight stared at Lionblaze as though she could hardly believe her ears.

"Without Bramblestar's body, Ashfur will have nowhere to hide," Lionblaze insisted.

"Are you sure of that?"

"I can't see any other way—"

"So you'd kill the cat who raised you?"

Lionblaze stared at her. "Do you think I find this easy?" Bristlefrost suddenly realized the golden warrior was trembling. "I care about Bramblestar too. He was like a father to me. But I'm not going to let that cloud my judgment. The cat ShadowClan is holding prisoner isn't Bramblestar. Bramblestar is gone."

Squirrelflight's tail flicked ominously. "You're making a lot of assumptions," she hissed. "One of them seems to be that I'm letting my feelings for Bramblestar guide me, instead of reason."

"Aren't you?"

Squirrelflight stretched her muzzle closer to Lionblaze. "I'm doing what Bramblestar would have done," she hissed. "I'm making sure that our next move is the right one before we make it."

Lionblaze held her gaze. "We don't know what Bramble-star would have done," he mewed. "We think we do, but the truth is, we didn't really ever know what he was thinking. If we had, we'd have seen right away that an impostor had stolen his body."

A growl rumbled in Squirrelflight's throat. "Are you saying I should have known it wasn't Bramblestar who came back after he died?"

Lionblaze didn't move. "You were closest to him."

Squirrelflight flinched, as though he'd lashed out at her with his claws. How could Lionblaze say something so hurt-ful? Didn't he know that Squirrelflight was already blaming herself for not having realized sooner? Heart lurching, Bristle-frost started forward, but Alderheart was already crossing the clearing.

He stopped in front of Lionblaze. "That's not fair!"

"Really?" Lionblaze blinked at him. "I'm only being hon-est. I'm grateful to Squirrelflight. I respect her. She raised me. But she's made mistakes before trying to protect cats she loves. Keeping the truth of my birth from her Clanmates was a bad decision, and letting Ashfur keep living inside Bramblestar's body would be another."

Bumblestripe grunted in agreement. "We should kill him and be done with it."

"The longer Ashfur lives, the more trouble he can cause," Mousewhisker agreed.

Bristlefrost's belly hardened with dread. She couldn't believe so many of her Clanmates were willing to risk

Bramblestar's life like this.

Twigbranch stared at them. "If we kill him, we might lose Bramblestar forever."

"Nonsense!" Mousewhisker's pelt ruffled. "He just needs a chance to get his body back. He'll never do it as long as Ashfur is living in it."

"You don't know that!" Birchfall padded to Squirrelflight's side. "Would you really take this risk and *kill* Bramblestar?"

Jayfeather whisked his tail. "Arguing won't solve the problem," he mewed. "The Sisters have arrived. Before we make a decision, we should consult them."

Lionblaze's eyes narrowed to slits. He glanced at his Clanmates, his gaze stopping when it reached his brother. "If you want to put your faith in a bunch of rogues, go ahead. I want nothing to do with it." He stalked toward the warriors' den. "When you're ready to do what must be done, you know where to find me." Pelt twitching, he ducked inside.

Bristlefrost fluffed out her fur as disappointment chilled her. She'd felt so sure that news of the Sisters' arrival would help. Instead, Lionblaze had stormed away, leaving the clearing eerily empty. She glanced at Squirrelflight. The Thunderclan leader seemed suddenly very alone.

Squirrelflight lifted her muzzle. "Let's not waste any more time." Her mew was hard. "I'm going to speak with the Sisters." She began to head toward the entrance.

"Take a patrol with you," Birchfall called after her.

She looked back at him, hesitating for a moment. Then she dipped her head. "Twigbranch." She looked at the gray warrior. "Come with me. Finleap and Alderheart, too."

Bristlefrost's heart quickened. "Can I come?"

Squirrelflight blinked at her. "You must be tired after your journey. Why would you want to go all the way back to Sky-Clan's camp now?"

The truth blazed across Bristlefrost's mind in an instant. *Rootspring will be there.* But she pushed the thought away. "I traveled a long way to find the Sisters. I'd like to see it through."

Squirrelflight paused, as if considering Bristlefrost's words. "Okay," she said finally, heading for the entrance. "Then let's go."

Bristlefrost followed the patrol as it pushed through the ferns hiding the entrance to the SkyClan camp. The damp fronds brushed her pelt. In the moonlight, which silvered the clearing beyond, she could see Snow and Sunrise sitting with Hawk between them. The other Sisters waited in the shadows while SkyClan's warriors hung back, their ears twitching as they glanced uneasily at their new campmates.

Leafstar crossed the camp and greeted Squirrelflight. "I'm glad you came." She glanced at Snow and the others. "The sooner we get this done the better." Bristlefrost guessed from her ruffled pelt that the SkyClan leader wasn't comfortable having so many strangers in her camp. "I've sent out messengers. Tigerstar, Mistystar, and Harestar should be here before long."

Bristlefrost's paws pricked. She was surprised Leafstar had acted so quickly in assembling the Clan leaders. The Sisters must be tired after their journey. Clearly Leafstar couldn't wait another moment to find out if they had the answers the Clans needed.

She scanned the camp. There was no sign of Spotfur. The queen must already have headed home. Rootspring was standing beside Frecklewish and Tree on the other side of the clearing. She blinked a greeting, longing to join him, but how could she when their Clanmates were watching? She glanced guiltily at Twigbranch and Alderheart as Squirrelflight padded forward to greet Snow.

The Thunderclan leader dipped her head as she reached the white she-cat. "Thank you for coming."

"You look tired," Snow told her.

Squirrelflight's eyes glistened with emotion, but she blinked it away. "A lot has happened since we last met."

As she spoke, ferns rustled at the entrance. Tigerstar barged through, his eyes narrowing as he saw the Sisters. Bristlefrost tensed. Tigerstar had been so hostile to the Sisters the last time the Clans had dealt with them. Would he cause trouble now that they were here? Puddleshine, Dovewing, and Tawnypelt followed him into the camp, and Squirrelflight greeted the patrol with a nod.

Tigerstar glanced dismissively at Snow and Sunrise. "Can they help us?" he asked Squirrelflight.

"Why not ask them yourself?" Squirrelflight narrowed her eyes.

Sunrise padded between them. "I know Tigerstar well

enough not to expect courtesy." Her whiskers twitched with amusement. Then her gaze grew solemn. "In answer to his question, I'm not sure we can help. There is a strange energy here." She exchanged looks with Hawk, who nodded.

"It feels like something odd is happening," she murmured. "It could be dangerous."

Dangerous? Fear wormed in Bristlefrost's belly. Could the Sisters really tell that just by standing here? She looked at the shadows between the dens, forcing her fur to stay flat. As the ferns rustled again, she stiffened and jerked her muzzle toward the entrance, relieved when she saw Mistystar lead Willowshine and Shimmerpelt into the SkyClan camp.

"Harestar is on his way," the RiverClan leader announced as she crossed the camp to join Tigerstar. "We saw him on the trail behind us."

"Good." Sunrise's gaze flitted around the clearing. "We can begin the ceremony as soon as he arrives."

Tigerstar narrowed his eyes. "Will you be able to find Bramblestar?"

"I don't know," Snow answered. "But there are many spirits around the lake. We can bring them here."

Tigerstar sniffed. "We don't need every spirit," he mewed. "Just Bramblestar."

"Aren't you looking for your ancestors too?" Sunrise tipped her head to one side.

"Let's start with the living." Tigerstar shifted his paws. "We can worry about the dead later."

Bristlefrost blinked at the ShadowClan leader. Had he finally been convinced it was still possible to save Bramble-star, even though Ashfur had stolen his body? She closed her eyes, hoping it was true.

As she opened them, she saw Sunrise glance expectantly at the camp entrance. "We should wait for Harestar. He will be here in a moment," the Sister mewed.

Can she hear the WindClan patrol? Bristlefrost pricked her ears but could hear nothing beyond the shifting of the gathered cats and the breeze rustling the bushes.

Sunrise swished her tail. "We will need the help of a Clan cat." She looked calmly around the clearing, her gaze stopping as it reached Rootspring.

Bristlefrost saw him stiffen, his eyes growing wide as Sunrise beckoned him forward with a flick of her nose. "Stand beside me," she told him.

As he crossed the dew-drenched grass, Bristlefrost's heart ached with sympathy. He clearly wanted to do his best to help, but she could see from the prickling of the fur along his spine that he was nervous as Sunrise waved Squirrelflight and Leaf-star out of the clearing with her tail, then nosed Tigerstar and Leafstar away as well.

She guided Rootspring to the center and stood beside him as the Sisters padded from the shadows and formed a circle around him. "We can begin as soon as Harestar arrives," she mewed softly.

Bristlefrost's breath quickened as Rootspring blinked at her. His eyes shimmered with fear. She tried to hide her own and blinked back at him reassuringly before the Sisters pressed in front of her, blocking her view. Would they really be able to summon spirits here? She moved closer to Twigbranch, her mouth suddenly dry as, behind her, the ferns rustled. The WindClan patrol had arrived.

CHAPTER 17

Rootspring's throat tightened as he watched Harestar lead Crowfeather, Breezepelt, and Kestrelflight into the SkyClan
camp. The Sisters bunched tighter together, closing the circle
around him until he could barely see the warriors who had
come to witness their ceremony. He could hear Tigerstar and
Squirrelflight greet the WindClan leader, but the wind was
rising, swishing through the branches that overhung the camp
so that he couldn't make out their words.

He glanced toward Tree, but his father was hidden with
the rest of his Clanmates behind the Sisters. He could still
feel the warmth of Tree's breath on his shoulder where he had
touched it with his muzzle, wishing him luck as Sunrise had
beckoned him to the middle of the clearing.

Rootspring wished he could still see Bristlefrost. He needed
her reassurance. His heart quickened as he saw her peek over
the top of Moon's head, her eyes round and beseeching. Was
she willing him to be brave? He blinked at her gratefully,
wishing she could be inside the circle with him. Just thinking
about it helped him steady his breath.

Sunrise crouched beside him, and the Sisters began to mew,

their voices merging into a soft ululation. As their calls rose into song, Rootspring became aware of the grass beneath his paws. He sensed energy flowing from his claws, snaking like roots into the earth. Around him, the Sisters' mewing grew louder, strengthening until it became a yowl. This was different from the song they'd sung for Spotfur's kits. Their cry was insistent, demanding; it seemed to melt into a single voice as they began to chant.

"Spirits of the forests, spirits of the hills, spirits of the wind and the water. Show yourselves."

Rootspring felt a sensation, like a wind ruffling his fur from the inside. As the Sisters carried on chanting, raising their voices again, he closed his eyes, pressing his paws harder against the earth to stop them trembling, aware only of the song and the exhilaration swelling in his chest. He felt like he could hardly breathe. Then the song stopped. Rootspring opened his eyes, his fur bristling. He saw ghosts all around him. They filled the clearing, crowding the camp, their translucent pelts just visible in the moonlight. Rootspring saw the Sisters shift uneasily. He stiffened as he saw their gazes widen. Something was wrong. His belly hollowed with dread as he recognized fear burning in the Sisters' eyes.

A new moaning drifted over the gathered cats, and Rootspring realized that it was coming from the spirits. He heard Tree wail too, from the edge of the clearing.

Terror edged his father's voice. "What have we done?"

"What's wrong?" Leafstar cried, turning an anxious circle.

"They're everywhere," Tree told her. "They're . . ." His mew faded, as though whipped away by a storm.

Rootspring knew why his father sounded so afraid. The spirits weren't like the ghosts he'd seen before. There was nothing peaceful in the way they stared at the living cats. They crouched against the earth, twisted like snakes, their fur spiked as they looked around them. Lips drawn back, they hissed, their eyes as black as holes. *They're in pain.* Rootspring shrank as fear ran icy claws along his spine. A white-and-orange tom met his gaze, eyes narrowed to agonized slits. *Stemleaf!* Rootspring swallowed back terror as, through bared teeth, a yowl seemed to tear itself from Stemleaf's throat. It echoed around the camp, more tortured than the scream of dying prey.

Rootspring stared urgently into Stemleaf's eyes. "What can I do?" he asked the Thunderclan warrior. He longed to help him as the other ghosts began to hiss, their pain hardening into rage.

Stemleaf stared at Rootspring, accusation burning in his eyes. Stiffening in fear, Rootspring pressed against Sunrise. She was trembling. He tore his gaze from Stemleaf's to look at the yellow she-cat. Horror darkened her eyes as she stared at the ghosts. Around her, the Sisters' pelts stood on end. *They've never seen this before.* Rootspring felt sick with dread. What was happening?

Around the camp, the Clan cats glanced nervously at one another.

Squirrelflight pushed her way between the Sisters. "Is

he here?" She looked desperately around the clearing. "Is Bramblestar here?"

Rootspring shook his head. "Not yet!"

Scanning the camp, he recognized Spiresight. The spirit had led him to Shadowsight when the young medicine cat had been injured and left for dead in the ravine. "Who are all these cats?" he called to the yellow-eyed tom. "Why are they in so much pain?"

Spiresight fixed him with a silent stare that seemed to beg him to understand.

"How can I help them?" Rootspring yowled. There had to be a way to end their suffering.

He strained to hear as Spiresight opened his mouth, but no words came from the yellow-eyed tom, only a piercing wail that spoke of pain Rootspring couldn't imagine.

Panic flooded his thoughts until he froze, too scared to move. Something evil was happening to these spirits. He began to tremble, a yowl of anguish rising in his throat. He tried to swallow it back, but it tore out of him, joining the anguished wails of the spirit cats.

Pale gray fur moved at the edge of his vision. Bristlefrost was trying to break through the Sisters' circle, pushing her way between Moon and Sunshine. "Let me through!" she wailed.

Moon pushed her away. "Stay back," she warned. "There's something wrong here." She was watching the ghosts. Some crouched like foxes preparing to attack; others bared their teeth in snarls, lunging forward a step, then retreating, as if trying to make invisible enemies run away. "They want to hurt us."

Growls rippled through the air. Hawkwing dropped into a battle stance, while Shimmerpelt lifted her hackles defensively. They looked warily around the camp, clearly scanning the shadows for an enemy they couldn't see.

Sunrise shifted beside Rootspring. "We must stop this!" She nodded to the other Sisters. "Send them back."

"No!" Alarm shrilled through Rootspring's pelt. "Bramblestar isn't here yet!" Squirrelflight was staring at him, hope fading in her desperate gaze.

But the Sisters had begun a new chant. "Spirits of the forest, leave us. Return to the hills and valleys."

"Not yet!" Rootspring darted forward, weaving his way between the spirits. He looked from one to the other. "Have you seen Bramblestar?" He wasn't sure they'd even understand. Some of these were cats he'd never seen before. He stopped in front of Stemleaf. "Have you seen him?" he begged.

Stemleaf stared back, his eyes wild with pain.

"Bramblestar!" Rootspring lifted his mew above the chanting. "Where are you?" He froze when he saw a figure at the edge of the circle. A tom, his translucent gray pelt fluffed out with pleasure, was watching the spirits. No pain showed in his eyes, only satisfaction as he gazed at the suffering cats. Rootspring's blood ran cold, as he realized which cat the dark warrior must be. *Ashfur!*

The Sisters kept chanting, and the rest of the spirits began to fade. Rootspring spun around. "Wait!" They couldn't end it now. Panic flared in his pelt as, one by one, the spirits melted into the moonlight and disappeared. Ashfur's eyes glittered for a moment before he, too, blinked out of view like a dying star, and the camp was suddenly empty of ghosts.

The Sisters fell silent, staring at one another, as though they could hardly believe what they'd seen. Slumping with exhaustion, they let the circle break.

Bristlefrost pushed her way through and rushed to Rootspring's side. "Are you okay?"

He realized he could hardly breathe. His fur still tingled as though a wind were roaring through him; the still air around him seemed to pulse with the echo of their presence. "They're still here," he breathed.

"Who?" Bristlefrost blinked at him. "The spirits? Were there a lot of them? Was Bramblestar with them?"

He couldn't answer. It would crush her. He wondered for a moment how she hadn't sensed so many cats crowding the clearing. Their suffering was so intense he could still feel it, like mist in the air, reaching through his fur and making him cold. "I don't think it was meant to happen like that," he mewed shakily.

Sunrise padded toward him, her ears twitching nervously. "I've never seen anything like it before," she murmured. "The spirits were angry."

Snow's eyes were wide. "It was like they wanted to attack us."

Moon and Tempest nodded.

Hawk stared at Snow. "Why are they in so much pain?" Outrage edged her mew.

Snow frowned. "I don't know, but they meant us harm."

Tempest flicked her tail. "I saw dead leaves falling from the trees."

Rootspring glanced around the clearing. There were no dead leaves lying on the grass now. Had the tabby she-cat imagined it?

Snow met his gaze. "Dead leaves mean bad spirits are around."

He swallowed. There had certainly been one bad spirit in the SkyClan camp tonight. "I think I saw Ashfur."

"What?" Tigerstar shouldered his way past Tempest as Leafstar crossed the clearing, Hawkwing at her heels. Mistystar, Squirrelflight, and Harestar hurried to join them. The Clan leaders looked bewildered; Rootspring had to remind himself that they hadn't seen the spirits or heard their wails.

He looked at Tigerstar. "He was right there." He nodded to the patch of grass where Ashfur had stood, watching the other spirits with cruel amusement.

Mistystar's pelt ruffled. "Could Ashfur have left Bramblestar's body?"

"He's done it before," Tigerstar told her. "Shadowsight's seen him do it."

Alderheart padded forward, pricking his ears. "That was in a vision."

"That doesn't mean it didn't happen," Tigerstar mewed grimly.

Rootspring narrowed his eyes. "What happened to

Bramblestar's body when Ashfur left it?" How could it live with no spirit inside?

"He said it looked like it was sleeping." Tigerstar paused, his gaze darkening. "Ashfur's been sleeping a lot lately."

Alderheart shifted his paws. "Do you think his spirit has been leaving the ShadowClan camp without us realizing?"

Rootspring's ears twitched. "I'm pretty sure it left his body to be here tonight." A thought struck him. "Perhaps *he's* the reason why the other spirits were suffering."

The Clan cats glanced nervously at one another.

Tigerstar frowned. "The Sisters seem to have given us more questions than answers."

Squirrelflight was trembling. "Did you see Bramblestar?"

Rootspring looked at her guiltily. "No."

As her gaze clouded, Alderheart added quickly, "If there were as many spirits as Rootspring says, perhaps Bramblestar was hard to spot."

Rootspring didn't correct him. He didn't want to steal Squirrelflight's last hope.

Tigerstar grunted. "He would have made himself known if he'd come."

Sunrise met the ShadowClan leader's gaze. "Perhaps something stopped him from coming."

Squirrelflight's eyes flashed with hope. "You mean he might still be around."

"Something very strange is happening here," Sunrise mewed slowly. "It might be better for you to move on from this place."

"Leave?" Leafstar's pelt bristled across her shoulders. "Sky-Clan traveled a long way to be here, fought many battles to establish our territory. Cats *died*. . . . No spirit is going to drive us away from the lake."

Tigerstar gave a nod, showing his teeth. "If spirits want the Clans' territory, they'll have to fight us for it."

Sunrise gazed at the two leaders solemnly. "That's what I'm afraid of."

As she spoke, rain began to batter the clearing. Great drops pounded around them as the clouds opened and wind ripped at the trees.

Leafstar narrowed her eyes against the storm. "This weather is too bad to travel in," she told the other leaders. "We can find room in our dens for you all."

Rootspring glanced at the crowded clearing. It had been hard enough to find nests for the Sisters. How would they find room for the rest of the Clan cats?

"RiverClan cats aren't afraid of getting wet," Mistystar told Leafstar, dipping her head. "We'll head home."

"So will we." Tigerstar had fluffed out his fur against the rain. "ShadowClan has the answer we came for."

Harestar's pelt was already slicked against his lithe frame. "WindClan has no wish to stay here."

Squirrelflight was gazing imploringly at Snow. "I'd like to stay." She clearly hadn't given up hope that the Sisters could reach Bramblestar. Rootspring felt a pang of pity for her, but his heart was beating eagerly. If Squirrelflight stayed, it meant Bristlefrost would stay too.

Sunrise tucked her paws beneath her as the rain hardened. "The Clans have a serious problem here." She looked earnestly at Leafstar. "We should stay close for a while. You might need us."

Leafstar dipped her head. "Thank you."

"In the morning, we'll make a camp nearby," Snow told her. "We know this territory well. There's a copse in the next valley where we can build temporary dens."

Tigerstar frowned. "Don't get too comfortable," he warned. "This is Clan land now."

Snow eyed him sharply. "If you want to keep it that way, you might need us."

"Can you fight spirits as well as see them?" Tigerstar mewed sourly.

"When spirits are affected by the sort of bad energy we felt here tonight," Snow warned, "they can take on physical form." She looked around at the Clan leaders. "And if they do, you'll need all the help you can get."

Rootspring stiffened. Was that true? He glanced at Tree, who had been hanging back, his pelt ruffled and dripping. Elsewhere, he noticed Tawnypelt sharing an anxious look with Mistystar, which made him wonder what horrible memories the two older cats shared.

Tree padded forward as Rootspring caught his eye. "We should get every cat out of this storm," he mewed.

Leafstar nodded. "Show the Sisters to their dens," she told him.

Tree dipped his head, signaling to the Sisters with a flick

of his tail before guiding them toward a temporary den woven between two bushes. Snow looked back at Squirrelflight, her eyes round with worry, then disappeared inside with the others.

Harestar was already leading his patrol to the entrance, Mistystar at his tail.

Tigerstar began to follow, hesitating as the others pushed their way through the fern entrance. He glanced back at Squirrelflight. "We'll meet soon to discuss what happens to Ashfur now." Rootspring pressed back a shiver. Tigerstar's words were ominous. Squirrelflight returned the Shadow-Clan leader's gaze nervously. "That was the purpose of this ceremony, wasn't it?" Tigerstar pressed. "To find out if Bramblestar could be reached. But if we can't reach him, and the spirits of our Clanmates are suffering because of Ashfur, we have to do something."

Rootspring guessed what Tigerstar meant by *something*. He was ready to kill Bramblestar's body.

Squirrelflight looked away without responding.

Leafstar dipped her head to the ShadowClan leader. "Let's discuss it once we've questioned Ashfur about what happened here."

Tigerstar's gaze darkened. He turned and padded out of the camp.

Hawkwing's pelt ruffled as he watched the ShadowClan patrol go. "We all know he's already made up his mind."

"I'm sorry." Leafstar blinked at Squirrelflight. "I know this isn't what you hoped for."

"No." The Thunderclan leader sat down, hunching her shoulders against the rain. Rootspring's heart ached with pity as she lifted her gaze to meet his. "Thanks for trying." Her mew was barely a whisper. "I wish you'd found him, but I know you did your best."

Around the camp, SkyClan began to melt away, taking shelter from the storm. Needleclaw caught Rootspring's eye as she followed her Clanmates toward the warriors' den. As the clearing emptied, she beckoned him to follow with a flick of her tail, but he ignored her. He hadn't finished here.

Squirrelflight stared at her paws. "I won't be able to stop them from killing him now," she mewed bleakly.

"Let's not get ahead of ourselves," Leafstar put in. "The final decision hasn't been made yet. We need to find out what Ashfur was doing here and whether he's responsible for what's happening to the spirits."

Squirrelflight lifted her head wearily. "How? There's no cat left to guide us."

Leafstar began to direct her toward a bracken den. "You should rest." She looked hopefully at Frecklewish, who lingered at the edge of the clearing. "Is there room in the medicine den for Squirrelflight and her patrol?"

"We can make room," Frecklewish told her.

Wordlessly, Squirrelflight got to her paws and headed after the SkyClan medicine cat. Alderheart followed with Finleap and Twigbranch at his tail, but Bristlefrost hesitated, watching her Clanmates disappear into the den before turning her gaze back to Rootspring.

He blinked at her. Leafstar and Hawkwing were heading for the leader's den. He guessed they needed to discuss what their next move should be. As they ducked inside, Rootspring was sharply aware that he and Bristlefrost were alone in the clearing. Overhead, the trees rocked in the wind. Rain thrummed against his pelt, but he hardly noticed it. He was with Bristlefrost. He met her gaze. "I'm sorry," he mewed. "I wish I'd seen Bramblestar. I know how much it meant to you."

"Sorry?" She looked surprised. Shaking rain from her whiskers, she lapped his cheek quickly. "You've got nothing to be sorry for. You were amazing tonight. I don't know what you saw, but you looked terrified. You saw it through, though. You're the bravest cat I know." Sitting back on her haunches, she looked at him, her eyes shining through the rain. "I'm proud of you."

Warmth rushed beneath his fur. His heart seemed ready to burst. Memories of the suffering spirits burned in his thoughts, but he suddenly felt less frightened of them. He was strong enough to face a forest full of spirits as long as Bristlefrost was with him.

CHAPTER 18

♣

Shadowsight crouched in the bramble enclosure, grateful that Ashfur was sleeping. The dark warrior lay between the roots of the hollow tree, light dappling his stolen tabby pelt. Last night's storm had passed, and sunshine was filtering between the pines. Ashfur's sleep was deep; he hadn't woken as Shadowsight treated his injuries, applying fresh poultices to the most serious wounds and making sure the rest were clean and beginning to heal. He'd worried at first that something must be wrong, but Ashfur's pelt wasn't hot and his breathing was regular. *He must just be exhausted after Lionblaze's attack.*

Shadowsight had no wish to wake him. Ashfur would only needle him about not being a medicine cat anymore, or about only being tolerated by his Clan only because Tigerstar was the leader. *Did your father send you here?* His pelt itched with irritation as he remembered the warrior's words. *Of course he did!* If he had a choice, Shadowsight wouldn't come near this place. And yet he was here, sitting beside Ashfur as he slept, one eye on Lizardtail and Mallownose as they guarded the entrance. As much as he disliked Ashfur, he couldn't risk letting any cat hurt him.

They're going to kill me. . . . If I die, you'll never get Bramblestar back.

Ashfur's words still rang in his head. The Clans needed him alive. And since Lionblaze's attack, he didn't trust any cat—even his guards—not to finish what the Thunderclan deputy had started.

Urgent mews in the clearing outside made Shadowsight stiffen. He crossed the enclosure and peered through the entrance. Alderheart, Frecklewish, and Hawkwing were talking to Tigerstar, their voices hushed. Why had they come to the ShadowClan camp? Shadowsight's heart quickened. Had something happened? He pricked his ears, trying to hear what they were saying, but they kept their voices low. Shadowsight ducked behind a tree as Alderheart glanced at the enclosure. He didn't want to be seen eavesdropping. He backed away as he heard paw steps drawing close.

Lizardtail and Mallownose moved aside as Tigerstar led Alderheart and the SkyClan cats into the enclosure. The RiverClan warriors' eyes were glittering with interest, but they didn't speak as Tigerstar padded past.

Shadowsight shifted uneasily as his father stared at Ashfur.

"How long has he been asleep?" He jerked his muzzle toward Shadowsight.

"All morning." Shadowsight frowned. Why did Tigerstar look so worried?

Alderheart padded past them and sniffed warily at the dark warrior's pelt. Frecklewish hung back. Hawkwing narrowed his eyes.

"Is something wrong?" Shadowsight blinked at them, still wondering why they'd come.

Tigerstar met his gaze. "The Sisters held a ceremony last night."

Shadowsight's fur pricked along his spine. *That's where you went.* He'd wondered why his father had slipped out of camp so late with Puddleshine, Dovewing, and Tawnypelt, but he'd grown so used to being left out now that he hadn't even tried to question Puddleshine before he'd left the medicine den this morning. His heart quickened. "Did they find Bramblestar?"

"No." Tigerstar exchanged glances with Puddleshine.

Alderheart stepped back from Ashfur. "There were other spirits."

Was that fear edging his mew? "Other spirits?" Shadowsight echoed.

Alderheart faced him. "Only Rootspring, Tree, and the Sisters could see them, but it sounded like the spirits weren't exactly friendly."

"Rootspring seemed to think they were suffering," Frecklewish mewed.

"The Sisters said they looked angry," Alderheart added.

Shadowsight's mouth grew dry. "Were they the spirits of dead warriors?" Why would warriors be angry with the Clans?

Frecklewish shivered. "There were warriors among them." Her gaze slid to Ashfur, who was still sound asleep. "*He* was with them, and he wasn't suffering."

Shadowsight's eyes widened. "But he was here. I checked

his wounds at moonhigh and he was—"

"Sleeping?" Tigerstar's mew was ominous.

"Yes."

Tigerstar leaned closer. "Like he's sleeping now?"

Shadowsight swallowed. "Yes." Was his father trying to say that Ashfur had somehow left the ShadowClan camp to join the Sisters' ceremony? He glanced at Ashfur, wondering afresh at the peculiar stillness of the dark warrior's body. Sleeping cats moved: Their pelts rippled; their tails twitched from time to time. His paws felt suddenly heavy as he remembered how stiff Bramblestar's body had looked when he'd seen Ashfur's spirit rise from it in the ThunderClan leader's den. *He looks like that now.*

Panic sparked in his chest as the truth began to dawn on him.

"Wake up!" Tigerstar suddenly darted toward Ashfur and hooked his scruff with his claws. He lifted the warrior and shook him.

Ashfur blinked open his eyes, stiffening for a moment as he saw Tigerstar, then letting himself fall limp. He slumped to the ground as Tigerstar let go, his gaze catching Shadowsight's. It glittered with meaning. *See?* Shadowsight stepped back as he guessed the warrior's thoughts. *I told you they're going to kill me.*

"Get up!" Tigerstar snarled, pacing in front of Ashfur.

Alderheart and Frecklewish watched without speaking.

Hawkwing's eyes narrowed with interest. "We've come to ask you a few questions."

Ashfur pushed himself to his paws and looked at the warriors, his lip curling. "You can ask me anything you like. I don't have to answer."

"Do you really believe that?" Tigerstar flexed his claws.

Shadowsight's breath caught in his throat. What was Tigerstar planning to do to Ashfur? He pleaded silently with the dark warrior. *Please, just tell him what he wants to know.*

Frecklewish padded closer. "Have you left the ShadowClan camp?"

Ashfur's eyes widened. "How could I?" He nodded toward Mallownose and Lizardtail. "I've been under guard the whole time."

A growl rolled in Tigerstar's throat. "We're not stupid," he hissed. "We know you can leave Bramblestar's body if you wish."

"Really?" Ashfur looked unconvinced. "If I could do that, why would I stay here, as a prisoner?" He glanced innocently around the bramble enclosure.

Tigerstar thrust his muzzle close to Ashfur's. "Rootspring and the Sisters say they saw you in SkyClan's camp with the other spirits."

Ashfur didn't flinch as Tigerstar's growl hardened. "And you believe them?"

Hawkwing's ears flattened. "Rootspring wouldn't lie."

Ashfur tipped his head to one side. "The Sisters are his kin, aren't they? They might have put him up to it."

"Rootspring is a loyal SkyClan warrior!" Hawkwing snarled.

Tigerstar glared at Ashfur. "Why would the Sisters lie to us?"

Ashfur's eyes widened. "Didn't you drive them from their camp?"

Frecklewish's ears twitched defensively. "They hold no grudge."

"And you killed their leader," Ashfur pressed. "Moonlight, right? That was her name?"

"It was Moonlight who persuaded the Sisters to help us," Hawkwing snapped.

"Did Rootspring tell you that?" Ashfur asked calmly.

"Yes! And I believe him." Hawkwing's tail flicked ominously.

Ashfur eyed the SkyClan deputy. "Did anyone else see her?"

"The Sisters saw her!" Frecklewish hissed.

Amusement twitched in Ashfur's whiskers. "Of course they did." He slid past Tigerstar and stopped a muzzle-length from Frecklewish. "Have *you* seen any of these spirits they claim to have seen? Have any of the medicine cats seen them?"

Frecklewish held her ground. "We don't have the same powers as the Sisters."

"So you trust a group of cats you hardly know when they say they can see something the Clans can't?" Ashfur's eyes shone with satisfaction. "What do you even know about them except that you stole their land? What do you know about their kin?" He didn't wait for an answer. "Tree isn't a real warrior, is he? He threatens to leave the Clans at the first sign of trouble. And now his son is making up stories about ghosts—stories that set one Clan against another and send you running to outsiders for help."

Shadowsight stared in alarm at Ashfur. Why was he trying to stir up trouble even now?

Ashfur went on. "Who fetched the Sisters back? A warrior with their blood running beneath his pelt. And what do they do when they get here? Stir all of you up with stories of spirits no other warrior can see."

A growl rumbled in Tigerstar's throat, but Ashfur hadn't finished.

"Do you really believe Rootspring's on your side?" Hawkwing's fur bristled as the dark warrior leaned closer to Frecklewish. "Do you?"

With a hiss, Hawkwing leaped at Ashfur, raking claws across his muzzle. "How dare you suggest that my kin can't be trusted!" He lashed out again at Ashfur, clawing his cheek. "Rootspring has earned his place as a SkyClan warrior!"

Ashfur backed away, crouching low, his gaze flitting around the Clan cats. No fear showed in his eyes. Shadowsight could see he was thinking. Why did the mouse-brain insist on goading these cats when they clearly wanted to hurt him?

Ashfur's gaze settled on Hawkwing. "Perhaps Violetshine should have chosen a better mate." He curled his lip. "Instead of a stray the Clans took in. At least then you'd be able to trust your own flesh and blood."

Rage flared in Hawkwing's eyes. He lunged at Ashfur and curled his claws into the dark warrior's fur. Lifting him like prey, he flung him against the hollow tree. Ashfur thumped against the bark and slithered to the ground as Hawkwing reared for another attack.

"Don't hurt him!" Shadowsight darted forward, but Tigerstar pushed in front of him. Relief swamped Shadowsight. The ShadowClan leader would stop Hawkwing from hurting Ashfur. Then Shadowsight's breath caught in his throat; his father's claws were unsheathed; anger twisted his face. Shadowsight froze. "What are you doing?" He stared in horror as his father lunged at Ashfur.

Panicked, he turned to plead with the others. "You have to stop them!" But Frecklewish and Alderheart didn't move. Mallownose and Lizardtail watched from the entrance. They were going to let this happen. And Ashfur wasn't even going to defend himself.

The earth seemed to tremble beneath Shadowsight's paws as his father sank his teeth into Ashfur's neck. Ashfur writhed beneath him, yowling. Shadowsight recoiled as the smell of blood filled the air.

Tigerstar flung Ashfur away and lashed out with his forepaw, striking the dark warrior's cheek. Ashfur reeled, staggering into the path of Hawkwing, who swiped a claw at his other cheek.

"Tell us if you've left this camp!" Tigerstar yowled.

Ashfur grunted, blood running from his face. "Is this the code you follow?"

"Tell us!" Tigerstar raked his claws across Ashfur's ears.

Ashfur backed away as Hawkwing swung another blow at the top of his head.

"What have you been doing while Bramblestar's body has been sleeping here?" Tigerstar demanded.

Ashfur gazed at him scornfully. "Claws can't help you now."

Eyes flaring with rage, Tigerstar raked his muzzle again, and Ashfur slumped beneath his paws.

"Enough!" Shadowsight leaped forward. He didn't care what his Clan thought. He couldn't let this happen. He ducked in front of his father and the SkyClan deputy. "He's had enough."

Tigerstar froze, his paw in midair, and stared blankly at Shadowsight.

Shadowsight flinched but held his gaze. "You mustn't do this."

The rage clouding Tigerstar's eyes died away. He staggered back, his hackles falling, while Hawkwing grew still.

Ashfur lay unmoving. Was he dead? Shadowsight pressed his ear to the warrior's chest. He was relieved to feel a heartbeat. But it was weak, and blood matted his fur. "I need herbs—" He gasped as claws hooked his scruff and jerked him backward.

"What are you doing?" Tigerstar glared at him.

Shadowsight blinked in disbelief. "I have to help him." Was Tigerstar going to let Ashfur die? "You told me I had to take care of him, remember?" Shadowsight searched his father's gaze. He hardly recognized the warrior staring coldly back. "You ordered me to protect him because no other cat would."

Tigerstar didn't move.

Anger flared in Shadowsight's belly. "I'm a medicine cat,

no matter what you say! I *have* to help."

He felt his father's claws unhook from his scruff. "You're right," Tigerstar growled hoarsely, dipping his head. "Take care of him." He turned away, stalking out of the enclosure and signaling with a flick of his tail for the others to follow.

Alone with Ashfur once more, Shadowsight ducked down beside him. Claw marks on his cheeks and muzzle oozed blood. One of his ears was ripped, and wounds showed on his flank where chunks of fur had been ripped out. Shadowsight pressed his ear to Ashfur's flank again. The dark warrior's breath came in gasps. *Don't die.* Shadowsight hopped over him and slid into the hollow tree, relieved when he saw cobwebs caught in the rotting wood. He scooped out pawful after pawful and carried them outside, where he began to press them into the deepest wounds on Ashfur's cheek.

He stiffened as Ashfur's eyes flickered open.

The dark warrior stared at him helplessly. "I told you," he rasped. "They're going to kill me."

Shadowsight swallowed. "He just lost control, that's all."

Blood bubbled on Ashfur's lips. "If Tigerstar can't control himself, how can he control his Clan?" His gaze fluttered weakly toward the enclosure entrance. Flaxfoot and Tawnypelt were watching through the gap. He looked back to Shadowsight, malice flickering in his eyes. "If your father doesn't kill me, some other cat will . . . and you'll *never* get Bramblestar back."

Shadowsight's paws shook as he tried to wrap cobwebs around Ashfur's injured ear. He didn't want to think about it.

Bramblestar *had* to come back.

Ashfur shifted his head heavily, wincing as he moved. "But we both know that killing this body won't make a difference," he murmured. "I can't be stopped, no matter whether this body lives or dies."

Don't listen to him. Shadowsight tried to block out Ashfur's words. If he'd refused to listen to this fox-heart from the beginning, none of this would have happened. His thoughts began to whirl. He'd seen hatred for Ashfur in his father's eyes. Like the Clans, Tigerstar had hardened so much that Shadowsight wondered what he might do next. And if they killed Bramblestar's body and Ashfur's spirit lived on . . .

"Only you can keep Bramblestar alive now," Ashfur whispered.

Shut up! Shadowsight closed his eyes, but how could he ignore him when the dark warrior might be right?

CHAPTER 19

❧

Rootspring padded into the camp, relieved to find himself bathed in bright sunshine. The warriors' den had been cramped and stuffy, with extra nests for the Sisters who'd slept there. They were awake now and already in the clearing, sharing tongues with one another. Macgyver and Plumwillow exchanged glances as they picked their way past Moon and Tempest, who were chatting beside the fresh-kill pile. Leafstar sat beside her den, eyeing her guests thoughtfully. Outside the nursery, Dewspring and Nectarsong watched Beekit and Beetle-kit explore a patch of long grass beside the camp wall. The kits' pelts were fluffed with excitement, and Nectarsong and Dewspring followed them with wide, anxious eyes. Rootspring felt a weak tingle of warmth and amusement. This was their first day outside.

Dewspring stiffened as Beekit darted from the grass and nearly crashed into Snow, who was washing at the edge of the clearing. "Look out!" He started forward, his pelt bushing as Beekit pulled up just in time. The large white she-cat blinked warmly at the kit, but Dewspring grabbed Beekit by the scruff and carried her quickly away.

Rootspring could hardly believe that the same clearing had been filled with glaring, hissing ghosts last night. He pressed back a shiver as he remembered their angry gazes and anguished wails. Perhaps it had been a dream. He looked around at the Sisters. *No.* The Sisters had seen it too. But he'd been the only one to recognize that it was Ashfur. Why had the dark warrior been there? And why had he seemed to take pleasure in the suffering of the other spirits?

Rootspring shook out his pelt and tried to focus on the present. He wondered if Hawkwing, Alderheart, and Frecklewish had questioned Ashfur yet. They'd left before dawn, promising to return with news. Another thought was tugging at him too. Bristlefrost had spent the night in the medicine den. Was she still asleep? He looked for a glimpse of her pale gray pelt, but she was nowhere to be seen. His paws tingled with anticipation. If they lived in the same Clan all the time, they could hunt together and eat together every day. *Or wake up in the same nest . . .*

Sunrise interrupted his wishful thoughts, padding to meet him. She blinked an affectionate greeting. "You did well last night," she told him.

"Thanks." He met her gaze. "But I wish we could have found out why the spirits were so unhappy."

"Why not ask them next time you see them?"

"Next time?" His tail twitched nervously. "Are you going to summon them again?"

"You don't need us to summon them." Her mew was soft. "You have the gift."

"I don't think I could manage so many spirits alone," he mewed.

"Of course you can," Sunrise told him. "The power is in you. You just need to learn to strengthen it, that's all."

Rootspring wasn't sure that he wanted to. It sounded scary. But if the Clans were in danger from the spirits, he might need to. "How do I strengthen a power I don't understand?" he asked Sunrise.

"Until now, spirits have found you, right?" Sunrise tipped her head to one side.

Rootspring nodded. "Right. Well, I've summoned Bramblestar on purpose before, but that was . . . hard."

"Okay." Sunrise sat down. "If you need to reach out to a spirit, it helps to have something of theirs. A piece of fur, or bedding they've slept in."

Rootspring's ears twitched uncertainly as she went on. Was it really so simple?

"Hold it in your paws," she told him. "And focus on the cat you wish to see. And use the earth."

"How?" He wondered suddenly if Tree had learned these skills. Or had he left the Sisters too soon?

"Lie down like this." Sunrise pressed her belly into the damp grass. "So the earth can feel your heartbeat. Do it every day so it can get to know you. Each time you do, your connection will deepen."

Rootspring copied her, his pelt prickling self-consciously. He noticed Nectarsong's gaze flash toward him but kept his focus on Sunrise. He'd have to practice this somewhere out of the camp. His Clanmates thought he was weird enough already. Dew seeped through his belly fur as he crouched low. "Okay."

"Feel your heart press against the earth with each breath," Sunrise told him.

Rootspring focused on his chest, aware now of his heart thumping, sensing the earth reverberating with each beat. He felt suddenly aware of every hair on his pelt, and as he breathed, he could feel his heartbeat slow as though it was falling into rhythm with something only it could hear.

"Do you sense it?" Sunrise whispered.

Rootspring nodded slowly. "I think so." He hoped he could. Perhaps he was imagining it.

Sunrise sat up. "That's all you have to do."

He blinked at her and got to his paws. "Will it be enough?"

Sunrise shrugged. "You must open your heart," she mewed. "Let the power flow through you, and trust it to find a way."

"I'll try." Rootspring hoped none of his Clanmates were listening to this conversation.

Sunrise lifted her tail. "It's time for us to go make camp." As the other Sisters began to get to their paws, Squirrelflight padded from the medicine den.

She hurried toward Sunrise. "Could you try to find Bramblestar one more time before you go?"

Sunrise blinked at her. "If he didn't appear last time, there's no reason to think he'll appear now."

Squirrelflight stopped beside her. "But we have to try."

"We won't be far away," Sunrise mewed softly. "If we see

him, we will let you know." She dipped her head. "It was good to see you again. I'm sorry it's in such unhappy circumstances." She nodded to Snow, who began to lead the Sisters toward the camp entrance. Then she padded toward Leafstar. "Thank you for giving us shelter," she told the SkyClan leader. She paused and gazed around the camp. "You've made this place into a fine home."

"Thank you." Leafstar dipped her head.

Sunrise turned and headed for the ferns, calling back over her shoulder: "If you need us, you know where to find us."

Squirrelflight's eyes rounded with disappointment. As she looked away, Sunrise hesitated at the entrance and beckoned Rootspring with a nod. He stiffened. Did she have more advice on using his powers? He hurried toward her, pricking his ears.

"Don't let go of Bristlefrost," Sunrise whispered as he reached her. He followed her gaze as it cut across the camp. Bristlefrost was padding from the medicine den. Rootspring's heart leaped. Her pelt was still ruffled with sleep. As she yawned and looked around the camp, a purr rumbled in Sunrise's throat. "You're in love with her, and she's in love with you."

"That's not true—"

Sunrise cut him off. "It's obvious," she mewed. "I don't understand why you need to lie."

"It's complicated."

Sunrise shrugged. "The Clans seem to make the easiest things difficult." She nosed her way through the ferns. "Take care of each other."

As she disappeared, Rootspring shook out his pelt. How could a Sister ever understand what loyalty meant to a warrior? He realized that Bristlefrost was staring at him. He whisked his tail and hurried toward her. There was no harm in saying good morning. After all, she was a guest of SkyClan. He was only being polite. And yet he wanted to say more than good morning. He had to talk to her before the Thunderclan patrol returned home.

His ears pricked as he passed Squirrelflight and Leafstar.

"There's no choice," Leafstar was telling the Thunderclan leader. "Even you must see that now."

Squirrelflight's mew was tight. "But we don't even know if Ashfur will really—"

Leafstar interrupted her. "It's the best chance we have to get rid of him."

Squirrelflight's pelt twitched. "What if it doesn't work? We'll have killed him for nothing. We know he can leave Bramblestar's body; what's to stop him stealing another one?"

He flattened his ears, not wanting to hear any more. There was nothing he could do in camp about Bramblestar. Right now he had something more important to do. "Come with me," he whispered as he reached Bristlefrost.

Her eyes widened. "Where?"

"Just follow." He padded around the edge of the clearing and slipped behind the warriors' den. Behind it, a gap in the bushes led to a grassy slope. He guided her up it, to where beech trees crowded the top, and padded between them, stopping where they opened onto a wide stretch of meadow. SkyClan's territory stretched before them, bright in the green-leaf sunshine. Flowers flashed among the long grass, which shimmered in the breeze.

Bristlefrost stopped beside him, her eyes round with worry. "Is something wrong?"

"No." He stared at her, his heart skipping a beat. Bristle-frost's fur glowed in the sunshine, and her neat, gray ears twitched eagerly as she waited for him to explain. "Nothing is wrong. Everything is right as long as we're here, together." He took a breath, pressing his paws into the earth for courage. "I love you," he mewed. "And I think you love me. I want to be together."

She didn't move, her gaze fixed on his, unreadable for a moment so that he wondered if he should have spoken.

"I love you," he mewed again, willing her to answer.

"I love you too." Her eyes sparkled. Sunrise had been right. She *did* love him. For a moment he felt he might burst with happiness. Then Bristlefrost's gaze clouded and he felt as though he were falling. His heart skipped a beat.

"But it doesn't matter what we feel." Her eyes glistened with sorrow. "We've been over this. We can't be together."

"It *does* matter what we feel," Rootspring insisted. "It mat-ters more than any rules. The Sisters think the Clan rules are wrong, and I agree. We make each other stronger. We'd be better warriors. Why shouldn't we be together?"

"But how?" Bristlefrost searched his eyes, as if she believed they were hiding an answer.

"We need to make a choice," he told her. "I can join Thunderclan, or you can join SkyClan. As long as we're together, I don't care which."

Bristlefrost held his gaze. "You *do* care. I know you do. You know exactly which of us you think should leave our Clan. You're hoping I will leave Thunderclan."

His tail twitched uncomfortably. He didn't want to admit it, but she was right. "It's only natural that I'd prefer it if you joined SkyClan. My kin are here."

"*My* kin are in Thunderclan," Bristlefrost pointed out.

"But SkyClan is stronger," he pressed. "Stronger than it's ever been. Thunderclan has been torn apart by what happened with Ashfur. Your warriors are leaving. Your leader doesn't even have nine lives. What if Thunderclan never recovers from this?"

"That's not a reason to leave." Bristlefrost sounded angry. "It's a reason to *stay*. Do you really think I could abandon my Clan when it's in trouble? If Bramblestar is really gone and the Clans kill his body, Squirrelflight will be grieving. How can I leave her to hold Thunderclan together all by herself? And I promised Spotfur I'd help raise her kits. You saw how scared she was. She'll need me." She paused, her breath coming quickly. "Don't you see? I *need* to stay in Thunderclan."

He stared at her. He hated that everything she said was true, but he loved with all his heart her desperate loyalty to her Clan.

"So?" She blinked away grief, her gaze seeming to reach so deep into his eyes, Rootspring had to force himself not to tremble. "The question is, would you be willing to leave Sky-Clan to join me?"

Rootspring stared back at her, searching for words. He wanted to say yes. Being with her was more important than anything else. And yet, to turn his back on his kin—Tree and Violetshine and Needleclaw? To walk away from a leader he believed in, and the Clan that had raised him? Words seemed to dry on his tongue. Bristlefrost's stare didn't waver as she waited.

"I'll have to think about it," he mewed quietly. Was he letting her down?

She nodded. "I understand." There was no reproach in her voice. "It's a big decision. Take as much time as you need." She looked away. "We should head back."

"Yes." Guilt jabbed his belly. He wished he could give up everything for her without hesitation. But it was more complex than Sunrise seemed to think. The Sisters thought the warrior code was wrong, but it was impossible for him and Bristlefrost to pretend it wasn't part of who they were. "It's best if we don't go back together." He nodded toward the path they'd followed. "You go that way. I'll use the entrance."

She nodded and headed back down the slope. Rootspring watched her go, his thoughts more tangled than ever. He shook out his pelt. He needed to think. He followed the hilltop and took the path down the valley that led to the camp entrance. As he pushed through the ferns, he smelled Hawkwing's scent. It was fresh. The SkyClan deputy must have returned from questioning Ashfur.

Hawkwing was standing in the clearing. Frecklewish and Alderheart flanked him as the patrol reported to Leafstar and Squirrelflight. Bristlefrost was already in camp, watching from beside the warriors' den.

"He wouldn't tell us if he'd left the ShadowClan camp," Hawkwing mewed. "And he didn't seem scared, even though we could have killed him right there."

Squirrelflight flinched. "Did you really think he would be?" she mewed. "It's not his body. He doesn't care what happens to it."

Leafstar flicked her tail. "It sounds like Ashfur's no use to us now."

Squirrelflight stared at her. "He's keeping Bramblestar's body alive."

"So you keep saying." Leafstar faced the Thunderclan leader. "But that doesn't get us anywhere." She dipped her head formally. "I think it's time your patrol returned home."

Squirrelflight seemed to freeze. "You're right," she mewed stiffly. "Thank you for giving us shelter and allowing the Sisters to hold their ceremony here." She nodded to Alderheart and Twigbranch, then padded toward the fern entrance.

Rootspring stepped aside as she passed, watching Bristlefrost as she hurried after them. She avoided his gaze, but he saw her fur ruffle as she slid past him and followed her Clanmates out of camp. He closed his eyes. Why wasn't this decision easier? He only wanted to be with her. Why couldn't he simply decide to leave SkyClan?

He turned and padded heavily toward the fresh-kill pile.

Tree would understand if he left, surely. What about Violet-shine? His mother might forgive him, but Needleclaw? Would his sister ever speak to him again if he followed Bristlefrost to Thunderclan?

He was so lost in thought, he hardly noticed Beekit and Beetlekit haring toward him. Squeaking with excitement, the two kits darted between his legs. Rootspring blinked in surprise and hopped nimbly out of the way. "Slow down!"

Beekit froze and blinked up at him. "Oops!"

"Sorry!" Beetlekit scrambled to a halt, his short tail fluffed out like a dandelion.

Beekit pricked her ears. "Who are you?"

Rootspring hesitated. Would Dewspring and Nectar-song have told their kits about their Clanmate who could see ghosts? He shifted his paws self-consciously, remembering how, as an apprentice, his denmates had teased him about having Tree as a father. Would these kits call him weird too? *I guess they have to know sometime.* He puffed out his chest. "I'm Rootspring."

Beekit's eyes widened. "Are you the one who brought the Sisters here?"

"You can see ghosts, right?" Beetlekit stared at him.

"Yes." Rootspring braced himself, ready to see fear spark in their eyes or amusement twitch in their whiskers.

Beekit purred excitedly. "That's so cool!"

Rootspring blinked at the white-and-tabby she-kit. "Is it?" He couldn't hide his surprise.

"Totally!" Beetlekit fluffed out his fur. "I wish I could see ghosts. It would be awesome."

Beekit pushed in front of her brother. "Can I be your apprentice?"

Beetlekit nudged her out of the way. "I want to be his apprentice."

"I said it first!" Beekit glared at him.

Beetlekit puffed out his chest. "But I'm older than you."

"No, you're not!"

"Yes, I am!" Beetlekit leaped on his sister and bundled her over. Tumbling across the clearing, they began to play-fight.

Rootspring watched them, happiness washing his pelt. He suddenly realized how far he'd come since the other apprentices had called him names. He'd never imagined he'd become a warrior that kits would *want* as a mentor. Maybe he belonged in SkyClan more than he'd thought. His weird powers were a strength now, something he could use to help his Clan. He gazed around the camp.

Sunlight dappled the clearing. Hawkwing was gathering a hunting patrol at the entrance. Kitescratch and Turtlecrawl were clearing old bedding out of the elders' den. These were the cats he'd grown up with, and the cats he'd grown strong to impress. Somehow he'd embraced his and his father's strange powers, and it had only made him a better SkyClan warrior.

Now his Clan not only needed him, but wanted him.

How could he think of leaving this place where he belonged?

CHAPTER 20

❧

Bristlefrost glanced again at the camp entrance. Early morning sunshine had flooded the hollow. The dawn patrol would be back soon. They had to be. She stretched and tugged impatiently at the earth. Why hadn't she woken earlier? She could have joined Lionblaze, Bumblestripe, and Cherryfall on patrol. Instead she was stuck in camp, frustration itching at her pelt.

Alderheart turned to face her. "If you're bored, you can help Flamepaw and Baypaw clean out the bedding." The Thunderclan medicine cat was with Brackenfur, dabbing mouse bile onto ticks that had lodged in the elder's fur while he'd been out in the forest yesterday.

Brackenfur wrinkled his nose at the bitter stench. "I don't think they need more help."

"No, we don't." Baypaw was dragging a bundle of crushed bracken from the elders' den. His pelt twitched irritably. "Cloudtail and Brightheart are already giving us plenty of advice."

Brightheart poked her head from the den. "Make sure you take the old bedding right out of camp," she told him.

"Bring ferns this time," Cloudtail called from inside. "Bracken is too prickly for Brightheart."

"But bracken stays fresh longer," Brightheart called back.

Baypaw rolled his eyes and dragged the old bracken toward the camp entrance.

Bristlefrost sat down. It seemed like every cat in Thunderclan was trying to stay busy. Mousewhisker, Finleap, and Larksong were clearing stones that had fallen from the rock tumble; Twigbranch and Birchfall inspected the camp wall for holes. Dewnose and Poppyfrost were helping Jayfeather clear brambles from the entrance to the medicine den, while Spotfur wove an extra nest for the nursery. Daisy, it seemed, had gone to help Smoky with his new kits while Bristlefrost had been away fetching the Sisters. She hoped it was just to help Smoky, and not because Daisy, too, was thinking about leaving Thunderclan for good. With Spotfur's kits coming soon, Bristlefrost would feel better knowing that the cat who'd helped raise generations of Thunderclan kits would still be around.

She wondered what Rootspring was doing. Was he out hunting with his Clanmates? Perhaps he was helping to clear away the temporary nests SkyClan had made for the Sisters. *Is he considering leaving SkyClan to be with me?* She shook out her pelt. She couldn't think about that. It felt wrong to wish he'd leave his Clan.

Bristlefrost looked at the fresh-kill pile. It was still full from yesterday. Lionblaze had organized so many hunting patrols that there was no point sending out more today, especially as the warm weather meant the prey would spoil easily.

Beside her, Spotfur was sitting back on her haunches and frowning at the nest she'd woven. "It needs moss," she told Plumstone.

"I'll fetch some." Plumstone got to her paws.

Bristlefrost lifted her tail. "I'll go." Anything would be better than staying in camp. She hadn't been able to settle since she'd returned from SkyClan's camp yesterday morning. She missed Rootspring, but more than that, she wished she knew what was going to happen next. Squirrelflight had hardly left her den, and Lionblaze was as sullen as a badger with a sore tail. If Bramblestar had disappeared for good and Ashfur's spirit could travel wherever it liked, the Clans had to do something. It would be crazy to wait for the dark warrior to cause more trouble. But what could they do but wait?

As she headed for the entrance, paw steps sounded outside camp. She hesitated as Lionblaze padded from the thorn tunnel, Bumblestripe and Cherryfall at his heels.

Lionblaze blinked at her. "Where are you going?"

"Spotfur and Plumstone need moss," she told him.

He frowned. "Warriors shouldn't go out alone now that we know Ashfur can roam the forest whenever he likes."

"I can take a patrol." Bristlefrost guessed some of the other warriors would be pleased to get out of camp too. Her Clanmates' pelts had been twitching since yesterday as though a thunderstorm were coming. It was probably why Lionblaze had been keeping everyone busy with hunting patrols.

"Okay." Lionblaze glanced around the camp.

Bumblestripe's tail flicked tetchily when it landed on him. "You want me to go on a moss-gathering patrol?"

Lionblaze narrowed his eyes. "There's more to Clan life than hunting and marking borders," he told the gray tabby tom.

"But *moss* gathering?" Bumblestripe huffed.

Cherryfall shifted her paws. "I don't know why we're wasting time tidying up the camp when there's a more important problem we should be dealing with."

Lionblaze eyed her sharply. "You mean Ashfur?"

She gave a slow nod. "We were supposed to decide what to do with him once we'd consulted the Sisters."

"I know." Lionblaze flexed his claws. "We should be dealing with him right now."

"Why don't we just get on with it?" Bumblestripe mewed.

Anxiety trickled along Bristlefrost's spine. Lionblaze had once seemed ready to kill Ashfur. If he thought he had the support of other warriors, would he revive that plan? And would anything stop him carrying it out? "We have to wait for the leaders to decide," she reminded him.

Lionblaze scowled. "Squirrelflight's clearly not ready to make a decision. She's trying her best, but her loyalties are divided. And truly, she's not a real—" He stopped, but Bristlefrost guessed what he was going to say.

She stiffened as the brambles at the entrance to Bramblestar's den twitched.

"Finish your thought." Squirrelflight padded out. She glared down at Lionblaze. "I'm not a real what?"

Lionblaze hesitated. Bristlefrost held her breath. Would he say it out loud? She was aware that her Clanmates had stopped what they were doing to stare at their deputy nervously.

He lifted his muzzle. "You're not a real leader."

Squirrelflight leaped from the Highledge and padded toward the golden warrior. She stopped a tail-length away. "What would make me a real leader?"

"StarClan," Lionblaze answered. "They need to give you nine lives."

"And how can they when they're not even here?"

"Getting rid of Ashfur might bring them back." Lionblaze held her gaze. "We have to do whatever we can. Maybe if we drive him out, Bramblestar will be able to get back into his body, and everything can go back to normal."

Squirrelflight half turned away from him. "That's not the answer. Hawkwing says that Ashfur has left Bramblestar's body more than once while he's been held prisoner, and yet Bramblestar hasn't been able to get back in." She blinked at the golden warrior.

Lionblaze's tail drooped. "What if . . . what if that means he really is gone for good?"

Spotfur left the nest she was weaving and padded toward Squirrelflight. "I know how hard it is to lose your mate," she mewed gently. "But perhaps it's time you accepted that Bramblestar's not coming back."

Squirrelflight stared at her wordlessly. Was that panic in the Thunderclan leader's gaze? She blinked it away. "I need to be sure," she growled. "If you kill Bramblestar's body while his spirit is still beside the lake, you might be condemning him to wander the forest forever. It's too great a risk."

Frustration flared in Lionblaze's eyes. "It's more of a risk if we do nothing at all!" he yowled.

"Lionblaze is right," Cherryfall mewed. "Ashfur could be planning anything."

"The more we delay, the more time it gives him," Bumblestripe chimed.

Lilyheart pushed past Bumblestripe. "Why do you need to rush this?" She glared at Lionblaze. "We have no proof that Bramblestar is gone."

"We have no proof that he isn't!" Bumblestripe snapped.

Bristlefrost stiffened. Her Clanmates sounded so angry. "Perhaps we should wait just a little longer."

"We've waited long enough!" Mousewhisker snarled.

Bristlefrost flinched, shocked by the rage in his mew. She glanced around the clearing as angry growls rumbled around the camp. Her Clanmates were glaring at one another. Was Thunderclan willing to fight over this? She tried to catch Alderheart's eye. Someone had to stop them. But the Thunderclan medicine cat was staring at the ground. Bramblestar was his father, and he clearly didn't want to get involved in this argument.

Bristlefrost turned to Lionblaze, but the Thunderclan deputy's eyes had narrowed to slits as he stared at Lilyheart with undisguised fury. Her heart began to race. *Please stop it!*

Stones rattled down the rock tumble as Squirrelflight bounded onto the Highledge. "Silence!" Her Clanmates froze as the Thunderclan leader's mew rang over the clearing. "We're not the enemy!" she yowled. "We shouldn't be fighting one another. We're Thunderclan. We *protect* one another. We're bound by kinship and loyalty and the warrior code. Some of you chose Thunderclan." Her gaze flashed toward Twigbranch, who lifted her chin proudly. "All of you have fought for your Clan, even when everything seemed hopeless." She looked at Spotfur. "Some of you are preparing to bring new life into Thunderclan. Kits need to be protected and loved and taught how to live as warriors, and I know they will be, because in Thunderclan we protect those who cannot protect themselves, and we help those who need to be helped." Her gaze flitted over Poppyfrost, Mousewhisker, and Lionblaze. "We live, not for ourselves, but for one another." Emotion swelled in Bristlefrost's throat as Squirrelflight looked around the Clan. "Every one of you has put your Clan before yourself in the past." She blinked at Bristlefrost. "No matter how young or inexperienced, you've all fought to protect your Clan. The bond that we've shared will not be broken now. We have all been through too much."

Bristlefrost blinked at Squirrelflight. Every word was true. She glanced nervously at her Clanmates, relieved as she saw their fur smooth. Lionblaze dropped his gaze. Lilyheart dipped her head. Twigbranch and Finleap touched pelts. The air seemed to soften as the Clan shifted self-consciously around the clearing. And yet Bristlefrost couldn't relax completely. A nagging worry told her that this peace was temporary.

Lionblaze padded to the bottom of the rock tumble and looked up at Squirrelflight. "You're right," he mewed. "Our Clanmates aren't the enemy; Ashfur is. We mustn't lose sight of that."

"But we still need to deal with him," Bumblestripe ventured quietly.

"Yes." Squirrelflight closed her eyes.

"We asked the Sisters to contact Bramblestar," Cherryfall mewed. "And they couldn't find him."

Lionblaze met Squirrelflight's gaze. "You promised that, if we tried everything else first, we could talk about killing Ashfur."

Squirrelflight stared down at him, her expression calm. Was she ready to agree? She lowered her head. "I did promise," she mewed slowly. "I can't deny that. But I won't be the first to call for Bramblestar's murder."

Lionblaze held her eyes. "Then perhaps it's time to consult the other leaders." As Squirrelflight hesitated, he went on. "If Ashfur has been leaving Bramblestar's body, we can be sure he's planning something. We need to act quickly."

Bristlefrost shivered as silence gripped the Clan. She felt as though ice had flowed into the hollow and frozen every cat in place. Lilyheart, Twigbranch, and Finleap looked at Squirrelflight, their eyes glittering with hope. Bumblestripe, Cherryfall, and Mousewhisker looked away, as if too ashamed to look at her.

"Okay," Squirrelflight mewed at last. "We will speak with

the other leaders, and I will abide by whatever they decide."

Bristlefrost's breath caught in her throat. Was Squirrel-flight really ready to agree to Bramblestar's death? The Thunderclan leader's eyes were too dark for her to read anything in them but pain. She turned away and padded into her den. The Clan began to return to their duties, as though the ice had released their paws and they were free to move once more. Bristlefrost watched Spotfur pad back toward the nursery. Her paws seemed to tremble beneath her. Was she ill? Bristlefrost hurried over.

"You look tired," she mewed anxiously.

"I am." Spotfur sat down. "A little."

"Let me finish your nest so you can rest." Bristlefrost grabbed the bracken Spotfur had been weaving and dragged it into the cool shelter of the nursery. Thriftear rushed to help her and they pushed it against the bramble wall. As Thriftear quickly tucked in the last loose ends, Bristlefrost slid outside and nosed Spotfur gently to her paws. Her heart was beating fast as she guided the queen inside. She was still shocked by how close Thunderclan had come to fighting. It was as though the Clan had begun to unravel like an old nest. So many of the strands that had held it together were gone. Bramblestar was missing, and Thornclaw, Graystripe, and Flipclaw had left. So had Snaptooth and Flywhisker. Did Spotfur really want to raise her kits here? Would Thunderclan be the same Clan she'd grown up in? Fear dropped like a stone in her belly. Bristlefrost didn't want to lose hope, but she didn't know how to hang on to it when they'd all lost so much. No cat could tell what the future held. This might be the end.

Wordlessly, she helped Spotfur into her nest. Perhaps Rootspring had been right about Thunderclan. It might never recover. She felt sick. Was it time to leave here and find a home somewhere else?

CHAPTER 21

❧

Shadowsight paused at the medicine-den entrance and unrolled the leaf wrap Mothwing had left for him.

Puddleshine looked up from the moss he was pressing into a nest at the back of the den. "Do you have everything you need?"

Shadowsight looked through the herbs bundled into the wrap, his heart sinking. There were hardly enough leaves to treat one wound, and Ashfur had plenty. Why had Mothwing been so stingy? With the long days of greenleaf ahead, there was no shortage of herbs. Did she *want* Ashfur to suffer? He pushed the thought away. Mothwing was a medicine cat. She'd never want any cat to suffer. Perhaps she didn't realize how badly Tigerstar and Hawkwing had wounded him. He blinked at Puddleshine. "I could use some more marigold."

Puddleshine nodded and headed for the herb store. "Anything else while I'm here?"

"Goldenrod." Shadowsight forced his fur not to prickle with frustration. It would be easier if he could just fetch the herbs himself instead of going through Mothwing and Puddleshine every time. He picked through the leaves Mothwing had rolled. There was nothing here to ease pain. "And some poppy seeds."

As he spoke, a shadow fell across the leaf. He looked up as Yarrowleaf slid into the den. She glanced at the leaf wrap as she passed, then blinked at Puddleshine. "You said I should come back so you could check my cough."

"I did." Puddleshine hooked out a bunch of marigold and tossed it to Shadowsight. "Take what you need," he told him. "I'll find you poppy seeds and goldenrod after I've checked on Yarrowleaf." He padded toward the warrior, but Yarrowleaf wasn't looking at him. She was watching the marigold bundle as Shadowsight reached out a paw to catch it.

"Who's that for?" Her eyes narrowed.

Shadowsight hesitated. The ginger warrior looked angry. She must know he'd been treating Ashfur. "Bramblestar's body is in rough shape," he told her. She had to understand he was trying to keep the prisoner alive for Bramblestar's sake. "I'm trying to heal it."

Yarrowleaf glared at Shadowsight as Puddleshine leaned down to listen to her chest. "You should have let Tigerstar and Hawkwing kill him."

Shadowsight's eyes widened. He knew he was the only cat who wanted to defend Ashfur, but he hadn't expected his Clanmates to wish him dead out loud.

Yarrowleaf padded toward him. "Don't you think we'd all be safer if Ashfur was gone?"

Shadowsight lifted his chin. "I'm still a medicine cat," he told her. "I have to try to save Bramblestar's body."

"Bramblestar is long gone." Yarrowleaf stopped a muzzle-length away. "You're just helping a dead cat walk around in his fur."

Shadowsight didn't answer. He *had* to believe that Bramblestar could return. If the Thunderclan leader had no way back to the living world, then it meant Ashfur had won. He quickly ripped a few marigold stalks from the bundle and wrapped them in the leaf. "I'll fetch the other herbs later," he told Puddleshine.

He grabbed the wrap between his jaws and hurried out of the den. He could understand why Yarrowleaf was angry, but she was a warrior, not a medicine cat. Sometimes warriors couldn't see past their own claws, and then it was his duty to do what was right.

The clearing was empty. It was sunhigh, and most of the Clan's warriors were on patrol. Only Tawnypelt and Gull-swoop were left in camp, sharing tongues with Oakfur in a small patch of sunshine outside the elders' den. Gorseclaw and Nightsky stood guard at the entrance to Ashfur's prison.

As Shadowsight passed the nursery, he heard voices from outside the camp. He pricked his ears. They didn't sound like ShadowClan. He dropped his bundle of herbs, licking his lips to clear the smell, then tasted the air. Thunderclan scent hung in the air.

Why? Shadowsight's pelt prickled. Had Thunderclan warriors come to harm Ashfur? He eyed Gorseclaw and Nightsky warily. Was RiverClan part of this too? He tried to look relaxed as he padded to the camp entrance and ducked outside.

A tree-length from the entrance, Tigerstar faced Lionblaze, Bristlefrost, and Cherryfall. Squirrelflight hung back a little way behind her Clanmates, watching grimly as Lionblaze spoke to the ShadowClan leader.

"You know what happened at the ceremony," the Thunderclan deputy growled. "The Sisters couldn't find Bramblestar."

Quickly, Shadowsight slid behind a swath of bracken and crept closer to the Thunderclan patrol. Staying low, he tried to remember what Lightleap had taught him about stalking prey. Keeping his paw steps as light as thistledown and his tail clear of the ground, he padded as close as he dared and stretched his ears, straining to hear.

Tigerstar eyed Lionblaze thoughtfully.

When he didn't speak, Cherryfall leaned her head forward. "Bramblestar's gone. He's not coming back."

Squirrelflight seemed to shrink beneath her pelt.

"We have to act," Lionblaze growled. "If what the Sisters said was true, Ashfur is already causing trouble among the dead. It won't be long before he starts causing trouble among the living again. It's time we killed him."

Shadowsight held his breath as his father's gaze flicked over the Thunderclan patrol. It stopped on Squirrelflight.

"I'm ready to kill him if you are," Tigerstar mewed.

No! Shadowsight dug his claws into the ground to steady himself as Squirrelflight padded forward.

"I understand why you're so scared of what Ashfur might do," she began.

Tigerstar curled his lip. "He doesn't scare me," he growled.

"He scares me." The Thunderclan leader hardly moved. "But I can't let you kill Bramblestar without defending him one last time. His spirit might still be near, and if we kill his body, I will never see him again." She struggled to keep her voice steady.

Tigerstar looked puzzled. He glanced around the patrol. "I thought you came here to ask me to help kill Ashfur, not to defend him."

"We came to sound you out and see what you thought," Squirrelflight mewed.

Lionblaze's gaze darkened with fury. "I thought we came here to kill—"

Squirrelflight glared at her deputy. "I will abide by the final decision of the leaders, but it has to be *all* the leaders, not just Tigerstar."

"There's always one more reason to wait," Lionblaze mewed through gritted teeth.

Squirrelflight ignored him, her gaze still on Tigerstar. "My Clanmates think I'm too close to Bramblestar to make a fair decision," she told him. "They may be right. I have to listen to them." Her paws trembled as she went on. "But I still think we need one last meeting of all five Clans to decide whether Bramblestar's body should die."

A blackbird chattered in the branch overhead. Tigerstar glanced at it as it fluttered away, then looked back at Squirrel-flight. "I understand," he mewed evenly. Shadowsight saw sympathy in his father's gaze. Tigerstar clearly knew how hard this was for Squirrelflight. How could he ask any cat to give up their mate for the sake of the Clans? But how could she refuse?

Tigerstar dipped his head. "If we're going to do this," he mewed, "we should have the agreement of all the Clans. If we're wrong, then we must be wrong together."

Lionblaze growled. "And if we're right, we need to act quickly."

"I'll send patrols to RiverClan and WindClan to tell Mistystar and Harestar there will be a Gathering on the island tonight," Tigerstar mewed. "You send a patrol to Leafstar."

"We'll go now." Without consulting Squirrelflight, Lionblaze flicked his tail toward Cherryfall and Bristlefrost. Taking the lead, he led them away.

Squirrelflight called after them. "Tell her we'll meet at moonhigh."

Tigerstar blinked at her. "I know how hard this is for you," he mewed softly. "But I don't think we have any other choice." He dipped his head and turned toward camp.

Squirrelflight watched him go, grief sharpening her gaze. Then she stiffened and opened her mouth, as though tasting the air. Shadowsight's heart lurched as she jerked her muzzle toward the bracken. She'd caught him eavesdropping.

Hot with shame, he crept from his hiding place. "I'm sorry."

She stared at him blankly, as though she hardly cared he was there. Her thoughts seemed distant. Was she thinking about tonight's Gathering? It would seal Bramblestar's fate. The leaders would vote to kill his body, and there was nothing she could do to stop them. Without speaking, she padded away. Shadowsight's heart twisted in his chest. She looked so defeated, her pelt slicked against her narrow frame. Had she given up all hope of saving Bramblestar?

CHAPTER 22

Rootspring pressed closer to Tree as Mallownose and Lizardtail pushed past him, following their Clanmates through the crowded clearing. The island was humming with the hushed mews of the gathered Clans. Above, Silverpelt stretched across the crow-black sky. Rootspring could see Bristlefrost sitting among her Clanmates at the edge of the clearing. He felt relieved when she caught sight of him and blinked at him reassuringly. He knew why this meeting had been called. He just hoped the leaders would make the right decision.

Harestar and Tigerstar were already sitting on the long, low branch of the Great Oak. Leafstar leaped to join them as Mistystar wove her way through the throng below. Squirrelflight was hunched in the crook of the branch, her pelt ruffled, as though it hadn't been groomed for a while.

Rootspring shuffled closer to his father. "This is her last chance to save Bramblestar," he whispered.

Tree followed his gaze to the Thunderclan leader. "I don't know if she'll be able to." He glanced around the gathered cats. "Every cat has heard about the Sisters' ceremony. They're convinced Ashfur is determined to cause trouble."

Rootspring's tail twitched nervously. "That doesn't mean Bramblestar should suffer."

"His suffering might already be over for all we know," Tree mewed darkly.

Rootspring remembered the spirits shimmering in Sky-Clan's clearing. There had been too many to count, but there had been no sign of Bramblestar. He shuddered as icy claws seemed to run through his pelt.

Plumwillow shifted beside him, stretching up to look over the ears of the cats in front. "Have they decided how to deal with Ashfur?"

Macgyver grunted. "It's about time we did something. A fox-heart like him shouldn't be allowed to rest while we hunt his prey for him."

As he spoke, Mistystar settled beside Squirrelflight in the oak, and Tigerstar got to his paws.

The gathered cats fell silent as the ShadowClan leader's gaze swept over them. "You've heard already that the Sisters were unable to make contact with Bramblestar."

Rootspring stiffened as Tigerstar looked straight at him.

"Tell them what you saw," the ShadowClan leader ordered.

Rootspring's pelt prickled nervously as the gathered cats turned to stare. "I—I saw other spirits," he stammered. He felt Tree's flank press his and forced himself to speak louder. "They were desperate, like they were in pain. They seemed angry."

"Were they warriors?" Lizardtail called from among the RiverClan cats.

"They weren't all warriors, but there were warriors among them. I saw several at a distance. . . . One of them was Stemleaf." Rootspring scanned the crowd, hoping Spotfur hadn't come. He didn't want her to hear that Stemleaf was suffering.

Tigerstar flicked his tail impatiently. "You also saw Ashfur, didn't you?"

"I think I did." Rootspring met his gaze.

"Did *he* look like he was in pain?" Tigerstar demanded.

Rootspring shook his head. "He was the only spirit who wasn't." He tried not to catch Squirrelflight's eye. He knew she was staring at him imploringly. But he had to tell the truth. "He looked pleased."

Murmurs of horror rippled through the crowd. Tigerstar's eyes sparked with angry triumph. "Ashfur is up to something," he mewed. "It's time we put a stop to it."

"How?" Macgyver called from the crowd.

Tigerstar flexed his claws. "We kill him."

Squirrelflight flinched, and heads dropped among the gathered cats. Hootwhisker stretched onto his hind paws, but said nothing.

Lionblaze scanned the crowd from the roots of the Great Oak, where he sat with the other deputies. "We can't let Ashfur use poor Bramblestar's body any longer," he growled.

Hawkwing nodded. "Without it, Ashfur couldn't stay in the forest."

"You don't know that!" Dovewing pushed her way through the crowd.

"She's right!" Puddleshine called from among the medicine

cats. "We don't know what Ashfur's capable of. If Rootspring saw him at the ceremony, it means Ashfur may not need Bramblestar's body to survive. He can move where he pleases without it."

Dovewing reached the front of the crowd and faced Lionblaze. "If we kill Bramblestar's body, Ashfur might just steal another!"

"Not unless another leader loses a life," Lionblaze snapped.

Dovewing's ears twitched. "What's to stop him stealing Bramblestar's body again and again? Are we going to keep killing him until he has no lives left?"

Squirrelflight's eyes widened with horror. As much as she wanted her mate to return, the idea of him suffering any more than he already had must be breaking her heart.

"You say he's gone"—her gaze flitted from Lionblaze to Tigerstar—"and then you say we need to kill him so he can return. You don't really have any idea what you're doing, do you? You think *murder* will solve everything." Her mew grew husky with grief. "Bramblestar has always been a loyal warrior and a good leader. He'd never murder any cat—not like this. He'd never give up, but you're ready to give up on him." She stared at the other leaders. "Please don't do this. . . ."

Silence gripped the Clans for a moment. Then Kestrelflight cleared his throat. "If Ashfur *is* torturing spirits, surely we have to kill him? We should do something to break his hold on the living. Perhaps then he'll have less power over the dead."

"You don't know that!" Squirrelflight gasped.

Tigerstar puffed out his chest. "We've argued enough!" he snapped. "We don't know what will happen, but we have to act and we have to act quickly! Ashfur is clearly planning something, and it's not safe to wait and find out what it is."

Harestar nodded. "He's already caused enough trouble in the Clans. Warriors have died because of him. We can't risk losing more."

Rootspring closed his eyes, wishing more cats would speak up for Bramblestar. He remembered the first time Bramblestar's ghost had appeared to him—how desperate the Thunderclan leader had looked as he'd begged for help. But it sounded as though the leaders had made up their minds. Angry whispers fluttered through the crowd.

"Ashfur must die," Lizardtail called.

Yarrowleaf curled her lip. "We should kill him before any other warriors die."

"Kill him," Emberfoot growled.

"Kill him!"

"Kill him!"

The cry echoed around the Clans, growing louder and louder until Rootspring flattened his ears against the yowls. He felt dizzy as Tigerstar gazed calmly at the gathered cats. Harestar dipped his head, as though acknowledging the will of the crowd.

Rootspring felt Tree stiffen. His father raised his muzzle and shouted over the noise. "Are the Clans so eager to kill in cold blood?" Around him, the yowling faltered and died away as the warriors turned to see who had spoken. Tree pressed on.

"It's been a long time since I was with the Sisters, but I know *they* would never deliberately sacrifice a cat in an attempt to change their destiny." He was staring at Tigerstar. "The Sisters only kill in self-defense."

Tigerstar narrowed his eyes. "This *is* self-defense."

Leafstar stepped to the edge of the branch. "Can you truly say that, faced with a cat like Ashfur, the Sisters wouldn't make the same decision? They seemed frightened of him when they contacted the spirit cats. . . ."

Harestar yowled to speak over the murmurs of agreement. "We'll be putting Bramblestar out of his misery. Isn't that the right thing to do? We'll be protecting his spirit."

Tigerstar nodded. "We'll be protecting *all* the spirits. If Ashfur is torturing our fallen warriors, I'm sure Bramblestar would want us to stop him any way we could."

Tree's gaze clouded with uncertainty. The Clans shifted in awkward silence.

Mistystar swished her tail. "The leaders must vote to decide." She nodded toward the end of the branch. "Any leader who thinks Ashfur should die will go there." Her gaze switched toward the trunk. "Any leader who thinks he should live, come to this end."

Squirrelflight, already huddled in the crook of the branch, pressed closer to the trunk. Rootspring felt a flicker of hope as Mistystar stayed beside the Thunderclan leader. Two of them wanted to give Bramblestar a chance. Tigerstar dipped his head and padded to the other end. He looked back expectantly until Harestar followed and stood beside him.

Rootspring's breath caught in his throat. Leafstar was hesitating in the middle. Her gaze flicked from one end to another.

The SkyClan leader shifted uncertainly. Which way would she go? Rootspring couldn't press back the desperation clawing in his belly. "I was one of the last cats to see Bramblestar!" he called out. "I know how much he wanted to return to the Clans. You can't kill his body. He still needs it. I know he does! He wouldn't give up this easily."

Dovewing nodded eagerly. "We can't even be sure that killing Bramblestar's body will stop Ashfur!" she yowled. "We might change nothing. We'd only be killing a cat who doesn't deserve to die."

Leafstar's paws trembled. Rootspring willed the SkyClan leader to agree. *Don't let them kill Bramblestar.* He realized he was holding his breath.

Leafstar dipped her head to Squirrelflight. "I'm sorry. But I have to do what I think is right for my Clan." She turned and walked slowly toward Tigerstar.

Bramblestar. The earth seemed to tremble beneath Rootspring's paws. They were going to kill him. He pressed his pads into it, praying for strength. What if the lost leader could never return? Rootspring swallowed back anger as shocked whispers filled the air. He turned his head, glaring at the warriors crowding the clearing. *This is what you wanted, isn't it?*

Tigerstar squared his shoulders. "Now we must decide who will kill him."

Mothwing padded forward. "I can give him deathberries,"

she mewed. "It will be easy to hide the juice and seeds in a piece of prey. It would be quick. He wouldn't realize he was dying until it was too late."

Tigerstar flicked his tail. "Ashfur must die like a warrior," he growled. "We must kill him with our own claws."

Rootspring swallowed. The ShadowClan leader's dark amber eyes sparked with satisfaction. Did Tigerstar want to rip Ashfur to pieces to avenge the attack on his son?

"I agree." Harestar lifted his chin. "That fox-heart doesn't deserve an easy death after all he's done to the Clans. The warriors he killed didn't have an easy death—why should he?"

Leafstar looked solemnly around the leaders. "Then we must kill him together." As her gaze reached Squirrelflight, the Thunderclan leader pressed herself harder against the trunk. "So that no one cat is to blame."

"I could never . . ." Squirrelflight's eyes were wide with horror. Her mew collapsed into a sob. How could any cat expect her to kill her mate?

Leafstar nodded. "I understand."

"Let's do it now." Tigerstar's eyes looked as hard as stone. They glittered with determination in the starlight as he gazed across the gathered cats. "Any cat who wants to be a part of this can follow." He jumped down from the oak, Harestar at his tail. Leafstar and Mistystar followed, pushing after him as he headed through the crowd.

Thunderclan, RiverClan, and WindClan fell back as they passed. SkyClan and ShadowClan watched them go with rounded eyes. Did they regret what they'd done? Then, one by one, warriors began to join the patrol. Crowfeather, Lion-blaze, and Hawkwing led the way. Lizardtail and Mallownose scurried after them. Bumblestripe and Emberfoot fell in as they passed.

Rootspring steadied his breath. This was actually happening. He glanced around the warriors left behind, instinctively searching for Bristlefrost. She was staring at him, her eyes bright with dread. He knew why she was scared. What would become of Thunderclan when Bramblestar was dead? And what about Squirrelflight? How could she ever look the other leaders in the face—or even her own Clanmates—knowing they'd murdered her mate?

Rootspring froze. Where was Squirrelflight? He looked toward the oak. The branch where she'd crouched was empty. He scanned the clearing. There was no sign of her. As Tiger-star led the way toward the tree-bridge, Rootspring saw the long grass quiver. He narrowed his eyes. A dark shape was hurrying ahead of the patrol. *Squirrelflight!* Where was she going? Foreboding wormed beneath Rootspring's pelt. What was she planning to do?

CHAPTER 23

❧

Bristlefrost gasped, her breath catching as she took in the empty branch where Squirrelflight had been huddled against the trunk. *Where's she gone?* She scanned the island clearing. Tigerstar was leading Harestar, Mistystar, and Leafstar to the long grass. Their deputies followed. More and more warriors had fallen in behind them, swelling the patrol until it seemed to spread like a shadow over the shore.

Rootspring was staring past them, his eyes bright with alarm.

She raced toward him. "Squirrelflight's gone," she gasped as she reached him.

"She ran ahead of them." He nodded toward the long grass. "She's probably crossed the bridge by now."

Bristlefrost's pelt sparked with fear. "She's heading for the ShadowClan camp," she breathed.

Rootspring's eyes widened. "We have to stop her."

Squirrelflight loved Bramblestar enough to give up her life, her leadership, her Clan. Certainty pressed like stone in Bristlefrost's chest. Squirrelflight would do anything to save her mate. "She'll fight us."

"If she gets to him before Tigerstar, the Clans will never forgive her."

"But she can't save him alone." What could one cat do against all the Clans?

"She can warn him they're coming," Rootspring growled. "She might help him escape."

"Maybe she's doing the right thing." Bristlefrost stared desperately at Rootspring. "Thunderclan needs Bramblestar back."

"What if he can't come back?" Rootspring's gaze was hard. She felt it pierce her like ice. "Squirrelflight won't be helping Bramblestar escape; she'll be helping Ashfur. And if she betrays the Clans like that, there will be no cat left to hold Thunderclan together."

Bristlefrost swallowed. He was right. Thunderclan was already falling apart; if it lost Squirrelflight, it might never recover. "Do you think we can stop her before she reaches him?"

"We can try." Rootspring headed after Tigerstar's patrol.

Bristlefrost raced beside him. "We can cut across River-Clan territory," she whispered.

Ahead, warriors were streaming across the bridge. She stopped beside Rootspring as they waited for the patrol to pass. "Why do you care so much about Thunderclan?" She searched Rootspring's gaze. "You're a SkyClan warrior."

"I care about you." His eyes glittered with starlight. "And I care about Squirrelflight. She's lost too much already. She mustn't lose her Clan."

Bristlefrost's throat tightened. Rootspring was the kindest, bravest cat she knew. Her heart felt like it would break. "If we save Thunderclan," she breathed, "I will stay with them."

He didn't flinch. "I know."

Love surged in Bristlefrost's chest. Rootspring was willing to fight to save something she cared about, even if it meant sacrificing his own happiness.

Ahead of them, the tree-bridge stood empty as the last of the patrol crossed, but Rootspring held her gaze. "I can't join Thunderclan for you," he mewed. "I belong in SkyClan. It will always be my home."

Bristlefrost froze. In a way, she'd known it all along, but grief still hit her like a wave. She let it flood her without fighting it. He'd made his decision and she understood it. If Rootspring left SkyClan for her, he wouldn't be the warrior she'd grown to love. And if she left Thunderclan for him, then all they had fought for together would mean nothing. It had to be this way.

The patrol was heading toward ShadowClan territory.

Rootspring jerked his gaze away. "Come on." He leaped onto the tree-bridge and raced along it.

Bristlefrost followed, digging her claws in to steady herself on the smooth wood. Stones shifted beneath her paws as she leaped onto the far shore. Ahead, Rootspring kept low as he streaked toward the reeds. He disappeared like a shadow among the stems. One eye on the patrol, she hurried after him. No cat had looked back to see them slip away. Once they were in the cover of the marsh grass, Rootspring picked up the pace. She stayed close behind him as they raced toward the ShadowClan border. Her breath burned and her chest ached, but she didn't slow. Squirrelflight was somewhere up ahead. Had the Thunderclan leader come this way? Had she also planned to stay ahead of the patrol by cutting across River-Clan land?

Bristlefrost tasted the air, but RiverClan scents drowned out every other smell. The dank stench of stagnant water filled her nose. Mud squelched beneath her paws. Stems pressed close on either side as Rootspring led the way, zig-zagging between the thick clumps of reeds. She prayed they didn't run into a RiverClan patrol. How would they explain their presence here?

The ground grew harder beneath her paws. The reeds opened onto meadow, and brambles spilled over a rise ahead. Pines grew there, and at last Bristlefrost smelled forest scents once more. The sharp tang of the ShadowClan border cut through the air.

Rootspring glanced over his shoulder, catching her eye as though reassuring her before he leaped up the slope and darted through a gap in the brambles. She began to catch up to him, her paws surer now on firmer ground. Thorns scraped her pelt as she pushed through the brambles. She let him lead, let him swerve between the pines, following his paw steps as he cut a line through the forest. How did he know which way to run? This terrain was unfamiliar to Bristlefrost. Did Root-spring know the way to the ShadowClan camp from here?

"Can you smell Squirrelflight's scent?" she panted. Perhaps he'd picked it up where she'd missed it and was following it now.

"No," he mewed. "But this is the quickest route to the camp. If Squirrelflight is trying to reach Ashfur before the patrol, this is the way she'll go."

"Can we get there before her?" As hope sparked in Bristlefrost's belly, she glimpsed orange fur between the trees ahead. "There!"

A warrior was racing through the forest a few tree-lengths ahead. *Squirrelflight!* Her ears were flat. Wind streamed through her pelt.

Struggling for breath, Bristlefrost ran harder. They had to catch Squirrelflight before she reached the ShadowClan camp. Rootspring pushed ahead, his paws thumping against the forest floor. Pine needles sprayed as he swerved to cut across Squirrelflight's path. The Thunderclan leader's gaze was fixed on the forest ahead. She didn't see him as he veered from behind a swath of ferns and flung himself toward her.

Bristlefrost slowed, pulling up as Rootspring slammed his paws into Squirrelflight's flank. He sent her thudding onto the forest floor. Her eyes narrowed into slits and she hissed as she scrambled up and faced her attacker.

"It's me!" Rootspring stared at her, but Squirrelflight's hackles were high. She lunged at him, claws stretched, and flung him onto his side. Hooking deep into his pelt with her foreclaws, she rolled him onto his back and kicked her hind paws into his belly.

"Stop!" Bristlefrost raced toward her. "We want to help you!"

Rootspring twisted from Squirrelflight's grip, but he didn't fight back. Instead he flattened himself to the ground and stared at her pleadingly.

She scowled at him, her gaze flicking once more toward the ShadowClan camp. "Leave me alone." She hared forward, but Rootspring reached out and caught her forepaws with his. She stumbled and rolled, swinging her muzzle toward him with a snarl. "Don't you understand?" Her eyes burned with fury. "Tigerstar's bringing a patrol to kill Bramblestar. I have to save him."

Bristlefrost stared at her. "You can't fight every cat in the Clans!"

"I can help him get away." Squirrelflight lashed her tail.

"They'll know who did it," Rootspring leaped to his paws. "They'll never forgive you." He thrust his muzzle closer. "You won't be saving Bramblestar," he mewed. "You'll be saving *Ashfur*."

"Thunderclan needs a leader!" Blood roared in Bristlefrost's ears. "If you do this, we'll have lost two—Bramblestar *and* you." She stared imploringly into Squirrelflight's eyes. "And we'll become the Clan that saved *Ashfur* after he tried to destroy us all. Do you think we could survive that, without a leader? Do you think Thornclaw, or Graystripe, or any of the others will want to return?"

Squirrelflight hesitated, glancing once more toward the ShadowClan camp, but less certainly this time. "It's

Bramblestar's body," she whispered. "How can he return if there's nothing for him to return to?"

Bristlefrost blinked at her. "How can he return if you help Ashfur survive?"

Squirrelflight stiffened. The determination in her eyes faded into grief. "Bramblestar might find his way back," she mewed helplessly.

Rootspring held her gaze. "If he could, don't you think he'd have done it by now?"

"You really think he's gone?" Squirrelflight's mew was taut with pain.

"I haven't seen him in so long. Even the Sisters couldn't reach him." Rootspring's pelt was still prickling along his spine.

Bristlefrost swallowed back pity as Squirrelflight seemed to sway. Was she going to collapse?

The Thunderclan leader shifted her paws to steady herself. Her flanks shuddered as she drew in a heavy breath. "I've imagined losing Bramblestar many times," she whispered. "In battles, to sickness, but never like this. I thought I'd have eight more lives to say good-bye, but he's gone before I was ready, and I can't let go of the idea that he's still out there."

"He's not," Rootspring mewed. "Something terrible is happening to the spirits around the lake. Perhaps it's better that he's not among them."

Squirrelflight lifted her head. "Do you think he's free from suffering, wherever he is?"

Rootspring returned her gaze. "I don't know."

Bristlefrost padded closer. "I can't imagine how hard it must be to let go," she mewed. "But you have to think of your Clan. You can't do anything for Bramblestar now, but you can hold your Clan together." She dug her claws into the earth. "You can rebuild Thunderclan as its leader. You can make sure it stays strong. Isn't that what Bramblestar would have wanted?"

Paw steps pounded in the distance. Beyond the ferns and the thick pines, the patrol was nearing the camp.

Squirrelflight glanced toward the sound, her eyes rounding with grief. "Bramblestar would always have chosen Thunderclan over his own life." Her emerald gaze glittered in the shadow of the pines. "If he must die, then Thunderclan must survive. I will do everything I can to save it."

Relief flooded like cool air through Bristlefrost's pelt. For the first time in a while, she heard clarity in Squirrelflight's mew. The Thunderclan leader meant to keep this promise.

Yowls echoed between the trees and a screech of pain rose above them. Bristlefrost shivered. Had Tigerstar and the other leaders killed Ashfur at last?

Squirrelflight stared toward the sound, her mouth opening as though she could hardly believe her ears.

Rootspring lowered his gaze. "Tree always says that every ending is a beginning."

Squirrelflight looked away, trembling.

Bristlefrost padded closer. She couldn't let Squirrelflight give in to grief yet. "Now it's time to rebuild Thunderclan."

CHAPTER 24
♣

"Did you hear that?"

"Hear what?" Shadowsight stiffened as Ashfur lifted his head and jerked his muzzle around, staring at the entrance to the bramble enclosure. Shadowsight had been watching the dark warrior as he'd slept, as still as dead prey. Now Ashfur sat up, his ears twitching as though a nightmare had woken him, and Shadowsight's pelt bristled along his spine. He strained to hear beyond the rustle of wind in the pines. The forest seemed to sleep, wrapped in moonhigh silence. Only a bird called, far away between the trees.

Ashfur got to his paws, his posture stiff and his eyes wide— he looked like a hunted animal. He tasted the air. "Something's changed." His gaze bore into Shadowsight's. "They're coming for me."

Shadowsight tried to push away the fear welling in his chest. He knew the Clans were meeting to decide Ashfur's fate. Had they decided the dark warrior must die? He glanced toward the entrance to the bramble enclosure. Stonewing and Grassheart were sitting guard. Their pelts were smooth, their shoulders relaxed. "You must have imagined a noise," he mewed, hoping it was true.

Ashfur thrust his muzzle closer. "They're coming for me," he growled. "I can sense it."

Shadowsight backed away, fighting back fear. "I can't hear anything." But so many cats wanted the dark warrior dead that he couldn't help feeling Ashfur was right. His thoughts whirled. Perhaps they *should* kill Ashfur. He had hurt so many cats and caused the death of more. *He tried to kill me.* It was dangerous to keep him alive. If Ashfur died, Shadowsight wouldn't have to care for him anymore. He'd felt his Clanmates' reproachful gaze each time he carried herbs to tend the prisoner's wounds. They hadn't forgotten that Ashfur had killed Conefoot and Frondwhisker. And, if Ashfur was dead, he wouldn't have to listen to any more of Ashfur's sly twisting of the truth. The dark warrior had told Shadowsight again and again that he would never be a medicine cat, that his Clanmates would never trust him, that their fates were intertwined. And yet Ashfur *mustn't* die, surely? Bramblestar needed his body. And would the Clans be any more than rogues if they could kill a cat in cold blood?

Ashfur leaned closer. His sour breath bathed Shadowsight's muzzle. "If they kill me, then you'll never get Bramblestar back." Trembling, Shadowsight met the dark warrior's gaze. "You were the one who sent him to the frozen moor to die," Ashfur pressed. "Do you think any of the Clans will forget that? They'll see you as Bramblestar's murderer forever."

"That's not true!" Shadowsight lashed his tail, but he knew Ashfur was right. He *was* Bramblestar's murderer. Perhaps it was time he accepted it and let go of the hope that the Thunderclan leader could return.

Ashfur stared at him as though he could read Shadowsight's thoughts.

Shadowsight glared back, refusing to be intimidated. "Why shouldn't they kill you?" He puffed out his chest. "Bramblestar's gone! His spirit hasn't been seen for a moon. You've done something with him and he's never coming back." Ashfur held his gaze. Nothing showed in the tom's eyes. "His body isn't any use to him," Shadowsight went on. "Why should you have it?"

Ashfur's gaze glittered, suddenly spiteful. "Are you *sure* he's gone?"

What game was Ashfur playing now? "He must be!"

"Why?"

The simple question made Shadowsight stiffen. "If he were still around, he'd have come to the Sisters' ceremony!"

"What if I didn't let him?"

Shadowsight felt cold. He could sense Ashfur's spirit beneath Bramblestar's flesh as his malignant gaze seemed to burn from the spirit world into this one. "What have you done with him?"

Ashfur's whiskers twitched. "Didn't I already warn you not to ask?"

Shadowsight remembered too clearly how, when his spirit had traveled to Bramblestar's den, he'd seen Ashfur's spirit rise from the Thunderclan leader's body. Ashfur's threat had been clear. *You shouldn't ask what became of Bramblestar. Not unless you want the same thing to happen to you.* He pressed his paws into the earth to stop himself trembling. "Let him go."

"You're so worried about Bramblestar's spirit." Ashfur narrowed his eyes. "Haven't you wondered about any other cat? Don't you realize how much power I gained when I discovered how easily I could move between the living world and the dead?"

"What do you mean?" Panic sparked in Shadowsight's pelt.

"No cat's spirit is safe from me."

Who else was Ashfur holding hostage? Shadowsight's breath caught in his throat.

Ashfur went on. "Have you forgotten Spiresight?" His eyes glittered malevolently.

Spiresight. Shadowsight remembered with a jolt the cat he'd looked up to as a kit, who, as a spirit, had saved him after Ashfur had left him to die in the ravine. As he stared in horror at the dark warrior, Ashfur's eyes lost Bramblestar's amber depth and grew pale until they shone yellow in the moonlight. Shadowsight stared, hardly able to believe what he was seeing as he recognized Spiresight's eyes staring at him from Bramblestar's face. He saw desperation there as Ashfur dropped into a crouch, his shoulders hunching in fear until Shadowsight knew he was no longer seeing the dark warrior, but Spiresight trapped beneath Bramblestar's pelt.

"Listen to him." Spiresight's mew was helpless with terror. "He has us all—" His mew broke into a gasp as he struggled to go on. "He'll force us to—"

His eyes closed and Bramblestar's body uncurled as Ashfur

seemed once more to claim it, driving out Spiresight's spirit as though chasing prey from its nest.

Shadowsight fought to control the dread surging deep within his chest. "What was that?"

"That was a warning." Ashfur stared at him. "I want you to realize how much is at stake and what will happen to the spirits I control if you let Tigerstar and the others hurt me."

"How do I know it's true?" Shadowsight forced his chin high. Ashfur had been trying to manipulate him from the start. "How do I know you're not faking this, too?"

Ashfur's pelt prickled angrily. As Shadowsight watched, his body began to change once more, this time straightening until Ashfur stood tall, his head high, pride showing in the smooth curve of his tail. Shadowsight's eyes widened as he recognized Bramblestar's posture. Warmth suddenly glowed in the impostor's gaze as though it was really Bramblestar staring back at him.

Bramblestar stretched his muzzle until it was a mouse-length from Shadowsight's. "Do you believe Ashfur could fake *this*?"

Shadowsight's heart quickened. He didn't know what to believe anymore. Ashfur was a liar down to his bones. He was twisted enough to do something like this, and yet could he really make Bramblestar's body look like a *true* warrior, as he was doing now, when he had the heart of a fox?

When Shadowsight didn't reply, Bramblestar went on. "Don't you think Ashfur has a plan? He wouldn't come back unless he thought he could get what he wanted. But he needs me to make it happen, and he can't get rid of me until he has what he wants. I'm still here. You didn't kill me."

Shadowsight's heart seemed to melt with relief as he heard Bramblestar's words. *I'm not a murderer.*

Bramblestar's gaze burned hotter. "But if my body dies, I die with it." His muzzle was a whisker from Shadowsight now. "There will be no chance to get me back."

Shadowsight pulled away, his mind buzzing. Was this just a trick by Ashfur to convince him to help him escape? Or was Bramblestar really pleading with him to keep him alive? Ashfur had convinced his whole Clan that he was Bramblestar for a while. *Why couldn't he convince me?* And yet, if there was a chance to save Bramblestar, shouldn't Shadowsight grasp it?

A yowl ripped through the still night air. *Tigerstar.* Shadowsight jerked his muzzle around as paw steps thrummed beyond the camp wall. The Clans were coming. He could smell their scents. And, from the fierceness of his father's cry, he guessed they were coming for Ashfur.

The dark warrior slumped to the ground. Shadowsight stared at him. His eyes were closed, his body limp. Shadowsight poked him with a paw. He was breathing, but they were long, deep breaths, as though he was sleeping.

The brambles shivered as Lionblaze stalked into the enclosure. The Thunderclan deputy's angry gaze flitted past Shadowsight and stopped as it reached Ashfur. Lionblaze curled his lip. "The leaders have voted," he told Shadowsight.

Shadowsight stared at him, his mouth too dry to answer.

"I've sent the guards away," Lionblaze told him.

"Where's Tigerstar?" Forcing himself to speak, Shadowsight glanced past Lionblaze. Surely the Thunderclan deputy didn't plan to kill Ashfur alone.

"He's outside with Mistystar, Harestar, and Leafstar," Lionblaze told him. "They'll join me once you've left." His eyes were dark with determination. "Go and wait with the rest of the patrol outside camp."

"Lionblaze." Tigerstar's mew sounded beyond the enclosure walls.

Lionblaze frowned and turned toward it. "What?" He padded from the enclosure.

As he disappeared, Ashfur scrambled to his paws. "You know what to do?"

Shadowsight blinked at him, wondering whose voice was speaking now. It sounded like Ashfur, Bramblestar, and Spiresight all at once, as though the impostor held all their spirits.

Ashfur stared urgently at Shadowsight. "You have no choice," he hissed. "Bramblestar will die forever, and you'll have killed him."

Shadowsight closed his eyes for a moment, his heart feeling as though it would burst as horror pressed into it like stone. Then he turned and padded from the enclosure.

The camp was empty, the guards gone. Only the leaders and Thunderclan's deputy remained. Lionblaze and Tigerstar were talking in heated whispers at the edge of the clearing, while Mistystar, Harestar, and Leafstar shifted nervously beside them.

"Are you sure you want to act for Squirrelflight in this?"

Tigerstar gazed questioningly at Lionblaze.

"Thunderclan must take as much responsibility as the other Clans," Lionblaze growled.

Shadowsight hurried toward them. "Before you do anything," he called, "there's something you should know." He padded past them, drawing their gaze from the bramble enclosure.

His heart pounded in his ears as they stared at him, their eyes bright with curiosity.

"Is something wrong?" Tigerstar leaned closer.

Leafstar pricked her ears.

"Ashfur isn't . . ." Shadowsight hesitated, letting his gaze flit from one leader to another. They stared at him. Harestar frowned as he let the pause lengthen.

"Spit it out!" As Lionblaze snarled, Shadowsight saw a shadow slip from the bramble enclosure. It flitted across the camp and headed for the dirtplace tunnel. He looked back at the leaders, but it was too late. Lionblaze's gaze had followed his. It jerked toward the narrow gap in the camp wall as a dark tabby tail disappeared into the darkness.

Lionblaze's pelt spiked. He swung his muzzle back to Shadowsight. Shadowsight backed away as the golden warrior unsheathed his claws. Eyes glittering, Lionblaze shook with rage.

"What in StarClan have you done?"

CHAPTER 25

❧

Rootspring watched Squirrelflight push her way through the ferns, her orange pelt no more than a pale shadow between the leaves. The yowls from the ShadowClan camp had died away, and he shivered as he wondered what had happened there once the patrol had arrived. Was Ashfur dead? He wondered suddenly if Bramblestar *was* still wandering the forest. Would he know that his body had been killed—that he had nowhere to return to now? Rootspring longed to see him again, to speak to him, to apologize. *I failed him.*

Bristlefrost shifted beside him, her gaze following Squirrelflight as the Thunderclan leader disappeared into the trees. "Where do you think she's going?"

"She said she wanted to go where she can be close to Bramblestar." Rootspring remembered the grief sparkling in Squirrelflight's eyes. "The *real* Bramblestar."

"But we don't know where the real Bramblestar is." Bristlefrost blinked at him.

Rootspring gazed between the trees. "I think she's heading for the Moonpool," he mewed softly. "It's as close as any cat can get to StarClan now."

Bristlefrost tipped her head to one side. "Do you think she'll be okay?"

Rootspring hardly heard her. A shaft of moonlight had caught Bristlefrost's cheek, so that her fur shimmered with silvery light. Her blue-green eyes were round, their dark centers wide. She looked frightened. Was he really going to live the rest of his life without her? He fought the urge to wrap his tail around her and draw her close. If she lived in a different Clan, how would he ever know she was safe?

"Do you think she'll be okay?" Bristlefrost mewed again, her eyes growing wider.

"Eventually," he murmured. "She's accepted that Bramble-star won't ever return to the lake. She can begin to mourn properly now."

Bristlefrost's eyes glistened. "Her heart must be broken."

Yes. Rootspring's heart ached too, for Squirrelflight and for himself. The Thunderclan leader had lost a mate she'd loved for countless moons. He was losing the future he'd hoped he'd spend with Bristlefrost. His throat tightened as he fought back grief. Bristlefrost was beside him now. He wanted to press close to her and feel her warmth. It might be the last chance they ever had to be alone. Instead he moved away. "I'm going to follow her," he mewed. "I think I can help."

"Shall I come?" Bristlefrost lifted her chin eagerly.

He shook his head. "I want to share with her what I learned from the Sisters," he explained. "It might be a comfort, to hear how the dead stay with the Sisters after they're gone, to continue their journey alongside them."

He saw tenderness in Bristlefrost's gaze.

"You're very kind," she breathed.

He dropped his gaze as heartache overwhelmed him. "I just want to make it easier for her."

Bristlefrost leaned closer. "Let me help too."

Rootspring turned away. "It's probably best she doesn't see a Thunderclan cat right now," he mewed hoarsely. "She has to be strong for her Clanmates; she won't want you to see her so weak with grief."

Bristlefrost reached out her muzzle and touched it to his shoulder. "Be careful," she whispered. "The Moonpool's a long way."

He felt the warmth of her breath in his fur. "I'll be fine." His mew was husky. Padding away from her, he didn't dare look back. They would never be mates now. This was as close as they'd ever be.

He felt as though he'd left his heart behind as he headed between the trees. There was an empty space in his chest, aching at its loss. He ignored the pain, forcing himself to focus on Squirrelflight's scent instead.

Tracking it along a rise, he followed it past the ditches, which cut furrows through ShadowClan's forest like claw marks. The scent was harder to trace as it reached Thunderclan territory, masked by other Thunderclan scents, but Rootspring kept his head low, opening his mouth to let the night air bathe his tongue, and found traces where Squirrelflight had skirted the SkyClan border. She was clearly heading for the far side of Thunderclan's forest, where trees gave way to moorland. He felt sure now he'd been right. She was going to the Moonpool.

He slid from the trees, padding into moonlight, and crossed the short stretch of grassy moor that led to a stream. Pausing, he scanned the hillside, where the stream cut a rock-lined path up to the Moonpool hollow. A shape moved among the boulders far ahead. Was that Squirrelflight? The shape moved in and out of the shadow of the rocks, weaving among them as it followed the stream. It must be.

Rootspring quickened his pace, not wanting to lose sight of her. The stream chattered beside him as he scrambled over the rocks. A breeze rolled down from the high moor, fragrant with heather scents. It slicked his pelt against his skin, and he lowered his head, moving quickly as he neared the waterfall that reached from the streambed to the lip of the Moonpool hollow. Squirrelflight was already climbing it. He could see her ginger pelt in the starlight now as she leaped from boulder to boulder and hauled herself up over the edge.

As the moon silhouetted her at the top, Rootspring hurried to the base of the waterfall and began to scramble up. He paused as Squirrelflight sat down, her head drooping. He ducked into the shadow of a rock and watched her as she sank into grief. He couldn't approach her now. The words he'd wanted to share about the Sisters and their connection to the spirits of their ancestors seemed suddenly empty. Perhaps they'd be a comfort later, but right now she needed to be alone, to remember Bramblestar and mourn his passing.

A tabby pelt moved at the edge of the hollow. Rootspring stiffened as he recognized the broad shoulders and wide head of a tom. He was padding along the edge of the hollow, his gaze fixed on Squirrelflight. *Bramblestar?* Rootspring narrowed his eyes. It looked exactly like him. Had his spirit found a way back to comfort his mate? Squirrelflight lifted her head and saw the tom heading toward her. Rootspring's heart leaped with hope as he saw her eyes light up.

Then she frowned, her pelt spiking along her spine.

Horror gripped Rootspring. *It's not Bramblestar....* His paws sparked with dread as the tabby slowed and stopped a tail-length from Squirrelflight.

"I'm giving you one last chance." The tom's mew was edged with a threat.

Ashfur! Rootspring stared at the dark warrior. How had he escaped from the ShadowClan camp?

Squirrelflight backed away, her hackles lifting. "Stay away from me."

Ashfur narrowed his eyes. "Don't you realize how I feel about you?"

"I don't care how you feel about me!" Squirrelflight bared her teeth. "I want Bramblestar back."

"He's not coming back." Ashfur's ears twitched. "I've made sure of that. I'm the only cat who loves you now. And I'm willing to forgive you for betraying me and making me a prisoner. Come with me. I can make you happier than you ever imagined."

Squirrelflight stared at him, her eyes glittering with disbelief. "Do you think I could ever be with the cat who killed my mate?"

Be careful. Rootspring silently pulled himself onto the next rock. *Don't make him angry.*

Hurt showed in Ashfur's eyes. "I've loved you through death." His mew was pleading now, like a kit desperate for food. "Doesn't that mean anything? I came back from StarClan to be with you. Bramblestar could never do that. No cat could. Don't you think you could learn to love me now that he's gone?"

Squirrelflight glared at him. "You killed him and stole his body!" she hissed. "You lied to every cat and tore Thunder-clan apart. I made my choice moons ago, and you've proven over and over again that it was the right one." She squared her shoulders, hate burning in her eyes. "I could never love you!"

Rootspring scrambled higher, panic pressing in his chest as Ashfur flattened his ears.

A growl sounded in the dark warrior's throat. "I'll make you wish you'd never made that choice." With a snarl, he flung himself at Squirrelflight. She reared and met his attack with a vicious swipe that raked his muzzle and sent blood spraying onto the rock. He spun toward her and hooked his claws into her shoulders, dragging her onto the stone. Leaping on top of her, he slashed her cheek with his foreclaws. She pushed up with her hind legs, flinging him away, and lunged at him with a yowl of fury as he rolled across the rock.

Rootspring leaped to the top of the waterfall and heaved himself over the edge. Squirrelflight was on Ashfur, churn-ing his belly with her hind paws. The dark warrior gripped her neck between his claws and rolled her onto her spine. She screeched with pain as she tried to twist free. Blood smeared the stone where she writhed. Showing his teeth, Ashfur dug his claws harder around her throat until Squirrelflight's shriek became a strangled yelp.

Rootspring hurled himself toward them, sinking his claws into Ashfur's pelt. Straining, he dragged him backward, shocked by the dark warrior's strength.

With a snarl of rage, Ashfur turned on him. "Warriors are like rats," he hissed. "No matter how many I kill, there's always another waiting to steal from me."

Rootspring's pelt spiked as he saw murder in Ashfur's gaze. The dark warrior lifted a paw and swung at his face, a blow so fierce that it sent Rootspring reeling away.

Blind with pain, Rootspring hit the rock, the hard stone knocking the wind out of him as he landed. He fought for breath and blinked away blood welling in his eye. He pushed himself to his paws and gasped for air, terror flooding his chest as Ashfur padded toward Squirrelflight. She was trying to scramble to her paws, but her legs buckled beneath her. Her gaze darkened with fear as it met Ashfur's. Helplessly, she lashed out at him, but he ducked and grabbed her scruff between his teeth. Growling ominously, he began to drag her along the spiral of dimpled paw steps, down toward the Moonpool.

Rootspring forced his breath to steady. The hollow swam before his eyes, his vision blurred with blood. He shook it away and, flanks heaving, staggered after Ashfur as the dark warrior hauled Squirrelflight's limp body to the bottom of the hollow.

The Moonpool reflected starlight, its surface unruffled in the shelter of the encircling rock. Rootspring stared in confusion as Ashfur waded into the water, dragging Squirrelflight with him. *Is he going to drown her?* Rootspring's paws shook beneath him as he stumbled after them. Ashfur pushed deeper into the pool, his eyes glittering with triumph as, with a grunt, he pressed Squirrelflight beneath the surface and disappeared after her.

Rootspring stopped at the edge, hardly able to believe his eyes. Panic surging beneath his pelt, he plunged in after them. As the chilly water soaked his fur, his thoughts flashed to the time he'd nearly drowned in the lake. Ignoring the memories, he waded as deep as he dared, circling the pool, reaching out with his paws to feel for Ashfur or Squirrelflight. *Nothing.* Taking a gulp of air, he ducked beneath the surface, his eyes stinging as he scanned the dark water for some sign of them.

There was no cat there. He flailed his paws, sweeping the water in a desperate search. *They can't have disappeared!* Bursting up through the surface, he scanned the hollow. It was deserted. He circled the pool again and again, sinking below the surface in case he could see some sign of Ashfur and Squirrelflight. But the Moonpool was empty. He was alone.

Struggling to the edge, he heaved himself out and shook water from his fur. The Moonpool shimmered, then grew calm, its surface unruffled once more as it reflected the star-specked sky.

Where had they gone? Shock reached like ice to his bones. How would any cat believe what he'd seen here? He stared at the water, hardly breathing. Water dripped from his pelt as he began to shiver.

Ashfur was alive, and he'd taken Squirrelflight to a place where only the dead could reach her.

CHAPTER 1

❧

The moon had slipped down behind the trees at the top of the ThunderClan camp; Bristlefrost guessed that dawn could not be far off. She paced restlessly around the edge of the stone hollow, so tired that every paw step was an effort, yet something inside her wouldn't let her keep still. And she was not alone. No cat was sleeping: Her Clanmates were also padding to and fro, exchanging nervous glances as their tails and whiskers twitched. Bristlefrost could feel their tension like strands of cobweb clinging to their fur, stretching from one cat to another until they enveloped the whole Clan.

Lionblaze and a few others were gone, and none of the remaining cats seemed to know what to do. *Because they're probably killing Ashfur in Bramblestar's body right now,* Bristlefrost mused. *How are we supposed to feel about that?*

Her heart lurched in her chest, as though buckling under the weight of the grief and fear flowing through her. She could not imagine ThunderClan without their wise and brave leader. Squirrelflight would be a most worthy successor, but without the guidance of their spirit ancestors, could she ever truly lead her Clan? Some of Bristlefrost's Clanmates had already left. Were the rest of them doomed to split up and become no better than rogues, without the warrior code to guide them?

How can ThunderClan ever come back from this?

At last she detected the sky beginning to grow pale, so that she could see the outline of the trees above her head. Dawn was breaking. The long and weary night was finally coming to an end.

At the same moment, she spotted movement at the opening of the thorn tunnel. Twigbranch, who was on watch, sprang to her paws, and Bristlefrost, thankful for something to do at last, raced across the camp to her side. She was ready for an invasion, or for the return of Lionblaze and his patrol, but instead it was a single cat who stepped into the clearing.

"Flipclaw!" Bristlefrost's joyful cry echoed around the camp.

Her brother had been one of the cats who had left the Clan for a "wander"—as he and some of the other cats had explained it, a "wander" was the chance to think things over in peace. None of the cats had been sure they would return to the changed Clan, so she had resigned herself to never seeing him again. Yet here he was, looking strong and vigorous, with a surprised expression as he gazed around the camp and saw every cat out of their den. Nuzzling his shoulder, breathing in his familiar scent, Bristlefrost felt a stab of hope that life would not always be dark and full of grief—that there might be a time when ThunderClan would live, and thrive, again.

More welcoming yowls broke out behind Bristlefrost as the

rest of the Clan bounded up to greet Flipclaw. Their sister, Thriftear, and their parents, Ivypool and Fernsong, thrust their way to the front of the crowd, almost overwhelming the young tom as they brushed their pelts against his, twined tails with him, and covered his ears with licks.

"Hey, give me room to breathe!" he exclaimed happily.

"I'm so glad you've come back to us!" Ivypool's purr was full of joy as she pressed herself against the kit she'd thought she might have lost forever. "It's been nearly a moon, so I was worried you wouldn't come home."

Bristlefrost stepped forward and met her littermate's eyes, hoping that he could see how pleased she was. Squirrelflight had told all the cats who'd gone on the "wander" to return to ThunderClan within a moon or they wouldn't be welcomed back. None of the others had returned except Thornclaw, an older cat who'd wandered home within a quarter moon, musing that he wasn't young enough to start over.

"I'm glad to be back," Flipclaw responded. "I faced so many dangers out there, it made me realize that if there has to be danger, I wanted to face it with my Clan by my side. I know now that ThunderClan is the right place for me. But . . . what's happening?" he went on, gazing at the cats swarming around him. "Why are you all up and about so early?"

A chorus of voices began to answer his question, but Flipclaw fixed his attention on Bristlefrost. "Tell me," he meowed.

"It's bad, Flipclaw," Bristlefrost replied. "The leaders have agreed to kill Ashfur, and it's happening now—or maybe it's already happened."

Flipclaw's happy expression faded; his jaws gaped and his eyes stretched wide in a look of shock and devastation. "But that means . . ." His voice died away as if he couldn't bear to speak the words.

"Yes, Bramblestar's body will have to die," Bristlefrost finished for him, her voice steady though her heart was wailing in grief and fear.

For a moment, every cat was silent, until Twigbranch spoke, clearly just trying to break the tension and move on. "Flipclaw, where are the other cats who left camp with you? Thornclaw has returned, but will the others come home?"

Flipclaw shook his head sadly. "We split up, a couple of days after we left camp. Graystripe and I went to the mountains to visit the Tribe of Rushing Water, where Graystripe's son Stormfur lives." His voice grew livelier as he continued. "It was great! I made friends with Stormfur's son, Feather of Flying Hawk, and he taught me how the Tribe cats hunt in the mountains, and then a whole bunch of rocks fell on me and I hurt my leg, but—"

"Wait," his mother Ivypool interrupted. "Did you say that *rocks* fell on you?"

"Yes, but it was okay." Flipclaw waved his tail dismissively. "But then—"

"You hurt your leg?" This time the interruption came from Jayfeather, pushing his way forward until he stood beside Flipclaw. "Which leg?"

"This one." Flipclaw lifted one hind leg, then, remembering that Jayfeather couldn't see what he was doing, gave him a prod with it. "Stoneteller healed my injury. I had to rest it for a few days, but it's fine now."

"It's not fine until I say it is," Jayfeather grumbled. "You'd better come to my den and let me check it out."

"Okay." Flipclaw sounded quite cheerful, and Bristlefrost reflected that if his leg had carried him all the way back from the mountains, there couldn't be very much wrong with it. "Anyway," he went on, "living with the Tribe made me realize that I wanted to come home and work to make ThunderClan as strong as it used to be. But Graystripe—"

"Yes, where is Graystripe?" some cat asked from the back of the crowd.

"I can't tell you where he is right now," Flipclaw replied, as other cats echoed the question. "All I know is that when he left the Tribe, he said he was going back to the old forest territories."

"What?" Cloudtail exclaimed, his eyes stretching wide and his tail flicking straight up in the air. "But that . . . that's mouse-brained! We left the old forest because Twolegs were tearing it down. There'll be nothing left!"

"There might be something," his mate, Brightheart, murmured. She rubbed her muzzle against Cloudtail's ear. "I'd like to go back and see it again."

"So would I," Birchfall agreed. "I was only a kit when we left, but I can remember our old camp very clearly."

Cloudtail snorted. "Even if it is still there," he meowed, "I can't understand what good Graystripe thought it would do, trekking all that way."

"He wanted to see if he could make contact with StarClan through the Moonstone," Flipclaw explained.

Murmurs of amazement rose from the cats gathered around him.

"Oh, if only he could!" Alderheart exclaimed fervently.

"I think he might," Flipclaw responded, his eyes bright with hope. "Graystripe's a clever cat, and if he thought it was worth making that long journey, then surely there's a good chance it will work."

Every hair on Bristlefrost's pelt prickled with reviving hope. *If Graystripe can get through to StarClan there, then maybe he can bring them back here, too. Maybe everything can get back to normal—at last!* More than that, Bristlefrost couldn't help wondering whether, if StarClan could return, they would be able to send Bramblestar back with a new life. *Maybe our leader will be himself again.*

"But Graystripe *is* going to come back, after he visits the old territory?" Fernsong asked.

Flipclaw nodded. "I think so."

"And what about Flywhisker and Snaptooth?" Cinderheart asked, slipping through a gap in the crowd to stand in front of Flipclaw. Her blue eyes were filled with anxiety. "As Ivypool said, it's been nearly a moon, and we've had no contact. Do you have any news of them?"

Bristlefrost could understand why the gray she-cat was so desperate to hear what had happened to her kits. No cat had seen or scented them since they had left, and most of the Clan—except for Cinderheart and her mate, Lionblaze—had been far too preoccupied with the Clan's troubles to give much thought to them. But Squirrelflight's deadline was approaching, and if they came back after that—if Squirrelflight held to her word—they would be turned away.

"They're okay," Flipclaw reassured Cinderheart. "But you probably won't like what I'm going to tell you."

Cinderheart blinked in confusion. "Why not?"

Flipclaw paused before continuing. "When Graystripe and I left, Snaptooth and Flywhisker were talking about trying out life as kittypets. So when I was on my way home, I detoured around our territory and headed for the Twolegplace, to see if I could find them. And I did—they're both living with a Twoleg now. I stayed—"

Flipclaw broke off as yowls and hisses of shock burst out from the cats around him. Spotfur hung her head, and Bristlefrost's heart ached with sympathy. *She's about to bear the kits of her dead mate, and now she's lost her littermates too.* She tried to give the queen an encouraging look, but Spotfur wouldn't meet her eye.

"Traitors!" Hollytuft growled.

Cinderheart whirled around to confront her daughter, her neck fur beginning to bristle. "How dare you!" she snarled. "Can you tell me that you haven't—that *any* cat hasn't—thought about finding some way of escaping from this awful mess that we're in? If you do, I won't believe you!"

Bristlefrost noticed Twigbranch and Finleap exchanging troubled glances. *They were Snaptooth's and Flywhisker's mentors,* she recalled. *I hope they're not blaming themselves.*

Alderheart rested his tail on Cinderheart's shoulder in a calming gesture. "Accusing your kin of treason doesn't help," he told Hollytuft. Turning to Flipclaw, he asked, "Didn't you try to persuade them to come home?"

"Of course I did!" Flipclaw retorted. "I stayed in the Two-legplace for days, catching the odd mouse or snatching bites of that terrible yuck the Twolegs feed their kittypets. I did my best to convince Snaptooth and Flywhisker to return to the Clan, but they wouldn't. Do you think I should have picked them up by their scruffs and brought them back as if they were kits?"

"No cat is blaming you," Ivypool told her son. "We just wish that—"

Whatever she might have said next was lost in the sudden noise of pounding paw steps coming from the thorn tunnel. Lionblaze burst into the camp with Bumblestripe hard on his paws. Both cats' pelts were bushed up, their ears flat and their eyes glaring with wild fury.

What now? Bristlefrost asked herself, her belly beginning to churn with apprehension. They did not look like cats who had just killed their leader's body; she would have expected sorrow, or even guilt, not this uncontrolled rage.

But as he took in the crowd of his Clanmates, Lionblaze came sharply to a halt. "What's going on?" he asked.

"Flipclaw is back!" Fernsong announced.

Lionblaze's gaze swept almost indifferently over the young tom. "Oh, hi, Flipclaw," he meowed. For a moment he gazed around with a hopeful look in his eyes; Bristlefrost guessed he was looking for Snaptooth and Flywhisker. When he found no sign of them, the hope in his eyes died; he didn't ask about them, even though Bristlefrost knew he had been worried about his kits. *He'll question Flipclaw later,* she told herself. *Right now, he has more pressing matters on his mind.*

"What's happened?" Jayfeather asked. "I can scent your anger. Did something go wrong?"

"It couldn't have gone more wrong," Lionblaze replied, his voice a rumble deep in his chest. "Ashfur has escaped his prison in ShadowClan."

A stunned silence met Lionblaze's announcement. Bristlefrost thought that the Clan must be so numb from the shocks they'd received over the past moon that they hardly knew how to react anymore. She herself didn't know what to think. Ashfur was free again to carry out whatever destruction he had planned next—but at least that meant Bramblestar's body still lived. Their leader might yet return.

"Weren't those ShadowClan mange-pelts guarding him?" Cloudtail demanded with a flick of his ears.

"Shadowsight helped him get away," Lionblaze explained. "And . . ." He glanced at Bumblestripe. "We think he was conspiring with Squirrelflight."

Bristlefrost stared at the golden tabby warrior, her whiskers twitching in confusion. At an emergency Gathering the day before, she and Rootspring had watched Squirrelflight beg the other leaders to have mercy on Ashfur to save Bramblestar's body. But the other leaders were sure that killing Bramblestar's body was the only way to get rid of Ashfur's spirit. When they'd left to carry out the grim task, Squirrelflight had snuck off—and Bristlefrost and Rootspring had intercepted her just in time to talk her out of freeing her mate's body. At least, that was what Bristlefrost had understood. Bristlefrost had come back to ThunderClan, but Rootspring had meant to follow Squirrelflight, to comfort her in her grief.

I wonder what happened, Bristlefrost asked herself. *Did Squirrelflight change her mind?*

"Yeah, ShadowClan is holding *Shadowsight* prisoner now," Bumblestripe put in.

"Their own medicine cat?" Cinderheart exclaimed. "Tigerstar's son?"

Lionblaze nodded. "Even Tigerstar can't protect him if he's acted against the Clans to save our enemies."

Bristlefrost found it hard to believe that the young medicine cat would choose Ashfur over the Clans, not after the way Ashfur had deceived him and tried to kill him.

"Shadowsight would never act against the Clans," Alderheart meowed, echoing Bristlefrost's thought. "If he really did help Ashfur escape, he must have had a good reason." His voice shook as he added, "I'm sure of it."

ENTER THE WORLD OF
WARRIORS

Check out WarriorCats.com to

- Explore amazing fan art, stories, and videos
- Have your say with polls and Warriors reactions
- Ask questions at the Moonpool
- Explore the full family tree
- Read exclusives from Erin Hunter
- Shop for exclusive merchandise
- And more!

Check Out the New Warrior Cats Hub App!

Download on the **App Store**

GET IT ON **Google Play**